Nick Oldham was born in Blackburn, Lancashire, in 1956. He has been a police officer since the age of nineteen, spending the majority of his service in operational roles. He is married and lives with his wife on the outskirts of Preston. A TIME FOR JUSTICE is his first novel.

A Time For Justice

Nick Oldham

HEADLINE
FEATURE

First published in Great Britain in 1996
by HEADLINE BOOK PUBLISHING

First published in paperback in 1997
by HEADLINE BOOK PUBLISHING

A HEADLINE FEATURE paperback

10 9 8 7 6 5 4 3 2 1

ISBN 0 7472 5462 1

Typeset at The Spartan Press Ltd,
Lymington, Hants

Printed and bound in Great Britain by
Cox & Wyman Ltd, Reading, Berks

HEADLINE BOOK PUBLISHING
A division of Hodder Headline PLC
338 Euston Road
London NW1 3BH

This book is dedicated to my dad, Edward Vincent Oldham, who has been my rock. Mum knows and approves.

ACKNOWLEDGEMENTS

To David and Lesley Briggs, and Ian and Gillian Carney – for their unfailing friendship over the years.

To Graham Street – for his firearms advice. All the liberties taken were mine.

To everyone who has lived with my ambition over the years – thanks for your support. You know who you are.

And to Sarah – who always had faith.

PART ONE

Chapter One

Hinksman never intentionally set out to kill innocent people. Not that he ever lost sleep when it did happen, but it was something he tried to avoid.

With that in mind, he set the timer on the bomb for thirty minutes after the car was due to leave for the airport. That way, he figured, even if there was a delay, the Daimler would be on the motorway when the bomb went off. The possibility of killing some other sucker was still there, of course, but at least it was minimised . . . to a degree.

And it was only a small bomb. That's all it needed to be – a block of Semtex no bigger than a slim paperback with a detonator pushed into it and a timer strapped on with insulation tape. The timer was nothing more than the switch-and-circuit-board mechanism from an automatic dog-feeder he'd bought the day before, cannibalised and adapted to his needs. It was powered by a small AAA battery. A ring magnet was attached to the bomb by super-glue.

The result was a plain, simple, home-made bomb. Just the right size to blow a Daimler limousine to smithereens.

It took Hinksman only seconds to put the bomb into place.

He'd parked his hired Ford Mondeo in one corner of the Posthouse Hotel car park near Lancaster and waited patiently for the Daimler to appear. It arrived on time.

The driver left it unattended and went into the hotel.

Hinksman had been counting on this; as he climbed swiftly out of the Mondeo, he sniggered. Security in this country was a complete joke! In the States, no car would ever have been left without a minder, even for a moment. Here in England, things were just so lax. So amateur.

As he walked alongside the limo his suitcase flipped open and the contents spilled out onto the tarmac. He cursed aloud, bent down and began to collect up his clothes. At the same time he clamped the bomb with a satisfying *clunk* firmly on the underside of the car, near to the petrol tank.

Stuffing his belongings untidily back into the case, he was suddenly aware of someone standing over him. He looked up and smiled.

'Damned suitcase,' he said.

'Can I help you, sir?' It was the chauffeur, eyeing him with suspicion.

'No, no,' he said in the clipped English accent he'd been perfecting. 'Clasp's broken, have to get a new suitcase. Thanks anyway.'

He stood up and walked across to the hotel, aware that the chauffeur's eyes were piercing into his back all the way. It was hard not to glance over his shoulder – but that would have given the game away. He kicked himself mentally for not noticing the man's return; it was only a small mistake, true, but big enough to have got himself killed. 'Shape up,' he told himself. 'Just because you're in England that's no reason to get slack.'

He booked into the Posthouse Hotel under false details and went immediately to his room.

Ten minutes later he was back in the foyer, drinking coffee, reading a newspaper and waiting for his targets to leave. He wanted to see the Englishman and the American off on their final journey. He was sentimental like that.

The two men were agonisingly late coming down to check out. When they eventually did appear, the reason for the delay became obvious – they each had a devastatingly beautiful woman clinging to their arm, and no doubt had been saying their goodbyes to them in time-honoured fashion.

Hinksman did not begrudge the men their last moments of pleasure. They had probably paid handsomely for it, judging by the quality of the women. These were no cheap whores, thought Hinksman.

The chauffeur met them at Reception and took their suitcases out to the Daimler while the men settled their accounts, in cash.

There were smiles, laughter and handshakes between the men and the hotel staff. Evidently they had been generous guests.

Hinksman took the opportunity to study them discreetly. This was the first time he'd actually seen in the flesh the two men who'd become a thorn in his boss's side. They didn't look anything special, but they'd begun to spread their activities in all directions without telling Mr Corelli or giving him his fair share – and therefore Mr Corelli was not pleased. They had been warned several times to get into line, but they seemed to be deaf. A somewhat unfortunate ailment.

And now they'd had the audacity to go into business full-time. They'd fixed up a deal right under Mr Corelli's nose.

Even though he was impressed by their acumen and daring, Mr Corelli was not a happy man.

He wanted them dead.

And what Mr Corelli wanted, he got.

Which was where Hinksman came in.

After the pleasantries, the group stepped out of the hotel into the damp morning. Hinksman checked his watch. The bomb was due to go off in sixteen minutes. By then they would be on the motorway racing to Manchester Airport. The flight to Miami left in ninety minutes and the American was due to be on it.

The chauffeur saluted and opened the rear door of the limo but only one of the men, the American – and his female companion – slid onto the plush back seat . . . leaving the two others on the kerb, holding hands like newlyweds.

Hinksman frowned.

The driver clunked the door shut, walked smartly round the vehicle and got in behind the steering wheel. He drove elegantly away, turning out of the car park towards the M6.

Leaving the Englishman behind.

Hinksman said 'Shit', softly to himself.

A few moments later, a 7-series BMW with tinted windows drove into the car park and picked up the Englishman and his companion. This car turned in the opposite direction to the motorway.

Hinksman put his paper down and cursed.

120 mph. Henry Christie looked up from the speedo at the profile of Terry Briggs, his partner in the pursuit of crime. Terry, concentrating on the driving, was completely relaxed; his hands rested lightly on the wheel, his head against the head-rest. His eyes, though, took in everything. They darted about continuously, checking the mirror, the road ahead, then the mirror again. All the time reading the traffic, anticipating.

Terry was a brilliant driver, and Henry Christie felt as safe as was possible under the circumstances. For the past eight years, ever since they had been PCs in uniform on crime patrol together, Henry had trusted the driving to Terry and never been let down.

A quarter of a mile ahead, a red Porsche 911 Turbo pulled out into the fast lane. Henry put the binoculars to his eyes. A puff of smoke from the exhaust and the Porsche became an even smaller speck.

'He's put his foot down again,' said Terry. 'If I do the same he'll clock us for sure . . . if he hasn't already done so.'

'True,' said Henry, lowering the binos, amazed – as ever – at Terry's vision. Eyes like a shit-house rat was the phrase which sprang to mind.

Following someone down a motorway wasn't easy at the best of times. It was even harder when the target was surveillance-conscious, was probably scanning police airwaves, and had about a quarter of a million pounds' worth of Ecstasy tablets on his back seat. He was also believed to be armed – with a Smith & Wesson .38 special, according to their intelligence.

'He's no fool,' said Henry, rubbing his eyes. It had been a long job. Two nights with no sleep chasing all over Scotland, dodging and hiding all the time. And now this, a hectic drive down from Glasgow . . . to where? Manchester, probably. Or Birmingham. Henry yawned. He was knackered, needed a shit, a shave and a shower, and was all too aware of his armpits.

'Drop back,' he said. 'Let Jim go through.'

Terry obediently floated the Cosworth into the middle lane.

Henry pressed the radio transmit button on the dash and spoke, his voice being picked up by the mike in the sun visor. Wireless workshops had told him that his transmissions couldn't be intercepted on this frequency – but he rightly treated that assurance with a pinch of salt. Too many jobs had gone wrong thanks to careless banter over the airwaves.

'Eyeball to back-up,' Henry said crisply.

There was a crackle of static. 'Go ahead.'

'Back-up make ground,' said Henry, 'then confirm eyeball.'

'Received.'

Moments later, from nowhere, the second car in the four-vehicle Regional Crime Squad surveillance team – a high-powered Vauxhall Carlton – smoothed effortlessly past them. The two detectives in it flashed V-signs at Henry and Terry, who returned the gestures.

'Fuckin' cops,' said Terry. 'Think they can get away with anything.' He dropped his speed back to a respectable ton as they approached the bridge over the River Lune. Two miles away to their right stood the city of Lancaster.

Henry fidgeted on his seat, adjusting the uncomfortable shoulder-holster which held the lightweight pistol under his left armpit. Crime Squad detectives were often armed when there was the possibility of confronting criminals believed to be carrying weapons – but it wasn't something Henry felt easy about.

* * *

Danny Carver was young and ambitious but not too intelligent. He had good looks and the muscles of a pit bull, and did not hesitate to do any 'sorting' – if any had to be done. But like most young and ambitious hoodlums who lacked the ability to look ahead, he didn't realise when he'd bitten off more than he could chew. Which is why, as he settled down in the back of the Daimler, thoughts of Corelli were far from his mind.

His mind was on one thing only – the woman sitting next to him; Leila, aged nineteen, had cost him almost £2000 for three days of service from a 'respectable' escort agency.

Two grand, he thought with a chuckle – but so what?

He could afford it. The deal he had just pulled off was going to net him millions. And that big fat Italian bastard could just fuck off! Who the hell did he think he was?

The Daimler sped silkily down the motorway.

Danny opened the drinks cabinet and helped himself to a generous measure of Glenfiddich. He leaned back and stretched his legs. There was plenty of room.

'Go down on me,' he told Leila.

She smiled and got to work on him without hesitation. If she made this one extra-special, she thought as she spied a bottle of Taboo in the cabinet, it might be worth a bonus.

The driver checked his mirror and saw what was going on. He adjusted it downwards for a better view.

By the time they were approaching the Preston exit of the M6 – Junction 31 which passed over the River Ribble – Henry and Terry were the last car of the team. They almost dawdled along at ninety, listening to the flashes of transmissions between the three cars ahead, all of which were well out of sight.

They still had the Porsche though. He wasn't going anywhere.

Leila used all her experience and know-how on Danny. Time after time she brought him slowly to the brink, and had him writhing in ecstasy across the back seat. Nibbling, licking, chewing, biting, sucking, gently blowing. Stopping. Starting again.

'Jeez . . . aahh . . . *Jeez!*' was all that Danny could say. He gripped her head, her shoulders, the car seat. He wanted to explode. And he wanted it to go on for ever.

'This is worth an extra two-fifty,' he gasped in a rare moment of lucidity.

Damn right it is, she thought, and reached for the bottle of Taboo.

'What the hell . . . ?' blurted Danny. She kept hold of him with one hand and unscrewed the cap with her teeth. She put the bottle to her full lips and swirled the liquor around like a mouthwash, then swallowed it. She looked wickedly at Danny.

'You'll like this,' she said, lowering her head to his lap.

Danny screamed. He shot bolt upright and banged his head on the car roof. Leila kept a grip and would not be swayed from her task, consummate professional that she was.

'God, that stings! It's fantastic!'

He ejaculated in her mouth exactly sixteen minutes after starting the journey.

They were halfway across the Ribble Bridge, in the middle lane of the motorway, travelling at 87 mph, when the timer, which should have been flicking open a bowl full of Pedigree Chum, brought together the two contacts of the bomb which Hinksman had stuck to the underside of the Daimler.

The device exploded bang on time. Just four seconds after Danny's climax.

The explosion ripped into the petrol tank, turning the fuel into a massive fireball of white heat which vaporised everything in its path.

The Daimler was hurled sixty feet into the air like a toy car thrown by a child. It somersaulted a dozen times before crashing back down onto the carriageway and then bouncing off the bridge into the river below.

Two BMWs which had been in the process of overtaking the Daimler on the outside were tossed like cardboard boxes in the wind over the central reservation, right into the path of the oncoming traffic.

On the inside lane, a minibus containing kids from a special school took the sideways brunt of the blast. The windows and side panels were destroyed as the '*whoosh*' of the explosion ripped into it and sent it skidding on its roof across the hard shoulder, where it smacked into the safety barrier. The barrier simply acted like a foot, tripping the vehicle up and sending it over and down into the river.

Two hundred metres back, Henry Christie saw everything happen in slow motion – images he would relive time and again in his dreams and in his waking hours. The horror was imprinted on his brain for ever.

Even from that distance, the force of the blast struck at their car like an angry demon on the rampage.

Terry fought valiantly to control the steering wheel, breaking his right thumb in the process. Despite his efforts, the Cosworth careered across the carriageway.

Henry wasn't sure whether he screamed or not.

They glanced off another car on the inside lane, skidded across the hard shoulder and onto the grass verge. They were jolted in their seats like dummies in a car commercial, held loosely in place by seat belts whose buckling inertia reels were tested to their outer limits. Henry cracked his head on the door jamb and on the side window. Fleetingly he felt his scalp split open.

Suddenly the front of the Cosworth caught something underneath. The vehicle flipped over, rolling along the verge until it spun back onto the hard shoulder and came to an unexpected standstill – on its roof.

Hanging upside down, like giant bats, Henry and Terry had a brief moment to exchange sidelong glances and check that the other was alive, before another car clipped them. Like a movie stunt, this car then screeched down the motorway on its side, sparks flying, for about fifty metres before it righted itself and abruptly stopped.

'Let's get out of here,' shouted Henry.

Terry, cool as ever, switched off the ignition.

Simultaneously they smacked their belt-release buttons and tumbled into an untidy heap on the inner roof. They scrabbled wildly for the door handles. Outside, they rolled onto their feet and sprinted up the banking to a height where they felt reasonably safe.

'You okay?' Henry gasped.

'My thumb hurts,' said Terry. He showed it to Henry. Already the joint was swelling. 'You've cut your head,' he observed.

'I know,' said Henry. He touched the open wound gingerly.

'And you screamed.'

'I thought so,' Henry admitted.

'We got off light,' commented Terry as they surveyed the scene.

The motorway was in chaos. Both carriageways were blocked by a mangle of vehicles of all descriptions – a total of seventy-two, reports would say later. Bodies were strewn about. Some moved and twitched, others did not move at all. Many were torn into bloody pieces. People were wandering around stunned. Others, uninjured, offered what assistance they could in the circumstances. On the northbound side the blue flashing lights on the first police Range Rover approached the scene.

'Buggerin' 'ell!' said Terry, taking it all in. It was the strongest expletive he ever used.

'Improvised explosive device,' said Henry.

'Eh?'

'It was a bomb.'

Terry nodded. He was holding his thumb.

They turned and looked at each other. Henry's face was covered in blood; blood in his eyes, nose and mouth.

Both remembered, visualised the blast.

'That minibus!' bawled Henry. He set off running towards the river. Terry, pain forgotten, ran behind him.

* * *

Hinksman checked his watch and smiled with a degree of satisfaction. A good job, half-done. He finished his lukewarm coffee, folded up the newspaper and went to the payphone in the lobby. He inserted the phone card and dialled an international number. While waiting for it to connect he hummed and gazed round.

Two men in suits entered the hotel. They looked flustered. Hinksman immediately identified them. *Cops*. He watched them stride across to Reception.

Puzzled, he put the phone down just as it rang and walked casually towards them.

They leaned on the desk, all bluster, business and tension.

His intuition proved correct as one of them flashed a warrant card and introduced himself. Hinksman heard the name – McClure – but not the rank. His sharp eyes caught the glimpse of a revolver in a holster at the man's waist, hidden by the jacket. Hinksman thought, An English cop *armed*?

He clearly heard the name and rank of the other policeman as he spoke to the receptionist, '. . . and I'm Special Agent Donaldson from the FBI – in America.' He showed his shiny badge of office – a badge Hinksman hated. He couldn't see a gun on him.

'We'd like a word with the manager,' McClure said. 'Quickly, please.'

Hinksman, trying to act naturally, turned and headed towards the exit. As the automatic door hissed open, knowing he shouldn't but unable to stop himself, he turned for one last look.

His third mistake of the day.

The American detective was leaning with his back on the desk, supporting himself with both elbows, fingers interlocked across his chest.

His eyes met Hinksman's briefly. It was almost nothing – but in that almost nothing there was the glimmer of something as the detective's eyebrows furrowed.

Recognition?

Hinksman went through the door. This time he didn't look back.

The ambulanceman draped a blanket over Henry Christie's wet, exhausted body and ushered the shivering detective towards the back door of the waiting ambulance.

Henry resisted. He turned to look back across the river, which was deep and fast-flowing, having been in full flood only twenty-four hours previously. The minibus was still lying where it had landed – threequarters submerged, the side uppermost with all its windows intact.

A police diver surfaced and signalled to his colleagues on the riverbank. Negative. Thumbs down. He refixed his face mask and disappeared under the water again.

Henry gritted his teeth. He looked up at the grey sky.

'C'mon, mate,' the ambulanceman said gently, trying to steer him away. 'You've done all you can here.'

Which, in the end, was nothing, the young detective thought bleakly.

'We need to see you're all right now.' He indicated Henry's head. 'That cut's a bad one. It'll need stitches. And if you don't warm up soon you'll catch your death.'

Henry wiped his face and looked at his hand. Blood, mud and water mixed in a paste. He sighed with resignation and nodded numbly. Then, out of the corner of his eye, he caught sight of a TV news crew heading purposefully towards him. A reporter holding a microphone was followed by a cameraman, lighting and sound man and a woman carrying a clipboard.

The reporter was talking excitedly into his mike as he approached. Henry recognised him from TV. The crew stopped in front of Henry and the ambulanceman, blocking their way.

The reporter spoke dramatically into the mike. 'Detective-Sergeant Christie, you and your partner struggled in vain to rescue the children trapped in the minibus. How do you feel, knowing that they've almost certainly perished?'

He thrust the mike into Henry's face.

How do I feel? Henry asked himself. He explored his body and mind for an answer. *Numb. Frustrated. Useless.* Emotions tumbled through him like a pack of cards being shuffled and suddenly they all welled up into one: anger.

His eyes blazed. 'Parasite!' he yelled, knocking the mike out of the reporter's grasp and lunging at him. He grabbed him in a clinch, as if they were dancing partners and shoved him backwards down the riverbank.

The reporter tried desperately to balance himself . . . but failed. He teetered, then fell into the mud with a loud scream.

Henry turned to the cameraman who had recorded the incident.

The man backed off.

Henry was about to say something, but in a flash of clarity he recognised the stupidity of his actions and the possible future repercussions.

Silently he walked over to the ambulance and was helped inside.

Hinksman held the phone away from his ear. Over 3000 miles separated him from the voice on the end of the line, but Corelli still managed to boom with a force that could burst an eardrum.

Hinksman let him shout. Mr Corelli was entitled. He was the boss.

As the tirade began to subside, Hinksman re-entered the conversation. 'The FBI are here too, for some reason – and I don't like it,' he said.

'I'll look into it,' Corelli promised, which meant he'd get some information from his highly placed, and highly priced, mole at the Bureau.

'So what do you want me to do?' Hinksman asked finally, although he already knew the answer.

'I paid you to do a job. You ain't done it yet. So go finish it, Sonny.'

Chapter Two

Following the bomb on the motorway, the casualty bureau at Lancashire Constabulary's force headquarters near Preston was staffed to its maximum and working at full stretch. A barrage of phone calls from all over the country clogged up the specially installed switchboard.

A squad of officers – sweating, ties removed – noted down details of relatives, friends and lovers who hadn't returned or called home. They reassured callers, promised to phone back, passed on the details to be cross-checked and answered the next one.

The dry-wipe boards on the walls told their grim stories.

Descriptions of bodies, clothing, vehicles. Names of the injured; those who could talk, those who couldn't, their descriptions and their condition.

Twenty-two people were confirmed dead so far – not including the kids on the bus. They had a dry-wipe board all to themselves. Nine kids, two social workers and the driver. Twelve extra – all either dead or missing. Six bodies had been recovered from the river by divers; two were still trapped inside the minibus – undoubtedly dead. Specialist lifting gear was awaited. It was believed that the four missing bodies had been thrown from the bus and washed away down the river. The Support Unit was now searching the riverbanks, but there was little hope.

Of the other twenty-two, twelve still remained unidentified.

Since the bombing had hit the national news the Bureau had logged over 1500 calls, and they were still coming in thick and fast. Many people were late home; their families feared the worst but they were simply stuck in the horrendous traffic jams which blocked the motorway for over twenty miles in both directions.

The Chief Constable, Dave August, listened to the way his officers handled the calls. He did not envy them their job. He had no desire to talk to distraught relatives. He had neither the patience nor the compassion.

Earlier he had visited the accident site by helicopter, but had quickly delegated the scene management to one of his ACCs. His job was back here at HQ, coordinating, overseeing – panicking.

In one corner of the room a news cameraman and a reporter – not the man who had accosted Henry Christie – had set up their equipment. The camera slowly panned the room. August made his way over to them and prepared to be inverviewed.

He was in full uniform, with gold braid and sharp creases. He was the captain at the helm, steering the ship, reassuring crew and passengers alike. Secretly he'd always wanted to be an admiral.

The arc light came on and a make-up girl dabbed at the shine on his nose. He stepped forward in front of the camera – which, incidentally, loved him.

Next to him, one pace to his right and slightly behind, but making sure she was in camera shot, stood his aide, Chief Inspector Karen Wilde. Karen wielded a great deal of influence over her boss. Not yet thirty years old, she was a graduate entry to the force – biochemistry being her subject – who had milked the system for all it was worth. She was alleged to be a ruthless manipulator who would sleep with anyone, male or female, of any rank, who could do her good. Part of her myth – an accusation often levelled at career-minded females in the police – was that she'd been afraid of working the streets as a Constable during her two-year probation. She was supposed to have avoided this un-pleasantness by long bouts of sickness, suddenly regaining full health once the probationary period was over and Bramshill Police College beckoned her to the fast track.

Like most myths, the one surrounding Karen Wilde was a combination of truth, lies and stereotyping from jealous male officers who hated the competition.

She had been married twice, briefly; her dedication to self-advancement had left both husbands gasping for air. It would not be long before her next promotion, and it was widely speculated she could become one of the few women to attain ACPO rank in the country. To make this a reality, her first priority was to ensure that Dave August got the Home Office Inspectorate post he so desired. With him there, pushing for her, the journey upwards would be very much smoother. Ten years tops, she calculated. She did a lot of calculating.

The Chief concluded his interview and turned to her. 'Well, how was I?' he whispered.

She fluttered her eyelashes at him. 'You performed well, sir, as always,' she said cheekily. 'However, the shipping metaphors were rather OTT.'

'When the day is done,' he said, 'I'll be docking in your harbour.'

'Wanna bet?' she said, and spun away.

Out on the motorway it was getting dark and cold. A wind had begun to howl. The carriageways were still blocked but traffic had started to move sluggishly now that diversions were slowly coming into effect.

Tomorrow the scene would undergo a fingertip search by specialised police, Army and forensic teams. The estimate was that the motorway would be closed for up to forty-eight hours while that was carried out. A major fuck-up, traffic-wise.

Not that Special Agent Donaldson nor Detective Chief Inspector McClure gave a toss about that. They were too busy trying to find out if Danny Carver was dead or alive.

Having confirmed that he hadn't caught the Miami flight

from Manchester, they concluded that the bomb must have gone off beneath the limousine that the hotel staff had seen him get into.

The problem was that they couldn't find the Daimler.

Both men stood on the hard shoulder of the motorway looking at the scrapheap-from-hell of vehicles littering the carriageways. They were not allowed to go any closer, the whole scene having been cordoned off. The centre of the area was a crater in the road surface some thirty feet in diameter, two feet deep. Smoke continued to rise from it.

Sipping sweet strong tea provided by the mobile canteen, they were glad of the warmth the liquid provided. Their stylish suits and thin shirts offered scant protection against a wind that whipped in fast and bitter from the Irish Sea.

In one hand McClure held a list of vehicles which creased in the wind as he tried to read it.

No Daimler listed on it.

No Daimler to be seen on the road.

The official line at the moment stated that this was a sick terrorist attack aimed at killing the maximum number of innocent people and disrupting the economic infrastructure. In the absence of the Daimler, McClure tended to agree with the assumption – even though the main suspects, the IRA, hotly denied all responsibility. It was true, he agreed, that this sort of thing would do the IRA cause no good whatsoever . . .

So where was the Daimler?

It hadn't turned up in Manchester at any of the usual haunts that were currently under surveillance.

Puzzling.

'Maybe they split up because they knew we were watching them and they've met up somewhere else,' McClure ruminated.

'Naw, I ain't having that,' drawled Donaldson. 'This is too much of a coincidence – all this and the word that Corelli had put a contract out on Carver. Then there was that guy back at the hotel. I know that face, I'm sure I do.'

They each took a sip of tea. It was burning hot. Blue and red lights flashed with greater intensity as the night crept in. Mobile floodlights lit up the scene eerily.

'Perhaps there's nothing left of it,' McClure suggested. 'It might be here in front of us, in a billion fragments.'

'Naw.'

Another pause. A cold gust of wind made them shiver. Then a thought hit each man at the same time.

'It's in the river!' they said in unison.

They threw down their paper cups and made for the mobile control room which had been set up about a mile away from the scene of the explosion.

A glorified caravan with radio and telephone equipment, an inbuilt console and a toilet, the control room was a bustle of activity. People went in and out. Radios blared. Messages were passed. Action was taken. It was a warm place, a haven of comfort in an increasingly cold night.

The ACC (Personnel) sat by one of the radio operators looking glum and tired. It had been a long day and it would be an even longer night. Times like this he wished he'd retired years ago.

He glanced up as Donaldson and McClure knocked and entered.

By the time the three men reached the riverbank, the crane was lifting the sad remains of the minibus out of the water. It gushed like a sponge. The body of a child hung limply out of one of the broken windows. The crane jolted. The body was dislodged and dropped back into the water.

A police diver, treading water nearby, grabbed it before it was washed away.

Slowly the arm of the crane moved round and deposited the bus on safe ground. A swarm of rescue workers moved towards it like ants.

The ACC, clearly upset, wiped his eyes and blew his nose. After pulling himself together he went to speak to the diving team.

Two hours later they located the Daimler. The crane

hauled its remnants out of the Ribble and dumped them on the bank. There was very little left of it to identify. There was nothing left of the occupants at all.

Henry Christie tottered unsteadily through the crowded Accident and Emergency Department of Preston Royal Infirmary. Although the casualties had been split between three other hospitals – Blackpool, Lancaster and Blackburn – even now, six hours later, the staff were still having difficulty coping.

Henry had not even reached a treatment room yet; they were all occupied. He had seen some distressing sights . . . people with both legs blown to tatters, horrendous head wounds. He felt guilty to be sitting there with just a cut head.

Eventually he had been stitched up by a harassed nurse who looked no older than his teenage daughter. Henry pitied her. She told him to come back for an X-ray in a couple of days and pointed him at the exit.

He looked pretty bad with his head partly shaved and eight stitches in a wound which seeped blood. His eyes were dark and circled, his skin pale and sickly, his clothes dry now, but crumpled and dirty. What he needed more than anything else was a drink – something very alcoholic.

As ever, Terry was ahead of him, sitting in the back of the traffic car detailed to take them home. His hand was in plaster and his demeanour reflected Henry's.

They were driven home by a traffic PC who sensed that any conversation would be less than beneficial to his health.

Eventually, Henry said, 'I lost my gun in the river.'

'Me, too,' said Terry.

These were the only words spoken on the journey.

Henry walked up the drive to his new home on the outskirts of Blackpool. He'd recently part-exchanged his old home for this 'executive' one – new, soulless, on an unfinished estate of similar houses.

The front door opened.

His daughters stood there, mute and fearful, as they watched his approach. It was too much for the youngest, Leanne, aged nine; she broke cover and dashed to meet him, clinging to his legs. He rubbed her hair, bent down stiffly and picked her up, almost squeezing the breath out of her.

'Daddy, Daddy,' she said in his ear. He could feel the wetness of her tears on his cheek.

'You should be in bed.'

'Mummy said I could wait up for you.'

His wife, Kate, appeared in the hallway as he reached the front door.

She had been crying too. Henry thought she looked very beautiful in her sadness.

'They said you'd been hurt but were all right. They told us to stay here and wait for you,' she explained, shrugging her shoulders.

Henry nodded. Leanne slid down him, but clung to his hand.

'We saw you on telly,' his eldest daughter, Jenny said. She was thirteen, dressed somewhere between a punk and a Sloane Ranger. Henry noticed she was wearing one of his shirts.

He was puzzled. 'Telly?'

'Yeah, pushin' that reporter into the mud. Deserved it, he did.'

'He was only doing his job, I suppose,' Henry admitted.

They all stood and eyed each other.

'Oh, Dad!' Jenny burst out suddenly. 'It must have been so awful.' Her arms went round his neck and she sobbed into his chest. 'Those poor kids.'

'It's all right, lovey, it's all right.' He patted her.

He reached out for his wife's hand and drew her towards him. He was dying to get hold of her and squeeze her tight. Tighter than ever before. So tight . . . God, he needed her . . . tight, tight, tight . . .

Chapter Three

As usual after a kill, Hinksman was in a state of euphoria. He drank too much in several pubs until he found himself sitting at the bar of a strip joint near the Winter Gardens complex in Blackpool.

He was happy. He'd negotiated two and a half million dollars for Carver and the Englishman, and he knew – because he'd checked – that the second third of the money had already been wired into his Cayman Island account and, as per his instructions, immediately redeposited in Jersey. Tomorrow one half of it would be in Switzerland. Corelli was an honourable man. That's why he liked working for him. Honourable and generous – but noisy!

So, one more kill and the balance of the money would be deposited. Then, unless Corelli had anything urgent for him, he'd take some time off. Get out of the gangsterland rat race and travel a little. Australia seemed a good idea. Maybe he'd buy another house – or an apartment. Miami beckoned. He could buy an apartment in the same block as Don Johnson. Perhaps they'd become pals. Yeah, that sounded good. *Me and Don Johnson getting legless, snorting together, scoring together, racing our Ferraris down the Keys.*

Hinksman smiled at the thought.

He looked around the club. It was a seedy, smoky place, well attended by a cross-section of humanity. Drinks were cheap but the strippers were past the first flush of youth. There were many similar places in the States and Hinksman felt comfortable in these surroundings.

For a while he watched the strippers then became bored

and concentrated on getting drunk. He wondered if there was a drug dealer in the place.

Just before midnight there was an interval and people gravitated to the bar. Hinksman, who disliked being crowded, withdrew to an empty table.

Within moments he was joined by a woman who sat boldly down without an invitation. Hinksman thought he recognised her and when she introduced herself it clicked.

'Hello, luv,' she said in broad Lancashire. 'Me name's Jane. Did y'like me act?'

'Ahh,' he said, remembering. He lied, 'Yes, very much.'

He'd seen her prance onto the small stage, thought she had flat feet and no rhythm and had turned back to his drink without watching her remove any items of clothing.

He looked closely at her now. Thirty going on forty, with crow's feet around her heavily made-up eyes, a multitude of broken capillaries on her cheeks that no amount of foundation would conceal and a slight double chin. No doubt she'd once been good-looking, he mused, but time and her profession had taken their toll.

'Drink?' he asked.

She smiled. Hinksman wished she hadn't. Her teeth were crooked and discoloured.

'Luv one. Champers?'

'You can have white wine,' he said.

She shrugged happily and beckoned a waiter.

When the drinks came she said, 'Thirsty work', put the glass to her lips and swigged three-quarters of it in one. Hinksman winced. *She's so goddamned vulgar*, he thought. *What the hell, I need some stress relief.*

'You a Yank?' she asked.

'What of it?'

'Y'all alone in town?' she leered in her best, mock-American accent.

He nodded.

She tilted her head. 'Well?'

He nodded again. The deal had been struck.

23

'Forty quid,' she said, businesslike.

He nearly choked on his drink. He wondered how much Danny Carver's whore had cost – God rest what was left of his splattered soul. A little more than forty pounds sterling. Even so, Hinksman quibbled. She was probably riddled with disease.

'I wouldn't pay that for a good-lookin' broad. Twenty-five. Take it or leave it.'

Unoffended, she bargained.

'Thirty-five.'

'Twenty-five.'

Seeing it was his one-and-only offer she accepted it with good grace. 'OK – but up front.'

'And anything I want.'

'So long as I don't get hurt. I'm not into that.'

'Deal . . . waiter! A bottle of champagne to take out.'

In the taxi Hinksman handed Jane a slim wad of five-pound notes. She stuffed them away in one practised movement, then moved a hand to his lap. As she unzipped him, and bent her head to the task, he suddenly yanked her upright by her hair.

'Wait,' he said.

'Ow, that fuckin' 'urt,' she wailed, rubbing her head.

He glanced sideways at her and smiled.

She shivered. She didn't like the look in his eyes at that moment. She thought he had the eyes of a madman. Suddenly she had serious doubts about the wisdom of this transaction.

'This couldn't have come at a better time,' Karen Wilde said to the Chief Constable. 'The way we handle it is very important.'

She was being very matter-of-fact, despite having re-moved her blouse and bra. She eased her skirt down her thighs and folded it neatly over the back of a chair, brushing a hair off. She stepped out of her knickers and stood there naked but for stockings and a suspender belt – totally

24

impractical and uncomfortable, but the Chief's favourite. As she unpinned her blonde hair and shook it out of the constricting school-marm bun, she went on, 'If we play it right – media-wise and result-wise – this could be your final stepping stone to the Inspectorate.'

'Maybe,' said Dave August.

'You've got to take control of this, make it yours, grasp the nettle.'

'Maybe,' he gasped.

He was lying completely naked on the single bed in the en-suite room which adjoined his first-floor office at headquarters. It was a room specifically designed to be used by the Chief should he or she need to work long hours or stay the night. Previous Chiefs rarely used it, preferring the detached police house which was in walking distance and within the headquarters' grounds. However, August had never even furnished the house. It might have encouraged his wife and kids to stay and he liked to keep them at arm's length – in the house he owned in Cheshire.

Karen walked across the small room and sat astride the Chief. She wriggled provocatively. He gasped again.

'The biggest crime since Lockerbie,' she mused, 'and it's happened on our patch. It's got great potential.'

'And so have you,' he breathed. 'Now c'mon, stop thinking about it for a while. That's an order, you scheming little minnie.'

She took no notice.

'Just suppose,' she pondered out loud, 'you put me in charge of the investigation.' She wriggled.

'But you've only ever done short secondments to CID. You'd be way out of your depth. And I need someone of at least the rank of Superintendent to head it.'

'I've given that some consideration,' she smiled.

'And . . . ?'

'That Detective-Super from commerce branch is on long-term sick. I could become Acting Superintendent . . . and anyway, running it wouldn't be that hard. Just a case of being a good manager. It's all done by computer these days.'

Before August had a chance to reply, she kissed him. Wet. Long. Lots of tongue. She swayed her hard nipples across his chest then ran her hand down his belly, grasping him firmly.

'How about it, boss?' she asked, rising for air. 'Can I? The media will love me.'

August chided himself. He wished he was big enough to say no. But she was bargaining from a position of strength.

'Would you take a fuckin' look at that, man!' whistled Agent Donaldson.

He dabbed the button on the hand-held remote control and rewound the video tape taken from one of the overhead cameras on the M6. Then he played it forwards one frame at a time. Even so, the explosion was so fast and devastating that the camera didn't really take it all in. It wasn't designed to do so.

One second the car was moving down the middle lane.

In the same second a huge flash filled the screen and the car was gone, replaced by chaos, death and confusion, with no discernible gap between the scenarios.

He and McClure watched it a few more times, mesmerised.

The picture quality wasn't that good. The tape had probably been re-used a million times. But it showed that the car was definitely a Daimler. And no doubt Danny Carver was in the back of it.

The Technical Services Unit would spend time enhancing the tape later. They promised wonderful things. The picture would be made clear with pin-sharp images and using their electronic wizardry they'd be able to enlarge selected segments of the screen. That way the number on the registration plate could be read and the faces of the people in the car might be identified (but don't hold your breath, they warned). And TSU could also speed up the

26

tape to 'mega-fast' (their description) and that way the explosion could be watched and analysed, conversely, in slow motion, bit by bloody bit.

With a *phtt* the screen on the TV fizzled out to blank, and Donaldson handed the remote back to the Control Room Inspector.

He and McClure left the Control Room together and walked across the car park at the front of the headquarters building.

'This certainly cocks the job up,' McClure said.

'A peculiarly British understatement, I would say,' remarked the American. 'But you're right, with Carver in pieces I'm back to square one with Corelli – and it was going so damned well.'

'All may not be lost,' said McClure airily.

'How d'ya mean?'

'Well, if you're right and this has Corelli's backing, then all we need to do is catch the killer, put him under pressure and we could have a lever to get to Corelli through him.'

'You make it sound so simple.'

'What about the guy you saw at the hotel?'

'A glimpse of someone I may have recognised isn't exactly evidence that he's a killer, even for British justice.'

'It's a start though, so don't forget that face. Think hard about it and keep it in your mind's eye. I've got an idea.'

'Which is?'

'Tell you later,' said McClure as they reached their car. He leaned for a second on the roof. 'If this is down to Corelli, then it shows what an evil bastard he is.'

'Evil?' Donaldson laughed briefly. 'In the last two years Corelli's put at least eight of his rivals out of business – that we know of. Another three are still missing, presumed dead. There's no evidence to link him, of course, just hearsay and bar talk. But they're down to him and he stays whiter than white. You've heard of the untouchables? He's fuckin' totally untouchable.'

'So who's doing the killings?'

27

'Dunno.' Donaldson shrugged his shoulders. 'Someone very good, someone we don't even know. Probably the guy who did this one. But I do know one thing . . .'

McClure waited, arms folded.

'If I was Danny Carver's English partner, I'd be shitting in my pants right now.'

'Why's that?'

'We expected both of them to be in that limo so it's safe to assume the killer expected the same. He's only done half a job.'

A grunting noise made them turn and look up at the building.

A dim light shone behind a curtain on the first floor.

'Someone's up late,' said Donaldson. He climbed into the car.

It was 1.30 a.m.

Jane the stripper lay awake on the grubby sheets listening to Hinksman's regular deep breathing as he slept beside her. The room, like the rest of the hotel, was musty and dank-smelling.

Her top lip throbbed from a cut on the inside where it had banged against her teeth. Blood seeped into her mouth. She shuddered at the salty taste. Her right eye was badly swollen and beginning to blacken; she could hardly open it. That too throbbed – a slightly different beat to her lip.

She moved a hand slowly up to her throat, slowly so that she would not disturb Hinksman, and massaged her Adam's apple tenderly, remembering how Hinksman, on reaching his climax, had clamped a vice-like hand around her windpipe and almost strangled her to death in an orgasm that was a torrent of violent, uncontrollable, jerking spasms.

The injuries to her lip and eye were punishments because she had complained about the near-murder.

When he knocked her around the room – a cold, clinical assault – she thought he got even more pleasure from the

28

violence than from the sex. His mad eyes had really been shining.

Hinksman moved onto his back. His mouth fell open. He snored.

Crazy American bastard, she thought.

Lying there, motionless and taut, she wondered if she would be able to get out of bed, dress herself and slide out of the room without waking him up. He'd told her that he wanted her to be there in the morning – so she could imagine what his reaction would be to find her fleeing the place: a worse beating than before. Yet to be there in the morning would no doubt entail another beating too.

She squinted sideways at him through her good eye. He seemed well gone. She moved slightly. He groaned. She went rigid again. He didn't wake.

From somewhere down in the bowels of the hotel a phone started ringing.

'Fuck,' she cursed under her breath and heaved a deep sigh. Until it stopped there was no point trying anything. Escape would have to wait. She glanced at her watch – 2 a.m.

The phone seemed to ring for ever. Then there was the mumble of a voice followed by footsteps on the stairs, getting closer to Hinksman's room. Jane fully expected them to pass. They didn't. There was a light knock on the door.

Hinksman continued to snore.

The knocking persisted, growing louder. Hinksman was not disturbed.

In the end Jane could tolerate it no longer. She tugged a sheet off the bed, wrapped it round herself and answered the door.

An unshaven man wearing pyjamas and a stained dressing-gown stood there. Heavy bags hung beneath his bloodshot eyes. It was the hotel proprietor, Pepe Paglia.

'Oh,' he said, surprised at seeing her. 'I want him.' He pointed with a nicotine-stained finger at Hinksman.

'Help yourself,' she said. 'He's all yours.'

Paglia went over to the bed and shook Hinksman. 'Wake up, come on.'

He was lifeless. A sustained effort was needed before he was finally roused; it was a fair while after that before he knew what was happening.

The woman kicked herself. Had she suspected he was this hard to wake when drunk, she would have been long gone.

'Phone call,' said Paglia. 'It's . . .' he glanced at Jane, turned back to Hinksman and whispered, 'Miami.'

'Jeez, what does he want?'

'Dunno. I said you were asleep but he told me I had to get you.'

'Right.' He rubbed the sleep out of his eyes with the base of his thumbs, pulled on his dressing-gown and padded barefoot out of the room, ignoring the woman.

Paglia was left with Jane. He dawdled, peered closely at her. 'Given you a belting, has he?' he said. 'If you want looking after properly you can always come to me. Great Italian lover.'

His face contorted into what could only be described as a leer. He thrust his hips forward with a jerk.

'God forbid,' she said. She wafted away his halitosic breath.

'Suit yourself,' he shrugged, and left the room, looking pleased with himself.

'Yuk,' she said when he'd gone, and shivered at the thought of him.

She dressed quickly.

Prior to leaving, she picked up Hinksman's wallet and quickly went through it. She couldn't believe her eyes. It was the first stroke of luck she'd had that night – or that year, come to think of it. Apart from credit cards, six of them, and driver's licence which she intended to sell on, there was about £1,000 in mixed Bank of England notes, and a thick wad of dollar traveller's cheques. And he'd only paid her twenty-five quid, the tight bastard.

'Criminal injuries compensation,' she muttered, pocketing the money.

She tiptoed onto the landing above the entrance hall where Hinksman was taking the phone call. She backed into the dark recess of an alcove and waited.

'Unfortunate,' she could hear Hinksman saying. 'But it's the name of the game ... innocents do die occasionally ... so where will he be? Who? Say that again ... Right, got that; I speak to him. Right, OK. I'll take care of it, don't you worry, boss. Take it as read. It's as good as done ... OK, OK, so long.'

In the shadows Jane's stomach tightened with fear. She prayed to a God she didn't really believe in: *Please, don't let him spot me hiding here.* She closed her eyes.

She heard him coming up the stairs.

She steeled herself to open her eyes again.

She almost let out a yelp. There he was. Less than three feet away from her! She could reach out and tap his shoulder. Surely out of the corner of his eye he must see her. Surely then he would kill her.

But Hinksman walked straight past her, yawning, massaging his neck muscles. His mind and senses were far away. She was undiscovered.

Still holding her breath, Jane gave him time to get round the corner before emerging like a ghost from the darkness and bolting down the stairs, along the hall and out through the front door – away from a man she never wanted to see again.

Sadly for her, this was not to be the case.

Chapter Four

The phone in the bedroom rang for a long, long time. Slowly it insinuated itself into Henry's brain cells and forced him into wakefulness. It was a fight against whisky, analgesic and a crack on the head. He lay listening to the shrill noise, not knowing what it was at first. Eventually he threw off the duvet and went over to pick it up.

'Yeah?' he croaked.

'DS Christie?'

'Yeah.'

'This is Linda in control room. If you're fit, you're requested to be at the murder incident room which has been set up at Preston police station at eleven o'clock for a briefing.'

'What time is it now?'

'Nine-o-five.'

'Right. I'll be there.'

'Are you OK for transport?'

'Yeah.'

He reeled slightly as a spell of dizziness hit him and put a hand to his forehead, steadying himself. His fingers brushed the tender stitches and shaved area on the left side of his head. He flinched at the touch. He felt old and stiff.

The house was quiet. Kate must have taken the girls to school and gone on to her part-time job at the insurance brokerage in Blackpool. She hadn't disturbed him when she left – or at least he couldn't recall it.

He had a long hot redeeming shower, brushed his teeth vigorously and gargled with TCP to get rid of the alcoholic residue. He emerged feeling almost alive.

He made a quick phone call to Terry – who was all right but had reported in sick – and with three Paracetamols down him (and a further supply in his pocket), a glass of skimmed milk to line his stomach, a quick peek in the mirror to remind himself how he looked – bad – he left for work just after ten, shaving as he drove with a battery-powered portable.

Hinksman was pissed off to find that the prostitute had vanished. He swore and checked his wallet. Empty. What a surprise.

He decided that if he had the opportunity, he'd track her down and hurt her. Rather more than he had done already.

As soon as his head hit the grubby pillow again he was asleep.

His heavy night, however, didn't prevent him from waking up before his alarm and turning out for a four-mile run along the promenade. It was no easy, laid-back jog, but a hard fast work-out designed to flush his system. By the end of it he felt clear and quick again. Ready for work.

Hinksman found the hotel proprietor in the kitchen. He helped himself to a slice of toast and a cup of coffee, after which he backed Paglia into the large, walk-in pantry and spoke to him.

'That bitch cleaned me out last night,' Hinksman hissed. 'I need money – pronto.'

'No problem. Ten, twenty, thirty pounds?'

'A grand.'

'What! I haven't got that sort of money.'

'Get it,' said Hinksman levelly. 'This afternoon. I need to buy things.'

'I can't,' he protested.

Hinksman reached out his right hand at the speed of a cobra striking, and clamped it round the little man's throat. From there he lifted him on tiptoes and slammed him back against a tall freezer which rocked precariously, the contents clattering around inside. Hinksman's grip tightened.

Paglia struggled for breath, gagging and choking, both hands fumbling in a pathetic attempt to peel Hinksman's fingers out of his soft skin.

'I said get it. You don't want to fall out with us, now do you?'

Paglia's eyes bulged. He managed to shake his head and Hinksman set him down.

'Good,' said the American. 'A very sensible person.'

Paglia coughed painfully and rubbed at his throat. Thumb and finger indentations were clearly visible on the skin.

'Mamma,' he whispered. 'There was no need for that.'

'You're obviously a man who needs to be made to understand. Now – I want that cash by this afternoon, OK?'

Paglia nodded forlornly.

Hinksman smiled. He went out, leaving the little man in the pantry, still not having recovered from his ordeal.

Hinksman walked through the hotel flexing his fingers.

That felt rather good, he thought.

The Chief Constable's office had a view across the sports field at headquarters. Dave August spent many a happy hour watching games from the window. Feet up, all calls diverted, all callers blocked. One of the few benefits of rank, he thought.

At ten o'clock that morning, the day after the M6 bombing, he was behind his desk, facing into the room. Two men sat opposite him.

Here was one of the drawbacks of rank, he thought sourly. Making unpopular – and bad – decisions and having to stick with them.

The ACC (Operations), Jack Crosby, a tough no-nonsense career detective was one of his visitors. He looked grave and unhappy. He'd spent all his service with Lancashire and had been involved in over 200 murder investigations – and got a result on all but one. He'd also been involved in career manipulation and politics at the highest level of the service, and could see right through the Chief's announcement. It was obvious what he was thinking. *Dick rules head.*

Robert Fanshaw-Bayley, the Chief Superintendent in charge of crime, was the other visitor. Despite his fancy-sounding name and appearance, he was as tough and hard-edged as Crosby, but ten years younger. He thought he'd seen and heard everything in his time, but the Chief's words left him gobsmacked.

August could see what effect his announcement had had, but there was no going back now.

'So I hope you'll give her your whole-hearted support,' he finished weakly.

'And there's no doubt about it – she's gonna need a hell of a lot,' said Fanshaw-Bayley. He clammed up as soon as the words were out of his mouth.

The Chief kept his temper. 'I admit she's inexperienced, but she's very capable.'

'And ambitious,' interjected Crosby. 'Isn't this what it's all about – ambition?' His Liverpool accent, normally un-detectable, became more pronounced.

'It'll be a good challenge for her,' August said. 'And yes, it won't do her career any harm.'

Crosby sighed. He pinched the bridge of his nose.

'This crime,' he said, 'is above career ambition. In my opinion, Ronnie Veevers is the man who should be running it. He's got the experience, contacts and ability to run such a large investigation. He did well on the Baxter shooting and that double murder over in Colne at the beginning of the year. And he wouldn't be heading it because he wants to become a Chief Constable – he'd be heading it because he wanted to catch the evil bastard that did it!' His voice had risen.

'If she wants some experience, boss, let her run with Veevers. Be his aide, his assistant or whatever – but don't let her have the reins. This is far too big to make mistakes.'

August sat back in his big chair. The leather creaked. He

indicated Fanshaw-Bayley. 'Robert, have you anything to add?'

'Plenty – but not here and now, except to say I agree with everything Mr Crosby has said.' He folded his arms and gazed past the Chief's shoulder, out of the window.

'In that case – meeting over,' the Chief concluded airily.

'What exactly does that mean, sir?' Crosby asked.

'It means that Miss Wilde heads the investigation.'

After they had gone Karen emerged from the en-suite. She'd been listening at the door.

'You were brilliant, boss,' she cooed.

'Mm,' he said doubtfully.

'Typical misogynistic CID, that's all,' she assured him. 'You've taken their toys off them and they don't like it so they're sulking. A boys' club, that's all it is. And I've got their ball and I'm going to play with it.'

'Don't you let me down,' August warned her.

'Would I? *Moi?*' She winked at him. 'Now, that briefing is set for eleven. I'll put it back to two, which'll give me time to get my hair done and sort out a few new working outfits.'

Inwardly, Dave August groaned.

Crosby and Fanshaw-Bayley walked side by side down the corridor towards Crosby's office. The corridor of power. Anyone who was anyone had an office along here.

Once behind his own closed door, the man exploded.

'I simply do not believe what I've just heard!'

He slumped down behind his desk and thumped it with his fist.

'Wilde has no experience of police work of any description. She's done all the secondments and training courses she needs to do to get where she is and nothing more. She's hardly set the world on fire, just played the system and won. She's nothing more than a competent administrator. Jesus, this is *appalling*. I wonder how long it is since she was last face to face with an actual villain? Or even a member of the public, come to that?'

36

FB listened to the tirade, nodding all the while.

'It does help,' he added, 'when you're shafting the Chief Constable at the same time.'

Crosby's eyes narrowed. 'We don't know if that's true. Let's turn some of that rumour into hard fact before it's too late. We don't want this investigation falling apart round our ears. We'll need to move fast. Can I leave it to you, FB?'

FB nodded.

McClure picked up Donaldson from his central Manchester hotel – paid for by the FBI – at ten-thirty that morning. Both men looked haggard through lack of sleep, but at least McClure had had the advantage of spending the night in his own bed with his own warm-arsed wife to spoon up to.

It had gone three when Donaldson had clambered into a bed which was cold and uninviting despite the plushness of the room. He missed having someone to get to grips with in the dark hours. In fact, he had missed someone for three years. Ever since his wife had disappeared with a beat cop from Fort Lauderdale who worked horrendous hours yet came home every day. Donaldson didn't really blame her. If he made it home once a week it was an occasion. He was thankful there were no children to worry about.

'Put a name to that face yet?' McClure asked as the agent slumped beside him.

'Can't say I have,' sighed Donaldson, 'but I'm sure I've seen it before . . . in the Corelli file . . .' He thought hard, screwing up his face. 'Or a bar somewhere . . . I dunno. Anyway, I'm going to do an ET.'

'A what?'

'You know – phone home,' Donaldson explained.

'Oh, right,' said McClure bewildered.

'I'll have someone look through the photos for me. I'm sure it's from one taken in a restaurant or bar. It's just tough that we've hundreds of Corelli in fucking restaurants.'

'Actually I have an idea that might just help on that score.'

'Whaddya mean?'

'Later, later,' said McClure. 'Just sit back and enjoy the ride.'

The gymnasium at Preston police station had been commandeered as the murder incident room. Since the early hours, furniture and equipment had been rolled in and placed on the canvas matting which had been laid to protect the gym floor. Four HOLMES terminals (Home Office Large/Major Enquiry System) were already up and running, waiting for information to be fed into them; four more were expected. Twelve phones had been rigged up. Desks were placed around the room, all equipped with stationery and wire baskets and a sign indicating who would be sitting there: *Receiver, Allocator, Coordinator, Exhibits Officer* etc . . . and the wall ladders around the gym were covered with whiteboards, blackboards and noticeboards.

Two coffee machines had also been installed.

It was going to be a long investigation.

The room was crowded for this initial briefing. There were forty detectives drawn in from around the county, twenty-odd uniform officers mainly from the Support Unit, some traffic cops, a handful of civilians and three Coroner's officers.

Those present were subdued but expectant and raring to go. Impatient too. After all, the first briefing at eleven had been cancelled. Valuable time was being wasted.

The atmosphere was quietly charged.

Despite himself, Henry Christie couldn't suppress a smile. He leaned back on the wall and looked around the room. He'd worked on many murders, been in this situation many times. Dying to get going, get your teeth into it. Knowing that maybe, just maybe, you'd be the one to feel the collar.

Particularly this one. This was almost personal.

His smile disappeared.

Especially this one.

* * *

Karen Wilde shuffled her notes into order, glancing through them once more, collating all the salient facts. She knew all there was to know so far, and she also knew exactly what she was going to say in the briefing which was – she checked her watch – five minutes away.

She stood up and paced the office she'd taken over – a small one on the third floor belonging to some pen-pushing nonentity admin inspector who'd moaned pathetically when she'd turfed him out. Silly little sod.

She straightened her suit then made her way towards the lift and pressed the button. The gym was several floors up. She tapped her feet as she waited for the lift to arrive.

It came. The doors creaked open. Two men she did not know stepped out. They peered at her office pass which was clipped onto the lapel of her new jacket.

'Chief Inspector Wilde,' one of them said.

'Acting Superintendent,' she corrected him, bustling past into the lift. 'Acting Detective-Superintendent, actually,' she said, pressing the button.

But the lift did not move. The man had stepped across the threshold, preventing the doors from closing.

'I believe you're running the investigation into the M6 bombing?'

'Correct.'

'Big job for a little lady like you,' said the other man. Karen noticed his American accent.

She said stonily, 'I don't know who you are, but I don't care for your attitude or approach. Now, I have a briefing to give, so if you wouldn't mind . . . ?' She waved away the man who was impeding the lift.

'We have some valuable information for you regarding the bombing,' he said.

'Can't it wait?'

'No.'

'Then you'd better be quick about it, hadn't you?'

Earlier that day, McClure had driven north up the M6.

He'd had to detour round Preston because the motorway was still closed, but within an hour they were in Lancaster. He drove into the Posthouse Hotel car park.

Donaldson was mystified. McClure had refused point blank to answer any of the American's queries.

'This better be fucking good,' said the FBI man, clambering out of the car.

McClure just smiled.

The two men stood side by side. McClure, still silent, pointed up at the hotel.

Donaldson's mouth dropped open.

Video cameras. Two of them. Each one positioned on a front corner of the building, recording views of the car park from different angles.

He spun round to McClure, grinning. 'You brilliant bastard! How in hell did y'know about these?'

McClure shrugged modestly. 'Just recalled seeing them yesterday, but didn't think much of it at the time.'

'Let's hope they work.'

The management were as helpful as on the previous day, allowing the detectives to view the tapes in a private room. It took only ten minutes to find what they wanted. Then McClure claimed the relevant tape for evidence and gave the manager a receipt.

'May I ask what all this is about?' the manager asked.

'Did the man we've just seen on the tape book a room?' McClure enquired, ignoring the question.

'Yes – he paid two days in advance.'

McClure looked quickly at Donaldson. 'Is he still in it?'

'I don't know. We'll have to ask Reception.'

'Let's do it,' snapped Donaldson.

'But what's it about?' the manager demanded.

McClure said, 'The M6 bombing.'

'Oh my God,' the man breathed. Then he pulled himself together. 'Right, come this way.'

Reception confirmed that the man had booked and paid for Room 111 but hadn't returned to it since yesterday, unless he'd sneaked back without their knowledge. The key had not been returned yet.

McClure and Donaldson conferred hurriedly.

'He could be in there, then,' McClure said. 'In which case we could do with an armed back-up.'

'He won't be there,' Donaldson said with certainty. 'And anyway, you gotta gun. Don't be a cissy.'

McClure paused, then made a decision. He nodded and turned to the manager. 'Give us a pass key to the room, please.'

The corridor was quiet and empty. A laundry basket on wheels was part-way along it, the room itself three-quarters of the way down. The two detectives edged slowly along. McClure held his gun in his hand. Sweat beads began to form on his head.

Donaldson grinned. 'You ever used that thing in anger?'

'Never even drawn it outside a range,' McClure whispered.

'Thought as much.'

The men stood on either side of the door. They eyed each other for a moment.

Donaldson knocked loudly and shouted, 'Good morning. Maid service.'

There was no response.

Donaldson inserted the pass key, pulled the handle down and pushed. The door swung gently open. There was nothing to see.

'Armed police! Come on out with your hands up,' McClure barked.

Nothing. He repeated the order. Still nothing.

In one swift movement, gun held in the classic two-handed shooting grip, he twisted into the short hallway, low, fast, his breathing controlled, but heart beating like a demented drum machine. Keeping low, he almost danced to where the short hallway widened out into the bedroom proper – where he exposed himself fully for the first time.

He expected a bullet in the head. It never came. The room was empty. He beckoned Donaldson in.

The American sauntered up behind him. 'Very good. You move well.'

'Thank you. Let's check out the bathroom before we get too cocky,' said McClure shakily.

It was empty.

'He booked in and fucked off when he saw us, I guess,' Donaldson mused.

McClure reholstered his weapon. 'I'll tell the manager to seal off this room until we can get Scenes of Crime to do it.'

Thirty minutes later they accosted Karen Wilde in the lift at Preston police station.

As they followed her down the corridor to her office, Donaldson said, 'What a bitch,' under his breath.

McClure merely raised his eyebrows.

'I'd like to fuck her though,' he added without moving his lips, eyes glued to her rear.

'Join the queue,' McClure retorted.

'Right, what've you got for me?' Karen said when they reached her office. She sat at the desk.

'I'm Detective Chief Inspector McClure from Greater Manchester's Serious Crime Squad and—'

'I'm Special Agent Donaldson, Karl Donaldson, FBI, based in Miami, Florida, in the United States of America.'

'I'm fully aware of the location of Florida. It's where Mickey Mouse lives, I believe.'

Both men shook her hand, Donaldson with a grave, piss-taking formality. 'And may I add what a pleasure it is to meet ya'll, ma'am?'

'You can add what you damn well like. Just get on with it – I'm busy.'

McClure opened his mouth but Donaldson cut in. 'Allow me . . . I'll try and sum it up in a nutshell.'

'Do try,' said Karen thinly, resting her chin on her thumb and forefinger.

'I work in the Organised Crime Department of the FBI and for the last five years me and my partner have been trying to nail a mobster called Corelli. Very rich guy, into

42

anything illegal you care to mention – drugs, prostitution, fraud . . . Anyway, we've been pretty unsuccessful.

'This guy Corelli has loads of business partners. One of them is a young punk called Danny Carver. Carver has been linked to Corelli for about three years. Suspected of being involved in some major stuff. I mean mega-shit – gun-running, drugs, massive commodity frauds, the whole caboodle. Eventually, Carver gets pissed because he does a lot of legwork but only gets a small percentage of the profit. So what does he do?'

'Do tell,' said Karen.

'Cuts loose and starts doin' deals himself without the boss but using his contacts. Cheeky, huh? Corelli ain't happy but he lives with it until Carver schmoozes into a deal that Corelli himself is actually tryin' to put together with a drug baron in Manchester, guy called Brown. Corelli is that far –' here Donaldson laid his palms together – 'from doin' business when Carver steps in and pulls the rug out from under him then sets up the same deal with Brown but with bigger percentages all round.'

'What does this deal involve?'

'Importing crack into the UK. Basically taking over the British market,' intercut McClure. 'Big money.'

'Millions,' affirmed Donaldson. 'Money that Corelli wasn't happy losing. The rumour is that Corelli put out a contract on Carver – but I stress it's only a rumour.'

Karen checked her watch impatiently.

'What we intended to do,' Donaldson said hurriedly, 'was to nail Carver, which wouldn't have been too difficult because he's a sloppy operator. Then we'd promise him immunity from prosecution, a new life, new I.D. – y'know, full-blown witness protection – in exchange for him testifying against Corelli. Might've worked,' he mused.

'Anyway,' he concluded, 'we fixed up this transatlantic cooperation exercise between the FBI and the Greater Manchester police – with the blessing from your Home

Office . . . and it was all going well until yesterday. Carver was—'

'What happened yesterday?' Karen interrupted.

McClure took over. 'We'd had Carver and Brown under obs for a couple of weeks. We knew they'd holed up in an hotel in Lancaster with a couple of call girls. It was our intention to pick up their tail yesterday morning, but we were late arriving at the hotel because we got snarled up in motorway roadworks. By then, both of them had gone.'

'How careless,' sneered Karen. 'This is very interesting, but what has it got to do with me?'

'According to the management,' said Donaldson, 'Carver had left in a Daimler with one of the hookers and Brown had gone off in a Beemer with the other girl.'

'A Beemer – what's that?'

'Sorry – a BMW,' explained Donaldson. 'Next thing we know – BOOM! Carver has a bomb up his ass.'

'Hang on. So you're saying that the car that blew up causing the M6 tragedy, had Danny Carver in it – and you might know who killed him and why?'

'Not exactly,' Donaldson stressed. 'I am saying that Carver was in the Daimler. I'm surmising that he was killed by a hit man who works for Corelli, because he'd usurped him on a big business deal.'

'How can you be sure that this Danny Carver was in the Daimler? There's nothing identifiable left in the car. It's not even recognisably a Daimler.'

'Just adding up the scores on the doors,' said McClure.

'Talk evidence,' Karen insisted.

'OK,' said Donaldson. 'Firstly we know that Carver was booked on a flight to Miami from Manchester yesterday. He didn't get on it – we checked.'

'Secondly we have a video tape here from the hotel –' he held up the cassette – 'which shows Danny Carver getting into a Daimler with a girl and being driven away. We've watched your tapes of the explosion from the freeway camera and it looks like the same model of Daimler. I'll bet when your forensic team get their results together they'll find the remains of three bodies.'

'I am definitely intrigued,' said Karen, beginning to squirm a little with excitement.

Donaldson went on, 'I saw a man in the hotel lobby yesterday who I recognise as having some Corelli connection – but the great thing is that the hotel video cameras pick him up arriving in a car, parking it, walking past Carver's limo and bending down next to it.'

'Really!' exclaimed Karen, barely suppressing her glee. 'Can you see exactly what he did?'

'No, because the film is a bit blurred. It needs enhancing. However, we *can* see that his suitcase drops open next to the car. He bends down to pick his clothes up and quickly reaches under the limo.' This was said by McClure. 'Good stuff, eh?'

Fucking bloody ace, Karen thought, but didn't allow herself to smile.

'Add to that the rumour about the contract,' said Donaldson, 'and I think we're onto something, don't you?'

'Possibly,' Karen said.

'Once you get a Technical Support Unit to enhance the numberplate from the motorway video we'll know for sure if it was Carver's Daimler or not.'

'I already have the number,' Karen said triumphantly, and read it out aloud from her notes.

'That's the one!' McClure confirmed. 'If TSU can do the same for the hotel video and lift the registered number from this guy's car, we could be well on our way.'

'And all I have to do is catch him,' Karen said. She looked expectantly at Donaldson. 'So, what's the guy's name?'

'That's the problem. I don't know. There is another problem too. I believe he's only fulfilled part of his contract. If we don't get him quick, he'll kill again.'

In spite of her tardy entrance to an already delayed briefing,

Karen Wilde handled the start of her first murder investigation with the assurance of a seasoned professional.

She stepped onto a raised platform at one end of the gym and called for quiet.

Within minutes she had them eating out of her hand. The irritability of the officers soon evaporated as she directed her considerable public-speaking skills at them. She concluded by naming the pairings of detectives and asking them to see the Allocator for their tasks in half an hour.

The investigation was underway at last.

Before leaving the platform she said, 'Is DS Christie here?'

'Yes, ma'am,' he said from the back of the room.

'My office – ten minutes,' she clipped and stepped down.

'Lucky you,' someone said to Henry.

'Why?'

'Spanking.'

Henry chuckled.

He knocked on the office door and entered. Karen was sitting behind her desk reading the initial pathology and forensic reports.

'Sit down,' she said, briefly looking up then returning her attention to the paperwork.

He sat on a chair opposite her and waited, wondering what job he was going to be given. He speculated. Must be interesting if she was giving it to him personally.

Eventually she stacked the papers neatly in front of her and looked at Henry.

'DS Christie,' she said at length.

'Yes.'

'How are you? You look awful, if you don't mind me saying.'

He shrugged. 'Don't feel too bad, just sore. Can't wait to get going with this, though.'

She frowned. 'Hm,' she said.

Henry's eyes narrowed. Something was wrong here.

There was a pause, then: 'Can you tell me how it is that

within the space of a few minutes yesterday you performed an action which reflected great credit on the force, followed by one which has brought us equal public disgrace?'

Henry's mouth sagged open. He clamped it shut with a clash of his teeth.

'Your action at the scene of the bombing in trying to rescue those children was commendable. Shortly afterwards, in an incident which was broadcast on nationwide TV, you threw a reporter down the riverbank. What do you have to say?'

Flabbergasted, Henry shook his head. 'Nothing.'

'Well, I can tell you that an official complaint has been made by the BBC. It alleges assault, abuse of authority, discreditable conduct and suchlike. Here . . .' She handed him a form.

It was the notorious Form 14, a Discipline and Complaints form. On it were set out the allegations in detail.

Karen cautioned Henry and asked him if he had anything to say. He shook his head sadly, on the verge of tears.

'D and C will be looking into it,' Karen said. 'In the meantime you can return to your normal duty.'

'I'm not on the investigation then?'

'No – you're too personally involved. It wouldn't be right, for your sake. Before you go, though, would you write out a detailed statement about what happened yesterday and submit it to the statement reader. OK, that's all.'

Chapter Five

Hinksman drove his hired Mondeo east across the county to Rossendale, an area of high moorland, deep valleys and towns clinging precariously to the hillsides like clusters of weather-beaten barnacles. He was making for a remote farmhouse situated high above Bacup which had fantastic panoramic views across the Tops towards the ugly sprawl of Greater Manchester in the south.

The house had been renovated and modernised and owed little to its agricultural origins. Now it was the type of house a wealthy accountant or stockbroker might have bought as a place in the country: private, exclusive, yet within commuting distance of work.

Hinksman looked around admiringly as he drove up the steep, winding track to the house.

He'd been there only four days previously. He'd hoped that a return would be unnecessary but . . . such is life.

He stopped at the large wrought-iron gates and pressed the button on the intercom.

'Yes?' came a metallic voice.

'We met last week,' Hinksman said. He glanced up whilst talking and waved at the camera discreetly lodged in the branches of a tall tree. 'You sold me some almonds.' The word 'almonds' referred to the smell given off by Semtex.

'I thought we'd finished our business.'

'You were wrong,' said Hinksman.

He took his finger off the button and returned to the Mondeo. He'd left the engine running.

After a short delay the gates swung silently open. He

nosed the car up the drive, and came to a halt on the gravel at the front of the house. He got out and leaned on the bonnet of the car for a moment, admiring the view and the other two cars parked there, a Bentley and a Ferrari. I'll treat myself to a Ferrari one day, he thought. It's a real good idea. Me and Donny blasting down the Keys together. Sure thing! The picture in his mind's eye made him smile again.

Footsteps crunched behind him. The man who was walking towards him from the house was about fifty, six feet tall and upright like the ex-soldier he was. Hinksman knew him only as Gaskell. He was an arms dealer, legit and properly registered with the local cops.

'You shouldn't have come here again,' said Gaskell, clearly worried. 'It's far too risky, and as far as I'm concerned, my business with you is concluded. I did a favour for Corelli because he'd done one for me many years ago; now we're even. I don't particularly want to be associated with someone who indiscriminately kills women and children.'

'But you *are* associated, buddy,' replied Hinksman. 'You gave me the explosive and the detonator. You're in it just as deep as I am – if I choose to make it that way.'

Gaskell looked hard at Hinksman, who returned the stare with the glimmer of a smile.

'But all those people!' Gaskell said, pained.

'Unfortunate, but it happens. Casualties of war.' Hinksman shrugged. He did not care.

Gaskell shook his head bitterly. 'I knew you were an evil bastard when I first saw you.'

'I do a job, that's all.'

'What do you want this time?' Gaskell asked after a pause, resigned to his fate. He knew he was trapped.

'Handgun. And ammunition.'

Gaskell sighed. 'You'd better come in.'

He led Hinksman through the house to a study on the ground floor at the rear. The walls were lined with leather-bound books. A plush desk with an inlaid leather top was situated in the bay window; on it was a PC – keyboard, monitor and printer, very state of the art. It hummed quietly. On one of the bookshelves was a TV which gave a split screen recording from cameras which protected the house. There were views of the front and rear. A VCR whirred dully underneath the TV.

Hinksman hadn't been here before. Their last transaction had taken place outside.

'Very nice,' he admitted.

Gaskell made no reply. He unlocked a desk drawer and took out a set of keys. He indicated for Hinksman to follow him.

Gaskell opened a door in the kitchen and went down a flight of steps. There was another door in the basement, this of steel construction with high quality locks. In one corner of the door was a stamp from one of the country's leading safe manufacturers.

Gaskell unlocked it and pushed it silently open. He reached inside and flicked a light switch.

Twenty metres away two soldiers with rifles appeared out of the gloom, charging noiselessly towards them.

Hinksman was impressed. 'Your very own firing range.'

'Yes,' said Gaskell. 'Inspected and certified by the Army and police. I test a lot of small-arms down here. I have a bigger range at the warehouse.'

He smacked a button on the wall. The targets at the end of the range clattered out of sight. The soldiers were charging no more.

Hinksman wandered down the range as Gaskell opened a steel cabinet in the safe area, behind the firing line.

He took another key out of this cabinet and bent down to pull back the carpet in the corner of the range, revealing a floor-safe. This he opened and heaved the lid off like removing a manhole cover. He drew out a heavy holdall which he placed with a thud on a table. He unzipped it. Inside was a collection of handguns – revolvers and pistols.

By this time Hinksman had returned from his stroll down the firing range.

'Everything in here is untraceable,' Gaskell told him. 'And nothing has been used in a crime before.'

'How can you be sure?'

'I'm sure.'

Gaskell pulled out four guns, two revolvers, two pistols, and laid them side by side on the table for Hinksman to inspect. 'All cleaned and oiled. Here –' he offered Hinksman a pair of plastic disposable gloves from a box.

Hinksman shook his head, declining.

'I like to feel a gun,' he said.

He picked up a model 469 9mm Smith & Wesson autoloading pistol with a 12-shot magazine which he slid out. Empty.

Gaskell delved into the bag and came out with a loaded one.

'If you want to try it, feel free,' he offered. 'Ear protectors are hung on the wall there.'

Hinksman reached for a pair and covered his ears. 'Can you time the targets?'

The dealer nodded.

'OK, six two-second exposures and vary the times when the targets aren't visible . . . anything up to ten seconds.'

'D'you want both targets?'

'Yep.'

Gaskell programmed in Hinksman's requirement as the American wandered to the 15-metre mark on the range. He shrugged his shoulders to loosen up, held the pistol with both hands, took a breath and signalled he was ready.

The delay seemed interminable, although it was only six seconds.

Then both targets swung into view. Suddenly, and for two seconds, Hinksman was faced with two heavily armed soldiers.

He reacted smoothly and quickly. His knees bent. He snapped into the weaver stance and, 'Ba-bam!' A double tap. The noise was incredible and so was Hinksman's speed and accuracy. In that split second of firing he put a bullet into each target. In the chest. On the heart. Then they were gone out of sight. Two seconds later – even before Hinksman had time to breathe out or consider how good his shooting was – the targets came back round again.

Again he caught them. Again both heart-shots.

Four gone. Eight remaining.

So far it was superb shooting. Gaskell was impressed and frightened. He quickly crossed the width of the range and picked up one of the guns from the table – a Makarov self-loading pistol. The targets swung back five seconds later: Hinksman amended his aim for these, drilling a hole in the forehead of each one with chilling precision. Six gone.

Gaskell checked the Makarov. The magazine was full. He eased one up the chamber and put the safety on. He didn't trust Hinksman. Didn't like the way he'd reacted to his feelings about the bomb. He thought it better to be in a stronger position when he came off the range with an empty gun, just in case. He wouldn't feel completely satisfied until the American had left.

The targets came round twice more in quick succession. Hinksman's aim stayed as remarkable as when he'd first started shooting. Two more shots to the head adjacent to the holes already there, followed by two more to the heart, forming a cluster any marksman would have been proud of.

Gaskell slipped the Makarov into the waistband of his trousers. He pulled his cardigan down to cover it.

There was a ten-second delay until the appearance of the targets for the last time.

An agonising wait.

Gaskell saw Hinksman's shoulders rise and fall and rise again with his controlled breathing.

The targets spun round.

And so did Hinksman. Fast. Only a millisecond behind the targets. Still with a double-handed grip. Perfectly balanced. Wonderful pirouette. He was now facing Gaskell.

The Englishman fumbled for his gun. But stuck there in his trousers, covered by the cardigan, he had no chance.

He'd hardly moved his hand before the first of Hinksman's bullets slammed into his chest. A heart-shot: dead centre. Perfect. The second bullet entered his head a fraction later, centre forehead, just above the bridge of his nose.

The arms dealer was almost lifted off his feet with the impact. He was thrown back against the wall where he stayed briefly pinned like a butterfly, arms high and wide, and then, already dead, he slithered into an untidy, bloody heap on the floor.

His chin lolled forwards onto his chest, exposing the gaping wound at the back of his skull where the slug had made its spinning exit.

Hinksman exhaled.

He looked at the gun and smiled. 'You'll do nicely,' he said. 'I wonder what else is on offer.'

Chapter Six

McClure and Donaldson got the registered number of the hired Mondeo from the hotel video. One PNC check later they'd got the name of the hire company to go with it.

Karen Wilde looked down at the hire documents which two detectives had seized and handed over to her in sealed plastic wallets.

It was a condition of the car-hire agreement that the person hiring the vehicle be photographed as part of the documentation process. Hinksman was no exception – but he'd worn a flat cap, glasses and a false moustache and moved his head when the receptionist pressed the button on the Polaroid. Result: blurred image.

Karen inspected the passport-sized photograph pinned to the corner of the hire agreement and compared it with the still that had been lifted and enlarged from the hotel video. Despite the disguise it was obviously the same man.

She read the agreement which gave the address of the hirer as Lytham St Annes, a seaside town south of Blackpool on the Lancashire coast. It was a fairly exclusive area.

McClure and Donaldson were sitting opposite her. Neither spoke as she peered at the evidence.

Her eyes rose from the document. She nodded.

'Good stuff,' she admitted.

'Yes, it's a good lead at least,' understated McClure. 'How's it going at the Posthouse Hotel room?'

'Scenes of Crime are there now. He obviously didn't spend much time there. Seems to have dumped his things, then done a runner when you two spooked him. Left his luggage behind. There could well be prints on his things, particularly toiletries. Looks like he had a drink from a glass of water, too.'

'Are you going to save the luggage for forensic?' Donaldson asked.

'Why should I?'

He looked at her like the rookie she was, but decided not to insult her. 'Well, from the video it looks like he kept the bomb in the case before clamping it underneath the Daimler.'

'So?'

He restrained himself from an impatient sigh. 'We now know the bomb contained Semtex; Semtex leaves traces on clothing. Could provide very good evidence.' Don't you know *anything*, he thought.

Smart-arse Yank, she thought sourly. 'I'll see it gets done,' she conceded gracelessly. 'So,' she went on, coming back to the hire document, 'with luck we'll be able to lift prints off this form and get the FBI searching their records. I don't hold out much hope though.'

'We'll get something,' Donaldson said.

Their eyes locked again. Briefly. Antagonistically.

McClure broke in. 'I still can't believe he had the audacity to hire a car himself – and from a company up here.'

'He's made a few mistakes,' said Karen. 'Yet you say he's a pro.'

'If he's working for Corelli, he's a pro. But even pros get careless,' Donaldson pointed out. 'He's operating outside his normal territory. He feels safe. He doesn't have the same sort of respect for British bobbies as he does for the FBI. He doesn't expect to get caught. He thinks it'll all be easy for him – and if I hadn't been here, it would have been.'

'Agent Donaldson,' said Karen, barely able to control her temper, 'we will catch this man, with or without your help.'

'Maybe.'

McClure tried to defuse the tension. 'What are we going to do about the address on that form?' He pointed to the hire documents.

'I'll send a pair of detectives round.'

'Is that wise?' asked McClure.

'Why not?' she shrugged. 'He's hardly likely to be there. The licence he's used is probably stolen or lost and the owner of it, who happens to be this guy –' she tapped the form – 'probably hasn't noticed it's gone or hasn't bothered to report it yet. Either way, he'll be sitting at home without a care in the world.'

'I don't think we should take that chance,' warned McClure. 'He's made a few mistakes so far, so maybe he's given us the address where he's actually holed up. OK, I admit it's unlikely but sending two unarmed lads round is a risk we shouldn't take.' He took a breath. 'That's my view, for what it's worth.'

Had it come from Donaldson, she would have dismissed it out of hand, but McClure's argument was reasonable in the circumstances.

'Go in with guns drawn and ready – is that what you're saying?

'Don't take a chance – *that's* what I'm saying.'

As McClure and Donaldson left the office, Karen picked up the phone and dialled an internal number. It rang and was answered quickly by the Chief Constable's secretary.

'I'm afraid he's busy just now, Miss Wilde,' the secretary said. 'He's meeting a member of the police committee.'

'I need to speak to him urgently, Jean,' Karen said.

'He's asked not to be disturbed,' the secretary said. She was one of the few who had hard evidence of Karen's affair with her boss and she disapproved of it.

'Jean,' Karen said slowly, as though making a point to a backward child, 'put me through to him now or I'll see that you end up transferred to some poxy little backwater copshop in the east of the county, typing up arrest reports for beat bobbies.'

'Very well. Hold the line.'

Joe Kovaks had spent the night cooped up in the back of an FBI surveillance van parked opposite a nightclub in downtown Miami. His partner for the stake-out had been a fat detective with a body-odour problem and a habit of breaking wind so spectacularly that their position was often in danger of being compromised. It made it worse that his partner was a woman. Had it been a man, Kovaks could've said something – or shot him – but what do you say to a woman who farts and stinks? He didn't know, so he called the job off at 4.30 a.m. They were getting nowhere.

He crept through his apartment an hour later, so as not to disturb Chrissy, his sleeping ladyfriend, and slid into bed, dropping immediately into a heavy slumber.

An hour and a half later, Donaldson called him.

'Look, Karl, what the fuck d'you want?' Kovaks hissed. 'It's good to hear from you but I've been on a job all night. Only just got to sleep, I'm shattered.'

Awoken, Chrissy rolled out of bed and padded naked to the toilet. Through his puffy eyes, Kovaks watched her.

'You been listening to the news?'

'On and off.'

'Hear about the M6 bombing?'

'Who hasn't.' Kovaks sat up, suddenly awake.

'Danny Carver took most of the blast. Or should I say, the late Danny Carver.'

'You're kidding me.'

'Absolutely not. I think Corelli had him hit.'

'Jeez . . . we'd heard some sort of whisper, hadn't we? Dog-feeder man, d'you think?'

'Can't be sure yet. Forensics are still piecing things together. Look, pal, I need you to do some digging for me. I'm sending a fax for you to the office. Two photos of the guy we think is the hit man. One's reasonably good, the other has him wearing some phoney disguise. And when I get 'em – sometime today, I hope – I'll send you a set of

57

dabs the fingerprint boys have lifted which may be his too. Run 'em through, will ya? See if they tie up with our fella. With me so far, buddy?'

'Anything else?'

'I think I've seen this guy before, on a photo with Corelli . . . sat in a bar or restaurant somewhere. When you get the fax, try and root out the photo, will ya? It could be the guy we've been after.'

'Oh, just like that? We've got over three thousand photos of that fat bastard, most of 'em feedin' his face.'

'Just do it, Joe. It's important.'

'Gotcha. No problemo.'

'What's Corelli been up to?' Donaldson asked.

Chrissy flushed the toilet and re-entered the room looking dopey, bedraggled and completely fuckable. Kovaks watched her slide in next to him.

'Nothing unusual,' he answered, as Chrissy cuddled up and squeezed him. 'Business, eating, fishing, eating, et cetera, et cetera . . . not always in that order.'

'Look, Joe, we really need to know who this hit man is. The British cops want to get him before he leaves the country. What I'm saying is, if the prints don't come back positive, this may be serious enough to approach Whisper.'

'Whoa! That's a big step – a decision for the Director to make.'

'Two dozen people are dead. A busload of little kids. I'd say we need to pull out the stops, wouldn't you? Plus, getting this bastard could lead us right up Corelli's ass.'

'Leave it with me, Karl.'

'The fax is on its way.'

'So am I.' Kovaks hung up and yawned hugely. Reluctantly he prised Chrissy away from his lower body. 'Got to go, sweetie. Sorry.'

'Fuckin' Fibbies,' she murmured. 'Hate 'em.' She turned over and snuggled back down into the bed.

'I can't make the decision for you,' Dave August sighed.

'No one said it would be easy . . . and I can't authorise a firearms team to turn out anyway. You'll have to go through the proper channels on this, otherwise things will start to stink even worse than they do already.'

'What do you mean?'

'You know exactly what I mean.'

'So I'll have to go creeping to that bastard Crosby for authorisation?'

'No – you'll have to put a reasoned argument to him and then, if he's satisfied, he'll give you the go-ahead to use a team.'

'You're no use whatsoever.'

She slammed the phone down, fuming, but knowing he was correct.

In Britain it wasn't as easy as in the United States, or anywhere else come to that, to deploy an armed police team. There had to be good reasons for it and the authorisation had to be made by an officer of at least the rank of Assistant Chief Constable. A Chief Constable, being of higher rank, could give the authorisation but procedure and protocol meant that, in practice, this would only be done if an ACC wasn't on duty. In this case an ACC was on duty. Jack Crosby.

Feeling nauseated, Karen dialled Crosby's number. Despite her pleas, he refused the request.

She wasn't surprised – it *was* fairly flimsy. Yet there was just the vaguest possibility that the man they were hunting might be at the address.

She frowned and pondered for a while.

The perfect compromise came to her in a flash.

After three phone calls she summoned McClure and Donaldson back into her office.

From inside a nondescript car parked at the end of the avenue, the two detectives watched the man drive past in his Audi. He parked in the driveway of his house and let himself in through the front door. He looked prosperous, not dangerous, but he lived alone – that much they had gleaned – and any man who lived alone in such a house (detached, four bedrooms, double garage) must have some questions to answer.

They gave him ten seconds before speaking on the radio.

'He's in – let's go,' said McClure.

Two vehicles screeched round the corner past them.

The first, a dark blue Support Unit personnel carrier, had darkened windows and steel grilles which protected the headlights, radiator and windscreen. It was a riot bus and looked like it meant business.

The second was an unmarked Rover 620i with two uniformed officers on board.

The carrier accelerated down the avenue and skidded to an impressive halt outside the house. Within seconds all the occupants had de-bussed in a well-rehearsed manoeuvre and were sprinting up the driveway.

Ten Constables, one Sergeant – not one under six feet tall. Each wore a specially designed riot helmet with the visor down, dark-blue flame-retardant overalls, leather belt, padded gloves, shin-guards, steel toe-capped boots and a kevlar bullet-proof vest. All but two were equipped with short round riot shields for extra protection.

Four men peeled off and raced down the side of the house to the rear.

The remaining seven, including the Sergeant, communicating by hand signals only, went wordlessly to the front door.

The two officers in the Rover got out at a more leisurely pace and took up a position which put their car between themselves and the house. Each held a ballistic shield in front of him.

The Support Unit Constables without the shields held a 'door opener' between them which was designed to be able to lever open any type of domestic door. They slotted the edge of the instrument into the narrow crack between the frame of the front door and the lock and heaved down together. The wood frame splintered and cracked immediately. The lock gave next. With the invaluable assistance of a size-ten boot, the door finally flew open – an operation that had lasted all of twelve seconds.

They stepped aside to allow their colleagues to pass.

'We're in,' the Sergeant said into the radio which was fitted in his helmet.

Cops with shields poured into the house.

'We're down the hallway. No sign yet.'

It was just before 6.35 p.m. When he came home, the owner of the house had gone straight to the lounge at the rear and switched on the TV quite loudly to catch a repeat of the news headlines.

He heard nothing – until the policeman's foot connected with the door.

Puzzled, he stepped into the hallway and into the middle of a nightmare. Around him surged what looked like an army from a science-fiction movie.

'Subject in sight,' shouted the Sergeant into his radio.

The man heard a voice from under a helmet scream, 'Come here, you bastard!' a moment before the mass of law and order drove him bodily through to the kitchen.

It was like being struck by an express train.

He smashed his head against the sink as he thudded down onto the tiled floor with the combined weight of three officers – almost forty stones – on top of him.

Head spinning, fearing death, short of breath, totally unable to comprehend the situation, he didn't need to be told not to try anything stupid.

'Subject overpowered and detained. No one hurt,' breathed the Sergeant into his radio.

Hinksman returned to his hotel room that evening, depositing a plastic carrier bag on the bed. He switched on the portable TV which was on the dressing table. It was badly tuned and the picture disappeared occasionally to be replaced by static for a moment or two. Karen Wilde was being interviewed by BBC North-West about the progress of the M6 bomb investigation. It was a live interview taking place on the steps of Preston police station.

Hinksman admired her looks and confidence and the way she handled herself. Very impressive.

Yes, she said, the IRA had been eliminated. Yes, they were following up many leads. There could be some truth in the rumour that it was a gangland killing; police were keeping an open mind. No, there had been no positive identification of the bodies in the car which was carrying the bomb. Yes, the bomb could have gone off accidentally, that was always possible. Over sixty detectives were now working full-time on the investigation. Finally (a withering look at the reporter here), yes, the officer who had assaulted their colleague was to face disciplinary proceedings, although no criminal charges were to be brought. Then: thank you and good night. Karen Wilde was a busy woman with work to get back to.

Hinksman crossed quickly to the window and peeked out. The street was quiet. No police activity. The TV interview had made him jumpy – but there was no way they could know about him, he reasoned. Then he remembered the two detectives in the Posthouse Hotel. Particularly the American.

He delved into the carrier bag and pulled out the video tapes he'd removed from Gaskell's house, once the arms dealer was dead. He placed them carefully on the floor. Then took out the gun, lay back on the bed with it held across his chest and closed his eyes.

Henry Christie flicked off the TV. 'Bitch!'

'Oh Dad, I was watching that,' complained Jenny, his eldest daughter. '*Emmerdale* is on soon.'

He tossed the remote control to her, and walked out into the back garden. It was a small, barren piece of land, all flat lawn and patio. A four-foot-high wooden fence was the boundary.

The evening sky was cloudy. Rain looked likely, but it was warmer than it had been.

His head hurt. His whole body ached dully.

Someone touched his shoulder. 'Hi,' his wife said. 'You OK?'

'After a fashion,' he said.

'Still smarting?'

'In more ways than one.'

'She's probably right, you know – keeping you off the job.'

'Look, Kate, I should be on that investigation! I should be tracking that bastard down. I deserve to be. I saw those kids drowning . . . Jesus . . . I'd like to get my hands on him.'

'Which is exactly why you shouldn't be on the enquiry.' She sighed and laid a hand on his arm. 'Why don't you take a few days off sick? Have a long weekend – be at home with the kids for a change. And me. They'd understand at work.'

'No.' He shook his head. 'I've got a drugs dealer to catch.'

4 a.m. Henry sat shivering in his front lounge as the semi-light of early morning filtered through the curtains. His teeth were chattering unstoppably. Yet he knew it was warm – the central heating was on full blast. But he was cold and clammy. He felt weak. He swallowed something back in his throat. It tasted of petrol.

The bottle of brandy found its way back to his mouth. The liquid gurgled down his gullet as though he were swigging back a pint of milk.

He only stopped when he began to choke.

Still he shivered. His whole body shook, convulsed.

Still he couldn't erase the vivid nightmare which had thrown him violently awake. Faces. Fingers. Clawing. Water.

The brandy went to his mouth again. Empty. He let the bottle slip out of his fingers onto the carpet and reached for the Bell's. The whisky went down neat on top of the brandy. Almost three-quarters of a bottle.

The room began a slow, sickening spin. Moving up, moving down, all in one flowing, churning motion. The petrol taste flooded back. He gulped it down again.

He slumped sideways on the sofa, breathing heavily, mind reeling like a roller-coaster, everything going round and round, him in the middle of it, unable to act, unable to stop it all and get off; drunk, shivering . . . then suddenly it all became ten times worse.

The dream surged relentlessly back. Those frightened faces, pressed against the glass. The rushing river. His failure. The muted screams. *His failure*.

Blackness came with a piercing, wailing sound and a bang-bang-banging from somewhere inside him.

The last blurred image he had before passing out was that of his eldest daughter standing by the door in her night clothes, a terrified expression on her uncomprehending face.

Chapter Seven

Joe Kovaks found the faxes from England wedged halfway down the pile in his pigeon hole. Drinking bitter black coffee from a plastic cup and grimacing with each mouthful, he looked at the photos. They were not brilliant reproductions but were clear enough to make an I.D. The prospect of sifting through thousands of photographs of Corelli and his cronies wasn't remotely appealing.

He was about to fetch Corelli's file when another fax was slapped down on his desk. It was the set of dabs lifted from the Posthouse Hotel room in Lancaster.

Kovaks scribbled a note marked *Urgent* and pinned it to the fax. He hurried down to the Fingerprint Bureau.

The atmosphere here was quiet and scholarly. Rows of computers, all logged into Printrak, filled the room. At each desk sat a fingerprint expert, dressed in shirt, tie, slacks and spectacles, the uniform of every fingerprint expert the world over, including the women. No one was smoking, so Kovaks took a final drag of his Marlboro and stamped it out on the corridor floor before crossing the threshold.

As he entered the room he wondered why anyone in their right mind would want to do this for a living.

He made his way over to a man peering at a magnified fingerprint on his computer screen. Blown up, it looked like the relief map of a mountain.

'Hi, Damian.'

The man spun round and squinted myopically at Kovaks. 'Joe, for heaven's sake, don't do that.'

'Oh, did I disturb you?'

'I was lost in a dreamworld of loops and whorls.'

'Sounds like a computer game.'

'But much more exciting,' Damian said. 'What can I do for you, Agent Kovaks?'

'Need a favour. It's urgent.'

'Always is with you. I suppose you want me to drop everything else and do your bidding.'

'Absolutely.'

He sighed good-naturedly. 'What the heck.'

'Thanks, Damian.' Kovaks gave him the fax.

Back in the office, Kovaks was surprised to see his partner from the previous night. Today she smelled quite sweet, but Kovaks noted the damp patches already beginning to form in her armpits.

'Hi, Sue,' he said amicably.

'I phoned Chrissy. She said you'd come in early, so here I am too.'

Kovaks groaned inwardly. This would mean trouble at home. Although he'd described his temporary partner to Chrissy, she'd had a look in her eyes which said, 'I don't believe you.' She was convinced Kovaks was working with a curvy blonde bombshell who was a weapons expert, karate black belt and had the sexual appetite of Pussy Galore. And now she'd heard her on the phone for the first time, which would only confirm her suspicions – on the phone Sue Mather sounded like a bimbo.

'I'm just doing something for Karl,' he explained. 'He phoned me from England.'

'Can I help?'

A flash of inspiration.

'Yeah, you can actually. I need to check Corelli's file but I've got to go and see the SAC. Do you mind?' He handed her the faxes and explained the task. 'Long-winded, I know. But very important.'

'Sure, Joe, anything.' She blinked clumsily at him in an attempt to flutter her eyelashes, but thank Christ she didn't pass wind.

He left her to it.

Two hours later Kovaks found Sue sitting at his desk drinking coffee and eating a doughnut. Eight cigarette stubs were in the ashtray, and another smouldered on the edge of the desk, threatening the woodwork.

She looked up, and waved. Kovaks stormed across the office.

'I asked you to do a job for me,' he hissed. 'Not sit there filling your fat face.' The words tumbled out spontaneously and he regretted them almost immediately.

Her good humour visibly evaporated. She had the look of a puppy kicked by its master for no reason other than bad temper.

Kovaks took a deep breath. 'Look, I'm sorry,' he said quickly. Totally inadequate. 'I didn't mean what I said.'

'Yes, you did,' she said petulantly. 'I may be fat but I don't need reminding of it.'

This was ground Kovaks didn't wish to cover.

'Forget it, huh? I'm sorry, honest.' He shrugged his shoulders and wore a suitably regretful look. 'Can we get back to square one? Pretty please?'

She sighed through her nose, her large shoulders rising and falling. A glimmer of a smile played on her lips. She nodded. 'OK.'

'Good. I take it you made some progress.'

'Sure have,' she said brightly. 'Here.' She rooted through some papers on the desk and pulled out the faxes. Attached to them was a black-and-white photograph. It was blurred, obviously taken from a moving vehicle, but clearly showed Corelli sitting at a table in a pavement café with another man – *the same one as in the faxes*. It was dated four years previously. Around the border was written: *Corelli dining with unidentified male. Carmel, Calif. No I.D. ever made.*

'Well done.' Kovaks patted her fleshy shoulder.

'Found it within five minutes,' she admitted. 'Then I got bored waiting for you, so I pigged out.'

'Of course, it doesn't really get us anywhere,' Kovaks brooded out loud. 'All it does is show us that Corelli once sat at a table with this guy. Not proof of very much, is it?'

'What exactly are you trying to prove?'

'Something big.' Kovaks picked up the photo and faxes and said, 'Come on, let's go and see a man about a don.'

As they walked away from the desk the phone began to ring. Kovaks groaned, but snatched up the receiver. It was Damian.

'Joe – got something for you. Haul your ass in here.'

Kovaks chuckled at Damian's dramatic turn of phrase as he hurried to the Fingerprint Bureau. He'd never heard the other guy say a bad word like 'ass' before.

As ever, Damian was sat at his station. His computer screen showed a set of prints.

His tie, however, was discarded over the back of his chair.

Heyyy, this had to be big, Kovaks thought. The guy had taken his tie off!

'What have you got for me?' he said.

Damian looked round. His short-sighted eyes lingered for more than a moment on Sue before returning to Kovaks.

'A match is what I've got. Several matches in fact,' he announced. His voice quivered with an undercurrent of delight.

Kovaks pulled up a chair and indicated for Sue to do likewise.

'You asked me to compare the fingerprints from England with the partial prints we have from the mob killings you and Karl are investigating.'

Kovaks nodded.

'I can confirm they match.'

'You certain?'

'Yes.'

'Wow. I take it we still don't know the guy's identity?'

'Whoever he is, he's not on record.'

'Oh well, can't have everything. Pity. Thanks, Damian. I owe you.' Kovaks shrugged and began to rise.

'There is something else, actually.'

Kovaks re-seated himself. 'Go on.'

'Just out of professional interest I did a further search with the prints from England and found some intriguing matches with partial prints from other crime scenes. This guy's been pretty busy.'

'Damian, don't keep me in suspense.'

'Well, I looked at the bombings, which as you know have happened all over the States. Here, Memphis, LA . . .'

'Yes, yes, I know,' said Kovaks testily.

'So I wondered if there's been any other crimes committed in the same places, on or around the same dates, that could've been perpetrated by the same man but weren't linked because we only had partial prints.'

'And I take it there were,' said Kovaks.

'Yep.' Damian smiled cheekily and raised his eyebrows at Kovaks and Sue. The smile for Sue lasted a fraction longer than it should. She giggled girlishly.

'Damian, just fucking tell me, OK?'

'Joe!' Sue rebuked him. 'There's no need to talk like that! He's only trying to help. And you really must stop swearing.' She beamed at Damian, who beamed back.

'Sorry,' Kovaks said contritely. 'Damian, do go on.'

'Thank you. You might be pleased to know that I've linked this man to seven other murders. The victims are prostitutes. All left with broken necks and killed at more or less the same time as the bombings. As well as being a professional hit man, your guy kills for fun too.'

'A serial killer,' breathed Kovaks. 'That's all we need.'

'The cops in England are on this guy's tail, but unless I can find out something more for them – and fast – they'll lose him and we'll all be back to first base,' Kovaks explained to Sue as they ran down the steps to the ground floor.

'What's the English angle?' she enquired.

'Long story – no time to tell it now, but amongst other things they think he killed all those people with that motorway bomb.'

'Jeez,' wheezed Sue, glad to reach the foot of the stairs. 'So what're you going to do?'

This was asked as Kovaks pushed open the security door leading to the public entrance foyer of the building. 'Well, the time for the subtle approach is long gone . . . oh shit!' He stopped in his tracks.

He'd spotted Lisa Want, pacing the foyer like a tigress. Fortunately, she hadn't seen him yet.

Kovaks began to reverse through the door. In his haste, he backed right into Sue, and trod heavily on her foot, crushing her big toe under his shoe like stepping on a walnut. She yelled in agony and pushed Kovaks away with such force that he lost his balance and belly-flopped onto the shiny marble floor.

Winded, bruised, he looked helplessly from his prone position all the way up the long, stunning, mini-skirted legs of Lisa Want.

'Joe, I'm sorry,' babbled Sue as she hobbled over to help him up.

Kovaks shrugged himself ungratefully out of Sue's meaty grasp and glared into the smirking face of Lisa Want, chief crime reporter on the *Miami Herald*.

'Joe,' she said, suppressing a giggle, 'what a spectacular entrance. You should be a stuntman.'

She was holding a voice-activated tape-recorder in one hand.

'Whatever it is, Lisa, I've nothing to say to you. No comment.'

She raised a finely plucked eyebrow. 'I've not asked anything yet.'

'Well, don't, then you won't be disappointed. Bye, Lisa.' He walked painfully away towards the exit, Sue limping behind.

Lisa followed. 'Do you have any comment to make about the motorway bombing in England?' she asked.

Stunned for a moment, he said, 'I don't know what you're talking about.'

'I have it on good authority there's a stateside connection. Can you confirm this?' She thrust the tape-recorder under his nose.

Kovaks shook his head, pushed on towards the door.

'What about the Mafia connection?' she probed deeper.

Kovaks still had nothing to say.

'Where does Corelli come into it? And Danny Carver? I hear Danny was killed in the bombing. Is it all connected with a drugs deal they were pulling? Is this the beginning of a gang war?'

They had reached the revolving door. Kovaks stopped. 'I don't know what you're talking about, Lisa. I've no comment to make to you about anything. And I never will have – OK?'

'C'mon Joe, give me a break. This is big stuff,' she pleaded. 'For old time's sake, huh?'

'It's because of old time's sake that I've nothing to say. Bye.'

In the car park the two agents walked towards Kovaks' Trans-am.

'Can I ask you a question?' Sue said.

'Sure.'

'You been sleeping with Lisa Want?'

'It was a mistake,' Kovaks openly admitted to Sue. They were being escorted through the corridors of Dade County Correctional Institute. 'I nearly lost my job over her. We were into a relationship but all she was doing was pumping me for information. Like a fool, I gave her some . . . pillow talk, and she used it as the bottom line for a scoop. It was pretty obvious where her information had come from. I got hauled before the Deputy Director and disciplined, while Lisa got the chief reporter's job. I learned a lesson.' He shrugged philosophically. 'We split up, and now I'll never trust another journalist as long as I live, even if they tell me they love me. They'll do anything just for that big story. Particularly Lisa Want. She'd sleep with her own mother if she thought there was a by-line in it.'

The prison guard in front of them unlocked the door to a visiting room. He allowed the two FBI agents to enter then locked it behind them.

A table, screwed to the floor, stood in the middle of the room. There were three chairs. A window of toughened glass overlooked a bare exercise yard.

The heavy metal door on the opposite side of the room led through to the innards of the prison. It was locked.

High in one corner of the room, out of reach but protected by a wire-mesh cage, was a security camera.

Kovaks and Sue sat down. They said nothing, looked expectantly at the door, waited.

It was a short wait. A key turned in the lock. Bolts were drawn back. The door, well-oiled, opened silently.

A prison warder appeared, followed by an inmate and another warder. The warders withdrew to the back of the room where they leaned against the wall, chatting quietly to each other. The inmate took the third chair.

Kovaks considered the man carefully. He was white, in his early thirties, and big – six feet four. But he wasn't fat. Through the ill-fitting prison garb Kovaks could see he was keeping himself in shape. The bulges were all muscle. His biceps were enormous and the veins stood out on them like strands of steel rope.

Kovaks said, 'Remember me, Whisper?'

The big man nodded. 'Never forget a face,' he said. The sound of his voice, as his name suggested, was a hoarse, rasping whisper, like a knife-blade scraping stone. Kovaks knew it was the result of receiving a blow to the throat in a street fight as a teenager. The damage to his voice box made him seem all the more sinister.

Kovaks also knew that the boy who'd hit him all those years ago had taken a knife through the heart.

Kovaks pulled out a pack of cigarettes and a lighter. Whisper took them without a word of thanks. He lit one – a Marlboro – inhaled deeply, exhaled slowly.

Kovaks retrieved the lighter.

'You can keep the cigarettes.'

Whisper nodded slight acknowledgement. 'So what the fuck d'you want, Agent Kovaks?'

'I'd like your help.' Kovaks knew there was no point in being coy. 'I've been to see the Special Agent in charge of the Miami field officer and spoken to the Deputy Director about you this morning.'

'Lucky you,' rasped Whisper.

'If you cooperate with us today to my satisfaction he'll make representations at your parole board to get the maximum reduction in your sentence.'

'Which means that, whatever happens, I'll still be in here for another five years.'

'That's true,' Kovaks said. 'But on the other hand, you could be in here for another twelve.'

Whisper blinked. 'I won't help you.'

'You don't know what we want.'

'I won't help you,' he reaffirmed. 'I don't help the law, particularly Feds.'

'Just like Corelli ain't helpin' you?'

'I don't know what you mean, bud.'

'Look, Whisper, we know you were working for him, taking all the risks for him, running the gauntlet with us and the DEA every time you came in with a plane-load of dope. And when you got caught he dropped you like a hot potato. Don't try to deny it now. We know you worked for him, Whisper, we know.'

'You don't know nothing.' Whisper's voice grated with a sneer.

'We *know* . . .' Kovaks' voice trailed off into thin air, leaving the words hanging there. 'And what's he done to help you, Whisper?'

'I don't know what or who you're talking about, asshole.'

Whisper took a deep drag of his cigarette, tossed it onto the floor and ground it out. 'End of discussion.'

He placed two hands on the table, pushed himself up. He towered briefly over the seated Kovaks. 'Bye bye, Agent Asshole,' he hissed. He turned and walked to the door.

Kovaks hadn't expected such an abrupt end to the proceedings. Something had to be done.

'Maybe he can't do much to help you in here,' he said to Whisper's retreating back, 'but he could at least help Laura out there, couldn't he? Laura and your daughter Cassie.' Kovaks was desperate. He was losing here and something had to be done to save the situation.

Whisper stopped in his tracks. He revolved slowly. His expression struck fear into Kovaks' heart.

'Yeah, that's right,' Kovaks pushed on, seeing he'd struck a chord. 'He's done nothing for her – other than exploit her. She was a real good-looker, your Laura. And she was clean, even though you were pushin' those drugs. Not now, baby, not fuckin' now!'

'What are you saying?'

'She's one of Corelli's hookers. Working downtown Miami in a sleazy club where the customer can get a five-minute blow job for fifty dollars. I've heard she does a hundred a night. Washes her mouth out between each one with antiseptic.'

'Liar,' Whisper said.

'Now she's a smack-head. A crack addict. With no money. Living in a shitty one-bedroom apartment over a grocery store with no amenities and your precious daughter on the at-risk register. The state are seriously considering taking her off Laura. That's how much Corelli's looked after your interests. He used you, now he's using her. Why do you think she never visits you? He won't fuckin' let her, Whisper, 'cos then you'll know.'

Kovaks had pushed hard and far and he knew it. Too far, too quickly. He had heard how deadly Whisper could be; now he found out at first hand.

Whisper moved so fast he took everyone by surprise. Kovaks had walked round the table as he'd talked and there was perhaps five feet of open space and nothing else between the two men. A mistake.

Whisper covered the gap in a movement so flowing and precise that the next thing Kovaks knew he was on his back. Whisper's huge paw-like hands were around his throat, squeezing, and Kovaks' eyes were bulging in their sockets.

'Fuckin' liar,' Whisper said. 'Fuckin' liar, fuckin' liar . . .'

His breath washed into Kovaks' nostrils. He began to smash the back of Kovaks' head repeatedly on the hard tiled floor.

Kovaks hit Whisper as hard as he could with a fist. It connected with the left side of his head by his ear and had no effect on the big man other than to encourage him to tighten his grip.

The prison warders moved in to assist. They tried to prise Whisper off, but he shrugged them away as easily as a man removing his coat.

Kovaks' vision began to distort. He felt faint. He knew he was going to die here. Strangled, head smashed to pieces in a fuckin' prison. His ears throbbed. Vaguely he heard an alarm sounding somewhere – a *whoop-whoop* noise. There were shouts. Screams. Footsteps running. He began to lose consciousness.

Then Whisper's head was yanked violently back.

He gave a yelp of surprise.

Kovaks' swimming vision took in the huge form of Sue hovering above him.

A big fist slammed down like a sledgehammer into Whisper's upturned face. His nose squelched and burst like a tomato. The fist smashed down again. Whisper released his grip on Kovaks' throat. His hands went up to protect his face.

The door flew open and two more warders ran into the room, batons drawn.

75

Now, four against one, even Whisper was defeated. He was bundled off his victim in a shower of blows, punches and kicks.

'You pack a good punch,' Kovaks croaked with admiration to Sue.

'I had to do something,' she said modestly, 'otherwise he'd've killed you. Those guards were useless.'

'I owe you one.'

'My pleasure,' she said meekly. She looked at the swollen knuckles of her right hand. 'I broke his nose, y'know.'

'You did good,' Kovaks agreed.

They were sitting in a cubicle at the Institute's hospital, a curtain drawn across for the sake of privacy. Kovaks had been treated and his throat had a bandage wrapped around it. No permanent damage had been done, according to the doctor. His voice was almost gone but in a few days, he was assured, everything would be fine again. Meanwhile he'd been advised not to speak too much and eat only soup and scrambled eggs.

The doctor drew the curtain back.

'Whisper wants to talk to you,' he announced.

Kovaks and Sue exchanged a surprised glance.

'Where is he?' she asked.

'We've just admitted him. He's down on the ward, first bed on the left.' The doctor pointed.

'How is he?' Sue enquired.

'He'll live.'

Curtains had also been drawn around Whisper's bed, denying the other occupants of the ward a view of the prison hard man beaten to a pulp. Kovaks and Sue ducked in and stood next to the bed.

Whisper looked bad. A real mess.

Other than the facial injuries inflicted by Sue, the warders had really gone to town on him. Obviously a lot of grudges had been exorcised. His left arm, wrist and all five fingers were broken; he had several broken ribs, as well as a smashed collarbone and a shattered kneecap. His face and upper body were a mass of welts, cuts, bruises and swellings. Several of the deeper cuts had been stitched and blood dribbled out of them onto the pillow and sheets.

His eyes were closed. His left had swollen up like a boxer's, round and big as a tennis ball, the colour purple. The other was merely bruised. He opened this one and peered sideways at his visitors.

'You wanted to see us,' Kovaks managed to whisper hoarsely.

'Can't hear you,' the big man said.

Kovaks leaned forwards, his mouth close to Whisper's ear.

'You wanted to see us.'

'Yeah . . . why you whisperin'?'

'Some bastard did my throat in.'

Whisper chuckled and winced with the pain which arced through his chest like an electric shock. When he'd reached equilibrium he said, 'Is it true – what you said?'

'It's true.'

'Fuck!'

'Help us,' Kovaks' voice grated painfully, 'and we can help her, Whisper. We'll get her in a re-hab scheme, set her up somewhere else and give her some cash to start a new life with Cassie – away from Corelli.'

'Nobody gets away from Corelli,' said Whisper, dismissing the idea. Then, 'But she's a good girl. She deserves a break. Will you do what you say?'

'I will,' said Kovaks, nodding.

'If you don't, I'll kill you when I get out of here . . . after I've killed Corelli.'

'I said I will,' said Kovaks, believing him.

'So what d'you want?'

Kovaks held out his hand. Sue gave him the photos.

'Who is this guy?' Kovaks held the prints so Whisper could see them without having to move. 'We need to know – urgently.'

77

Whisper looked hard at the photographs with his good eye. His breathing was painful and laboured. The analgesics were only just beginning to take effect.

'Why?' he asked.

'We think he killed a lotta people – including a busload of kids – on Corelli's orders.'

Whisper winced. 'I don't know him.'

Kovaks stood up, disappointed. 'Shit.'

'I mean I don't know him personally, but I know he's Corelli's top hired killer. Jimmy Hinksman, that's his name. Corelli keeps him pretty much tucked away. Talk is he used to be Special Forces but got kicked out for some girl trouble. That's all I know about him. Real mystery figure. Ahhh . . .' He gasped as he adjusted his position slightly. He waited a moment for the pain to settle.

Someone walked down the ward and stopped near to Whisper's bed. Kovaks heard the sounds of the doctor's voice murmuring in muted conversation. A female voice replied – a nurse. Footsteps walked past the bed. Kovaks returned his attention to Whisper.

'I only seen him once and I got the evil eye when I asked who he was. Real arrogant bastard. Did he do Danny Carver?' asked Whisper.

'How the hell did you know that?' said Kovaks, taken aback.

'News travels fast – even in here.'

'Where do we find him?'

Whisper shook his head slightly. 'In America he could be anywhere. But if he's in England, I know somewhere you could try.'

Chapter Eight

Donaldson perched on the Allocator's desk in the incident room, a phone cradled between his left ear and shoulder. 'Hey, Joe,' he was saying, 'you done good, pal. I'm real sorry about your injuries.'

The fax machine in the corner of the room beeped into life.

'It's coming through now,' Donaldson said into the phone.

At the machine, Karen Wilde and Ken McClure stood bleary-eyed.

It was 7.30 a.m. They had worked through the night interviewing the man arrested at Lytham the evening before. They had pushed to the limits allowed by the Police and Criminal Evidence Act, initially denying him access to legal representation in the hope of making a quick break-through. They had also broken the rules during the course of the interview – by their oppressive and intimidatory conduct, but in the end they had nothing on him. His driving licence had either been lost or stolen but he didn't know where or when. They dusted him down at 5 a.m., promised to pay for any damage caused at his home and sent him on his way without an apology. They hadn't been in the mood to apologise to anyone.

As they packed up, the phone rang.

Kovaks.

The first sheet came off the fax. It read, *With the compliments of Joe Kovaks, FBI, Miami, Florida, US.* There was a little photo of him beneath the wording. Karen groaned as she saw it. Under her breath she muttered, 'Another idiotic Yank.'

The next one came through with excruciating slowness. It was so damn slow that Karen was sure the machine had gone on the blink. She tapped her toes angrily. When the printing was complete, she grabbed the paper and read it several times before handing it to McClure.

She could hardly contain herself.

McClure read it out loud: *'Fingerprints identified from military file as belonging to James Clarkson Hinksman.'* He looked up and grinned. 'Got the bastard.'

Page three came off the machine. It was the photo from Corelli's file, showing the big Italian and Hinksman at a restaurant.

Page four showed an old photograph of Hinksman, passport size, dressed in a military uniform. Page five contained brief details of a military career which had come to a halt four years previously when he was dishonourably discharged following a court martial. The next four pages were an expanded summary of his service record. The last page listed all the murders of prostitutes that the fingerprints linked him with.

There was nothing else.

'At least now we know who we're looking for,' said Karen, 'although we haven't got a clue where he is. He may no longer be in this country.'

'Perhaps we should get his mug splattered all over the media,' McClure suggested.

'We will.' Karen turned to Donaldson. He was still on the phone, scribbling something on a scrap of paper.

'Thank your colleague for me,' she said. 'He's done a fantastic job.'

Donaldson finished writing. 'My new boss says thanks, Joe. Me too. Great job.'

He hung up and, smiling broadly, picked up the fax of Corelli and Hinksman. 'I knew I'd seen that face before. We have literally thousands of photos of Corelli but I remembered this one. I think I did quite well.'

'I do too,' Karen conceded with more warmth than she intended.

'So, we've got a real top hit man on our hands. Now, what's all this nonsense about not knowing where our Mr Hinksman is?' He held up his scrap of paper. 'He's on vacation in Blackpool.' He attempted a poor Lancashire accent. 'Land of cloth caps, donkey rides and mucky postcards, tha' knows, lass.'

'Give me that!' laughed Karen. She snatched the paper.

She read it and punched the air with a fist. 'Yes, YES, YES!'

Joe Kovaks leaned back in his chair and interlocked his fingers behind his head. He chuckled in disbelief, but consoled himself that even the best brains sometimes failed to see simple solutions to complex problems. He couldn't believe they'd never checked the military file, yet all it had taken was the press of a button on Damian's magic fingerprint machine and – hey presto! Mr James Clarkson Hinksman, Mafia killer extraordinary, was exposed. Jeez, how could they all have been so dumb, he thought. That bastard could have been fried over a year ago. If that harpy Lisa Want ever got hold of this, she'd have a field day exposing the inefficiency of the FBI.

He sighed at the stupidity, but wasn't too upset because it wasn't normal procedure to cross-check the military files.

Just then, Sue appeared in the doorway, virtually filling it. She'd just showered in the ladies' rest-room and changed into a jogging outfit which she kept in her locker. At least she would smell all right for a while, Kovaks thought cruelly, but then regretted it. She'd more than proved her worth today.

'Good result,' he said pleasantly, his voice carefully low.

'Yep,' she agreed.

'Good ole Damian. Workaholic, that guy.'

'I like him,' she admitted.

Kovaks took a deep breath and consulted his watch. 'Look, I know it's late and all that, but would you like a drink on the way home? Just a quickie, by way of celebration.'

'I'd love one,' Sue said, 'but . . . I've made other arrangements.'

As if on cue, Damian appeared at the office door. Hair combed, jacket brushed, tie straight. Like a nervous teenager on a first date.

'Damian's offered to take me home,' Sue said apologetically. 'Raincheck?'

Relieved somewhat, Kovaks nodded. 'Raincheck.'

Sue danced as lightly as was possible towards Damian, breasts bouncing uncontrollably, lighting up Damian's eyes with lust. She gave Kovaks a salacious wink, then disappeared with the slightly built fingerprint expert, arm threaded through his.

'Rather you than me, pal,' Kovaks said under his breath.

As he pulled on his jacket the phone chirped. It was the switchboard operator. 'Joe?'

'I'm just on my way home.'

'Dade County Correctional Institute left a message for you. You went to see one of the inmates earlier.'

'Yeah?' Kovaks' stomach dropped.

'He's been knifed to death.'

It was 11 a.m.

The unmarked police car raced at 120 mph down the motorway towards Blackpool. The driver was a PC from the motor driving school. McClure and Donaldson sat silently in the back of the car re-reading the faxes from America. Karen Wilde sat in the front passenger seat, brooding, staring intently ahead. Angry.

The confrontation she'd recently undergone with Crosby and Fanshaw-Bayley had set the whole thing back several hours, although in the end she'd got her own way and a firearms team had been deployed to Blackpool for a briefing.

After receiving the information from America, Karen had decided to see Crosby face to face to ask for a team this time. She walked straight into his office. Fanshaw-Bayley was also there.

'Ahhh,' said Crosby looking up from his desk. 'I was just about to summon you, miss.'

'I need authorisation for a firearms team,' she began breathlessly. 'We think we've located—'

Crosby slashed his right hand through the air as if he was executing a karate chop, stopping her in mid-sentence.

'You deliberately disobeyed my orders yesterday, miss, and now you want me to sanction another team?'

'What d'you mean, sir?'

'I said "No" to your request yesterday.'

'You did, yes.'

'Yet you utilised the Blackpool ARV,' he stated.

Her mind whizzed. What was going on here? 'It was a compromise,' she said defensively.

'It was disobedience of a direct order,' he shouted. 'Implicit in my "No" was the fact that you were not, repeat *not*, to use armed officers for your little fiasco.'

She looked quickly at FB who smirked, enjoying her discomfort.

'I didn't use a team,' she said, trying to regain her composure.

'You used armed officers!'

'Yes,' she said, exasperated. 'I used the ARV. They are on twenty-four-hour cover in every division and can be used for day-to-day jobs just like any other patrol in the county. They were there as insurance. They didn't draw their weapons, neither did they get involved in the raid. It was a sensible move, if you ask me.'

'No one's fucking asking you! You disobeyed my orders, pure and simple.' His face was red with rage; he was screaming in classic Scouse.

'I protected my men,' she insisted. There was no way she was going to back down and admit she was wrong – particularly with FB looking on.

'And it wasn't even the man you were after, just some poor innocent bloke . . .'

'Whose driving licence was used by the biggest mass murderer since Lockerbie.'

Crosby wasn't to be diverted now. He was in full flow. 'You used excessive force in entering his house and now I believe we're faced with a huge bill for trashing the place.'

'Trashing is not the term I would use. Damage was caused, yes, but it was minimal. The cost of repair will be relatively small.'

'I am tempted to have you disciplined for this,' Crosby growled.

'What? So you can have your investigation back? Because your beloved CID aren't running the show? Grow up, Mr Crosby . . . I know you don't like me, or the fact that I've got this job, but I'm doing it to the best of my ability and I'm *that* far off getting a result.' She held up her thumb and forefinger with just a sliver of daylight between them. 'And I won't be browbeaten or bullied by the likes of dinosaurs like you two . . .'

'Dinosaurs!' he blasted.

'If you want to sulk, then do so. But if you hinder the investigation, so help me God, I'll bring you down – and you, FB.' She pointed a finger at Fanshaw-Bayley.

'So what's it going to be?' she demanded. Her mouth was a tight angry line. Her eyes had large bags under them the colour of prunes and she'd been wearing the same outfit for a long twenty hours. Her hair felt like straw and she needed a bath followed by twelve hours' sleep. What she *didn't* need was this shit!

'The answer's no,' Crosby said.

She wheeled round and marched out of the office.

Two minutes later the tension that had been welling up inside Crosby's chest reached a climax. It burned up through his arteries like razor blades on fire, from his heart to his left arm and up the side of his face.

He clutched himself.

Then keeled over off his chair onto the floor with a crash, taking the contents of his desk with him.

FB looked on bemused for a moment before he realised what was happening.

His boss was having a major heart attack.

Whisper had been moved to a side ward, but other than that no one had touched him. He still lay on the hospital bed in his dying position: head lolling to one side, arms hanging loosely off the bed. The nurse who'd discovered him had tried to save him. She'd ripped the bedclothes off him and torn open his pyjamas, but it had been too late for Whisper. Despite all his gurgling and blowing of bubbles of blood through his nose and mouth, he was already dead.

Kovaks' weary but sharp eyes gazed at the wounds. There were at least twelve punctures in the chest around the heart and innumerable ones in his face and neck. One of his eyes had been gouged out, an ear sliced off and his cheek carved open. Kovaks could see Whisper's teeth through that particular wound.

Blood was everywhere. The bed was soaked, his body was drenched in it. Crimson was splashed ten feet up the wall behind the bed and across the floor. It had started to congeal in tar-like clods on the tiles. There were many footprints in it. It had been a frenzied attack.

Kovaks was puzzled.

He looked quickly from the body to the blood splashes and back to the body. A police photographer asked him to step aside while he took more shots from a different angle. Another photographer was videoing the scene for evidential purposes.

The stills man bent down on the far side of the bed. His camera flashed. He stood upright and said, 'Have you seen this?' He pointed down to the corner of the room.

Kovaks walked over carefully.

A piece of thick, pink, blood-oozing meat lay on the floor skewered by a knife. The knife was thin, as long as a stiletto but with one jagged cutting edge. Kovaks had no doubt he was looking at the murder weapon.

He had no doubt, either, that he was looking at Whisper's tongue. The message it conveyed was not lost on him.

He turned to the local sheriff who was standing at the door. 'I assumed he'd been killed out on the ward and his body moved here after.'

'Apparently not.' The man shrugged. His thumbs were tucked into his gun belt. He seemed slow-witted, but Kovaks knew not to underestimate such people.

'I'll be moving a team in here,' Kovaks informed him, 'but we'd sure appreciate your cooperation. I think that together – our skills and your local knowledge – we'll crack this.'

The sheriff smiled. 'Us and the FBI, working together? Sure thing,' he said, pleased.

'And obviously we'd like to set up an incident room to run from your office, if that meets with your approval?'

'Yeah, sure. From my office. No problem.' His smile widened even further.

'But first can you tell me where I can locate the nurse who found him?'

The sheriff cocked a thumb. 'Down there. She's pretty shook up.'

Kovaks strolled down the ward, muttering, 'Keep 'em sweet, keep 'em sweet.'

The eyes of the patients were on him. Some sneered at the sight of the badge pinned to his lapel. None spoke. He doubted if any ever would.

The nurse was a middle-aged lady whom he'd seen earlier. She was sitting in an office, her head buried in her hands, being comforted by the bored-looking doctor whom Kovaks had also met before. As Kovaks came to the door the doctor immediately ushered him back out.

'She is in no condition to be interviewed yet,' he said. 'I've given her a tranquilliser to get her this calm. Her husband should be here soon to take her home.'

'When will I be able to speak to her?'

'Tomorrow at the earliest.'

Kovaks nodded. 'OK. Can you tell me why Whisper was transferred to that side ward, doc?'

'To aid speedy recovery. He needed complete isolation, in my opinion.'

'Did you see anything that might be of use to us?'

'Such as?'

'Such as who stuck a knife into him a million times.'

'No, I didn't and frankly, I don't have the time to talk to you just now. I need to care for this nurse, then I need to get the hospital back to normal.'

'When can I see you then?'

'Ask my secretary. Make an appointment.'

Jack Crosby was still alive when he was slid on a stretcher into the back of the ambulance some fifteen minutes later, but only just. His heart and breathing had stopped at one point, but FB's half-remembered first-aid training had saved him. For the time being at least.

Karen watched the ambulance race away, blue light flashing. She was standing at a first-floor window.

The small crowd of people who had gathered outside dispersed slowly, leaving only two standing there: a pale, shaken FB and a worried-looking Chief Constable. FB began talking animatedly, arms waving, fingers pointing, voice obviously raised.

Karen's mouth twisted sardonically. 'I wonder who he's talking about,' she said under her breath.

She watched them turn and walk into the HQ building, FB not letting up for a second.

Karen made her way to the Chief Constable's secretary's office and sat down to wait. A wave of tiredness enveloped her. This was the longest single uninterrupted period she had ever worked in her life. It was all she could do to prevent herself falling asleep.

Jean, the secretary, glanced up at her.

'I do hope he's all right,' she said.

'I do too,' said Karen. She meant it.

'Is there anything I can get you? You look exhausted.'

Just a warm bed and a stiff drink. Karen shook her head, too tired even to speak.

'Don't blame yourself,' Jean said softly. 'He's been warned about his condition often enough. It was only a matter of time.'

Karen managed a wan smile.

FB and Dave August entered and the Chief went straight into his office without acknowledging Karen. 'I'm not to be disturbed,' he announced. 'I'm going to call Mrs Crosby.'

'Boss . . .' Karen began, getting to her feet.

'Disturbed by no one,' he reiterated and slammed the door.

FB turned to Karen, 'This is your doing,' he said with vehemence. 'None of this would've happened without your incessant ambition.'

'Don't become a bigger fool than you already are, FB. I wasn't to know he had a dodgy heart.'

'It was common knowledge.'

'Common to whom, dickhead?' she challenged. She sat back down and folded her arms, determined not to enter a no-win, no-profit argument.

The intercom buzzed on Jean's desk. 'Get a car to pick up Mrs Crosby from home and take her to hospital. Then arrange for mine to pick me up from the garage. I'm going to see him too.'

'Yes, sir.'

Karen came to an instant decision. 'This is preposterous,' she said, striding across to the Chief's door. Jean opened her mouth to remonstrate, but Karen burst through the door before she could utter a word and crashed it shut behind her.

Blackpool Tower came into view. In ten minutes they would be at the central police station where the firearms team had been told to assemble for the briefing.

Karen sighed heavily as she thought back to her head-on confrontation with Dave August, Chief Constable and lover.

'I said I was not to be disturbed.'

'I still need a firearms team,' she said. 'There's no ACC on duty now – only you can authorise it.'

'FB was right – you *are* a bitch. There's a man lying near to death and—'

'And there's also a killer on the loose who needs catching,' she cut in. 'Life goes on, especially in this job. So does death by murder. It doesn't stop because someone's ill. Now do I get the team or not?'

'Yes . . . now piss the hell off out of here.'

As she reached the door, August added: 'And by the way, if this murder isn't bottomed in twenty-four hours, you're off the investigation and I'm handing it over to someone with more experience.'

They were slowing down now as the motorway narrowed into a two-lane road and they entered Blackpool.

Karen sat back and cleared her mind, concentrating on the task ahead.

Pepe Paglia mooched, hands in pockets, down the street on which his small hotel was located. He was still rather depressed at having handed a thousand pounds in cash over to Hinksman the day before. On the other hand he felt reassured that Corelli would reimburse him handsomely in the not-too-distant future. That was the good thing about family ties, however tenuous; a favour for a favour.

He entered a newsagents and picked up a copy of that day's *Sun*. In the back room of the shop a TV was switched on, showing a lunchtime news bulletin. Paglia was not really paying it much attention. He was too busy choosing goodies for his sweet tooth. He glanced up by pure chance and saw the screen as he picked up a Mars bar. His mouth dropped open.

Paglia almost sprinted back to the hotel, arriving breathless and weak, in desperate need of a cigarette.

* * *

They commandeered the parade room at Blackpool Central police station for the briefing. The firearms team was already assembled when Karen, McClure and Donaldson arrived. There was one Sergeant and twelve Constables, including two women. All were dressed in lightweight blue overalls, ballistic vests and caps. Each wore a pair of Reebok trainers. They were checking numerous weapons between them as they waited: handguns, rifles, semi-automatic pistols, MP5s, stun grenades, CS gas launchers. They were like a small, well-equipped army.

Karen stopped in her tracks and surveyed them. It was the first time she had ever seen such a team. They exuded calm, confidence and good humour. And efficiency. They were an efficient killing machine.

Karen cleared her throat and moved to the front of the room, aware for the first time of the magnitude of the chain of events that she might be just about to unleash.

She introduced herself and her two colleagues.

The ceiling of Hinksman's room had many cracks in it and some dampness in one corner. He lay on the bed, hands clasped across his chest, staring blankly up at it, when Paglia rushed in without knocking.

Even though the door had been flung open, Hinksman had reacted instinctively as soon as the handle had started to move downwards. He rolled off the bed, grabbing the revolver which was on the bedside cabinet, twisting himself onto his knees, using the bed as cover; by the time Paglia actually stepped into the room he was greeted by the sight of a black muzzle pointing directly at his chest, the hammer on its deadly backwards journey.

Paglia froze. His jaw dropped.

Fortunately, Hinksman saw who it was and eased the hammer back into place with his thumb. He stood up angrily.

'Jesus H Christ,' he cursed through gritted teeth, 'I told you – knock and wait. Next time I'll kill you. That's a promise.'

Paglia gulped. 'Sorry,' he blabbered, 'but I thought you should watch this.'

He switched on the portable TV. The top story was being wound up with an artist's impression of the man police were after in connection with the M6 bombing. The sketch was Hinksman, of that there was no doubt. It captured his features exactly, right down to the cruel, piercing eyes. Killer's eyes.

Hinksman watched scornfully. 'So?' he spat. 'It changes nothing.'

'Oh,' said Paglia, bemused by the calm reaction.

'Because they think they know what I look like means nothing. They don't know my name or where I am, do they?'

'Right, right,' said the hotel-keeper. 'I thought you should know, that's all.'

Hinksman nodded. 'You did right.'

When Paglia had left, Hinksman switched the TV off and lay on the bed again. The drawing had been a very good likeness – and that was a niggling worry. There was no way it could have been drawn from someone's memory. It was a lift from a photograph, Hinksman suddenly realised. But which one?

Maybe it was time to quit this Godforsaken little country after all. Get the job done and get out. In the meantime, Hinksman decided, he'd hole up somewhere else. In a city. Manchester or Liverpool – somewhere he could just fade into the background.

The telephone rang in the reception area. Hinksman heard Paglia answer and then the sound of footsteps running upstairs.

This time Paglia knocked and announced himself nervously through the closed door.

'Come in, you idiot.'

'Phone for you,' said Paglia, out of breath again.

'Who is it?' Hinksman asked sharply.

'Only one other person knows you're here.'

Hinksman shouldered Paglia out of the way and sprinted down to take the call.

Only a minute later he was back.

He started to pack. Quickly.

Paglia hovered at the bedroom door. 'Problem?'

'Big problem,' said Hinksman, stuffing his clothes into a holdall. 'They do know who I am and what's more, they know *where* I am.'

And not only that, Hinksman thought as he looked at Paglia, you know far too much about me.

Chapter Nine

The briefing was over. The team was ready to move.

Karen had been as honest as she could be about the situation, which pleased them all. Normally briefings were couched in half-truths, downright lies and need-to-know, which could put team members in unnecessary danger. Here, she laid it all on the line, laid it on thick that Hinksman was a killer out of the top drawer, who knew how to kill well, had been trained to do it efficiently and probably enjoyed it too.

They got the message.

'Do you have any further questions?' she asked as she packed her notes together.

The team leader, Sergeant Macintosh, a well-built officer over six feet tall, who looked as if he would take no messing from anyone, asked: 'Where has the information about the hotel-keeper come from?'

Karen looked at Donaldson.

He coughed and replied, 'From a reputable Mafia source in Florida – a man who's presently serving time.'

'And how much do we know about this Paglia fellow?'

'Very little, other than he's been in this country for thirty years, generally in the hotel or restaurant trade. He's got a family connection with a Mafia boss we're currently investigating – and family connections mean a lot to these people. It would appear that over the years he's given refuge to many Mafia members en route from either Italy or the States.'

'So what do you think, Sarge?' Karen asked.

'Ideally, I'd like to seal off the whole area, evacuate the surrounding buildings and then go in, preferably with a floorplan of the hotel . . . I mean, we don't know how many other guests there are, how many staff, even if our man is there.'

'I know, it's a far from ideal situation,' agreed Karen, 'but we need to move quickly and get to him before he's alerted.'

Macintosh nodded and pursed his lips. He consulted a large-scale map of the relevant area of Blackpool. Everyone in the room had a copy.

'In that case,' he said, 'we'll back and front the place. I'll send a couple to the rear of the premises and, once they're in place, we'll hit the front and take it from there.'

'I'll leave it up to you, Sarge. You're the pro.'

'Thanks,' he said with a trace of irony. 'OK guys and gals, let's move.'

The firearms team were parked up three streets away in their 'battle-bus': an armoured personnel carrier with one-way bulletproof windows which enabled occupants to see out but no one else to see in, giving the vehicle a sinister appearance.

Karen's car drew up behind.

In the back seat Donaldson and McClure were poring over one of the street maps, muttering to each other.

Over her shoulder, Karen said, 'What the hell are you two prattling on about?'

'Prattling?' asked Donaldson. '*Prattling*? A peculiarly English term, is it?'

Karen managed her first smile in several hours.

'We've been trying to think like Hinksman,' said McClure. 'He's hardly likely to park his car outside the hotel, so we were just wondering where it might be – if he's still got the same hire car, that is.'

'I think we'll have a mosey through the highways and byways in this area,' said Donaldson, circling an area of the map with his finger, tilting it so that Karen could see. 'It's near enough to be in walking distance, but far enough away . . . if you know what I mean?'

'Mosey? What the hell is mosey?' she said with another grin. 'It's a long shot,' she added dryly.

'It'll give us something to do while the boys and girls are playing Cowboys and Indians,' said Donaldson.

The side door of the battle-bus opened. The team disembarked. They were all tooled up to the back teeth.

'They look like a SWAT squad,' remarked Donaldson. 'And I thought England was *s-o-o-o* backward.'

On a word from Macintosh they sprinted away. The team leader gave Karen a quick thumbs-up and followed.

The operation was underway.

Karen's stomach churned over. The colour seeped from her face as she thought, What have I done?

'We'll keep monitoring the radio,' McClure said, pocketing a personal radio which was tuned into the secure channel being used by the team. He patted the snub-nosed revolver at his side, arranged his jacket to cover it smoothly and climbed out of the car.

Before joining him, Donaldson leaned forwards and laid a reassuring hand on Karen's shoulder. He knew she was worried about the operation and troubled about something else, but he didn't know what. 'Relax, it'll be OK,' he told her.

She nodded numbly. 'Yeah, sure it will.'

Events were now out of her hands. All she could do was wait. And wait. And wait.

The two detectives confined their search to a small cluster of roads, back streets and alleyways about 200 metres in a direct line from the hotel. McClure had the PR in his pocket turned up loud enough for them both to be able to hear what was going on. It remained eerily silent for quite a number of minutes as the firearms team moved into position using verbal and visual signals only.

In the first few roads they checked there was no sign of Hinksman's car. They didn't really expect to find it.

As they turned into another street there was a brief transmission on the radio.

'Alpha in position.'

'Roger Alpha,' they heard Macintosh reply. 'We're at the front door now.'

McClure nodded at Donaldson, who said, 'Knock, knock,' in his best John Wayne drawl.

'Sierra – we're in through the front door. No opposition.'

They were inside. It was rolling.

Everything went dead again. For ever, it seemed.

Two things then happened almost simultaneously.

McClure and Donaldson walked into a quiet side street. And there it was: Hinksman's car.

'Bingo,' gloated McClure.

And the radio went berserk.

'Civilian down, civilian down. Head wounds, looks bad.'

'Sierra to Alpha, Sierra to Alpha – take care at the back, he may be coming. Get ready.'

'Alpha received.'

They heard Karen interrupt. 'Superintendent Wilde – situation report, please.' She sounded wound-up.

'Sierra to Superintendent,' Macintosh began, then was cut off.

'Shit, I wonder what's happening,' gasped McClure.

'Don't sound good,' commented Donaldson.

Macintosh's transmission was cut into: 'Basement door opening.' It was a calm, clear message. A woman's voice. 'Someone's coming out.'

McClure and Donaldson looked at each other, neither caring to speak.

A moment's silence descended on the radio. Then a male voice screamed, 'It's him, it's him.'

A transmission carrier must have stuck down then. There was the sound of footsteps running. Breathlessness. Rustling of clothing. A shout: 'Armed police. Stop and drop your weapon. I said throw down your weapon!' Panic rising in the voice. A gun shot. A heavy, rushing noise. A groan. More footsteps. Panting. Rustling. Then: 'Officer down! Assistance, assistance . . .' This was the female voice again. Another sharp crack, like a whip, very loud, distorted, as though next to the microphone: a gun shot close up. Then silence. Again.

'Fuck!' uttered McClure. 'What're we going to do?'

'Sit tight,' said Donaldson firmly.

The radio traffic started again. 'Charlie One, in pursuit on foot.' It was another female voice. The message became garbled. More panting. More running.

'He's gotta be making for here,' said Donaldson. 'Gotta be, c'mon.'

The radio crashed to silence once more.

Donaldson grabbed McClure's sleeve. 'Let's get hidden – and get that fuckin' gun of yours ready. It is loaded, isn't it?'

'Yes, yes,' said McClure.

They vaulted over a low garden wall and ducked down into a crouch behind it. Out of sight, but with a direct line of view to Hinksman's car.

'You can't give him a chance,' Donaldson whispered urgently into McClure's ear, prompting him. 'We take him by surprise and you shoot the bastard. Got it?'

McClure nodded.

He had the two-inch-barrelled Smith & Wesson in his hand. His sweaty hand. His shaking hand. His slimy forefinger quivered uncertainly on the trigger.

The seconds ticked by with a slowness that was physically painful.

The radio stayed silent, almost as though it had all been a nightmare. Or maybe he wasn't coming. Had he gone in another direction? Had they got him? Had he been arrested – or shot?

A figure appeared out of an alleyway about halfway down the street and walked in their direction. Seventy metres away. More of a trot than a walk. But there was no concern in the stride. No sense of urgency. Whoever it was didn't seem to be in much of a rush. A bag was being carried in the left hand. A holdall. It couldn't be him, surely.

'It's him,' said Donaldson.

The heads of the two detectives dipped an inch instinctively.

'Let him get to the car,' Donaldson said between his teeth, his lips not moving. He glanced sideways at his nervous partner.

'If he goes to the driver's door we'll have the advantage because his back'll be towards us.' That was McClure thinking out loud, his mind racing.

Hinksman got to the car, checking his shoulder as he fumbled briefly with the key for the door. He went to the driver's side, dropped the holdall to the ground and slid the key into the lock. He hadn't seen the detectives. They rose slowly from their hiding place.

'Armed police,' shouted McClure, pointing his gun at Hinksman's back and stepping over the garden wall. 'Stay exactly where you are. Don't move a fuckin' muscle or you're a dead man – understand?'

Hinksman froze. Then nodded.

'Shoot him,' Donaldson encouraged McClure. 'Do it now.'

McClure motioned to Donaldson to keep quiet with a chopping action of his free hand. 'Now put both your hands on the roof of the car so I can see them.'

Hinksman's left hand slid up and he placed it on top of the car, empty, the key in the lock. His right hand was still tucked up at the front of his body. Out of sight.

'Don't give him the chance, Ken. Shoot the bastard,' said Donaldson, verging on sheer anger.

'Both fuckin' hands,' yelled McClure at Hinksman.

'OK, OK,' said Hinksman.

McClure was moving forwards, concentrating totally on the killer in front of him, forcing fear and everything else to the back of his mind into a compartment to be unlocked later at leisure.

Donaldson was a wary two steps behind him. His head was shaking. His eyes kept moving heavenwards. 'Come on Ken, put him down.'

'No, Karl, it's not the way we do things over here.'

There was one more garden wall to step over. No higher, no broader than the last. But McClure's concentration was so absolute he misjudged his stride as he stepped across, snagging the top of it with the toe of his left shoe.

He stumbled, lost his balance and crashed down onto one knee with a yelp of pain.

Hinksman, who'd watched the approach in the wing mirror of the car, swung round fast, the gun in his right hand hot from previous firings.

McClure had regained his feet, but for a few seconds he was open and totally vulnerable. These were the few seconds Hinksman needed to loose off two rounds. They slammed into the detective's chest, blowing him backwards like a candle flame being snuffed out by a gust of wind.

The impact of the bullets propelled him into Donaldson who caught him with a hand under each armpit and, winded himself, staggered sideways with the weight and momentum of McClure's body. The two detectives crashed to the ground in a macabre embrace. McClure landed half on top of Donaldson, pinning him there, trapping him.

As they'd fallen, McClure's gun had skittered away out of reach.

Donaldson desperately tried to heave McClure off.

Hinksman sauntered up to them, a smile of victory playing cruelly on his face. His gun hung at his side, literally smoking. He was full of confidence.

He tossed his gun across to his left hand, clicked the magazine out and dropped it onto the ground where it tinkled merrily on the concrete pavement. His right hand delved into his jeans pocket and emerged holding a new magazine. He slotted it in without looking, his eyes holding Donaldson's in a death-warrant gaze. He transferred the gun back to his right hand.

Donaldson gave up trying to dislodge the wounded McClure, whose shirt-front was a soggy mass of bright red blood.

He lay there under McClure's dead weight, unable to move.

Hinksman stood arrogantly above him.

'Well now, Fibbie,' he said. 'So you wanted him to shoot me? Naughty, naughty. This is England. They play by the rules here. You should know that. Not like you fuckers . . . Anyway, can't stay even though I'd love to chat. Y'know, I ain't never done an officer of the law before today, but I guess there's always a first time for everything . . . and in your case, Fibbie, a fourth time.'

Hinksman pointed the gun at Donaldson's head as the significance of the words sank in.

The detective swallowed something big and hard and it stuck in his throat. His eyes squinted as he braced himself for the impact. He wondered what it would feel like.

Hinksman eased the hammer back. His forefinger curled onto the trigger. Only the lightest touch was now needed.

Donaldson thought of blackness for ever.

There was a shout. A female voice.

'Armed police! Drop your weapon!'

Donaldson and Hinksman looked. Twenty metres away stood two uniformed officers from the firearms team. Both had their revolvers drawn, both were in exactly the same weaver stance: left foot forward, guns held in the right hand, supported by the left, fingers on triggers – aimed at Hinksman.

A tense moment of silence passed when nothing happened.

'Drop your weapon and raise your hands,' the female officer reiterated.

Hinksman's gun was pointing at Donaldson. He glanced back down at him and smiled briefly. Donaldson thought he was going to pull the trigger.

Without warning the American moved quickly, becoming

a blur of speed. He pivoted on his heels, crouched down and cracked three earsplitting shots off at the officers. He threw himself to one side, grabbed his holdall and did a body roll down in front of his car. He leapt to his feet in one flowing motion and sprinted away without a backward glance, keeping low as he went.

The male officer had gone down with a scream, clutching his right bicep, his gun skidding away under a car. The woman dived sideways for cover behind a car after managing to fire one shot in reply.

Donaldson, powerless to do otherwise, simply watched Hinksman run down the street and turn left into an alleyway and disappear. He looked at the female officer who was flattened on the floor, breathing heavily, as white as a sheet.

'It's safe now,' Donaldson called out. 'He's gone. He won't be back.'

It took a while for her to pluck up enough courage to stick her head out for an instant.

The other officer, the one who'd been shot, struggled up into a sitting position, leaning against a low wall where he remained, sobbing as he held his injured, limp arm. Blood poured through his fingers.

Donaldson gently eased McClure off him and laid him out on the pavement. Thankfully he was unconscious.

'Shit,' said Donaldson on seeing his colleague's bloody front.

He ripped open the shirt to inspect the wounds. They were very bad. The bullets had gone into the left side of his chest. Brilliant, deadly shooting.

McClure was breathing, but with every breath big bubbles of blood were being blown out of the holes. He wheezed and gurgled as the breath came and went.

'Shit,' Donaldson said again, hopelessly.

McClure's eyes opened. They were glassy, unfocused.

'It's OK,' Donaldson said. 'Just hold on, pal.'

The eyes came to life. He looked up at Donaldson.

'Can't feel a thing,' he gasped with a twisted smile.

'Don't worry, it's not bad. You'll be fine,' he lied smoothly.

'No . . . no, I won't be. I should've shot him, shouldn't I?'

'Yep,' Donaldson acceded.

'Couldn't do it . . . couldn't shoot a man in the back. Not the way we do things round here.'

'I know . . . Now don't speak . . . save your energy.'

McClure coughed, spraying Donaldson with a fine mist of blood.

Donaldson ran a hand over his face.

When he looked, McClure's eyes were closed. Donaldson knew he was dead.

Crosby's face was ashen, his eyes sunk into black, hollow sockets. His breathing was laboured, but for the time being he was stable and surrounded by machines that continuously monitored his condition. He was also awake and quite compos mentis.

FB sat at the bedside. Crosby's wife stood out in the corridor talking in hushed tones to the Chief Constable.

'You saved my life,' Crosby said quietly through the oxygen mask. 'Thank you.'

FB nodded. 'Training took over. It was nothing.'

'As good a cliché as any,' said Crosby. 'Now you make sure you get that investigation back off that cow.'

'I will,' said FB.

'And do her. Do her well. If you can, get her thrown out of the job. Do it for me.'

'I'll do it, even if it takes for ever.'

'Good man.'

Crosby's head dropped back onto the pillow. His eyes closed.

FB actually felt a tear form and roll down his cheek. 'I'll get her if it's the last thing I do,' he said softly.

The machine which monitored Crosby's heart-rate

changed its tone to one continuous note. It took a moment to register with FB – by which time two nurses had rushed into the room and an alarm bell was sounding somewhere. More medical staff arrived within seconds, crowding round the patient, pushing FB out of the way.

He retreated to the door, standing by Mrs Crosby and Dave August.

Five minutes later it was over.

Crosby was dead.

FB stormed down the corridor muttering, 'That bitch is history.'

Karen sat alone in her borrowed office at Preston police station. She did not want to see anyone. She wanted to sit by herself for as long as possible as the day darkened to try and comprehend the enormity of what had happened.

Three policemen dead. Another injured. Shots fired. A member of the public dead too – that being Pepe Paglia whose body the firearms team had found on entering the hotel. He'd been shot through the head. And to cap it all the person responsible had got away. Been allowed to escape.

Basically the biggest single fuck-up in the history of Lancashire Constabulary. And it was all her fault.

Karen rubbed her face with her hands.

And for a classic post-script, Jack Crosby had died. Apparently she was to blame for that too.

How long was it since she had had any sleep? Many hours. Yet she doubted whether she could sleep now even if she had the opportunity. Her dazed mind raced around and around like an Indy car on an oval track.

There was a soft knock on the door. Donaldson crept quietly into the room. Bloodstains had dried on his clothing. He hadn't had a chance to change yet.

'OK?' he enquired.

'No, not really,' she admitted truthfully. She was on the verge of tears, struggled to keep them back.

'I have a little more bad news, I'm afraid.'

She sighed and shrugged her shoulders. 'Go on.' She wasn't sure how much more she could take.

'I've just spoken to Joe Kovaks; he tells me that the guy who gave us the information has been killed. Stabbed to death in his hospital bed at the prison. Even had his tongue cut out.'

'Oh God,' she uttered. She stood up shakily and crossed to the window which overlooked the town. In the distance the River Ribble snaked away towards the sea. She shook her head in disbelief.

She couldn't stop it. She began to cry with gut-wrenching sobs that racked her body, made her shoulders judder.

Donaldson crossed to her and placed an arm around her. She turned instinctively into him and buried her face in his blood-stained shirt. It was a great effort to prevent himself from crying. Ever since McClure had died, he'd shut his mind to it so that he could get on with what had to be done. Now that time was over. Family had been told. Statements had been made.

He stroked Karen's hair. It felt coarse and grubby. Stale.

She tilted her head and looked up. Tears flooded her eyes, pouring down her cheeks. Make-up ran, lipstick smeared. She would have been the first to admit she looked a mess.

'I'm sorry, Karl,' she said.

The door opened before she could finish.

FB and a sidekick strutted businesslike into the room.

'Oh, this is fuckin' great,' he shouted. 'Straight back to your old tricks and the bodies are still warm. I should've known. You're an uncaring, unfeeling slag. Yes, a fuckin' slag and you'll never be any different.'

Karen and Donaldson had stepped a pace apart from each other. They were speechless.

'Right – collect your things. You're off this investigation as of now and you're also suspended from duty pending a full enquiry.'

'Suspended?' she said in disbelief. 'On what grounds?'

'Neglect of duty, disobeying a lawful order, bringing the force into disrepute . . . you name it, lady, it's there. Unfortunately you'll be on full pay. May I have your warrant card, please? As of now you're banned from entering any police station, other than as a member of the public. You must go home and remain there until D and C contact you.' FB was in full flow. 'Do you know how many lives you've destroyed by this thoughtless operation? And do you care? I'll bet not.'

Karen couldn't answer.

'Let up, will you, pal?' Donaldson cut in.

'You shut it, Yank,' snarled FB, pointing. 'You're not involved in this.'

'Not involved?' Donaldson stepped forward and grabbed FB's lapels, heaved him onto his toes and whacked him back against the wall. They stood nose to nose. 'Not involved, you asshole? My friend died in my arms today, you little shit. *Not involved?* I oughtta punch you into next week.'

His big clenched fist drew back. FB braced himself, wondering what time-travel would feel like.

Karen caught the fist before it connected. 'Karl, Karl. There's no need for that. It won't do anyone any good . . . and please, let me fight my own battles.'

'But it'd make me feel so damned good,' he said, reluctantly dropping the sweating FB.

Numbly, Karen rummaged through her handbag until she found her warrant card. She placed it photo-up on her desk. She collected her coat, slung it around her shoulders and walked out of the office, averting her eyes from everyone else's.

'Good fuckin' riddance,' FB called out childishly. 'And stay away from the Chief – he doesn't need your poison.'

'You be quiet,' Donaldson warned him. He came up close to FB again. 'I don't know you, but you sure got bad manners and if she hadn't stopped me your teeth would be stickin' outta your ass now – because I'd've smashed them that far down your goddamned throat.'

Donaldson hurried out of the office after Karen, but she'd already caught the lift. He ran down the stairs into the car park – just in time to see the back end of her car pull away into traffic with a screech of tyres.

Chapter Ten

The surveillance was back on.

The suspected drugs dealer in the Porsche was gunning down the west-bound carriageway of the M55, heading out towards the Lancashire coast. He was averaging about 100 mph – not particularly excessive for such a car – but it showed he was fairly relaxed about things and didn't think he was being followed. What he didn't know was that a sophisticated tracking device had been fitted to the underside of his car and was emitting a powerful, easy to follow signal to the four-car RCS surveillance team, the nearest of which, two miles behind, was driven by Henry Christie.

This is an absolute piece of cake, Henry thought, alternately watching the tracking monitor fitted to the dash, the road ahead, the road behind. He'd only managed to get hold of the tracker by a combination of accident and theft early that morning. In their tiredness, another RCS team, going off-duty after an unsuccessful night's work, had forgotten to lock it away. So Henry nicked it.

He was alone in his car. Terry was still off sick with his broken thumb and Henry didn't really feel inclined to be working with anyone else at that stage. He wished to avoid talking about the bomb and its unpleasant aftermath. He just wanted to be at work, doing something, chasing someone, taking his mind off it. He did have a constant dull headache he couldn't rid himself of, though, due to the bump on his temple. That was reminder enough.

When the bomb exploded, the surveillance operation on the dealer had obviously gone to rat-shit. They had lost him for the time being and it had taken Henry and his team the best part of that day to relocate him and his car in Manchester and then get into position once the tracker had been fitted.

The tracker had proved to be a godsend once the target had started to move, about 8 p.m. The team had followed him without a hitch around Manchester for about twenty minutes and eventually onto the motorway network. He'd taken the M61 out of the city, picked up the M6 north and cut left onto the M55 where he was now, at two minutes to nine.

Henry hadn't a clue what he was up to, nor where he was headed. Because of the bomb they were starting from scratch again. Presumably he'd sold on his Ecstasy tablets. Henry hoped he was going into Blackpool to do some wheeling and dealing in the pubs and clubs where perhaps he could be caught red-handed.

It would be nice to arrest him in Blackpool, Henry thought. That way he could go straight home. See his wife and children. Even if it was late. He hadn't given them much time recently and he wanted to change that. They all needed a holiday and he vowed that as soon as he could arrange some leave they'd scoot off to sunny Spain.

On the final few miles into Blackpool, where the M55 narrows into a normal two-lane road, they hit the tailback of slow-moving Illuminations traffic, inbound to Blackpool. Hundreds of cars crammed full of families, all drawn by the world-famous lights fantastic. Everyone, including the Porsche, was forced to a snail's pace.

Henry decided the time had come to move up into visual contact with the target. He accelerated, executed a few hairy overtakes, causing some swerving, swearing, fist-shaking and angry horn blasts, and slotted in two cars behind the target.

Leaning forwards, he pushed the button to switch on the car radio. It was 9 p.m. He hadn't heard any news today. He tuned in to Radio Lancashire and almost crashed into the car ahead when the announcer calmly reported the deaths of three police officers in a firearms incident in Blackpool where the person responsible had managed to evade capture; the same person, incidentally, wanted for questioning in connection with the M6 bombing.

It was 9.30 p.m.

The public house on the promenade was busy, packed to the doors. Henry Christie squeezed in, his eyes roving the bar, searching for his man who he was sure had come in here. He shuffled sideways in between the crush of people, ensuring his left arm always lay tight across the revolver in his shoulder-holster. His compact Sig Sauer which he'd lost in the river had been replaced temporarily by a more bulky short-barrelled .38, which in comparison felt like a bazooka stuck under his arm. He would be glad when his new Sig arrived.

The smell of sweat, beer and cigarettes intermingled with the sound of raucous laughter, banter and loud music blasting from the video jukebox. Two huge screens hanging precariously from the ceiling showed the group Take That strutting their pectorals. It was a typical youngsters' pub. A good place to buy and sell gear – drugs, that is.

Henry still couldn't see his man but was sure he was in there somewhere.

Since he'd parked his Porsche some ten minutes earlier in one of the back streets behind the promenade, Henry, in a panic, had ditched his own car and tracked the man on foot.

On the face of it, the target seemed unaware that he was being followed. Unfortunately this indicated to Henry that he wasn't up to anything unlawful – yet.

The only problem Henry now had was that his mini personal radio, strapped to his belt at the small of his back and wired up to a discreet earpiece, a tiny mike pinned on the collar of his windjammer and a transmit button on the palm of his left hand, had packed up. In other words the battery had lost its charge, the bane of every policeman's life; and like most cops Henry hadn't brought a spare. So he was alone without any immediate means of contacting the rest of his team. All they could do was pinpoint the Porsche and sit on it until the target returned. Henry knew they would do this as a matter of course, but he cursed his own stupidity and short-sightedness for insisting on working alone, just because he felt like Greta Garbo.

He circled the room feeling more and more ancient by the minute as he brushed past young girls who looked no older than his thirteen-year-old daughter Jenny. He half-expected to see her face in the crowd.

Then he spotted his man.

Henry froze. He'd almost walked right up to him. He took a step back and a group of youngsters spilled into the vacuum he'd created.

The target was actually sitting in one corner of the room, in an area separated from the rest of it by a fancy wrought-iron, thigh-high railing. He was at a table together with another man and a woman. Lounging on the wall behind them were two casually dressed gorillas, whose eyes constantly scanned the room. Bouncers? Bodyguards?

Interesting, whatever.

Henry pushed his way to the bar. After an interminable wait he bought a bottle of Bud, declining the glass offered because it seemed to be the fashion to drink it straight from the bottle. Must be hip, he thought, and hiply took a cool, refreshing, fizzy swig. He then engineered a position by the edge of a slot-machine where he could see his target yet remain unseen himself.

The area the three sat in was like a total exclusion zone, even though there were two vacant tables. When a young couple innocently decided to sit at one of the tables, the gorillas swooped down from their tree and blocked the way menacingly.

Unwisely the young man remonstrated. He must have said a few harsh words; one of the gorillas responded by punching him hard and low in the stomach. Bent double with pain, he was quickly led away by his girlfriend. The gorillas loped back to their station.

The other people in the pub who'd witnessed the incident looked in another direction, not wishing to get involved.

Henry's eyes narrowed. An over-the-top reaction for no reason at all, he thought. They were certainly a nervous crew behind that wrought-iron fence. But what worried him most was the glimpse of a firearm when the jacket of one of the bodyguards inadvertently swung open. A bulge under the jacket of the other told Henry he was similarly tooled up.

The detective's attention moved to the man in the middle. He was obviously the boss.

Henry didn't know him, his face rang no bells, but suddenly he found himself very interested.

He was quite a young man, in his early thirties, fit-looking with jet-black hair, a neatly trimmed moustache, a swarthy complexion and the dark, all-seeing eyes of a predator. His clothing was casual but expensive; Ralph Lauren polo shirt, beautifully cut chinos and loafers. No socks. A slim, understated watch was attached to his wrist and a chunky gold chain encircled his tanned neck. He was good-looking, exuding an air of confidence, wealth and violence. It seemed to Henry that he would have looked more at home on the Costa del Crime, rather than here in Blackpool, the Costa del Shite . . . because there was one thing Henry Christie *did* know about this man, simply by looking at him : he was a top flight criminal, a major player. Henry would happily have bet his next month's expenses cheque on the fact.

Yet, despite the outward appearance of calm, something in his manner, a fraction below the surface, told Henry he was unsettled. His non-verbal signals betrayed him.

The girl who sat next to him was positively gorgeous – a black chick who looked young enough to be jailbait. One of her hands rested provocatively at the top of the man's thigh and she stuck close to him as though superglued, laughing in all the right places. Her short, low-cut dress left little to Henry's imagination and he soon found himself unconsciously trying to peer up her legs.

But this was no girlfriend. Everything about her screamed hooker; expensive hooker. And she looked uneasy, too. Her brown eyes never stayed still for an instant. Her shoulders were taut. She was very, very nervous.

Henry finished off his Bud and returned to the bar. This time he had a less fashionable bottle of non-alcoholic lager which tasted bitter after the slightly sweet American brew.

As he glanced casually around the room, Henry spotted another man watching the trio. He was mid-height, with blond hair and a moustache. Pretty nondescript, though he looked vaguely familiar. A moment later the man had gone. Henry thought nothing of it, resumed his position by the bandit and took a long drink from his bottle. Ugh. All the flavour brewed out with the alcohol.

He was about to make a phone call into the Blackpool Communications Room for them to pass on his present position by radio to his team when the three got slowly to their feet.

They were on the move.

Henry swore.

The boss man nodded to his gorillas. One of them took the lead, forging a way through the throng. The three slotted in behind with the other gorilla taking up a position at the rear, his right hand hidden underneath his jacket. They went out of a door at the rear of the pub.

Henry gave them a few moments, then followed.

Karen answered the door in her bath-robe.

She'd had a long hot soak and a shower. Nothing could shake the sense of disaster in her mind, but at least she was now clean and ready for bed. She'd just rolled the quilt back on her double bed when the doorbell rang.

She was tempted to ignore it, but found she couldn't.

Dave August stood there, swaying slightly. His official car, the Jaguar, was parked with one wheel on the kerb, unattended. Obviously he'd driven there by himself. Yet he smelled of alcohol. His eyes were watery and bloodshot.

'What the hell do you want?' Karen asked.

'To explain?' he said meekly. Then: 'Oh, come on, Karen. You owe me that at the very least.'

'Do I?' she asked resolutely.

'Look, can I come in, or shall we continue to conduct our business in public?' He was having a little difficulty stringing the words together.

She considered slamming the door in his face then relented, allowed him to enter.

She followed him into the lounge. He knew the way. It was a beautifully furnished room, much money having been spent on the tasteful décor.

August turned to her as she came in behind him. 'Karen,' he began, his arms outstretched.

'Not so fast, David,' she told him coolly. 'You said you wanted to explain something. If you think you're going to get a fuck after the way I've been treated, you're well off the mark.'

August backed off. 'Very well,' he conceded, tight-lipped.

He plonked himself loosely down on the plush sofa and crossed his legs. She perched on a chair-arm. Her robe fell open, revealing her thighs. She quickly pulled it back and covered up, though not before August had seen.

'Well, I'm waiting,' she said at length.

'I . . . I don't really know where to begin,' he stuttered. 'Look, could I have a drink?'

'I think you've already had enough.'

'Please.'

Karen sighed impatiently. She fixed him a large whisky, dropped an ice cube into it and handed it to him. 'Thanks,' he said. Most of it then hit the back of his throat. 'That's better.'

Karen's mouth twisted into a line of disapproval.

'You know I'm suspended, don't you? Barred from entering any police station in the county. Even had to hand my warrant card in. I feel so humiliated!'

August nodded. 'Yes, I know. I sanctioned it.'

'*You* sanctioned it? I don't believe this.' She stood up and paced the room. 'I should've realised.'

'I was under pressure to do something. Can't you see, after all that's happened?' he pleaded.

'From Fanshaw-Bayley, no doubt.'

August dropped his gaze and stared at the gas fire, confirming Karen's words. 'I'd been backed into a corner. I had to do it. I didn't want to . . . I just had to.'

'You're the fuckin' Chief Constable, for God's sake. No one can make you do anything you don't want to. You've simply kow-towed to FB and the CID again, haven't you? You weak-kneed bastard.'

'It was nothing personal, honestly, Karen. Purely professional.' He pronounced it 'perfeshinall'. 'I have to distance myself from you.'

Karen had had enough. 'Get out, Dave. Now. I don't want you or any other copper in my house.' She began to sob. 'Just get out and stay out!'

He stood up, exhibiting all the classic signs of a drunk: unsteady on his feet, eyes glazed, speech slurred. And like a drunk, reasoning wasn't part of his make-up.

'This doesn't change anything between us, does it?' he leered.

Karen couldn't believe what she was hearing. 'Get out – now!' she screamed.

'But I want you.' He moved towards her and grabbed her arm. She caught the look in his eyes – wild, unpredictable – and started to struggle.

'No, Dave,' she begged, trying to free herself from his grip. 'Just leave. Don't make things any worse.'

'You bitch. You use sex as a weapon over men and you don't like it when it's used against you!' He slapped her hard, open-handed, across the face.

She reeled back, stunned by the ferocity of the blow and its unexpectedness.

He lurched forward and took hold of one end of the belt around her robe. He wrenched. It unfastened. Her robe fell open.

'You've always thought you had power over me, but you were wrong,' he said. 'I'm the one in charge. I'm the boss. I decide what happens to you.'

He slapped her again. She lost her balance and fell back across the sofa. Her head swam in a sea of unreality. This could not be happening.

'You owe me . . . for what I've done for you, you owe me,' he grunted. He threw himself at her, straddling her, pinning her arms down, his whole weight on her. She struggled uselessly, pointlessly.

He forced his mouth down onto hers.

Chapter Eleven

Henry cautiously poked his head out of the pub door and looked both ways down the poorly lit street. Other than for parked cars it was deserted and quiet, though he could hear the Illuminations traffic passing the front of the pub.

To his left a narrow alleyway ran down the side of the pub, separating it from the next building along, which was a guest-house. It was a dead end, a place that smelled of dustbins and dogshit. They could be doing some sort of a deal down there, he thought. It was difficult to see into the gloom.

As he let his eyes adjust themselves to the darkness, a big man emerged from the dark shadows just inside the alley.

One of the gorillas.

Before Henry had time to react, a clenched fist shot out hard, catching him on the jaw. As Henry reeled away, head hissing and humming, he became dimly aware that another man was also rushing towards him: gorilla number two.

The men grabbed him with big, strong, no-nonsense hands, and heaved him into the alley, out of the street, so that this business could be transacted privately. They threw him down between two metal bins like a rag doll. Henry's right shoulder connected hard with the top edge of one of the bins as he fell. It toppled over and its smelly contents covered him.

'Right, you bastard,' he heard one of them say, 'Stick this.'

Henry tried to roll himself into a protective ball as the two men rained kicks into him without mercy. When they kicked him in the face, everything went black; his brain seemed to implode. Then his senses returned as quickly as they'd disappeared, and the situation became very clear.

He was going to die or get maimed unless he did something very quickly.

Self-preservation is a wonderful motivator.

He scrambled wildly to his feet and ran blindly between the dustbins to the dead end of the alley where he turned at the wall, facing his attackers.

They walked slowly down towards him.

He tried to get his breath. This was a hard thing to do, for each time he inhaled, a searing pain stabbed through his chest. He could feel blood flowing down his nose – taste it in his mouth, salty, sickly. And there was an unnatural wetness on the left side of his face. His stitches had burst open. Blood was pumping out of the newly opened wound.

They came closer. Gorilla number one laughed and sneered in one.

Then there were two unmistakable clicks. Henry saw the shimmer of two blades. Flick-knives. Christ. His spirits sank again. Henry was no fighter. He'd done the occasional self-defence class, was quite fit – as he had to be, to carry a firearm. He'd had his struggles and tumbles with burglars, drunks and yobs like any cop, and he'd been assaulted a few times – but he'd never faced a situation like this before, alone, terrified and without hope of assistance. Fuckin' Greta Garbo, he thought bitterly.

But he had one ace up his sleeve, or under his armpit to be exact. He reached under his soiled jacket for his gun.

Which wasn't there.

It must have fallen out when he'd been thrown into the dustbins – yet he was certain his holster had been fastened properly. Shite!

With this option gone his eyes searched quickly through the darkness for a weapon of some sort. The apes were fifteen feet away. He knew he had to make the running now. He had to take the initiative from them, otherwise he was beaten.

He flung himself to the left, snatched up a black plastic dustbin and heaved it down the alley at them. Its innards spilled everywhere as it went. They sidestepped it easily. Henry saw the knives glint in their hands. His mouth went very dry as fear swept though him like fire though a building. He wanted to beg for mercy, but knew these two wouldn't show it. So he fought on.

This time, instead of a whole dustbin, he picked up a lid and held it like a shield in his left hand.

'Right you bastards, come on,' he growled, sounding more confident than he really was.

He waved them forwards with the fingers of his right hand, like football supporters do when enticing the opposing fans to a fight. They came, as he knew they would. He made like he was going to step back but at the last possible moment he lurched at them. The nearest one to him copped the heavy metal lid right across the side of his head. It made a very satisfying *clunk* on connection. He went down like a jelly, a surprised scream frothing from his mouth.

Henry faced the next one smiling.

The gorilla looked worried now as Henry's eyes fixed on his face. Henry was determined to give none of his own fear away.

The knife lunged at him, but the move was telegraphed and slow. Henry jumped sideways, twisted round and smashed the dustbin lid down on the exposed, extended arm. The knife fell harmlessly away. The man cowered, holding his arm, his back to the wall.

Henry reversed down the alley, fully aware that all the man had to do now was draw his weapon and slot him. Suddenly, there was a blinding flash at the back of his right ear. His legs went wobbly. He turned around, stunned – and *whack!* – another blow hit the side of his head. At this double whammy Henry's legs gave up the ghost and crumpled beneath him.

Someone had sneaked up on him from the shadows.

He hit the ground, his fall slightly cushioned by a

mattress of debris from the overturned bins, and passed out. Seconds later he woke up, face down in the mess.

As he tried to push himself up, somebody placed a foot on the back of his neck and pressed hard. He nearly blacked out again, then the foot came off, the pressure was released and blood flowed back into his brain.

The same foot hooked itself under his shoulder and rolled him over so he was face up, looking heavenwards. He blinked and tried to regain his senses.

He heard a man say, 'Well, you're a couple of wankers. Fuck knows what I pay you for . . . no, don't say a fuckin' word, I'm not interested. Wankers!' he spat. 'I'll sort you out later.'

Several seconds passed before Henry's eyes focused properly. When they did he saw three faces glaring down at him: the target, the man with the Ralph Lauren polo shirt and the black girl.

'Back with us then?' asked the target.

'What the hell d'you think you're doing?' Henry demanded. He started to get up again. The target shoved the sole of his shoe into Henry's chest and rammed him back down. The pain in his ribs gripped him in its razor-encrusted vice.

He decided to stay where he was, without complaint, get his breath completely back, compose himself, measure the situation and if at all possible, run away.

The man in the Ralph Lauren top, who Henry christened Ralphie, said, 'He's all yours,' to the target.

The target squatted down on his haunches. 'I want to know who you are and why you're following me.'

'Me? I don't know what you mean.'

The target looked up at one of the gorillas – the one Henry had clattered on the head. 'Kick him once,' he ordered.

'Pleasure.'

Despite bracing himself, tensing his muscles as best he could, it wasn't much use: it still hurt.

'Now,' said the target softly, after the kick had been well and truly delivered, 'why are you following me?'

The stubborn side to Henry's character refused to give in so easily. 'I'm not, honest.'

'See if he's got any I.D.,' the target said to one of the gorillas, who gleefully reached down and rifled through Henry's pockets. His hand emerged with a leather wallet. He said, 'He's wearing a holster, but there's no shooter in it.'

'See if you can find it,' said Ralphie.

Henry eyed the people standing over him, ending up on the girl's face. If he'd expected any vestige of sympathy or concern from her regarding his plight, he was mistaken. Her mouth wasn't quite so lovely when it was folded into a snarl of contempt. She looked like she could have happily spat on him.

The target pulled everything out of the wallet. Three five-pound notes went sailing down the alley, one or two receipts went with them. His Barclaycard was tossed to one side after being twisted beyond use. A driving licence was extracted along with his warrant card. The target read them in the available light before showing them to Ralphie.

One of the gorillas arrived back bearing Henry's gun between thumb and forefinger.

'Found this in all that shite,' he said.

'Give it to me,' snapped the target, clicking his fingers.

He handed the gun over. The target looked at it, smiled, leaned over Henry and forced the muzzle into the soft flesh underneath his chin.

'So you're a cop, eh?'

'Yeah.'

'Do you think that makes a difference to me? Do you think that'll stop me from pulling this trigger? Eh?' He was becoming more and more angry and wound up as he spoke. 'Do you think that'll stop me from splattering your brains into the chop suey?'

'Don't know,' said Henry, his eyes wide, nostrils flaring.

He could smell the target's aftershave. It was overpowering. 'Probably not,' he conceded.

The target pushed the gun harder into the flesh. Henry heard the hammer being cocked. Oh God, I'm going to die in an alley full of shit, he thought.

'Now why the fuck are you following me?'

'Part of an operation . . . we suspect you of being a drug dealer.'

'Is that all?' He sounded disappointed.

'Yes.'

'Why the gun? *Why the fuckin' gun?*' he was screaming at Henry.

'I carry all the time . . . part of my job . . . Crime Squad,' Henry bleated. There didn't seem much point in beating about the bush now. It was no great earth-shattering secret.

The target rocked back on his haunches. Henry heard the man's knees crack. He looked up at Ralphie who was lounging by the wall with the girl.

'Shall I pop him?'

'Your problem, not mine,' said Ralphie unhelpfully.

Why couldn't you say no, Henry thought.

'I think I will.'

The target looked back down at Henry and opened his mouth to speak.

Before any words could come, however, there was the sound of a gun shot, and the target's head disintegrated. His mouth, still opened wide, vomited blood and brain out onto Henry's chest.

The girl screamed. Ralphie shouted some sort of warning. There were running feet, confusion.

For a few moments the target stayed where he was in a squatting position before keeling forwards across Henry's thighs and lower abdomen, twitching like mad in his death throes. Henry saw that the back of his head was missing.

The man who'd fired the shot stood at the open end of the alley. Even in the poor light Henry knew he'd seen him before; just a short time ago in the pub.

He held a gun in his right hand.

'Get him! Get him!' Ralphie screamed in panic at his men. He dived for cover behind a wheelie-bin, dragging the girl down with him.

Henry, trapped under the weight of the dead man, could not move.

The two gorillas reacted with predictable slowness. As they fumbled for their weapons, the figure at the end of the alley took his time, aimed slowly, and picked off each of the bodyguards with a shot to the chest. They were out of the game even before their weapons were in their hands.

Henry lay there terrified.

The man started walking down the alley to where Ralphie and the girl were hiding.

She was crying.

Ralphie was immobile. He exchanged a glance with Henry, whose expression said nothing.

'Stand up,' the man ordered Ralphie. He ignored Henry and the girl.

'No, please, don't, don't, what's this all about? Please, I haven't done anything.'

The target finished squirming. Henry eased himself to one side underneath the weight and his right hand slowly snaked out towards his revolver which was still in the target's outstretched right hand.

'I said stand up.'

Ralphie, quivering, got slowly to his feet.

'Face the wall,' the man said. He spoke with an American accent.

The gun was six inches further than Henry could reach without drawing attention to himself.

'*Nooo!*' screamed the black girl. She was already on her knees, her hands covering her face, rocking back and forth like a baby in a cot.

Ralphie faced the wall, his nose pressed up to the brick-work.

The man walked across to the girl and gave one violent

blow to the back of her head with his revolver butt; she fell silent. He went to Ralphie then and said, 'You know what this is for, don't you?'

'No.'

'Double-crossing Corelli. No one does that, Mr Brown.'

'Look . . . Jesus Christ!'

'Too late for Him.'

He pulled the trigger four times, putting the bullets into the back of Ralphie's head. Ralphie jerked into the wall with the impact and slithered to the ground. The man didn't bother to check if he was dead: he knew. Even whilst Ralphie was slithering he was walking away down the alley.

Shocked for an instant by what he'd witnessed – an execution – and still unable to believe it, Henry heaved the target's body off himself, prised the gun out of his dead fingers and pointed at the man's retreating back.

'Stop!' he shouted. He aimed the gun, but his hand was shaking.

The man barely glanced round before turning left at the top of the alley and disappearing.

Henry, who'd shouted his command from a seated position, rose quickly to his feet. He looked at the bloody scene which surrounded him. It was like a street in the capital of Rwanda, littered with bodies. The girl moaned.

Henry knew he had a decision to make. He made it quickly.

He went after the man.

Running was very painful. His ribs jarred each time a foot crashed to the pavement. He kept his left arm pressed tightly across his chest in a V-shape to support himself.

As he ran he checked that his gun was loaded, releasing the cylinder with the thumb of his right hand and flicking it back into place when he saw the chambers were full. On his belt at the small of his back was a leather ring which held a spare speed loader primed with six more .38s. The gorilla had missed it when searching him, as he'd missed the PR.

He veered out of the alley and ran in the direction of the promenade. About a quarter of a mile ahead of him the Tower loomed, bristling with lights.

He soon hit the Golden Mile. And people. Hundreds of people. He couldn't see the killer.

'Get out of the fuckin' way,' he screamed, repeating it as he ran. The crowd opened for him like the Red Sea as people scattered. Not surprising as it must have frightened the life out of everyone to see Henry careering towards them in his present condition.

Blood was still pouring from the reopened cut on the side of his face, as well as from his nose and mouth. His face was battered black and blue by the assault and his hair was in total disarray, matted with an unpleasant mixture of blood and cold, rotting food. There was a large area of blood and gore right aross his chest where the target had emptied the contents of the back of his head. With Henry's left arm wedged where it was, it must've looked like he'd sustained a massive injury of some sort.

His clothing was torn and filthy.

And he was waving a gun about.

And he was screaming like a madman.

He was only vaguely aware of the shouts, the music blaring out of the amusement arcades, the cars nose to tail, moving with desperate slowness one-way up the promenade.

Suddenly the man was there. Dead ahead. Unaware that Henry was behind him.

'Fuckin' stop now,' Henry yelled.

The man either didn't hear or took no notice.

Henry bellowed again. Still no response.

Quickly he pointed his gun out across the promenade to the Irish Sea and fired a high shot, using the recoil to re-aim at the man.

'Stop now,' Henry said.

The man stopped. But in a blur he turned. There was a gun in his hand. A child ran aross the gap, pursued by his mother – in the instant that the man fired. She took the bullet intended for Henry and pirouetted into the road on top of her child.

Henry weaved to retain his view. The man ran into the line of traffic and sprinted between the cars crawling up the promenade.

'Shit-fuck!' uttered Henry, aware now, if he wasn't before, he was in pursuit of a one-man killing machine.

Hinksman had been pleased to the point of smugness by the way things had gone. The information had proved correct, the hit had gone well, he had earned the last part of his money. Now all he had to do was get lost in the crowd, make his way to Manchester, then leave this Godforsaken country. He was already thinking about the Great Barrier Reef.

He hadn't bothered to find out who the goons were beating up. He'd simply eliminated everyone who appeared to be a potential threat – good, sound practice – then taken out Brown, finished the job. Four into the back of the head – a classic professional hit.

Now, as he twisted away into the traffic, he bitterly regretted not shooting the man on the ground. He hadn't seemed a potential threat, just some half-dead loser. How was he to know the bastard was a cop?

Hinksman rolled spectacularly across the bonnet of a car like a stuntman, much to the surprise of its occupants, and started to put some distance between himself and the cop.

He glanced round. Yes, he was coming.

Hinksman upped his pace, running north along the promenade, between the cars and coaches, zig-zagging, keeping low, constantly checking over his shoulder.

Stubbornly the cop remained there.

To Hinksman's left were tram-tracks which were laid adjacent and parallel to the road, used by the quaint trams which ran from Blackpool to Fleetwood in the north; on the other side of them was the wide pavement area for pedestrians only, then the railings of the sea wall, then the sea itself. Two hundred metres ahead was the North Pier, jutting out into the night. To his right was the Tower.

Hinksman's mind raced. He quickly calculated how many bullets he had left in the magazine. He'd fired seven in the alley and one at the cop – the one which had hit the woman. That left him with four. The cop had fired one of his own; Hinksman had registered the fact that the cop's gun was a six-shot revolver of some sort, so he was one up. If the cop was any good, one bullet could be a major advantage if it came to a confrontation. And Hinksman didn't like anyone having any advantage over him.

He released the magazine and stuffed it into his waistband, replacing it with one from his back jeans pocket.

Twelve to five. Good odds.

He swivelled from the hip and fired two in the general direction of the cop, knowing he'd miss but be close enough to scare him.

Then he was running again.

At the junction of Talbot Square, the Illuminations traffic had ground to a complete halt at the traffic lights. Hinksman looked behind. The cop was still there, but some distance away, more wary in his pursuit since the warning shots.

Hinksman had reached the point where he had to decide whether or not to carry on northwards or turn inland into town. The latter was a manoeuvre he wasn't completely happy about as it would give the cop a better target.

Then he had the answer.

In the stationary, nose-to-tail traffic sat a blonde woman in a red, open-top BMW, hood down, gazing at the Illuminations, unaware of Hinksman's approach.

He came alongside her, stopped by the driver's door, opened it, and before she could even scream, he grabbed her by the hair and threw her out onto the road where she landed on her backside in a bewildered heap.

'Thanks darlin',' he said and slid into the driver's seat, slamming the door, taking possession of the car. He was pleased to find it was an automatic gearbox. Selecting

Reverse he put his foot down and rammed into the car behind, a Metro driven by an elderly man.

Hinksman laughed, gave him a wave with the hand holding the gun, and pushed the stick into Drive.

Now, with room to pull out of the line, he virtually stood on the accelerator pedal and yanked the steering wheel to the left.

His plan was to drive across the tram-tracks, onto the pedestrianised area and head up north where he would abandon the car and go to ground.

A perfect plan. Except for one major flaw.

The car accelerated very quickly – it had a fuel-injected 2.5-litre engine. Unfortunately, within moments Hinksman was travelling so fast that there was no earthly chance of avoiding a collision with a south-bound tram which seemed to appear from nowhere, bearing down on him at the stately speed of 10 mph.

He saw it, but could do nothing about it. It was just there. Ten tons of trundling tram. Unmissable.

The front of the car hit the front of the tram head on, and there could only be one winner. The bonnet crumpled with the impact and the tram ploughed the car a further fifty metres down the tracks before the whole mangled mess ground to a screeching, spark-flying halt.

Although Hinksman braced himself against the steering wheel, he couldn't stop himself head-butting the windscreen. He sat there in the wreckage, dazed for a moment, amazingly still clutching his gun.

Then instinct took over.

He extricated himself from between the seat and the dashboard, feeling severe pain in his left leg. He slid over the side of the car and dropped to the ground on his hands and knees. He picked himself up and ran – ran like a drunk, staggering from side to side, feet hardly able to keep him upright. Not knowing where he was going, just aware that he needed to get away, despite the pain.

* * *

Henry Christie was right behind him, less than ten metres away. He could see that the man was injured. It was only a matter of time and patience now. There was no speed in him any more. Henry slowed down himself, keeping a safe distance, glad of the opportunity to get his own breath back.

Hinksman weaved on across towards the sea wall. Just before the railings he stumbled, tripped and slumped onto his knees. He remained there for about thirty seconds, wavering. The gun slid out of his grasp and clattered beside him. Eventually he turned himself round and sat down, head in hands.

Henry circled him, gun at the ready, unsure of his next move.

When Hinksman looked up, his mind was clear again, the pain in his leg dreadful.

The cop was standing in front of him, gun pointed at his head.

Hinksman chuckled.

'You're under arrest,' Henry said. His gun quivered nervously. It was the first time he'd ever pointed it at anyone. 'Put your hands on your head – now.'

Hinksman shook his head. 'You turn around and walk away,' he told Henry. 'And you get two million dollars. That's a promise.'

'Hands on your head,' Henry said.

'Okay, three million. Just think. Three million dollars. What could you do with that, cop?'

'I said you're under arrest. Now do what I say, or I'll shoot you.'

'Fuck,' winced Hinksman as a pain shot up through his leg like a million volts. 'This is your last chance – three and a half million. And remember, I just saved your life too.'

'Perhaps you should've killed me when you had the chance.'

'Maybe I'll just have to kill you now.'

He looked for his gun, saw it within reach of his hand.

'If you move, I'll shoot you,' Henry warned him again. His breathing had become shallow, body tensed up.

'No, you won't. You're a fuckin' terrified limey cop with no guts. You don't shoot people. I'm gonna pick this up and blow your fuckin' head off. Just watch.'

'Don't make me do it,' Henry said quickly, doubting whether he could. 'I can do it . . . I *will* do it. Now *put your hands on your head!*'

'Fuck you,' spat Hinksman. He reached out for the gun.

And Henry shot him.

Chapter Twelve

Donaldson drew up outside Karen's house, which was in darkness. He switched off the engine, killed the lights and sat there for a while wondering what his reception would be like if he managed to pluck up enough courage to actually go to the door and knock on it.

He had almost made the decision to drive away when he thought, What the hell. He had nothing to lose. It had taken him long enough and a bucket full of sickly charm to get the switchboard operator at headquarters to give him the address, so there was no way he was going to let that go to waste.

Added to that, he desperately needed someone to talk to. He was very much alone in a strange land and the only friend he had, had died in his arms earlier that day.

Plus he thought he was falling in love. And that was a very odd, unsettling feeling – one he hadn't experienced in a long time. It surprised him because when he'd first met Karen Wilde not very long ago, he'd detested her.

Something fundamental had changed over the course of the day. He'd seen a side of her after the Blackpool shootings that he was certain no one else had. It had touched him deeply. Now he couldn't get her off his mind no matter how he tried.

He wanted to find out how she felt about him. If there was something there, even the vaguest hint or possibility, he'd decided he would stick by her through this traumatic period and try and make things work out – professionally and personally – despite his living in Florida and she in Lancashire.

Light-headedly, he'd thought, Love will find a way – a thought that confused and disturbed him, but made him giggle at its silliness at the same time.

He checked his watch. 10.45 p.m. Too late? *Naah!*

He got out of the car.

It's a nice house, he thought as he strolled up to the front door. I could spend time here. He raised his knuckles, then saw that the door was actually slightly ajar.

He pushed it slowly. It swung open to reveal a darkened hallway. Donaldson tensed up, feeling his skin crawl. Something was wrong.

'Karen?' he called out from the threshold. 'Karen, it's me, Karl Donaldson.'

There was no answer, just a creeping silence.

Puzzled, slightly worried, he stepped inside and called out again. No response.

Then he heard a sound from upstairs. A creak, a movement of sorts; a murmur.

Instinctively his right hand slid under his jacket for his gun, which, of course, wasn't there. He cursed under his breath and went silently up, one stair at a time, pausing on each. On the landing he stood still, allowing his eyes to adjust to the darkness, getting his bearings. He listened hard.

Four doors, all closed, led off the landing. Three bedrooms and a bathroom, he assumed.

Cocking his head to one side, he attempted to pinpoint the source of the noise, which was a cross between a muffled sobbing and retching.

Where was it coming from? Not from behind the first door, nor the second. He crept along to the third. A little sign made of ceramic screwed to the door said *Bathroom*.

Donaldson hesitated. He had visions of a killer dog, all fangs and saliva, lying in wait for him, hungry for an intruder.

He knocked.

The sound continued.

He turned the handle and eased the door slightly open, prepared to slam it shut if necessary. Inside was complete darkness. He fumbled, found the light switch and pulled the cord. Bright lights from the six spots set in the ceiling lit the room; an extractor fan whirred into life.

Inside was a large corner bath with shower, a bidet, toilet and washbasin.

And the source of the noise.

Karen was curled up into a ball on her knees, her back, bottom and soles of her feet towards the door, squeezed down into the floorspace between toilet and bidet, her face pressed into the carpet. She rocked slowly back and forth like a baby. Her sobs were muffled, but they shook her body with violence each time one erupted. She was completely naked.

'Karen?' Donaldson said. 'It's me, Karl Donaldson. What's up?'

'Go away,' she sobbed into the floor. 'Go away, Karl. Leave me alone.'

Donaldson swooped down to her level on one knee. He touched her back with trepidation; she shrank away. 'Karen, what the hell's the matter?' He was painfully aware of her nakedness. 'Come on,' he cooed. 'It's me, Karl. Look at me. Talk to me. Tell me what's happening.'

She rose slowly to her haunches, her hands covering her face. She continued to cry; Donaldson continued to make reassuring noises. Slowly he prised her fingers from her face. His mouth fell open in shock at what he saw.

'Christ, Karen, what's gone on? Come on, tell me.'

She almost choked as she said, 'I've been raped.'

'I want a round-the-clock armed guard on this fella until we get him to a police station. In fact, deploy one of the firearms teams to do it; get them to work a rota out between themselves, get them to live here if necessary. Fuck the expense. I'll authorise it.'

This was said by Fanshaw-Bayley while striding down a

corridor at Blackpool Victoria Hospital. It was directed at the Duty Inspector from Blackpool Central police station who had already posted two armed men at the bedside.

'And I want them here as of now!'

'Yes, sir!' said the harassed Inspector, who began gabbling instructions down his personal radio.

'Now where the hell is he?' FB interrupted.

'Who, sir?'

'The killer, you idiot.'

'Just down to the end of this corridor, turn left, last door on the left . . .'

FB increased his pace and left the Inspector standing. He completed his sentence to FB's back. 'The one with the two bobbies outside . . .' His voice trailed off and he scowled at FB.

As FB reached the door, a doctor emerged from the room. FB introduced himself.

'How is he?' he then asked.

'He'll be OK. He's got a hairline fracture of the skull – not as serious as it sounds – a broken left tibia, and a certain amount of bone damage to his left foot where your man shot him, but he'll walk again. Eventually. He'll need surgery on it tonight.'

'Thanks, Doctor. By the way, you do know who the man is, don't you? What he's responsible for?'

'I have been informed, yes.'

'So you know he's under arrest and in our custody. There will be policemen with him every second of every minute of every day. He's highly dangerous, not to be trusted and never to be left alone.'

'This man is ill,' protested the doctor.

'Oh, he can have his treatment – but he'll have cops with him every inch of the way, even if it means cops with surgical gowns on. They'll be there to prevent his escape and to protect members of staff. The man is a killer, a ruthless, bloody killer and cannot be trusted. I can't stress it enough. If I could, I'd handcuff him to the bed.'

'That's going a bit far.'

'If it's necessary, I'll do it,' said FB, his words hanging in the air.

The doctor's gaze locked onto his; FB's won hands down. 'Message received and understood.'

'Thanks, Doc. Knew you'd understand.'

FB went into the room where Hinksman lay in bed.

His head was bandaged; a drip fed into his arm. A cage held the bedclothes off his feet. His eyes were closed and sunken. They didn't open when FB came in.

FB regarded him for a moment. Then he turned to the two uniformed Constables who were in the room. Each had a gun holstered at his side.

'Has he said anything yet?'

They shook their heads.

'He says anything, you remember to note it down, OK? And watch yourselves. This man is a cunt. If he does anything you don't like, shoot him again – this time through the head, not the damned foot. Got that? You have my express permission.'

'Yes, sir,' they said in unison.

FB took one last look at Hinksman, nodded curtly at the officers and left the room.

Out in the corridor, the two PCs who were guarding the door from the outside were surprised to see a Detective Chief Superintendent punch the air with a fist of victory and jig down the corridor.

Henry walked back from the X-ray Department and handed his X-rays to a nurse at the Casualty Department. He sat down wearily on a chair in the waiting area and closed his eyes. He was completely wiped out.

A few minutes later the casualty doctor called his name and beckoned him into a cubicle where he hoisted himself onto the edge of the examination couch.

His X-rays were pinned to a lighted panel on the wall.

There were shots of his head and chest.

'Not too much damage,' said the doctor. 'Broken nose which will heal in its own good time. There shouldn't be a problem with it. There won't be any breathing difficulties and it won't be deformed.'

'Good,' said Henry. 'I'm ugly enough.'

'Two cracked ribs . . . and they'll heal themselves too. A couple of weeks and you'll be as right as rain. I'll get a nurse to re-stitch that head wound and you'll need a couple of stitches in that bottom lip. You'll have two cracking black eyes and plenty of facial and abdominal bruising and swelling, but time and rest will see it right. Take aspirin or Paracetamol for the discomfort. You'll be a hundred per cent again – in due course. Now, I'll get a nurse to do the business.'

'Cheers,' said Henry, at which point his nose began to bleed again, gushing forth in a torrent down his chest. He tipped his head back as instructed. The bleeding stopped quickly.

'It may have a tendency to do that for a day or two,' warned the doctor.

'So how's the girl?' Henry asked the doctor, referring to Ralphie's ladyfriend who was in one of the other cubicles with a policewoman for company.

'Fine, fine . . . stitches and a sore head. Mentally very much on the edge, I'd say. She's witnessed some very heavy stuff.'

'Know how she feels,' said Henry bleakly.

'OK now? Bleeding stopped? Good. I'll send that nurse along.' The doctor slipped out between the curtains to be replaced a moment later by FB.

Henry peered up at him. He knew FB well and had worked in local CID under him some years before.

'Detective-Sergeant Christie,' said FB.

'Hello, sir.'

'You look like shite, Henry,' FB said truthfully.

'Feel like shite.'

A nurse came in and commenced to repair Henry's face.

FB said, 'Once she's finished, come and see me in the café and let's have a chat. I want to know everything that went on tonight.' He shook his head in wonderment. 'That was brilliant shooting, y'know. In the foot! Absolutely a-maz-ing.'

'Thanks, sir,' said Henry. He didn't have the heart to tell him he'd meant to shoot the bastard in the chest but his gun hand had been shaking so much that he couldn't aim properly. Still, Henry thought philosophically, might as well perpetuate the myth that I'm a dead shot, capable of winging suspects at will.

'Proper little hero, aren't you?' said the nurse sardonically. Then she dabbed something nasty on his cuts that made him scream.

At a public payphone on the hospital, FB called the Chief Constable's home number to give him the good news. Mrs August answered. The Chief wasn't there. She'd expected him hours ago. FB thanked her and said he'd try later. He looked up another number in his Filofax and thought, I wonder . . .

Donaldson poured out two cups of instant coffee when he heard Karen coming down the stairs. She had been in the bathroom for twenty minutes and spent a further twenty in her bedroom.

Her eyes were puffed up and swollen; a combination of being slapped and crying.

Donaldson caught his breath when he saw her. Anger welled up in him and all he wanted to do was exact some form of revenge.

He handed one of the cups to her. She thanked him with a nod of the head and sat down on the sofa. The front room was warm, cosy and made her feel safe. Donaldson had drawn the curtains and put the gas fire on. Karen held the cup in one hand and rested it on the palm of the other, feeling the warmth of the liquid permeate through to her skin. She stared blankly at the gas flames which leapt up through imitation coals as though it was a real fire.

'Do you want to talk?' Donaldson asked. 'I don't mind listening,' he said gently.

A tear rolled slowly down her cheek. She wiped it away with the back of her hand. 'You've turned out very sweet. I didn't like you at first.'

'The feeling was mutual,' he admitted.

She sighed, took a sip of her coffee. 'I have a very bad reputation, you know. People think I'm a slut and I suppose to some degree they're right. But I've only ever been a slut as far as this job is concerned. I wanted to go as far as I possibly could, I wanted to get to ACPO rank, but I realised very quickly it was an uphill struggle in a man's world and that I would simply have to take them on at their own game if I was going to get anywhere.

'They talk about equal opportunity and equality of the sexes, but it's all lip service. If you're a woman it's twice as hard because you're always up against old-fashioned ideas and old-fashioned men – no matter how young or trendy they are. Ever heard of canteen culture? It rules the job here, don't know what it's like in America. This must be one of the most out-dated, slow organisations in existence, the police. D'you know how often I've had my bum smacked or my breasts tweaked? D'you know how often I've been told to get my pretty little backside up them stairs and put the kettle on?' She shook her head in wonderment.

'People will tell you that I've slept with whoever needed to be slept with to get where I am today. Those are the rumours. Ever heard of "Rumour Control"? It exists in the police. And do you know exactly how many people I've slept with, to get where I am today, Karl?'

'No,' he said patiently.

'Not a one,' she said. 'I'll admit I've schemed and manipulated and flirted and played people off against each other – but I haven't slept with anyone. I've worked damn hard, studied damn hard and put myself out for the sake of advancement, but I haven't slept with anyone . . . with one exception. The man at the top. Dave August. Our beloved leader.'

She paused, tucked her dressing-gown tightly around her legs. 'Dave August was different. I got my job as his Staff Officer fair and square. I had the qualifications: the degree, Bramshill, the Media Studies courses . . . It was only after that we fell in love. Or at least I fell in love with him.

'He's married. Wife's a stunner for her age . . . and he's got two teenage sons. He said he'd leave her for me. I believed him. Same old stupid story, I suppose. Naïve mistress . . . I've been married twice myself, no offspring though. Both marriages were a joke. Neither could hack being the husband of a career lady. I promised myself never to get involved again, but then along comes doe-eyed Dave August. He wanted to get on, I wanted to get on, so I decided to help him so that he could help me in return. Was that so wrong? Helping someone I loved?'

'No, it wasn't,' said Donaldson.

'I groomed him to be good on TV. The camera loves him now, you know. He's had more TV exposure than any other Chief Constable outside the Met. All down to me . . . and I'll be honest, I did use my personal influence on him to get me on this investigation. I thought I'd stuff one up the CID. They still operate the "Token Woman" syndrome, though they'd deny it. An empire run by dinosaurs and I thought I could take it on. I should have known they'd close ranks on me in the end. God, it would have been wonderful . . . and we were so close to cracking it, too. Then it all went wrong. Jack Crosby dying, FB hating me, believing all those lies about me . . . those poor policemen dying, Ken McClure – Christ, I'm so sorry about him – and then Dave believing all that poison from FB. All the men clubbing together like a wagon train in a circle, protecting themselves from the evil woman . . . and suddenly I'm the villain and Dave thinks he's been manipulated by me, that I've used him. In truth, he's the one who used me; used my skills, fucked me when he should have been at home with his wife . . . No doubt he'll still get his Inspectorate post and I'll be left in his wake. Oh God, it's all so complicated.'

'So what are you going to do about tonight?'

'Nothing.'

'What? You can't do nothing! He raped you and beat up on you!'

'Can you see me going into the local copshop and telling them their Chief Constable's just raped me and given me a slapping? Get real, Karl. There's nothing I can do.'

'Well, there's something *I* can do – kill the fucker or at least make him eat shit.'

Karen shook her head slowly, a sad smile on her face. 'No, you'll do nothing of the sort, Karl. I decide what happens here. It's my body he violated, my mind he twisted, my face he punched.'

'At least go for a prosecution,' Donaldson pleaded.

'And what good would that do? He'd more than likely be acquitted. It would come out that we were having an affair. It'd just soil reputations for no good end result. I'd just be stirring it for the sake of vindictiveness . . .'

The shrill ring of the phone interrupted the words. Donaldson picked it up without thinking and said, 'Hello.'

'Is that Agent Donaldson?'

'Yes, who's that?'

'Chief Superintendent Fanshaw-Bayley. My, my, fancy you being there. May I speak to Miss Wilde, please – that is, if she's not too breathless.'

'Fuck you,' said Donaldson. He handed the phone across to Karen. 'It's that creep Fanshaw-Bayley.'

Karen took a deep breath and said in her best telephone voice, 'Yes sir, can I help you?'

'I suppose this is a stupid question now, but is the Chief there?'

'No.'

'Has he been there?'

'Yes – about two hours ago.'

'You *have* been busy . . . Oh, by the way, we've caught your man. Goodbye.' He hung up.

Karen handed the phone back to Donaldson.

'What the hell did he want?'

'Just to rub it in,' she said unhappily. 'They've caught Hinksman.'

'Damn!' Donaldson hung his head. 'So, what are you going to do?'

'Nothing. Get through this discipline thing then take some time off, go on holiday. Forget about promotion. Try and wangle a Chief Inspector's post in a quiet town out in the sticks somewhere, then maybe think about the future, once I've got my head back on line.'

'You shouldn't let it rest. It's wrong that he won't suffer one way or the other. He needs knocking off his perch . . . and I'd love to be the one to do the knocking. But if you've made your decision . . .'

'I have, Karl. Thanks for your concern.' She held out a hand and he took it. Her skin was soft and smooth. She smelled wonderful. He looked at her lovely face, now all swollen, longing to tell her how much in love he was, but this was neither the right time nor the right place.

After he'd rung home, Henry hobbled stiffly into the hospital snack bar and sat down next to FB. He felt slightly better, the painkillers beginning to take effect.

'Just what the hell is all this about?' Henry demanded of him. 'The M6 bomb, today's stuff . . . What's going on, boss?'

'I'm not all that sure,' FB admitted. 'For reasons you don't have to know about, I'm a little out of touch with this investigation, but I intend to put that right from now on. Oh, did you know Jack Crosby died today too?'

'Yes, I'd heard.'

'One of the old school,' FB said reminiscently.

Thank God he's gone then, Henry thought to himself.

'Anyway,' said FB, slapping the table top and bringing

his thoughts back to the present, 'I know that bitch Wilde told you to take a hike, but I want you back as of now, OK? I'll sort it with your DCI. And forget about that complaint made by the BBC – I'll fettle that for you too. As far as I'm concerned, that bastard deserved to get thrown into the river.'

Henry nodded. 'Thanks, boss. I would like to apologise to him at some stage, though.'

'Whatever.'

'So, do I get the opportunity to interview Hinksman?'

'No. That would be bad practice. I've already assigned a team for that. What I want from you is background, so that they can go into the interview fully briefed. I need to know exactly what's going on as soon as possible. I believe there's some Mob connection here. I suggest you liaise with a guy called Karl Donaldson. He's an FBI agent who was working here with Ken McClure on a related matter. Get a background to Hinksman, everything you can about him. You know what I mean. From birth onwards. I don't have to spell it out for you. I want a report on my desk by four p.m. tomorrow. Don't worry –' he put up a hand to reassure Henry – 'just a brief summary for starters; after that I want you to go into some depth. OK, Henry?'

'Yeah, sure,' said Henry.

'Actually you don't sound too sure. Problem?'

'I was going to report sick.'

'Get the fuck out of here! Don't be a nancy boy. You're a detective, aren't you? We don't go sick, or didn't you know? Beside which, I want you at headquarters at seven a.m. sharp tomorrow. Live interviews for local radio and Breakfast TV.'

'You are fuckin' joking, boss.'

'Nope. Best bib and tucker. And be there. That's an order. You're a national hero, my boy.'

Just before 4 p.m. the following day, Henry Christie placed his initial summary, as requested, on FB's desk.

'Sir' (he had written), 'I have liaised with Agent Donaldson at your suggestion, as well as detectives from the Serious Crime Squad in Manchester, and I have compiled this quick report which I hope goes some way to explaining the events of the past few days. All it is, really, is a jotting down of the things I've learned today, plus some of my own thoughts, in no particular order. I think it makes interesting and disturbing reading.

1) The reason Agent Donaldson was in this country and working with Ken McClure (the Serious Crime Squad, Greater Manchester Police) is that he was building up a file of evidence against Danny Carver (victim of the M6 bomb). Carver was a big underworld player from Florida who had connections with a very big Mafia boss called Tony Corelli. It appears that Carver used to work for Corelli, but decided to go his own way and double-cross him by pulling off a drugs deal with a Manchester criminal called Jason Brown. Apparently Corelli had already been in negotiation with Brown, but had failed to reach agreement. Carver had seen the opportunity and done a deal himself (conservative estimate £10 million EACH!). Donaldson's idea was to catch Carver bang at it and use this as a lever on Carver to grass on Corelli, who he has been after for many years.

2) Corelli was upset that Carver had done the deal and there was already a rumour picked up that a contract had been put out on Carver. It doesn't take a great deal of imagination to guess that if this is true, then he may have also put out a contract on Brown.

3) Hinksman is believed (now) to be the chosen hit man.

4) Hinksman is ex-Army and spent some time with the Delta Force, the US equivalent of the SAS. He is therefore highly trained in the art of killing, use of explosives, firearms, etc and is very dangerous. He has no previous convictions as such. (He was thrown out of the Army because of his liking for beating up prostitutes and was also suspected of raping and murdering a woman officer, but nothing was ever proved.) He may have been recruited by

Corelli about four years ago. Now that his I.D. is known, the FBI can link him (via fingerprints and forensic) to eight other Mafia-related murders across the US involving bombs triggered by timers from pet-food dispensers. He's one bad bastard. He can also be tied in with several murders of women (mainly prostitutes). He therefore likes killing as a profession and a hobby. He seems to have been kept very secret by Corelli, with good reason. He's an élite killer, not your normal run-of-the-mill mobster-cum-gunman. If we can get him to talk, he will be very valuable to the FBI.

5) So Carver was the real target of the M6 bombing. It is also believed that Brown, too, may have been a target. He should have been in the car with Carver.

6) Brown, as we now know, is the one who got shot in the alley by Hinksman. He was the target. Everyone else was just in the way. I don't yet know much about Brown, but the SCS in Manchester do. He was a big player, into many legit things such as pubs, clubs and gambling joints. He was also well into drugs and had very good connections in Manchester (where he was based), particularly in Moss Side. The deal he pulled with Carver was supposed to be for the importation of crack. But what was he doing in Blackpool? I don't know, but I'd lay odds he'd got legit businesses there too, fronting his drugs-pushing activities. (Amusement arcades are ideal.)

7) Apparently Brown was part of a loose criminal syndicate in Manchester. His demise could well have been orchestrated by Corelli and his own pals. (How did Hinksman find him in Blackpool – inside information?) But that's pure conjecture on my part.

8) Just a word about Corelli. He's a Mafia godfather (Yes, they do exist!) whose sphere of operations is mainly Florida and the Caribbean. He runs an extensive criminal organisation which consists of drugs, gun running, commodity fraud, tobacco smuggling, people smuggling, prostitution and gambling. These criminal activities are fronted by highly lucrative legit businesses ranging from

hotels, fast-food joints, nightclubs, building and transport companies and other leisure businesses such as deep-sea fishing trips, etc. His personal net worth cannot be accurately estimated, but he is believed to be a billionaire.

9) Having said that, most of this is purely conjecture by the FBI as Corelli has no convictions whatsoever. He once faced a murder indictment, but walked. He is continually investigated by the tax authorities, but keeps his books spick 'n' span. Without doubt he is the driving force behind the mayhem of the last few days.

10) We don't know the half of what's going on, but this international cooperation between crims worries me.

11) I'll bet we haven't seen the last of Corelli.

12) I don't think we'll ever get to the bottom of this.

13) (Unlucky for some): Prepare yourself for a crack epidemic in the north of England.

14) I'll bet the killing hasn't ended yet.'

Henry signed his name.

Then he went down to his car and drove home and went straight to bed, exhausted and very sore.

Chapter Thirteen

Most of Henry's predictions began to come true as he placed the summary down on FB's desk.

A silver-grey Bentley Mulsanne pulled up smoothly at the International Arrivals door at Manchester Airport and collected two people, a man and a woman, who had just landed on a flight from Malta.

The man was called Lenny Dakin, the woman Cathy Diamond.

Dakin settled himself back in the plush upholstery and said to the driver of the Bentley, 'Is it all over?'

The driver nodded. He wore a peaked cap, like a chauffeur, which was slashed to hide his cruel eyes. Although he also wore a uniform, he looked very uncomfortable in it. He could only be one thing – a villain. But not as big a villain as Dakin.

'Yes, boss, it's over,' said the driver. 'With a certain degree of complication.'

'Which is?'

'The American was arrested. Bad luck really, but he's been locked up. Got shot in the process.'

'Badly?'

'No.'

'But the job was done? Carver's dead and so is Brown?'

'Yup,' the driver confirmed.

'So I'm free to trade?'

'Absolutely,' said the driver.

Dakin turned to Cathy Diamond. His teeth were gritted in a smile. 'Yes,' he hissed. She beamed at him, her eyes playing over his face. She slid a hand onto his thigh and squeezed.

'Darling,' she said.

They embraced victoriously, all the while Dakin keeping an eye open to judge her reaction to the news.

'The way is clear now,' he said, breaking off and kissing her. 'Partnerships are just so much fucking crap.'

He reached for the car phone – the one fitted for the rear passengers – jabbed a number in and looked at his watch. 'It'll be morning in the States,' he said to himself. Whilst waiting for the connection he rocked impatiently, yet remained smiling and happy.

Once the call got through there was a further delay while Corelli came to the phone. Then he was there.

'It's done,' said Dakin excitedly. 'Everything is clear. They're both out of the game now. We can go ahead with the original deal.'

'Good, good,' said Corelli.

'One hiccup though,' said Dakin cautiously.

'What?' snapped Corelli.

'Your man has been apprehended, so I'm led to believe.'

'So you're led to believe?' repeated Corelli incredulously. 'What does that mean? Do you not *know* what's going on in your organisation? Has he, or hasn't he? Do you know – or NOT?'

'Look, I've been out of the country for a few days. I thought it best. I've only just been given the news. I'll look into it, OK?'

'I want him to have the best legal representation available. Do not spare expense. You will fund it.'

'No problem,' said Dakin. 'So when are we likely to meet?'

'I have heard the sad news that one of my relatives has recently died quite tragically in Blackpool. He will be buried in about four days' time. I will be coming for the funeral. Maybe then . . . I will try, but I have some business to attend to over here first.'

'Until then.'

Corelli hung up. Dakin was left holding a dead phone to his ear for a few seconds before he realised there was no one else at the other end.

'We are on a roll, honey,' he said enthusiastically to Cathy.

'Sweetie,' she purred.

'Don't spare the horses, James,' Dakin instructed his driver.

The Bentley slid onto the motorway and its speed soon hovered around the 100 mph mark.

Lenny Dakin was forty years old. He was a Scot, born and raised in the slums of Glasgow. Right from the start he had gone into crime, establishing a gang of young hoodlums who terrorised the neighbourhood, putting old people and shopkeepers in fear of their lives and property.

In his teenage days he had had two run-ins with the Scottish police which resulted in prosecutions; one was for petty theft for which he was convicted and the other was for a robbery where he got off at court. He was fifteen then and hired one of the best, and most bent, criminal lawyers in Scotland, showing how successful he was, even then. He was arrested on numerous other occasions, but with no end result.

By the time he was twenty, Lenny had become one of those self-styled gangland bosses for which Glasgow is famous. For a good eight or nine years he was very much the king of his wing of the castle. He was into everything in a small-time way: bribery, extortion, prostitution, burglary, theft and handling stolen goods. It was all pretty unsubtle stuff. He controlled his part of town very nicely thank you, but he didn't reckon on the big boys moving in. Which they did in ruthless style.

There was a bitter underworld feud between Dakin's gang and two others who had come together to oust him. It was the time of the 'Clyde Murders', as the press liked to call them. Eight people were found dismembered throughout Scotland, all villains, and not one murderer caught, but each body linked to Dakin and his sordid war.

In the end it got too much for him. He had a lot of muscle, but not as much as the other two gangs put together. Dakin knew when he was beaten. He held a summit meeting in secret with the other two gang leaders and came to an agreement – namely, that he would give up the struggle, put his men under their control, cut his own losses and split. Alive.

He'd realised he was close to becoming another one of the Clyde bodies.

He moved south to Manchester where his sphere and scale of operations expanded dramatically.

In a loose partnership with Brown, whom he'd met previously (the criminal underworld is a small underworld), he embarked on a series of violent armed robberies throughout the north-west of England, mainly with Sec-uricor vans as targets. It was very big stuff, as Dakin intended it to be, netting them more than two million pounds in a period of less than nine months.

This was to be the financial bedrock of their empire.

Dakin had previously decided where the true fortunes were to be made in crime – drug dealing. And he set about achieving his goals with a vengeance.

He and Brown made several journeys to Australia and the Far East where they established contacts, couriers and routes. After some initial blunders, mainly as a result of not bribing the right officials, business began to boom. Their first ever deal grossed them a profit of over one million pounds. By the end of their first two years in operation they had amassed over five million pounds each.

This time Dakin planned everything carefully.

He was never in a position where he could be compromised, and if he ever felt he was in any danger he dropped the deal or made a killing. Three doubtful couriers who knew too much and talked too loudly got bullets in the back of the head.

He also invested wisely in legitimate businesses with real profits, real management structures and good accountants who were paid excellent money to launder drugs profits through these businesses and offshore companies that existed in name only. He owned a small chain of supermarkets, six chemists, a dozen newsagents, several specialist wine importers, four pubs and a discotheque.

But his business relationship with Brown was always on shaky ground.

Their characters were not really compatible.

Dakin, tough, businesslike, careful; Brown, flash, unpredictable, volatile, careless and unprofessional.

Some of these things Dakin could forgive, but he suspected Brown of two serious transgressions, neither of which he could prove.

One was that he shortchanged on deals.

The other was that he had bedded Cathy Diamond.

Brown's lack of professionalism was his undoing; things came to a head during negotiations with Corelli.

Dakin had realised that even more money was to be made by dealing with the Colombian drug cartels. They were much more organised than the Asian drug barons, whom Dakin could never truly bring himself to trust. Something about their manner. He always expected a knife in the back.

Feelers put out amongst the international criminal fraternity led him and Brown to Corelli's organisation, which acted as wholesalers for Colombian operations in Florida.

Talks began slowly and tentatively between Corelli and the Britons, though they never actually spoke to the big man himself, only his distant intermediaries. One of these was Danny Carver.

It was during the course of these negotiations that Carver struck up a friendship with Brown. They were very much alike, sharing the same taste in cars, women and gambling.

Neither was happy with his lot.

Carver was ambitious to make it alone.

Brown was continually getting pain and grief from Dakin for the smallest thing and he'd grown to hate the man. He wanted out.

The result was they engineered a side deal which failed to include either Corelli or Dakin.

When Dakin discovered the deception – and the amount of money involved – he secretly flew to Florida where he had an urgent meeting with Corelli. Here, he told him the facts as he knew them: behind their backs, Carver and Brown were about to make twenty million pounds sterling, conservative estimate.

Corelli had nodded sagely. He knew of Carver's disloyalty. It had been going on for some time now. Other deals had been struck and Carver had been warned several times, but this was the last straw. Corelli had shown remarkable restraint so far. Now it was time to act.

Corelli promised to dispose of both Carver and Brown, for the sake of the business, nothing personal, then to resume talks with Dakin.

He had been true to his word.

Dakin was impressed and a little overawed. Now it was up to him to show Corelli that he was also a man of his word and get the best criminal lawyer in the country to act for the hit man. Fuck the expense.

Firstly, though, he had a little problem of his own to sort out.

The Bentley was driven to Dakin's modernised farmhouse in the Ribble Valley, set high on the banks of the river, overlooking the ancient Roman fort of Ribchester.

The first thing Dakin did was call his solicitor, to whom he paid a great deal of money as a retainer. After a polite threat from Dakin – 'I'll cut yer articles off' – the less than enthusiastic solicitor promised he would make his way to Blackpool and engage himself to act for Hinksman.

After this brief conversation, he summoned his driver and said one cold sentence to him.

'Get me Reeve.'

Gerard Reeve, dressed in only his underpants, held back the curtains and peered out of the hotel window. It was mid-morning and the Lake District village of Grasmere was milling fairly busily with its tourist trade, most of which centred on its main asset – William Wordsworth.

Just below the village, the lake itself lay gently and serenely, like a sheet of smoke-blue glass, unruffled and beautiful.

Reeve stared intently out, searching for something that could give him a clue. Anything. A car which did not seem to fit, a man perhaps, who did not give the impression of being a tourist. Anything to warn him that Dakin had caught up, because he knew that Dakin was after him. He did not have to be told he was on the run, and until he could leave the country he would always be in danger.

His sharp eyes roved and flickered once more, nervously taking everything in.

But there was nothing. *Yet.* He knew he would soon have to move.

'Come away from the window.'

He allowed the flimsy curtain to fall back into place and turned to face the female who lay stretched out naked on the bed. This was the third time that morning he'd been to the window.

'He'll never find you here,' she said.

Reeve did not actually agree with her. Dakin had very long, sticky tentacles and he never underestimated him.

'You don't even know if he's after you,' the lady went on, 'so come back to bed, eh? Let's have a good time.'

'I'm taking no chances, Janine. Once I've got all my money together, we're away.'

'Where to?'

'Spain, maybe . . . dunno.'

'Sounds nice, but I think you're overreacting.'

'Browney's dead, so's that American – plus every other

poor bastard in Lancashire. And I'm next in line. I was going to do the legwork for Browney and if Dakin knew about Brown's double-cross, he's bound to know about me too. I'd never be able to bluff my way out of it, never.'

He stood in the middle of the room, rubbing his chin with a hand, thinking. 'How the hell did he find out about Browney's plans? Fucked if I know. Who on earth could have told him?'

'Come on back to bed,' Janine said, a little too abruptly. 'Come on, babe, I'm dying to get hold of you.' The last thing she wanted was for Reeve to start thinking things through. He might be slow, but not that slow.

'I don't know . . . I think we should fuck off.'

'There's always time for sex,' she pouted.

'OK,' he said with a smile. 'You win, but let's make it quick. We're out of here ASAP.'

He crossed the room. She wriggled down the bed to prepare for business.

After peeling off his underpants – which had the words *Hot Rod* emblazoned across them – he stood by the bed, erection swaying, deciding what he wanted.

He stood well over six feet tall and had a build to match, large wide shoulders, flat muscular stomach, solid thighs – all areas of skin which over the years had become a canvas for wild tattoos. Hearts, daggers, girls' names, swords, ships, guns; many brightly coloured, others merely blue outlines. Only his head and neck remained free.

'Well?' she said, eyes dancing, breasts a-quiver.

He straddled her, letting his testicles (tattooed to re-semble two leather footballs hanging in a basket) rest on her body just below her well-proportioned breasts. She cradled these balls in the palm of her hand, crushing them gently, making him hiss. Then she took his erection (tattooed to look like a rocket) in her other hand. She knew what he wanted. She began a slow, rhythmic movement with flutter-ing fingers along the length of his cock.

Her experienced touch brought him to the point of

orgasm many times, but she then held back from the final fast strokes that would have allowed him to shoot forth his sperm.

It was almost agony for him.

His penis was huge and throbbing in her hands, but she refused to let him finish.

Then, as he approached orgasm for the umpteenth time, an axe smashed through the thin hotel door, sending splintering wood into the room.

This time Janine rubbed for dear life.

The axe-head was twisted round and heaved back, ripping out the panelling.

'Oh come, come, come,' Janine breathed as though she hadn't seen or heard the interruption. She held his organs tightly in her grip, refusing to let go.

'God, they're here!' he shouted.

'I know, I know,' she responded.

Reeve tore himself from her grasp, painfully. He hopped across the room to where his jacket was slung over a chair. Sperm shot everywhere in uncontrollable spurts. On the bedclothes, on the bedside cabinet, on the floor.

He fumbled for his gun which was in his jacket.

The door was battered and burst from its hinges. Three men stepped into the room, one being Dakin's driver, still dressed in his chauffeur's uniform.

The first man through the door was a small, lithe man, no bigger than a jockey. He had a baseball bat in his hands which he wielded with great accuracy across the back of Reeve's head.

In Miami it was almost ninety degrees. The city was sweltering under the curse of a heatwave, but on the boats taking day-trippers sightseeing around the bay there was a slight breeze coming off the water.

'And over there, to your left, is the home of Gloria Estefan, Miami's very own superstar,' said the captain's voice over the loudspeaker. Everyone's attention on the boat turned to the beautiful waterside mansion of the star in the hope of catching just one glimpse of her. There was no sign of the singer, nor any sign of life, just as there had been no sign of any other of the celebrities whose homes the boat had passed on its journey.

Eamon Ritter hadn't bothered looking. He'd been on the bay trips many times and could easily have taken over the commentary should the captain suddenly have fallen ill.

Instead he made his way inside to the empty bar, ordered a beer and sat down to sip it from the bottle by a window. He gazed out at the stunning skyline of Miami and marvelled, yet again, at the foresight of Julia Tuttle from Ohio. Hardly one hundred years ago, she had bought some of the Biscayne Bay swampland and reckoned she'd build a city.

Even she would have been surprised at the melting-pot metropolis she'd spawned.

The door opened. Ritter looked casually round. A middle-aged woman entered the room and went to the bar. Ritter remembered she'd boarded the boat with her husband. It was unlikely that she'd be the one he had to meet.

Ritter had earlier boarded the boat at the waterfront near to Bayside, the new shopping complex. He'd got on first and discreetly studied every other tourist who'd boarded. He couldn't for the life of him work out which one was Corelli's man or woman. He'd tried it every time, but failed, and been surprised when the least likely person actually approached him.

He looked out of the window and took a sip of the beer.

The other reason he checked everyone was to make sure he wasn't being followed.

'Upper deck, seats at the rear,' a voice said.

Ritter spun round. This time it was a girl, late teens, early twenties maybe. She wore big round sunglasses and had her hair pulled back tightly from her face into a ponytail. She had a nice, wide mouth, small upturned nose and was very tanned and pretty in an impish way. She was wearing a loose vest-like top which hung open around the shoulders and a pair of cut-off jeans revealing long, slender legs. On her feet were flip-flops.

Ritter remembered her boarding, but had dismissed her as being too glamorous.

Before he could reply to her instruction, she walked past him, out of the bar.

Suddenly his throat went very dry and constricted, as it always did at this time of betrayal. He began to pour with sweat; his stomach knotted and butterflies danced through his intestines.

He took a long pull of the beer, stood up and made his way to the upper deck which was laid out with seating for the tourists. There were many vacant seats. This voyage wasn't overly crowded as it wasn't the height of the season.

The girl was sitting alone at the back of the boat, leaning against the railing, one leg wedged in the back of the chair in front of her. She was drinking Coke from a can.

'Mind if I sit here?' he asked.

'Suit yourself,' she said with a sneer of uninterest as though she was fending off a pass.

Ritter sat. He extracted his sunglasses from his shirt-pocket and manoeuvred them onto his face.

'Miami's a wonderful city, don't you think?' he stated. These were the words, the phrase, that meant everything was OK to proceed.

She came straight to the point.

'He wants to know what Donaldson is doing in England.'

Without hesitation, Ritter told her.

When he'd finished, she said, 'How close are you to him?' meaning the FBI to Corelli.

'Donaldson and Kovaks are tasked to get him, as he already knows. It's their main function at the moment. It's difficult to say how close they are, but now that Hinksman's in custody, I'd venture to tell him to watch out. It could be the beginning of the end, unless he's careful.'

'It could be the beginning of the end for you too, Agent Ritter.'

'Don't you even begin to threaten me, lady. You're just a messenger, not a player, so do your job and messenge.'

She gave a short laugh, then got to her feet. 'Don't be surprised if those agents get a warning shot.'

'Then tell him not to be surprised if they bag his ass. They're good – very, very good.'

'And he's even better. Your money will be in the usual place. By the way, he thanks you for the information about Whisper and his big mouth. Excuse me.'

She sidled past him, her crotch provocatively at the height of his nose and only inches away. He could smell her and she smelled excellent. Ritter held himself back from letting a hand brush her outer thigh. She walked away from him down the deck, her ass swaying like a catwalk model.

Ritter tilted his head back and emptied his beer down his dry throat.

It was 8.30 p.m. British time. Cathy Diamond was seated behind a desk in a plush, well-appointed office, filing her already perfect nails with an emery board. She blew off the last of the shavings and was about to pick up her nail-polish when Reeve, flanked by two armed men, was led into the room.

He was past struggling and allowed everything to happen without trying to stop it. He knew he was doomed.

Two floors below, a supermarket belonging to Dakin had just finished trading for the day. The office staff had all gone home, as had the staff from the shopfloor. One or two members of the cleaning team were still there but, with the two hard men posted outside the door, there was little chance of an interruption.

Cathy looked at Reeve through half-closed eyes. He caught her gaze and thought, 'Bitch. If I'm going down, so are you.'

The two men seated Reeve on a chair in the centre of the room prepared ready for his arrival.

His head lolled forwards, chin on chest. He didn't have the strength or the desire to lift it and look around him. He just wanted to get it over with.

Cathy pressed the button on the intercom and said, 'He's here.'

A couple of seconds later the door to Dakin's office opened and the man himself strutted out. He strode across to Reeve and lifted his head, careful not to get any blood on his hands from the wound at the back which was now crusted over.

'Hello Gerry, old mate,' said Dakin.

'Lenny,' was all Reeve could manage to say.

'Good, good,' said Dakin soothingly. 'At least you're with us. I told them not to hit you too hard. My, though, that's a nasty cut. Does it hurt, buddy?'

'You could say that,' slurred Reeve.

'Well, that's the name of the game, innit? You make a decision and you open a door. You have to accept what comes through it, doncha? Agree?'

Reeve's head shook drunkenly, but he made no reply.

'Do you agree, Gerry?' Dakin's voice rose. Then he struck him across the face, putting his whole weight behind the blow. Reeve was lifted bodily off the chair and crashed to the floor. As he picked himself up he realised it wasn't a carpet he'd fallen on, but a polythene sheet. The type used by painters and decorators to keep paint off the carpets. Or by executioners to keep blood off them.

Reeve groaned inwardly.

'Sit him back up,' Dakin ordered his men.

They heaved him back into the chair.

Reeve rotated his jaw. It was already swelling up from the blow.

'Now then Gerry, let's have a tête-à-tête, eh?'

'I've nothing to say.'

Dakin guffawed. 'Now that's not altogether true, is it?'

Reeve looked contemptuously up at his tormentor, his breathing short, laboured. He remained defiant, said nothing.

'OK, have it your way,' sniffed Dakin, 'but I want to tell you this, Gerry –' he wagged a finger as though he was giving a ticking-off to a schoolboy – 'I know everything: you and Browney and that stupid American. In fact, you were all stupid. Doing the deal without me was bad enough, but crossing a Mafia godfather? Tut, tut. Now that strikes me as the very height of stupidity, Gerry. Men like Corelli don't forgive – whereas I do have that capacity.' He held his hands over his heart in an angelic gesture.

'Bollocks,' spat Reeve. 'It's fuckin' obvious you've made your mind up. You ain't going to forgive me for nothing. Otherwise why the sheet, eh? You cunt.'

'Gerry, I'm affronted. I was going to paint the room.' Dakin could hardly contain his own laughter.

'Yeah, with my fuckin' brains. I've seen *Lethal Weapon Two*, as well,' said Reeve. 'So come on then, how did you know? I didn't tell anyone, nor did Browney. It was a fuckin' secret.'

Dakin sighed, shook his head sadly. 'Pillow talk. It's amazing what a man will tell a woman at his weakest moments, Rocket Man.'

Reeve closed his eyes in despair as it all dawned on him. Janine. The bitch.

'So now you know what it's like to be double-crossed, don't you?'

'Well, I do have one thing to say,' Reeve spouted. 'It's about that slag there.' He nodded in Cathy Diamond's direction. With satisfaction he saw her sit upright. A worried look crossed her once-smug countenance.

'Browney screwed the arse off her – behind your back. They were laughing at you. Best blow job ever, he said.' Reeve raised his eyebrows and gave a short laugh. '"Know what it's like to be double-crossed, eh?"' He mimicked Dakin's Scottish accent.

Dakin swallowed. His lips pursed. 'Kill him.'

One of the gunmen stepped forwards, a silenced revolver in his hand.

It was over in a second. Reeve's body lay sprawled out on the polythene, the back of his head virtually removed by the bullets, a sea of hot blood lapping around him.

Dakin regarded the body a few moments prior to turning slowly and walking towards Cathy Diamond. She sat rigid, terrified. She'd dropped her nail file and polish at Reeve's revelations and her hands hadn't moved since.

As Dakin approached her she shook her head desperately. 'It's not true, Lenny. It's not true.'

He leaned across the desk, grabbed her by the hair and pounded her face repeatedly into the desk top, his anger overflowing. When he'd finished his frenzied assault her features had been mashed to a gory pulp. She was barely conscious, moaning. He let her head drop onto the desk.

He looked at the gunmen, pointed at her and cocked his thumb like the hammer of a gun, then left the room.

At the end of its journey the boat berthed back at Bayside. Ritter was last off, pausing long enough to ensure that no one was waiting to give him a reception. He watched the girl walk towards the shopping complex. He'd made no effort to speak to her further during the remainder of the trip, though he had watched her, wondering who she was, why and how she was involved with Corelli. Then he wondered how and why he himself was involved. Easy answer. Greed.

He glanced up at the replica of the *Bounty* moored further up the quay, the one used by MGM for the film *Mutiny on the Bounty*. Quite appropriate, he thought wryly.

Once on the quayside he made his way into Bayside, twenty-five thousand dollars richer. One step closer towards a prosperous retirement which he proposed to take as early as decency would allow. His fund consisted currently of an apartment in the Caymans, a small boat, and three hundred thousand dollars which was earning steady interest in the Cayman Islands. As soon as it reached the half-million mark he'd retire with a good pension, the interest on the capital, and hit the Caribbean. It was all worked out.

He failed to notice a happy couple sat on a low wall near to the waterfront. They were very much engrossed in each other and the picnic they were sharing.

As Ritter walked smartly past them the woman looked up purely by chance.

Puzzled, she said, 'Isn't that . . . ?'

'Who?' said the man.

'Naah, can't be. What would he be doing here?'

'Who?' asked the man again.

'I'm sure that was Eamon Ritter.'

'Well, so what? Maybe it was, maybe it wasn't,' said the man, doing what he thought was a passable imitation of a Jew.

She burst into a fit of giggles, her big fat shoulders shuddering with laughter. It was nice to be in love, laughing at things that would have been blatantly unfunny otherwise. She took a huge bite of her pastrami on rye sandwich, the mayonnaise dripping delightfully down her double chin.

Chapter Fourteen

Four days later Hinksman was discharged from hospital into the eager hands of waiting detectives.

The doctor said he was fit to detain, but must be allowed frequent rest periods and breaks during interviews, and must take his medication as and when prescribed. If he felt faint, complained of dizziness or was physically sick, the police surgeon should be called out or he should be brought back to hospital immediately. The impatient detectives raised their eyes to the heavens, but there was no way they were going to jeopardise this one by breaking the rules. For a start, too many cases had been lost in recent years by over-zealous cops bending the law and secondly, Hinksman was accompanied by his solicitor.

Hinksman was taken under armed escort to Blackpool Central police station.

Around the perimeter of the station were armed patrols who had been detailed to guard the building twenty-four hours per day whilst Hinksman was held there. Their MP5s were clearly visible, held openly across their chests for everyone to see and be warned. The police were taking no chances on this one.

At the station he was presented to the custody officer, who, after hearing the circumstances of the arrest, authorised Hinksman's detention to secure and preserve evidence and to obtain evidence by questioning. He booked him into the computerised custody system and gave him his rights: the right to free legal advice, the right to have someone informed of his detention and the right to consult a copy of the *Codes of Practice*.

Because he was with his solicitor, Hinksman did not choose to exercise his other rights at that time.

Fifteen minutes after arrival at the station he was taken to an interview room where the first of a series of taped interviews began. On and off, with breaks, the interviews would last all day.

The legal process had begun.

Chrissy woke up about 10 a.m., which was quite early for her. She worked behind a bar in an hotel in Fort Lauderdale which stayed open until 3 a.m. She never generally hit the sack until gone four which wasn't as bad as it seemed because Kovaks often finished work late (or early, depending on your viewpoint) and they often met tired, yet horny, in bed and indulged in great pre-dawn sex, which set them up for a long morning's sleep.

That particular morning, though, Joe Kovaks was on office hours. He'd left the apartment at 7 a.m. and Chrissy had the bed to herself.

Two things had woken her.

The first was her bladder, the second the thump of some mail coming through the door.

She slithered out of bed and took care of the first problem before traipsing naked down the hallway to sleepily retrieve the mail.

It was a package adressed to her from *National Geographic*, the size and weight of one of their excellent magazines. Which was all very nice, except she didn't subscribe to it.

She frowned, slipped a finger under the flap and started to open it.

Sue was walking down a corridor in the FBI Field Office in Miami, clutching a batch of mail underneath her crossed arms. She was smiling sweetly to herself and humming as she contemplated love, life and happiness. And more particularly, Damian's penis. Eamon Ritter was striding purposefully down the corridor in her direction.

'Good morning,' she said pleasantly to him.

He responded with a grunt; didn't bother looking at her.

'Did you go for a sail around the bay?' she asked as they passed, shoulder to shoulder.

'What?' he said, stopping in his tracks.

'Yesterday,' she went on innocently. 'It was my day off. I went down to Bayside – saw you walking up from the waterfront, near to the *Bounty*. Just wondered if you'd been for a sail around the bay.'

He looked coldly at her and shook his head. 'No,' he said. 'You're mistaken!'

'I'm sure it was you,' she persisted naïvely. 'In fact, you were wearing that suit.'

'I said you're mistaken.'

'Oh,' said Sue, belatedly realising from his tone of voice that he wanted her to be mistaken. 'Yes, I must be. Sorry.'

He gave her a look which made her shiver, then turned and stalked away.

She watched him for a mesmerised second or two, disgusted at his abruptness, and went on her way towards Organized Crime with the mail held more tightly to her bosom.

'Yeah, they've been interviewing him all day,' Donaldson said on the phone to Kovaks. It was 4.30 p.m., British time. 'But he's said nothing whatsoever. Exercising his right to silence, apparently. Won't even state his name for the tape.'

Kovaks sighed. 'Only to be expected,' he said philosophically. 'Is he represented by a lawyer?'

'Yeah. They call 'em solicitors over here.'

'An appropriate name. What's his history?'

'Connected to big-time local crims. Haven't got any further with him, though.'

Sue trundled into the office with a wave for Kovaks. Only a couple of other agents were in the room, sat at their desks, jackets off, deep into compiling reports. She distributed the mail around various desks, concluding with Kovaks'. 'Thanks,' he mouthed over the phone call and put his hand to his lips, forefinger and thumb-tips touching, indicating that a cup of coffee wouldn't go amiss. She nodded and made her way to the machine in the corner.

Kovaks slotted the phone in between his shoulder and left ear, leaving his hands free to deal with the mail.

'So what's your role now?' he asked Donaldson.

'Background. Working with a Detective Sergeant called Henry Christie . . .'

'Ain't he the one who arrested Hinksman?'

'Yeah. Seems a good guy, but his nerves are shot to hell. We're putting together everything I know that's of value for the investigation over here. How's Whisper's murder enquiry coming along?'

Kovaks was sifting through his mail as he talked. He flicked to one side a couple of envelopes which he knew contained intelligence bulletins, and opened another which contained a letter requiring a quick response. He finally came to the biggest envelope – one from the *National Geographic*.

'Wall of silence,' he told Donaldson. 'I'm not happy with the doctor, though. He's a creep and I don't trust him. So, are we going to extradite Hinksman?'

'All in good time.'

Kovaks picked up his letter-knife and slid it into the top of the envelope. He was already looking forward to a free magazine.

'We'll let the Brits go through their legal process first,' said Donaldson. 'They've got enough to stitch him up and convict whether he says anything or not. We'll try and get him after that. Anything new on Corelli?'

'Naw . . .' The knife went in as if it was cutting butter. 'Still waiting for permission to tap his house down in Key West. I think he does a lot of business down there.'

Sue appeared in front of him, holding two plastic cups of steaming coffee.

The envelope opened as the knife came out the other side. Kovaks saw the wires immediately. He shot out of his seat, dropped the phone, shouted, 'Oh Jesus shit – BOMB!' and threw the envelope across the room where it smacked on a wall and dropped to the floor. He flung himself at Sue and forced her to the floor; out of the corner of his eyes he saw the other agents in the room drop instinctively down out of sight, taking flimsy protection from their desks. The coffee Sue had been holding went everywhere as Kovaks landed on top of her. She was too surprised and winded to say anything other than, *'Ungph!'*

Nothing happened.

Kovaks rose slowly to his knees. 'Keep down,' he warned the others. He peered over the top of the desk at the envelope which lay innocently on the floor. Two wires poked out of it. Shaking, his heart pulsating to the point of bursting, he reached for and picked up the phone which dangled on its wire over the edge of the desk. He could hear Donaldson shouting at the other end. 'Joe, Joe! You OK, Joe?'

'Yeah, yeah,' he breathed. He looked down at the prostrate figure of Sue who hadn't moved. Her dress had ridden up to reveal her plump thighs and skimpy underclothes. 'I think I've just opened a letter bomb – but it didn't go bang. Speak to you later.'

He slammed the phone down.

'I think we're OK, people,' he announced. 'If it was going to blow it would've done by now.'

Gingerly the other two agents appeared from hiding. Kovaks held out a hand to Sue and heaved her into an unladylike sitting position, legs akimbo. She grinned her lopsided grin at him and said, 'You don't need an excuse to throw me to the ground and leap on me, you know.'

He chuckled with a slightly hysterical undertone, but before he could confound her with an off-the-cuff witty remark, the phone on his desk rang out. He answered it. 'Kovaks.'

'Agent Kovaks?'

'Speaking.'

'Broward Country Police here, Fort Lauderdale. Sheriff Tomlinson.'

'Yep?'

'You live up here with a lady called Chrissy Strand?'

'Yep – why?' Kovaks asked cautiously. His eyes flickered to the envelope on the floor.

'I'm sorry, but I've some bad news, sir. She's in hospital. Some kind of explosion at your apartment this morning . . . We think it could've been a letter bomb. It went off in her face.'

It was a one-room apartment over a row of sleazy shops near to Flagler Street in downtown Miami. In one corner of the room a baby cried itself hoarse in a cot. It was poorly cared for, a scrawny child, its growth stunted perhaps for ever by lack of proper feeding and loving attention. Its diaper stank and probably hadn't been changed for twelve hours. It was soiled and wet. Underneath, the baby's skin was red-raw and sore. And the baby was hungry, but it couldn't have kept anything down because of a recurring stomach infection.

But it hadn't always been this way.

In another corner of the room lay the baby's mother on a low camp bed with a thin mattress and brown, stained sheets.

She was a black girl, nineteen years old.

She hadn't always been this way.

Not many months ago she had been beautiful, big and full of life.

Now she lay there half-listening to her baby's screams of anguish. But they were noises that only vaguely registered in her ears. They were miles away, of no consequence. What was immediate was that her head was swimming and she was in a different, crack-induced world.

She was on a high, but it wasn't all that high. She needed some more. The last hadn't taken her far enough up. She'd seen the peak she wanted to conquer in the distant mist, but it had remained just out of reach. So she needed a lot more, but for the moment this would have to do.

She closed her dry eyes and ran her hands down her naked body, quivering with the sensation in her head.

Once her body had been beautiful, desirable.

Now she was thin and wasted. No one, no man, could possibly want to make love to her. Her bones stuck out hard and cold, her thin legs looked like they had rickets, her once large firm breasts were shadows of their former selves. Her nipples, once rich and scarlet, were pitiful and lifeless.

All she retained was her mouth.

That was still sensual, her lips thick and moist.

And that was how she made her living, with her mouth. She was good with it – the very best. Last night forty customers queued up and testified to the fact. At fifty dollars each that made two thousand dollars, and it wasn't her best night by any means. All she got though was a measly two hundred, a hundred and fifty of which went straight back to the man for dope.

And the baby cried in the corner.

The mother sat up, desperate for more. She searched frantically for some in her bag. There was none, but she already knew that anyway.

Then the door opened and two men came into the room. One was THE man.

'Oh God, thank God,' she breathed in relief, not even beginning to wonder why they'd come, just pleased with her good luck. 'I need it, man, I need it. I've got fifty dollars left here.' A hand slid under the pillow and came out clutching a wad of crumpled dollar bills.

The man crossed to her.

With the flat of his hand he smacked her hard and accurately across the face. 'Get the fuck out of here – *now* – and take that little piece of Whisper-shit with you.'

'I don't understand,' she whined, holding her face. 'What's going on? What've I done? I need it, man. Please!'

'You're being evicted. He's decided,' said the man,

pointing upwards as if to heaven, 'that he don't like bitches in any way connected to people who talk to the law. Now, nigger, get your clothes on, you skinny, ugly bitch, collect that thing and get out. From this moment on, you're a homeless person – and you can thank Whisper for that.'

Joe Kovaks had a four-hour wait before they let him in to see Chrissy. Part of the time he was accompanied by Sue who plied him with sweet black coffee from a nearby dispenser and machine-gunned him with small talk, which included her minor clash with Ritter. Everything went in one ear and out the other before eventually starting to irritate him. In the end he told her – not unkindly – to go, explaining that he needed to be alone.

She understood and left reluctantly, only to be replaced almost immediately by a young detective from Fort Lauderdale who got Chrissy's personal details from him, then a statement. It was like getting blood from a stone. Kovaks didn't feel very much like talking. He wanted to sit and brood. He spoke in angry monosyllables where he could and didn't feel any remorse or empathy for the detective. Fuck him, he thought. Just fuck him.

All Kovaks wanted to do was see Chrissy. Until then, he wasn't interested in making anyone's life easy. What the fuck were they doing with her?

When the detective left, muttering and bearing a statement a rookie would have laughed at, Kovaks sat there alone at last . . . but only for a short time. In less than five minutes a nurse turned up and asked him to accompany her.

He dropped the stub of his cigarette into his cold coffee, and stood up on quaking legs. He wanted to see her, yet he didn't. He wanted, yet dreaded, the moment. With this conflict battling inside him, he followed the nurse.

For the first time in his life he was totally shocked and speechless as he stood at the door of the Burns Unit and looked at the pathetic charred figure of Chrissy Strand, the woman he had definitely grown to love.

In truth he couldn't see all that much of her. There was a spaghetti-like mess of tubes running across and into her body and arms. A suit that looked like it was made of a combination of plastic and tinfoil covered her upper torso and a sheet was drawn up to cover the part of her body from her stomach downwards. A hairnet, rather like a shower cap, was on her head and the whole left side of her face was concealed by gauze. Her hands and arms were covered with plastic bags.

He gasped in horror as he saw her blackened hands, burned like an overcooked joint. He held onto the door jamb for support.

She looked awful and the expression on his face registered his shock and disbelief. His Chrissy.

At least she was unconscious and pumped full of drugs for the moment. For the moment.

Hi-tec machines surrounding the bed monitored her functions. Kovaks looked quickly at the displays. They all seemed to be pinging healthily enough.

He took a deep breath and approached the bed.

He wasn't sure how long it was that he stood there. Two minutes. Could have been twenty.

'Mr Kovaks?'

He jumped back into the real world and turned round. A young man in a classy suit offered a hand. Kovaks took it and they shook. Kovaks' puzzlement was cleared up when the man said, 'I'm the surgeon who operated on Chrissy. Dr Jefferson. I believe you're her boyfriend?'

'We live together as man and wife. We were going to get married.'

'Right, right.'

'So, how is she? No bullshit, please.'

'Come – let's discuss it out here.' He indicated the corridor.

Kovaks followed him out, amazed at how young and inexperienced he appeared. He couldn't have been over thirty, with a face like a baby, all chubby and rubicund. But he exuded an air of confidence and ability that Kovaks found reassuring, coupled with an outwardly relaxed persona.

The doctor leaned against the wall and waited for a couple of chattering nurses to pass. He cleared his throat. 'Right . . . obviously she's very badly burned. The device, or whatever you want to call it, was designed to pour out a flash of flame as the recipient opened the envelope. Normally that would result in hand, facial and neck burns. I say normally because most recipients would probably be fully clothed when opening mail. Chrissy hadn't got dressed.'

'Which makes it worse?'

The doctor nodded.

'She works late.' Kovaks felt he had to explain her nakedness for some reason. 'She'd probably got straight out of bed when she heard it fall through the door. We can hear mail coming in quite clearly from the bedroom.'

The surgeon shrugged. 'Whatever.' He went on: 'The problem is that there was no protection whatsoever from any clothing. Therefore much of her chest, upper arms and neck were burned as well as her hands and face. It was actually the left side of her face that took the brunt of the flames. The right side is hardly touched at all. A great deal of her hair has been burned off too.'

'So what's the bottom line? What's the future?'

'At this early stage it's difficult to say. She will be badly scarred, but plastic surgery can do wonders. She'll be OK physically. Her eyes are unharmed and in itself, her body remains in good shape. It's the mental side that'll be the biggest problem. All I can say is this: don't think too much of the future at the moment. Let's take each day as it comes. She'll need a great deal of support,' he added.

Kovaks nodded. His eyes watered over. 'She'll get it,' he said resolutely, biting his bottom lip, trying to hold back the tears.

The doctor laid a hand on his shoulder. 'Good man. Does she have some family?'

'Chicago. I'll speak to them.'

'OK. I don't think there's much point in you staying around here at this time, Mr Kovaks. She'll be sleeping for many hours yet. If you want to be here when she wakes up, come in tomorrow about eight a.m. But go and get some rest yourself. You've had a very exacting day so far and you'll need all your strength for Chrissy . . . won't you?' He raised his eyebrows questioningly.

'Yeah, you're right,' said Kovaks, acknowledging the sense. 'Look, if you don't mind I'll have a few more minutes with her before I go.'

'By all means.' They shook hands again. 'Good night. I'll see you tomorrow.'

'Thanks, Doc.'

He watched the surgeon walk away and thought that he rather liked the man. Talked straight from the hip, as it were. He believed Chrissy was in safe hands, which took a weight off his mind.

Kovaks spent a few minutes sat by Chrissy's bed, staring blankly at her, listening to the shallow breathing, his mind in turmoil. He wondered what the future would hold for them. Not eight hours ago it was very rosy. Now it was all upside-down, with its guts twisted out and fed to the scavengers. In his mind's eye he kept seeing her opening the package, just as he'd done. The whoosh of the flames. Her screams of terror.

Bastard. Whoever had done it. *Bastard*. It was a warning, wasn't it? And at that moment in his life, there was only one possible source – Corelli. The Mafia godfather had just told the FBI to go fuck themselves.

At the door he took one last look at Chrissy. She stirred momentarily, then moaned slightly. He willed his thoughts to transfer from his mind to hers, to penetrate the pain and the drugged state. *I will be there for you,* he told her. *Whatever happens, whatever the outcome. And whoever has done this to you will suffer. They have bitten off more than they can chew. I'll find them, I promise you, and justice will be done. I promise you. I love you.*

With that he turned and walked out.

In the hospital foyer his heart dropped as he saw the waiting, predatory figure of Lisa Want, accompanied by a photographer.

The camera flashed a dozen times.

Then Lisa Want swooped on him like an osprey on a fish. Her portable tape-recorder was running.

'How is she, Joe?'

Kovaks stopped dead and opened his hands wide as if to say, 'Got me.'

He looked levelly at her, then said, 'If you don't get out of my way, Ms Want, I'll break that fuckin' tape-recorder over your head and shove the batteries right up your pretty little ass – and you can quote me.' He shoved past her.

Unfazed, she persisted. 'Agent Kovaks, is it true that you also received a letter bomb, which failed to explode?'

No reply. It was true, of course. But how the hell did she know?

'Is it also true that it was wired *not* to explode?'

No reply. But also true. According to the bomb disposal expert who'd defused the device, it was a real live bomb but wired purposely not to detonate. Its sole purpose, therefore, was to frighten its recipient. But again, how the hell did she know? The office had decided that news of this package would not be released to the media, so who had told her?

'Why do you think you received the bomb? Is someone warning or threatening you to keep off a case? Is this all connected with your on-going investigation into the Corelli crime family? How do you feel? *Are* you intimidated? Has Chrissy regained consciousness yet? Can we get in for a photograph of her? How is your investigation progressing? Are you going to answer any of these fucking questions or not? Come on, Joe, give me something!'

Kovaks paused at the door. 'Turn that off,' he said, pointing to the tape-recorder.

Meekly, she obliged.

'It's quite obvious to me that you've already been given something, Lisa. Some of the questions you've asked indicate to me that someone in the FBI office in Miami is feeding you stuff you shouldn't know. I haven't a clue who it is and I don't think you'll tell me –' here she opened her mouth to protest – 'no, don't speak,' he ordered her. 'Let me finish. I know you'll deny it and that's fair enough, but I'll tell you this: when I find out who it is, whoever it is, regardless of rank, gender, race, length of service, length of penis, whatever, whoever – when I find them, they'll wish they'd never been born, never joined the FBI, never fucked you. Their feet won't touch the fuckin' ground – and nor will yours, because I'll go for your throat too and you'll be before a court faster than you come. Now, if you want to turn that machine back on, I'll give you a comment.'

Speechless, she pressed the record buttons.

'No comment,' he said, smiled, turned and walked out of the hospital.

Kovaks drove home in a bleak, black mood. He hit the bottle and his mood became darker and deadlier. How could he prove that Corelli was the man behind the bombs? The simple answer was that he couldn't. It wasn't as though Corelli, or even one of his hired hands, would go to the trouble of popping round or phoning to say, 'Back off – you've been warned.' Corelli would just assume that Kovaks was intelligent enough to get the message.

And now that Whisper was dead – the only chink in Corelli's ring of steel – there was no way they could tie Hinksman and Corelli together. Everything he'd told Kovaks before being knifed to death wasn't worth the breath it had been whispered on.

They were as far away as ever.

Once again, Corelli was out of reach. Untouchable.

Kovaks had started with a full bottle of Jack Daniel's. A quarter of it had slid effortlessly down to his empty stomach and then very quickly up to his head, clouding his judgement.

Drink makes people do rash things.

Holding the bottle by the neck, he stormed out of the apartment – down the blackened, burned hallway – and out to his car on the street below.

Without hesitation, other than the drunken delay caused by the problem of getting the key in the ignition, he drove south towards Miami.

He drove quickly, recklessly, with no regard for other road-users. With one hand gripping the wheel and one hand around the bottle, frequently necking mouthfuls of the fiery liquid contained therein, he was fortunate not to have caused a serious accident.

Once in Miami itself, he did a left onto MacArthur Causeway and headed out in the direction of Miami Beach and the Art Deco section where Corelli had a house. It was a 1930s mansion really, surrounded by a high wall, high security and a two-acre manicured garden with peacocks and arty statues.

Kovaks drew up at the high, wrought-iron gates. They stayed closed. A camera up on the wall focused on him and he waved at it. Still nothing happened. He staggered out of the driver's seat and rang the intercom set in the wall.

'Yeah?' came a voice. Friendly? No.

'FBI – let me in. I wanna see Corelli,' slurred the agent.

'Goodbye.' The intercom went dead.

Kovaks continued to lean on the buzzer whilst peering drunkenly through the gates up towards the house which was discreetly half-hidden by trees and topiary.

Eventually the front door of the house opened and two men in tracksuits meandered down the driveway. They walked on the balls of their feet. A tough guy's walk. Rolling shoulders, twisting hips. Smug. Each man carried a pump action shotgun. Kovaks recognised them as a couple of Corelli's minor heavies. He sneered at them, the drink making him much braver than he should have been under the circumstances.

They arrived at the gate. Their expressions remained

impassive but superior. One stood slightly behind the other, to one side, the shotgun held across his chest. The one at the front did the talking.

'What you want?'

'I wanna see Corelli – OK, bud?'

'Go away.'

'Let me see him.'

'You gotta warrant?'

'Don't need one – I'm backed by the power of Federal law,' Kovaks spat stupidly.

'Bye bye,' said the talking heavy. To reinforce his statement he laid the barrel of his shotgun on a cross member in the gate, pointing the weapon about chest-height at Kovaks. He pumped it. It was a deadly sound. 'You don't go right now, I'll have to phone the cops and tell 'em I had to shoot a drunken intruder.'

Kovaks stiffened. The insinuation got through his drunkenness. 'I just want to talk to Corelli,' he said.

'Well, he ain't here.'

'Where is he, then – Key West?'

The heavy checked his watch. 'By now he's about halfway across the Atlantic.'

'Why, where's he going?' Kovaks asked too quickly, making the heavy realise he'd said too much.

'Just shove it, man,' he said, beginning to lose his cool, his voice rising up towards agitation. 'You don't go, I pull this trigger.'

Kovaks conceded defeat and rolled back into his car. He slammed it into reverse and screeched backwards out of the driveway. He pulled away with the flourish of a boy racer, a finger for the two heavies and a head out of the window shouting, 'Fuck you, assholes!' It was the most original insult his drink-sodden mind could manage.

He reached across the passenger seat, swerving dangerously into, then out of, the path of an oncoming car, and fumbled for the bottle of JD. With an angry horn sounding in his ears he took a hefty swig of what should have been sipped without spilling a drop. He was quite proud of the accomplishment.

'So he's goin' to England, eh?' Kovaks murmured. 'Better let that cunt Donaldson know.'

His right foot went down heavy on the accelerator and the big engine roared with pleasure as it picked up speed.

Halfway back across MacArthur Causeway he heard a distinctive sound right behind him: the shriek of a police patrol car siren, the one blast that meant 'pull over'. Kovaks checked his rearview mirror and saw the car behind him, two officers on board, roof-lights flashing. He drew into the side of the road as smoothly as his state would allow and stopped with a lurch. He rested his hands on the top of the steering wheel where they could be seen.

One of the officers stayed half-in, half-out of the patrol car. The other one approached Kovaks with the caution of bad experience and good training. His right hand rested significantly on the butt of his holstered revolver.

Kovaks stayed where he was and awaited instructions.

'Get out of the car, please sir, and place your hands on the roof. Re-eal slow, like.'

Kovaks obeyed every word to the letter.

At the end of these formalities, when it had been established that Kovaks was unarmed, the officer said, 'Is this your car, sir?'

'It is.'

'We've received a report of a possible drunk driver in the Art Deco area, in a red Trans-Am.'

'Who made the report, officer?' Kovaks enquired politely.

'Anonymous caller, sir – but obviously correct. I can smell alcohol on your breath, your eyes are glazed over and you have slurred some of your words. I therefore suspect you to be drinking and driving. I am therefore requesting you to provide a breath specimen for a breathalyser test.'

'I don't suppose it'll make a difference if I tell you I'm a Federal Agent?' he asked hopefully.

'You don't suppose right, sir.'

Kovaks closed his eyes in despair. Bubbled by the Mafia. The perfect end to a fucking perfect day.

Chapter Fifteen

The wide-bodied jet touched down smoothly at Manchester Airport, despite the strongly gusting cross-winds. As is the norm in many airports now, the arrival was not heralded by tannoy, but merely blipped up on the numerous TV monitors dotted around the terminus.

Henry Christie and Karl Donaldson watched the plane taxi to the gate and the motorised steps be driven, rather like small, controllable dinosaurs, to the front and rear doors of the plane. The doors were heaved open and after a pause the first of the passengers began to disembark.

Donaldson held his breath.

Henry noted his tension.

Then the American said, 'That's him,' and pointed. 'The guy in the suit. He's brought one of his goons with him.'

Henry looked through his binoculars, focused them on Corelli as he clambered down the steps at the front of the plane.

'So that's what a Mafia godfather looks like. Looks more like a grandfather,' commented Henry.

'Don't let looks deceive you. That's one of his strengths. People are taken in by him.'

'But I'm well pissed off with this,' Henry moaned. 'He just doesn't fit my stereotype. Isn't life complicated?'

'Sure is, Henry,' Donaldson muttered bleakly.

Henry gave Donaldson a sidelong glance and wondered what was on his mind. 'Let's get down to Customs,' he said, 'and make his entry into Limey as uncomfortable as possible.'

'Good idea,' agreed Donaldson, pleased at the prospect. 'Pity that the only way we can get at the bastard is by getting him stopped and searched. He should be on Death Row by rights.'

They began to make their way down from the public viewing gallery.

Donaldson thought about the rushed telephone call he'd received about two hours earlier from Joe Kovaks. He'd called from the copshop in Miami where he'd been taken following his drink-drive arrest. He'd been released after giving a blood sample which would be analysed before any court proceedings, but they wouldn't give him his car keys back until he provided them with a negative specimen of breath. So he'd been very unhappy.

Even though the situation had been pretty tragic for Kovaks, Donaldson could barely contain his mirth at the predicament and its irony; the bare-faced cheek of the Mafia and how one quick phone call had put Kovaks' job on the line – because the FBI had a tough policy on lawbreakers within its own ranks. Drink-driving in particular was frowned upon. Several agents had been fired because of it. But Donaldson's amusement had waned, then turned to anger and horror when Kovaks told him about Chrissy . . . and then burst into tears down the phone.

The two lawmen had already introduced themselves to Customs and the airport police. They took up a position behind screens, together with one of the airport detectives and a Customs officer, from where they could see through one-way windows into the baggage reclaim hall and both Customs channels, green and red: Nothing To Declare and Goods To Declare.

By prior arrangement two armed cops – with revolvers and MP5s on open display – had been posted to the Customs area. Not that problems were expected. Corelli wasn't stupid. They simply wanted the godfather to feel under pressure when the uniformed Customs officers singled him out from the other passengers in order to search his luggage.

It all went according to plan.

Corelli and his aide collected their bags from the conveyor belt. Corelli had a small sports bag, his aide a large suitcase and flight bag. They placed them on a trolley and headed to the green channel.

The Customs officer with the detectives spoke quietly into his radio. The uniformed officers in the green channel nodded at their boss's instructions which they received via their earpieces.

Corelli and his man came into view.

The two armed cops were clearly visible.

Seconds later Corelli had been drawn to one side and directed to a long table where another Customs officer awaited them with a smile. The table was directly in front of the screen which Henry and Donaldson were behind, giving them, as planned, an excellent view of the proceedings.

Corelli and his man were smiling, as though they expected this to happen. They were patient and courteous, and carried out the requests of the Customs officer without rancour. Not once did they show irritation or annoyance.

'He's fuckin' enjoying this,' hissed Donaldson. He was the one showing irritation and annoyance. 'I just wanna put one on him. I really do.'

'Obviously something he'd foreseen,' said Henry, less bothered.

He studied both men through the one-way window.

Corelli was about fifty years old and overweight. He was short and rotund, but carried his poundage quite well. His face was wide and his skin dark, betraying his Mediterranean origin. He had eyes which were lit with humour and a beguiling smile which he flashed regularly as he shared a joke or two with the Customs officers. He reminded Henry more of an accountant or bank manager – or maybe a successful salesman. He looked ordinary, decent, law-abiding, middle-aged and fat. He wouldn't have drawn a second glance in a street.

'Know anything about the other guy?' Henry asked Donaldson.

'Lots. He's Corelli's main bodyguard, trusted right-hand man, but not a policy adviser or anything like that. He organises Corelli's personal protection and anti-surveillance. Name of Jamie Stanton. An ex-cop, actually – did about five years with the NYPD before he went bad. Got busted for selling drugs to fellow officers, then moved into the security business, personal protection mainly. Worked with one or two controversial businessmen and union organisers before gravitating to Corelli. I think he's probably very good – so good that he hasn't been tested in any situation yet, and he's made Corelli very surveillance-conscious. We've wired his home twice – both times sussed – and he never uses his own phone to do business, unless he can't help it because they're nearly always tapped. He's also a fitness freak. Jeez –' Donaldson shook his head – 'if he came across, it'd be gold for us, but that's just wishful thinking. He's dedicated to Corelli and paid very, very well.'

Henry saw that Stanton was a tough-looking man in his mid-thirties who oozed violence coupled with intelligence. A dangerous combination. He was chunky, strong-looking, with shoulders like a swimmer. He did fit the stereotype, Henry thought with relief. His eyes were watchful. His movements were those of a man accustomed to reacting quickly should the need arise, but otherwise he conserved energy, a bit like a cat. Everything was held back for that vital thrust. Yet he too was smiling and cheerful, though on closer inspection his countenance wasn't as convincing as Corelli's. He'd been told how to react if stopped and didn't really like acting the pleasant man. Henry made a mental note to watch him very carefully should their paths ever cross. He hoped they wouldn't.

The baggage search was over, the clothing and toiletries – for that's all there was – had been replaced.

Before moving away Corelli looked past the shoulder of the Customs officer at the one-way window behind which

Henry and Donaldson lurked. He gave a cheerful wave of acknowledgement. Then he and Stanton – who scowled – walked towards the arrivals hall.

'Bastard, bastard, bastard,' Donaldson muttered, wringing his hands in frustration.

'Suddenly I feel very small,' said Henry. He thrust his hands deep into his pockets. 'I don't now think this was a good idea, to have him searched.'

'Why the fuck not? It inconvenienced him, didn't it?'

'And brought us down to his level, Karl,' Henry said like the critical parent. 'We should be better than this. It's not as though we were likely to find anything, was it? He'd hardly have had a case full of crack, would he?'

Grudgingly Donaldson said, 'Suppose you're right . . . but I still enjoyed it.'

'And that's all that matters,' Henry said sarkily. 'C'mon, let's see who he meets up with.'

Out in the bustling arrivals hall they were just in time to see Corelli and Stanton being led out of the building by a man in a chauffeur's uniform.

They pushed through the crowd.

When they emerged outside, all they saw was the rear end of a large, plush saloon car pulling away from the kerb. A Rolls-Royce with personalised numberplates.

Donaldson cursed and fumbled for his pen and a piece of paper, hoping to get a note of the number.

'No need,' said Henry, laying a hand on Donaldson's arm. 'I know who owns it – a guy called Lenny Dakin. RCS have run surveillance on him a few times but got nowhere.' He pursed his lips thoughtfully. 'Now I know what Jason Brown was doing in Blackpool. Dakin has some business interests there. Looks like they could've been working together, maybe. Looks like Dakin could have set up Brown for the hit, maybe. Looks like Dakin and Corelli are now business partners . . .'

'Maybe,' the two men said in unison.

★ ★ ★

The charge of murder in English law is a very simple charge.

At 10 p.m., after a full day of interviews, a detective brought Hinksman, who was on his crutches, before the custody officer. Also present was Hinksman's solicitor.

'Just listen to what the officer has to say to you,' the custody officer told Hinksman.

The detective began to speak, reading from the charge forms. 'You are charged with the offence shown below. You do not have to say anything. But it may harm your defence if you do not mention *now* something which you later rely on in court. Anything you do say may be given in evidence. You are charged that at Blackpool in the County of Lancashire, you did murder Jason Brown. This is contrary to common law.' The detective looked up at Hinksman. 'Do you wish to make any reply to the charge?'

Hinksman, who had simply stared at the wall as the charge was read out, continued to do that. He acknowledged no one and refused to take his copy of the charge.

'You're not getting bail,' the custody officer said, 'because I have reasonable grounds to believe you'll fail to appear, or that you'll interfere with the administration of justice by intimidating witnesses if you're released. You'll be appearing at court tomorrow when there'll be an application for a three-day remand in police custody to allow us to question you about many other matters. Do you understand?'

No response.

The custody officer beckoned two gaolers. 'Take him back to his cell.'

They led him down the corridor and ushered him into a cell, slamming the door shut behind him, but leaving the inspection flap open. One of the gaolers sat down on a chair in the corridor outside the cell as it is normal procedure in Lancashire to keep all persons charged with murder under constant supervision.

In the cell Hinksman propped his crutches up and lay down on the bench-bed. The mattress was thin and covered with tough, thick plastic. He pulled a rough blanket over himself and stared at the ceiling.

Two thoughts circled around in his head: escape and revenge.

Henry and Donaldson drove back to Blackpool. The American had checked out of his Manchester hotel and moved into one in the resort while he continued to work with Henry on the Hinksman case.

On the journey Henry told him all he knew about Dakin, which was precious little. He'd actually heard nothing about the man for some time and would have to check with the RCS office in Bolton about the current state of play. He seemed to have slipped quietly out of the limelight.

They arrived at Blackpool Central police station just before 10.30 p.m.

After checking the custody office to find out whether Hinksman had been charged or not, Henry invited Donaldson up to the social club which was on the top floor of the station. Donaldson accepted. Both men were eager for a drink.

They sat at the quiet bar. Henry drank lager with a whisky chaser whilst the American contented himself drinking straight out of a bottle of Bud.

Conversation drifted from topic to topic as the drinks went down. Cops all over the world find it easy to talk to each other. They discussed their careers and enjoyed exchanging a few war stories. Eventually the subject turned somehow to Chief Inspector Karen Wilde. Henry was speechless when he was told about her treatment and then her rape.

'But you must not tell anyone,' Donaldson insisted. 'She wants it that way, wants to try and forget it and get on with her life.'

Henry whistled softly. 'I see her in a whole new light

now,' he confessed. 'I completely hated her, to be honest, but I never really considered things from her perspective. You seem to know an awful lot about her in such a short time. You soft on her?'

Donaldson coloured up and squirmed. He took a sip of his beer. 'You could say that,' he said with a slight trace of bitterness. 'I've fallen in love with her, I think. But she doesn't want to know – which, I suppose, is fair enough at the moment.'

'Why have you told me all this, Karl?' Henry asked.

'Dunno,' Donaldson shrugged, looking at the bubbles in his beer. 'So much has happened over the last few days, and although it might sound a little soppy, I just needed to get some of it off my chest. I just wanna talk to somebody and you're the nearest . . . and you seem a pretty decent guy.'

'Cheers,' said Henry doubtfully.

Two ladies who'd been sitting at the far end of the room near the snooker tables came to the bar to buy drinks as the last orders were called. Whilst waiting, one of them turned to Henry. He looked at her and smiled, vaguely recognising her. She was very good-looking and oh, so young. About twenty. She smelled delicious.

'You're Henry Christie, aren't you?'

'Yes I am,' he said. 'And who are you?'

'Police Constable Natalie Atkinson and this is Alex,' she said, thumbing at her friend. 'She's a PC too. We've just started here from training school.'

'Oh, very nice,' said Henry. 'I hope you have a good career.'

'That's a very nasty cut on your head,' she said. She laid a cool finger on his forehead.

'It is,' he agreed. His stomach leapt at the touch.

'You're a bit of a hero, aren't you?' she asked. Her eyes were wide and bright and moist as she gazed up at him. 'And you've shot a man, haven't you?'

'No to the first; yes to the second,' he said modestly. Who would be corrupting whom, he wondered idly, if this went any further. 'But,' he added, 'I'm not proud I shot anyone.'

'My friend and I are going on to a nightclub. Would you and your friend like to come along?'

'Oh, I don't know,' said Henry, flattered. He checked his watch. 'What about you, Karl?'

Donaldson had picked up the gaze from Alex. 'To be honest,' he said, 'I'd like to let my hair down for an hour or two, especially after the events of the last few days.'

'You're an American!' blurted Alex, sidling over to him. Donaldson nodded.

'He's an FBI agent,' Henry said.

'Wow,' Alex said, truly impressed.

'So, you coming along then, or what?' Natalie asked. 'We're going to the loo. It'll give you a minute or two to make up your minds.'

The ladies excused themselves.

Henry and Donaldson eyed each other uncertainly for a fleeting moment. Both men's faces cracked into smiles.

Henry, slightly affected by drink already, slapped his left hand onto his right bicep and jacked up his fist.

'What the hell does that mean?' asked a perplexed Donaldson.

'It means I could give her one,' said Henry dirtily.

'You mean . . .?'

'Fuck her, I believe is the international term,' said Henry.

'Doesn't mean that in the States. It means "Up Yours".'

'Same thing,' laughed Henry.

'You English, there's no hope for y'all.'

They finished their drinks and stood up as the ladies came back from grooming themselves. Henry felt light-headed and dizzy and a little out of his depth, but what the hell! A bit of a razz wouldn't do anyone any harm, would it?

'You game for a laugh?' he asked.

'Sure thing,' affirmed Donaldson.

In the lift Natalie slid her arm through the crook of Henry's. She inspected him minutely with big seductive eyes. Then she smiled. 'Can I kiss you?' she asked politely, turning to face him properly and snaking her arms around his neck, completely ignoring the other two in the lift. Henry took in her scent again. Its vapours intermingled intoxicatingly with the liquor which already clouded his brain and therefore his judgement. He knew he shouldn't. 'I've never kissed a hero before,' she said, drawing his face towards hers, his mouth towards hers.

His arms went round her waist. She felt so slim. He pulled her eagerly towards him. She responded, grinding her hips into his.

They kissed.

Two hours of negotiation, planning details, finance, profits, routes and couriers had passed before Corelli leaned back in his chair, stretched and yawned. In the grate a fire burned and spat ferociously. On a rug in front of it lay Dakin's two Dobermans, sleeping soundly.

Dakin smiled. 'Care for another drink?' he asked Corelli.

'A small bourbon,' said Corelli. He stood up and went to the window, looking out into the darkness that was the Ribble Valley. Light from the moon made the river itself look silver in the bottom of the valley.

Dakin handed him a glass. 'Do you like my house?'

'I do,' said Corelli, 'and your hospitality and your business ability.'

'Good, I'm glad.'

Dakin held out his glass. Corelli chinked his against it.

'Here's to the future and shared prosperity,' said Dakin.

They each took a sip of their drinks.

'There is, however, one problem to be resolved,' Corelli said thoughtfully.

'What's that?' Dakin sounded guarded. 'I thought we'd covered everything.'

'Oh, we have, businesswise. Now, the man the police arrested . . .'

'Hinksman,' nodded Dakin.

'As part of our arrangement, and to show your good will

towards me, I should like you to ensure that he does not remain in the custody of your fine police department any longer than necessary – if you see what I mean.'

Donaldson was still awake when the knock came on the door of his hotel room. He was savouring the feel and warmth of a woman in his bed, even though she was virtually a stranger. But that didn't matter to him at that moment. He felt good and relaxed and proud that he'd been able to perform so well after all this time.

The knock came again.

He wasn't sure whether he'd actually heard it the first time, or even if it was his door. He glanced at his watch. Just gone four. Puzzled, he eased his left arm gently from under the sleeping shoulders of Alex and sat up slowly on the edge of the bed so as not to disturb her.

There was another knock, louder, slightly more urgent this time.

He pulled on a pair of shorts and went to the door. He opened it to see Karen standing there in the corridor.

She was crying. Her eyes were pools of clear water. Streams ran down her cheeks. She looked lost and beautiful. Donaldson's heart went out to her when he saw how misshapen her mouth became as she cried and tried to hold it back, and how much her shoulders juddered with each sob.

'Karen,' he said.

'Karl, I'm sorry – I just needed someone. I need to talk to somebody . . . I haven't got any friends.' She almost choked on the word friends. 'I feel so alone . . . I want to talk to you. I'm cracking up, I think. My head, it's just spinning round and round . . . won't stop. I need someone to hold me. You don't mind, do you?'

'No, I don't.' But he couldn't help looking over his shoulder back into the room.

Karen saw the glance and followed it with her own eyes.

Disturbed by the noise, Alex was sitting up in bed yawning. The sheets had tumbled to her waist.

'You've got someone in there,' said Karen. It wasn't an accusation. There was sadness in her tone.

'Yeah,' Donaldson said. 'I mean . . . she's nothing. I'll get rid of her – she can go.'

Karen suddenly took control of herself. She shook her head. 'Don't bother, Karl. I'm sorry, I shouldn't have come without phoning first. It was stupid. But I expected . . . Oh, it doesn't matter.'

She turned and walked towards the lift.

'Karen – wait!' He started to panic.

The lift doors opened immediately. Half-naked at his doorway, Donaldson watched helpless as she left.

'Karen,' he shouted. 'Karen, I love you.'

As though she hadn't heard or didn't give a damn, she stepped into the lift, but did not turn round to face him. Her back stayed towards him.

The doors closed. The lift hissed and began to descend.

Donaldson closed his eyes and dropped his head forwards into the palms of his hands.

Chapter Sixteen

Henry slithered into work at nine the following day, not feeling particularly well nor particularly proud of himself. He'd got home just after 4 a.m. and sneaked into bed in a drunken stupor in the belief that he'd managed it without waking his wife; as the reality of the sober world hit him he realised there was no way this could have been the case.

Kate, however, hadn't said a word. She'd been her normal cheerful self, waking him up prior to setting off for her own work. She'd kissed him gently and placed a glass of orange juice on the bedside cabinet.

With his aches and pains and breakages, it took him about twenty minutes to get dressed.

He grabbed a coffee in the canteen which he intended to drink in the office. On his way to the lift he was waylaid by Natalie in police uniform. Henry took comfort from the fact that she looked worse than him – but she was on the early shift and could have only managed an hour or so's sleep at most. It didn't stop her being gorgeous though. And that perfume . . .

'Did you enjoy last night, hero? I did,' she said.

'Yes, yes I did,' Henry coughed. He vividly remembered the sex in the car. It was a long time since he had fucked in a back seat. He'd forgotten how difficult it was. But it had been good, fast and exhausting. Different. A change.

'What about tonight?' she asked.

'Oh, I don't know,' he said. 'Commitments, y'know?' He knew he should have said no, quashed it there and then, but could not bring himself to do so.

She nodded understandingly. 'Give me a call if you get free. I'll be in all night.' She tiptoed up and gave him a less than subtle peck on the cheek which was witnessed by several others.

I can handle this, he thought as he made his way to the office. No probs. I can handle this.

Donaldson was already in the office, sifting through paperwork, a visitor's badge on his lapel. Much to Henry's disgust he looked positively healthy.

'Mornin',' Henry croaked and sat down heavily, jarring his ribs painfully. 'I feel about nine thousand years old.' He rooted through the drawers in his desk for an aspirin. He knew they were there somewhere.

'Howdy,' said Donaldson.

'Good night?' Henry enquired of him, knowing he'd taken Alex back to his hotel room.

'So so,' he said. 'Good points and bad points.'

'Oh,' said Henry. He couldn't work up the energy to pry. He found and devoured two pills, swallowing them with his coffee. He wiped his mouth and said, 'To business. Let's try and find out what Mr Dakin's been up to recently, and also where he and Mr Corelli are holed up.'

'I have an idea where they might be today,' said Donaldson.

'Oh?' said Henry. He was about to ask when the phone rang.

'DS Christie – can I help you?' It wasn't a good line for some reason. 'Sorry, just hold on a second.'

Some of the other detectives in the office were laughing and talking quite loudly, making it difficult for him to hear. He shouted, covering the mouthpiece first: 'Will you lot shut your gobs! I can't hear a fuckin' word. And it *is* the Chief Super on the line.' Silence clamped quickly down. Henry returned to his phone conversation. He wrote furiously and listened intently.

A few moments later he hung up.

'Well, Karl, sorry about this, mate, but I've been taken

off this investigation as of now. We've got another murder – a double one, in fact.'

Henry drove all the way east across the county of Lancashire to the Rossendale Valley. He had two Detective Constables from his office as company. All three men had been assigned to the Murder Squad.

On the moors above Rossendale there are many quarries, both used and unused. These workings scar a bleak but beautiful landscape. It was to an old stone quarry above the town of Whitworth in the most easterly part of the valley that Henry drove that day.

He knew the way well. He'd served in that part of the county as a young uniformed PC on the beat and returned occasionally, to see friends made in that era of almost twenty years ago. It was an area he knew quite well and missed. He often thought of it with the affection of distance and time. The harsh winters, the placid summers, the contrast of hill and valley – all things lacking in the western half of the county.

The road he took now was rough and pot-holed. Only cautious driving prevented the bottom being ripped out of the car. However, they arrived at the scene without mishap.

It was a bustle of hectic police activity – cars, vans and cops milling everywhere. But thankfully no blue flashing lights. Henry did not wish to add to the apparent chaos and parked well away, walking the remaining distance, much to his companions' muttering annoyance. The only place a detective likes walking to is a pub.

A Detective Chief Inspector from the Division strode out from a cluster of worried CID men and greeted Henry, shaking hands. 'Oh good, my Murder Squad,' he said. However, he seemed more concerned with money matters than catching a killer.

'Bad do, this, lad,' he said glumly in his cloth cap accent. 'The bloody division's on its last legs financially and I don't know where the money'll come from to finance this. Bloody bankrupt us, it will. Headquarters'll have to dig in for this.'

The economic aspects of the affair didn't particularly concern Henry. If he'd wanted to juggle figures, he'd have become an accountant. That was his argument. All he knew was there had been an alleged double murder and he wanted a chance at catching the culprit. The money would come from somewhere. It always did. It had to.

He commiserated with the DCI. Then: 'What've we got, sir?'

'Two mutilated bodies down disused quarry workings,' said the DCI. 'Found a couple of hours ago by a man who'd been shooting rabbits in the area. No idea, as yet, who they are. Man and a woman by the looks. Doctor says they could've been here for up to a week. Decaying quite quickly now, apparently. Trail's cold here, I'd say.'

'What about the mutilation?'

'They're both face down at the moment, but it looks pretty extensive from what we can see.'

'Jealous lover?'

'Nope, looks like a professional job.'

'Hell,' said Henry, heart sinking. 'Makes it more difficult.' Then his spirits soared again. 'Never mind, the cost might ruin the county for good and we'll all be made redundant so it won't matter anyway.'

'Very funny,' murmured the DCI. But there was the glimmer of a smile on his face.

He led Henry towards two disused workings which had been dug side by side many years before behind a dilapidated redbrick stone-crusher. Both workings were roughly the shape of huge upturned and sunken ice-cream cones, about thirty metres across. They were partially filled with rainwater, old tyres, junk and the rotting hulks of abandoned cars that had been pushed over the edge.

The two bodies had been discovered in the right-hand excavation in relation to Henry's approach.

He carefully went to the edge and looked over.

From where he stood it was a sheer drop to the water's

surface, but to his right was a grassed pathway clinging to the inner circumference of the working which led down to a ledge about twenty feet below the rim. It was a wide ledge and he could see it clearly. It was the scene of the crime.

'This area is used a great deal by kids on scramblers,' said the DCI into Henry's ear. 'Surprises me they haven't been found earlier.'

Henry raised his eyebrows. 'If you don't look, you don't see.'

'No, suppose not,' admitted the DCI.

There were the only two living people on the ledge at the moment. One was the Scenes of Crime photographer, who was combining stills and video shots of the scene. The other was the Home Office pathologist, Dr Baines. He was dressed in an all-in-one disposable paper suit, with plastic gloves and plastic shoes. He looked like a painter and decorator.

The bodies themselves were tucked virtually out of sight under the bonnet of the decomposing shell of an old car which was on its roof. As Henry looked at the scene all he could see clearly was a naked foot, half-covered in grass.

'Have a look,' urged the DCI. 'The pathologist should have completed his initial by now. Time to go and get them turned over.'

At the top of the path stood a uniformed PC with a clipboard and pad. On the ground next to him was a supply of paper suits, plastic shoes and disposable gloves. He issued Henry and the DCI with a full set each and instructed them to put them into evidence bags when they'd finished at the scene. This way there was less chance of any vital evidence being carted away on the clothing and shoes of heavy-footed coppers.

It was not a simple task to get the suits on over normal clothing. Henry and the DCI jigged about comically for a while. Once dressed, Henry led the way down to the scene.

On the ledge he nodded at the doctor who, on recognition, smiled broadly at the detective. They had previously spent several revelrous nights together.

'Henry, you old bastard!'

'You not been struck off yet?' Henry asked lightly.

'No . . . the dead tend not to complain.'

They shook hands, despite their disposable gloves.

'So what d'you think?' asked Henry. 'Suicide pact?'

Baines chuckled. Then he became serious. He moved his large head from side to side, pursed his lips and thought for a moment or two.

Henry liked him very much. He was young, just forty, and for the position he held that was good going. He knew his job well, so well in fact, that Henry felt in awe watching him work. Henry enjoyed being in the presence of people who knew their specialised fields intimately and he was honoured that Baines classed him as a friend. Henry looked upon himself as a jack-of-all-trades. Their friendship also assisted their professional relationship no end when at the conclusion of an investigation they knew they would be out together on the town, celebrating success (or failure) in some dive of a nightclub. But now, in all seriousness, they both became the two pros they were.

'From here,' the doctor said, 'I'd say they've been rolled down that slope behind you.' He pointed to the steep side of the quarry. 'Or maybe pushed out of a car.'

'We'll get it checked for tyre-tracks,' the DCI cut in. 'Forensic can do that. They'll be here soon.'

'And they've come to rest under this car,' Baines concluded.

'And . . .?' Henry urged.

'Can only see one of them really, and not very well. A male. I'd say the other's female, but that's to be confirmed. He looks like he's had his brains blown out. Not pretty. Been butchered too. Can't say an awful lot about that either, yet.'

'Bloody messy,' commented Henry.

'So how do you want to recover the bodies?' the doctor asked. His question was directed at the DCI.

All three men turned to consider the problem.

The bodies had rolled down the slope and come to rest underneath the bonnet of an overturned car which looked like it had been there for years. It was badly rusting, had no windows intact, no wheels and probably no engine. It might once have been a Vauxhall of some sort, Henry thought, one of the bigger ones, but he couldn't be sure. They had wedged next to what used to be the front windscreen.

Henry knelt down and looked. The bodies were face to face, both naked, trussed up together in a large polythene sheet. One arm had come free and protruded into the cab of the car through the windscreen. Henry noticed that there was no hand on the end of it. For a brief moment he was stunned. He pulled himself together.

Baines squatted down next to him. 'As I see it,' he said, 'there's three options. One – drag them out by hand. Two – get your lads down here to do the heave-ho and roll the car away . . .'

'And the third?'

'Get a crane to lift the car away inch by inch,' said Baines. 'But,' he admitted, 'there are problems with each.'

Henry waited.

'The first one will be very messy and unpleasant – and we might do something silly like pull one of their legs off, or head off, or something. Fraught with danger, as they say. The second one is OK, but as you can see, from where we are, as soon as the car is rolled over, it will topple down the quarry on top of all those other cars which is a good sixty-foot drop. So if there's any evidence in the car, it'll be a pain recovering it.'

'And what about option number three?' asked Henry. 'It's like a TV game show, this.'

'Best of the lot,' enthused Baines.

'Why?'

'Everything is preserved. The only problem is that the crane might destroy any tyre-marks which are up at the lip of the quarry.'

'Unless we get forensic to move their arses and do the

business up there asap,' said Henry. 'Yep, I'm for that one.'

They stood up simultaneously.

'I don't want to put a damper on this,' said the DCI, 'but where the hell do you intend to get a crane from? It'll cost a fortune to hire one.'

'No problem,' said the doctor. 'There's a working quarry half a mile up the road from here. Plenty of cranes there. I'm sure if you ask nicely enough they'll oblige.'

'Something tells me,' said Henry with a smile, 'this is a decision already made.'

Donaldson knocked hard. There was no reply. He looked through the downstairs windows, shading his eyes with his hands, then went round the back of the house to check the rear garden, but it was clear there was no one at home.

Next he tried the neighbours. No one could help him.

Then he sat in his car on the road outside the house. He felt an incredible empty sadness pervading his whole being. She was gone. He had lost her. She didn't want to see him now.

And there would be no time to tell her what he felt.

He swore at the girl from the London office of the FBI who had contacted him that morning to tell him the news: he had been recalled to the States. The British cops didn't need him any more. He had done his job. His flight had been booked from Manchester for the following day. He was expected to be on it. It gave him just enough time to attend Ken McClure's funeral.

He punched the centre of the steering wheel in abject frustration, and cursed aloud.

Fanshaw-Bayley arrived at Rossendale's public mortuary. He looked a worried man. With good cause, as Henry was soon to find out.

After a cursory inspection of the two bodies which were laid out on the slab, still encased in their polythene coffin, he beckoned Henry and the DCI outside.

He sighed before he talked. 'Severe money problems here,' he began. 'And manpower.'

'So what's new?' asked Henry.

'Different this time,' said FB. 'I've been to see the Chief this morning and he's told me we cannot afford to launch a full-scale murder enquiry on this one. Basically there's no money left in the coffers. We feel we need to keep resources channelled into the M6 bombing so we tie up all the loose ends. And that means keeping the majority of the squad working on it for at least another two weeks. As and when it winds down, we'll release officers to this enquiry – unless you finalise it first.'

'Well, judging from this,' Henry said, 'there won't be any quick result here.'

'So what's the set-up?' asked the DCI.

'You're the head of the investigation, and Henry here will run the operation itself.'

'What?' said Henry nonplussed. 'Shouldn't it be a DCI at least?'

'The divisional DI is off sick and I've no one else available,' said FB. 'Anyway, they're only toe-rags, these two, crims topped by crims by the look of it. So it's your baby, Henry. Look on it as a reward for Hinksman.'

'Another good decision by the Chief,' said Henry sourly.

'Look,' said FB, a hard edge coming into his voice, 'I don't particularly like it either. But it's all about money these days, and that's something the county doesn't have much of . . . and I don't like a DS talking that way about the boss. He's under a great deal of pressure at the moment, what with Jack Crosby dying.'

Amongst other things, Henry thought.

'And we're making the best of a bad job – OK?' concluded FB.

'No, not really,' said Henry truthfully. 'We always make do in the police. Pisses me off, it really does. But what choice do I have?'

'Absolutely none,' said FB.

'How many men will I have?'

'Ten detectives.'

'Ten! Jesus! Impossible.'

'I'll try and get one of the support unit teams to assist too. That'll give you another ten PCs and a uniformed Sergeant. But no overtime, either.'

'Can't be done,' said Henry, shaking his head.

'You'll have to do it,' insisted FB.

'I am not happy, not one little bit.'

'It's not your job to be happy or not,' said FB shortly. 'You'll do as I say, understand?'

Glumly, Henry nodded. He began to realise now why Karen didn't much like FB.

FB turned to the DCI. 'You keep the media sweet, OK?'

'I'll do me best, sir.'

Creep, thought Henry.

'Let's just hope we don't get any more murders this year.' FB swivelled back to Henry. 'Oh, by the way, I'm satisfied you've done enough background re Hinksman. Well done. I've spoken to the FBI office in London and told them they can take their agent back. We don't need him any more.'

'But Corelli's landed in Manchester! I sent you a memo. He's hobnobbing with Lenny Dakin. Karl Donaldson's input could be crucial. We really need him and his knowledge.'

'Unfortunately he's going back to the States – tomorrow, I believe.'

'So who's going to keep an eye on Corelli then? This connection has the makings of a big one – and there are the links with the M6 bombing too. Rumour is that Corelli put the finger on Carver and hired Hinksman to do the dirty business.'

'Just pass your info onto the incident room and let them handle it,' said FB dismissively.

'But we need someone in the know!' Henry stressed.

'Unlucky,' said FB finally. 'He's going and that's that. Right, I'm off now. Hope you catch someone.'

Henry and the DCI watched FB's car drive away.

'I take it you knew this was going to happen,' Henry suggested.

'I had an inkling,' admitted the DCI.

'Thanks a bunch,' said Henry, throwing his hands up in the air. He turned and made his way back into the mortuary, talking to himself. 'Fine, fine, a double under-world killing, ten jacks to sort it, no bloody overtime. It's not a problem, I can handle it, I can handle it – I'm a Sergeant, aren't I? I should be off fuckin' sick.'

He felt completely overwhelmed and out of his depth. It was probably the last thing he needed at this time.

Baines stood by the slab, smock on, plastic gloves on, cap on, mask on, dissecting-knife at the ready. An attendant stood by his side. The Scenes-of-Crime photographer was standing halfway up a stepladder, video at the ready, in a position to record the whole post mortem.

'Problems?' asked Baines. 'Politics?'

'With a capital "P",' said Henry. 'But I can handle it. If you're ready, let's get on with it.'

'Lights . . . camera . . . action!' said Baines. His knife descended towards the polythene wrapper.

The post mortems carried out by Dr Baines were thorough and remarkably smelly.

Death, thought Henry, has a peculiar tang all of its own. Always the same – musty, dirty, clinging to clothing for hours, even days after. That was why he hated having to attend post mortems.

He was not physically sick, nor had he ever been. He knew of cops who couldn't face PMs even after a dozen years. But it was no big deal, nothing to be ashamed of.

Once, early in his career when he'd been a PC, he had sat through four in a row, one after the other. He'd not been remotely affected by any of them, despite the fact that one had been a road accident victim and another a child.

All he hated was that damned smell.

Today's PMs were not even as bad as some he'd had to attend, of people who'd been dead for weeks, gone bloated and bad. Today's victims had bellies that had been slit open and thus all the gases which normally accumulate had been able to disperse. Even so, they reeked strongly.

It took Baines four hours of hard toil to complete the task. He was sweating heavily when he finished.

Once he'd scrubbed himself down, he and Henry adjourned to a nearby public house for a confab.

The doctor was a troubled man.

'The bullets killed them both, as you saw. Massive brain damage. No doubt in a couple of days' time you'll have the exact calibre of weapon and other information from ballistics.'

'Couple of months, more like,' said Henry.

'Both were mutilated after they were shot, and very skilfully too. Sharp instruments, good technique. You'll never get a match on dental records and you'll never be able to build up models of their facial features. The only leads you've got are the bullets that I recovered from the woman and the man's tattoos. I think that's where the killer made his mistake – by wrapping them in polythene and dumping them where he did. The circumstances have acted to preserve the outer skin, which is fortunate for you.'

'And the missing hands suggest they might have criminal records,' said Henry. 'LCRO are checking files re the tattoos. We might get lucky, but I think it could be a long slog. Smacks of a London gang-killing, this. Could be a real ball-acher.'

'Yeah,' said Baines. He took a sip from his glass. He was drinking bitter. 'I reckon they were murdered and then passed on for someone else to chop up. Someone who is good at it. It's relatively easy to pull a trigger, but to dismember a body takes certain skills. Know what I mean?'

'Like a sicko?'

'Or a doctor.'

'Or a pathologist. You're pretty sick.'

'Yeah,' laughed Baines. 'I am.' He sighed and dredged his brain. 'Something rings a bell, but I'm not sure what.' He thought, but came up with nothing. 'Nope . . . it won't come, Henry.'

He drank the last of his pint. 'I'll let you have a full report on the PMs, probably late tomorrow.'

Henry nodded. 'If you do recall anything at all, will you let me know personally?'

'Sure, Henry.'

The detective stretched and yawned.

'Henry, can I say something?'

'Fire away.'

'Don't let this thing overburden you. You look pretty worn out to start with and I know what you've been through recently. I'm not preaching or anything like that, but watch yourself, OK? And that's from a friend and a doctor.'

Henry said, 'Don't worry about me, I'm as tough as old boots.'

The funeral was a miserable affair, made worse by the incessant drizzle which rolled in from the Irish Sea like a fine cloud. There were just a handful of people in attendance and the ceremony only lasted as long as it had to. The coffin, bearing the murdered body of Pepe Paglia, was lowered into the ground with a thud as it touched the bottom of the sodden grave. Within moments of the soil being scattered on it – earth to earth – the mourners began to move away, relieved it was over.

Two men strolled to a Rolls-Royce parked nearby. A chauffeur rushed out of it, opened the rear doors for them and when they were settled, the big car pulled sedately away.

Another man stood by the cemetery gates. He was not a mourner. He was a watcher. His hands were thrust deep into his raincoat pockets. The collar was pulled up. His hair was plastered to his head. He'd watched the arrival and departure of everyone, but his interest centred on the Rolls-Royce and its occupants.

The big car lumbered towards him down the narrow cemetery road. He stepped out into its path.

The chauffeur said, 'Trouble, I think, Mr Corelli. What do you want me to do?'

Corelli and Stanton leaned forwards.

Jamie Stanton recognised the man quickly. It was his job to do so. 'It's that fibbie, Donaldson.'

Corelli laughed. 'Pull over next to him.'

'He might be armed,' Stanton warned. 'He might do something stupid.'

'No, he won't. He's in England. He can't afford to,' said Corelli with certainty.

The car rolled to a halt by Donaldson, its brakes exhaling a soft sigh. Corelli's electric window opened and he looked up at the agent in the rain.

Neither man spoke for a moment.

Donaldson merely stared impassively down his nose at Corelli through half-closed eyes. He was chewing gum which he masticated like a cow chewing the cud. He blew a bubble which burst with a crack.

Corelli smiled.

Eventually Stanton shouted, 'What do you want, dickbrain?'

Donaldson leaned forwards, keeping his hands in his pockets, and looked into the car, his grey eyes level with Corelli's.

'I want *you*, Mr Corelli – and I shall get you. There's nothing more certain. I'm gonna get you for all the pain, misery and suffering you've caused.' His voice was level, emotionless, frightening. He felt very in control.

Corelli blinked, but was not daunted.

Stanton leaned over his boss. 'Let me take the fucker. There's a grave back there and it's big enough for two.'

Corelli wagged a lazy finger at Stanton. 'No need for violence.' He then addressed Donaldson. 'Pass my best wishes to Mr Kovaks' ladyfriend. I believe she met with an unfortunate accident. Perhaps you should take note of it,

Mr Donaldson . . . and be wary yourself. Accidents are always happening.'

'You don't even begin to intimidate me, you son of a bitch,' said Donaldson, feeling his composure evaporating. It took a great deal of effort not to reach in and rip the Italian's head off. He'd made a conscious decision to keep his hands firmly in his pockets for just such a reason.

'Who's trying to intimidate whom here?' said Corelli calmly. 'You seem to be intent on frightening me for some reason I fail to comprehend. Me – a man with no criminal convictions who has just attended the funeral of a close relative. All I was doing was simply offering advice from one human being to another. Let's just leave it at that.'

'I'm gonna have you. One day you'll walk into a courtroom and never walk out again, I promise you that. From one human being to a sack of shit.'

'We'll see,' laughed Corelli.

He pressed the button on his electric window. It rose slowly and the car moved away.

'Who the fuck does he think he is?' growled Stanton, frustration boiling up in him.

'An FBI agent – one of the Untouchables. But he's wrong. I'm the one who's untouchable.'

Henry sat down in the room which had been commandeered as the incident room at Rawtenstall police station, which was the only decent-sized station within reasonable travelling distance of the murder scene. The room was normally used for lectures but even so it wasn't really large enough to house a full-scale murder enquiry. But it would have to do. After all, this wasn't a full-scale murder enquiry.

One HOLMES terminal had been installed in the corner of the room. All being well there would be someone to operate the damned thing tomorrow.

It was 9 p.m. Henry had dismissed his team, with the exception of the two who'd travelled with him from Blackpool, and told them to be ready for a briefing at 8 a.m.

the next day. He wanted the show to be on the road for 8.30.

The question of overtime had been raised, as always. Cops are very money-minded. Henry had told them that there would be as much as necessary – in direct contravention of FB's warnings. He was sure that FB had been bluffing and they had all gone home happily contemplating December's pay cheques.

Henry quickly scribbled a list of lines of enquiry to action the following morning. These included finding the origins of the polythene sheet and the rope wrapped around it; the tattoos on the man, checking Missing from Home files countrywide, ballistics liaison for a quick analysis of the bullets; liaison with Surrey police who had contacted him already to say they had a similar murder – unsolved – on their books, as had Northumbria and Kent; liaison with forensic to chase up the tyre-track impressions taken from the scene.

That would be enough to get the enquiry underway.

When the uniformed support team arrived he also had a few ideas for their deployment: house-to-house enquiries in Whitworth and a fingertip search of the scene.

An appeal by radio, TV and the press would be launched too.

He put his pen down and slumped backwards in his chair. This is ridiculous, he thought. Nine-thirty showed on the wall clock. Over twelve hours worked already on very little sleep and he didn't anticipate getting much more in the next few weeks either. Travelling every day from Blackpool was going to be a hell of a strain too: something like an eighty-mile round trip every day. It was a daunting prospect. His head throbbed at the thought. He rubbed his eyes. They were becoming sore and gritty.

He knew he should go home, get to bed and fall into a good long sleep to get himself up for tomorrow. That's what he knew he should do for the best. But he didn't.

He lifted the phone and called home. Kate answered, sprightly, glad to hear from him. He made some weak excuses – lies, really – and prepared her not to expect him until the early hours. Murder enquiry, work to do, God knows when he'd finish, all the responsibility . . . blah blah blah. All crap.

However guilty he felt, though, it didn't stop him from phoning another number. Natalie answered. Yes, she'd be more than pleased to see him. He could come round at any time.

'Come on guys, let's hit the road,' he announced.

The three of them went downstairs and headed out through the ground-floor communications room which was buzzing with activity. A harassed uniform Inspector looked up from a desk. Henry recognised him. He'd last seen him fifteen years before when they had both been PCs.

Henry acknowledged him.

'You will not effing believe this,' said the man, shaking his head.

'Try me.'

'Another suspicious sudden death. A firearms dealer has been found by one of his business associates out on the moors. Looks like he's been murdered, shot in the head and chest. Probably been there a few days, by the sound of it. I'm just on my way for a looksee. Want to come?'

'Thanks, but no thanks,' said Henry with an apologetic shrug. 'Got enough on my plate at the moment.' He joined his two colleagues who were already sitting in the car, one in the driver's seat revving the engine.

Henry dropped into the back seat. 'Blackpool, my man – and give it some wellie!'

PART TWO

Chapter Seventeen

When Henry Christie woke up, his head felt like it was on fire. He couldn't remember too much about the night before, other than it had been heavy, but lack of memory wasn't unusual these days. What he did know was that he'd drunk too much and now he was suffering from it – again.

He lay there, fully awake, keeping his eyes firmly closed, knowing that soon he would have to move. He had to go to Crown Court that morning and the vestiges of professionalism and pride which remained in him would not allow tardiness.

Keeping his eyes still firmly shut, he swung both legs out and sat on the edge of the bed. The fire raging through his brain became a series of major explosions. He groaned, but he knew that the only way to get going with a hangover of this magnitude was by moving quickly and with purpose, rather than slowly and sluggishly which merely prolonged the pain and discomfort.

Over the last six months Henry had become an expert at hangover recovery.

When he eventually opened his eyes, he was surprised to find it wasn't as bad as he'd expected. The curtains were closed and the daylight filtered through them diffused and manageable. Pure daylight on tender pupils was something he knew he couldn't have handled in his present state.

He heard a murmur behind him. He looked sharply round.

With some shock he saw a woman lying there asleep. He tried hard to recall some of the details, but his alcohol-riddled brain cells refused to cooperate. All he could do was stare at her rather blankly and unbelievingly.

The sheet was around her waist. He pulled it carefully back to cover her up, still wishing he could remember how it had been, why it had been, wishing also that she wasn't here in his bed. He sneered contemptuously at himself, then staggered, evading discarded clothing, plates, bottles and glasses, through the bathroom door and underneath the shower.

He ran the water as hot as he could bear it. The fine, hard jets worked on his salty body, dislodging the dried sweat of the night from his hair, chest, armpits and limp genitals. It refreshed him considerably. In five minutes he was almost awake; in ten he definitely was.

After drying himself he wandered back into the bedroom, a large fluffy bath towel wrapped around his middle. He was shaving with a battery-powered portable which was losing its charge and seemed to be ripping whiskers out rather than slicing them off.

The woman was awake. She must have heard him moving about. She was propped up on one elbow and watched him come into the room with a smirk on her face. Her hair had been combed and she'd applied some lipstick rather inaccurately. The top half of her body was exposed and the sheet was draped across the bulge of her midriff. It looked to Henry as though she'd spent some time preparing this position for him. She reminded him of a photo of a 'reader's wife', rather tacky and desperately unsexy.

He couldn't bring her name to mind, though he knew she was one of the cleaners at the police station who'd worked there for years and had acquired a terrible reputation. Monica, he thought. Rather than ask her he just nodded slight acknowledgement and walked across to the wardrobe, still shaving. One thing he did know, because it sprang to mind, was that she was nearly ten years older than him.

I'm not sure I believe this, he thought. It wasn't the first time he'd thought this in the last few months.

'Good morning, Henry,' she said at length.

He grunted something in reply. His back was towards her and it must have seemed like an insult, even if he didn't mean it that way, when he let the towel drop and bent down to pull on a pair of Y-fronts.

Then he began to dress in his best suit.

'Well?' she said, beginning to sound irritated. She sighed and flopped back onto the bed, her large white soft breasts suddenly losing their shape like two cakes sinking in an oven. She scrabbled the sheet furiously back and kicked it off. She became still, lying there, one leg pulled coyly up, the other straight out. Absolutely naked and unashamed. Then she allowed the leg which had been pulled up to fall to one side, giving Henry a splendid view of the pubic area.

He went cold.

'Well, did you have a good time last night?' she asked him playfully. 'I certainly did.'

'Yeah, sure I did,' said Henry. The details were hazy, but he knew they'd had intercourse, after a drunken fashion. He pulled his jacket on quickly and grabbed a tie before rushing to the door of the flat. 'Got to go to work, Monica,' he said apologetically as he crossed the room. His hand went to the door handle, where he paused and took a deep breath. He turned to face her with the courage of a mouse.

'Look, it was a lovely night and everything, but—'

'Yeah, I know,' she said with resignation. She pulled back the covers. Anger coupled with disappointment creased her face. 'Same old story. All right, I'll let myself out. And by the way, I'm called Maureen, not Monica, wanker!'

He hesitated, his eyes unable to meet hers. A second later he was through the door and trotting down the stairs.

The only way out of the flat was through the veterinary surgery which occupied all of the ground floor. A Doberman was on the operating table and the vet was carrying out an unsavoury operation on the dog's bottom. She looked up and nodded at Henry as he drifted through to the back door which led out into the rear yard and then the back alley.

Outside he came to a bone-jarring halt and caught his breath. He felt as if he were about to hyperventilate. What the hell had possessed him to pick her up, he demanded of himself.

He shook his head in a physical attempt to overcome this early-morning mental haze. His eyes felt like sandpaper as they scratched over the eyeballs beneath. He rubbed at them with his knuckles and then looked up at the day.

The rain had stopped. A weak yellow sun was poking its nose through some broken grey-white cloud. There was some blue sky beyond. Seagulls circled overhead and the salty smell of the Irish Sea hung in the air.

It was a nice day for the start of a major criminal trial.

He unlocked the driver's door of his recently acquired twelve-year-old Austin Metro and clambered into the small car. The engine fired up on the third attempt. He rattled down the cobbled back alley and pulled into the light traffic on the main road. He headed out towards the motorway, his eventual destination – if the car kept going – being Lancaster, almost thirty miles and fifty minutes away.

Once again he had time alone; time to consider just how radically his life had been turned upside-down.

On the stroke of 8.30 a.m. the gates at Risley remand centre were flung open to release a convoy of police vehicles. Lancashire's force helicopter hovered above.

They were scheduled to arrive, all being well, at Lancaster Castle approximately one hour later. This would leave ample time for the prisoner to be given his new cell at Lancaster prison, confer with his lawyer and prepare himself for his court appearance.

The hooded figure of a police marksman in a dark green combat-style anorak patrolled the battlements of the medieval castle. He was equipped with his personally issued, personally adjusted sniper's rifle and a pair of high-powered binoculars. He paced the ramparts slowly, policeman's pace, keeping an ever-vigilant eye on the scene below. Pausing briefly to talk to a similarly dressed and armed colleague, he pointed to something in the distance across the rooftops of Lancaster. Both men put their binoculars to their eyes. It was nothing to worry about. Moments later they resumed their beats.

Down at street level, all the approaches to the castle were covered and kept under constant police surveillance. Dozens of uniformed officers, some with dogs, either patrolled the streets or maintained strategic static points.

Many of these officers were armed too, handguns hidden as discreetly as possible in hip-holsters covered by their tunics. So that the weapons could be drawn quickly if necessary, the tunics were fastened with Velcro strips rather than buttons. Each officer was well practised in flipping up his tunic with one hand and drawing with the other before bouncing down into a firing position, weapon aimed and ready.

High-ranking officers with tense faces paced nervously around, checking and re-checking their Constables and Sergeants, keeping them on their toes, never allowing their watchfulness to waver.

The Chief Inspector from Lancaster had already had just about enough of Chief Superintendent Fanshaw-Bayley that morning. Despite constant reassurances that everything had been covered, FB mithered and moaned, and was getting on the Chief Inspector's nerves.

Fortunately the Superintendent was called back to the station, giving the other officer some much-needed relief and an opportunity to have one last slow look around the perimeter of the building and then check inside the court-room itself, which had already been searched several times by specially trained teams.

Near the entrance to the Crown Court, which, para-doxically, was at the rear of the castle, three Portakabins with eighteen telephone lines had been installed for press use. TV companies were setting up transmitting equipment. Press men and women mixed with TV reporters, comparing notes. Every national British newspaper was represented, as well as all the radio and TV companies. There were also many American journalists and TV companies present to cover the trial, which was expected to last a month and had caused a storm in the States.

The Chief Inspector walked past the mêlée of media, many of whom had arrived several days before and checked into hotel rooms which had been pre-booked for several months.

There was an expectant, circus-like atmosphere amongst them.

At the Crown Court entrance, more armed officers were on duty. The muzzles of their revolvers poked out from beneath the hems of their tunics.

Public access to the building had been restricted and everyone entering the court was searched three times: once manually, twice electronically. Even the Chief Inspector.

The officer submitted to the search with dignity and patience, scanning the entrance foyer as the searches progressed.

Here the presence of armed officers was less subtle.

Two officers from the district firearms team lurked at the back of the room. They were dressed in their dark blue work overalls, complete with kevlar body armour and ski caps. Holstered pistols hung at their sides. One had an MP5 machine pistol slung casually across his chest; the other had a pump action shotgun held firmly across hers, loaded with heavy shot capable of smashing a car engine block to pieces or bringing down a charging bull elephant.

Both officers looked sinister.

Once the searches were over, the Chief Inspector walked through the court. Because of the showpiece nature of the trial, it was being held in the Shire Hall, possibly one of the most magnificent courtrooms in the country. Built in a neo-Gothic style with a high vaulted ceiling, its inner walls decorated with one of the largest collections of heraldic shields in the world, it was an ideal setting, steeped in tradition and legend.

The Chief Inspector looked round the room.

Two PCs patrolled it. They were unarmed. The High Court Judge who was presiding over the trial had been consulted and had stipulated that armed police officers would not be allowed into her courtroom, no matter what the apparent threat was. No amount of reasoned argument from the police could shake her.

The Chief Inspector consulted her watch. 8.45 a.m. Something should be happening.

Suddenly the personal radio crackled into life.

On a cue from the force control room, officers in reflective jackets strode out into road junctions and stopped all traffic. Lancaster city centre came to a standstill.

A chauffeur-driven car escorted by police motorcycle outriders threaded its way through the streets, past the stationary traffic and up to the castle, parting at the entrance to the Crown Court.

Already decked out in wig and robes, the High Court Judge stepped out of the back of the car, accompanied by the High Sheriff of Lancashire. Smiling affably, posing momentarily for the media, she walked into one of England's most secure courthouses and gaols.

The police officers on guard around the castle breathed a sigh of relief. That the was the first hurdle over with. At least the Judge had arrived alive, safe and well.

The Chief Inspector smiled with a trace of triumph. Time for breakfast.

She left the court and made her way on foot towards the police station which was on the other side of town.

For the first time in six months, Karen Wilde felt reasonably content with herself and life in general. She was back in the land of the living, instead of that dazed state of rape trauma which seemed to dog her every hour, asleep or awake. There was light at the end of the tunnel at last.

Yet she also felt slightly nervous.

Karl Donaldson was listed as one of the essential prosecution witnesses and it was very likely that they would meet at some stage. After all, she was in charge of the security operation at the castle and she would be in attendance every day the trial was running.

She wondered if he actually wanted to see her again.

She knew for sure she wanted to see him.

By 9 a.m. the prison escort was already on the M6, travelling north, passing the Preston exit, the helicopter overhead all the time, watchful like a kestrel.

On the opposite carriageway was the site where Hinksman's car bomb had exploded; now repaired, the road surface bore no sign of the devastation of that day.

High up on the grass banking though, someone had erected a stone cross which was surrounded by bunches of flowers of remembrance to the people who had lost their lives. Motorists often stopped illegally and dashed from their cars up the grass to drop off wreaths or bouquets. The motorway police turned a blind eye to this practice.

The escort was moving at a good pace.

At its centre was the 'prison bus' – a Leyland Sherpa personnel carrier with a 3.5-litre engine, easily capable of sustaining 90 mph, as it was doing that morning. The inside of the van, behind the front seats, was an inbuilt cage made of steel. Inside this sat Hinksman and two police officers. He was handcuffed. The officers were unarmed. He had not spoken during the journey so far, but had been compliant.

At the very rear of the van there was a space between the end of the holding cage and the back doors, in which a bench seat had been installed. Two armed officers sat there, one having the key to the door.

There were two people up front, driver and passenger.

Four other vehicles formed the escort. All high-powered, unmarked police cars, but fitted with blue flashing lights set into their front grilles and blue lights on the rear window ledges.

Two were at the front of the Sherpa, two at the rear.

They literally forced their way through the traffic, while at the same time preventing any other vehicle from passing by ruthlessly blocking any overtaking manoeuvre – just on the off-chance it might be a hostile act. It was textbook security escort driving and these officers had it off to perfection.

Two hundred metres behind the escort was a Mercedes saloon car being driven by Lenny Dakin. He drove with one hand on the wheel, the other holding a voice-activated tape-recorder. He spoke continually into the machine, recording his thoughts and observations all the while.

This was a recce run to see how it was all handled by the cops.

It worried him. They were good. Very professional, taking it all very seriously indeed. 'Shit,' he swore into the tape, not for the first time.

He realised he had a hell of a task ahead of him and that he hadn't yet formulated an action plan to carry it out. And there would only be one chance after this morning.

They were now north of the Blackpool turn-off.

Suddenly the escort veered sharply out towards the fast lane, from the middle lane which it had been hogging.

A second later Dakin saw the reason why: some fool in a clapped-out motor had been day-dreaming and forgotten to look in his mirrors. Without warning he had pulled out into the middle lane from the slow lane, causing all manner of chaos.

No accident happened.

The man in the car panicked when he realised the problem and swerved back into the slow lane. Within a matter of seconds the escort was past him.

A few moments later Dakin passed him too.

Dakin stayed with the escort all the way. It wasn't difficult to be inconspicuous as there was a fairly substantial build-up of traffic behind the police cars and being part of it drew no attention to him.

They came off at Junction 33, south of Lancaster.

From here they headed north up the A6, through the small town of Galgate, past the university and into Lancaster itself. Obviously warned by radio, the cops in Lancaster had ensured that all traffic was running in favour of the escort. They sailed through town and up to the castle where the prison doors were opened and the prison bus drove in.

Hinksman had been delivered with only the whisper of a hitch.

And Lenny Dakin had decided how he was going to get him out.

Henry Christie swore out loud as he looked in his rearview mirror and realised what he'd done. Lost in his thoughts, he'd allowed his Metro to drift unexpectedly across to the middle lane; the earshattering sound of sirens confirmed he'd landed slap-bang in front of a police escort which was conveying a prisoner and didn't intend to take any more.

He yanked his steering wheel down to the left and waved an embarrassed apology as the escort sped past him. The cop in the front passenger seat of the Sherpa indicated to Henry that he thought he was a dickhead. Henry didn't really disagree.

He looked into the rear of the Sherpa, but the smoked side windows prevented him from seeing anything other than vague, indistinct shadows inside. But he knew it was Hinksman. He was glad to see they weren't taking any chances with the bastard.

When settled back into the slow lane, he tried to concentrate more so as not to be a danger to other road-users.

He failed to spot Lenny Dakin's Merc sigh past him.

Henry's mind gradually returned to his previous thoughts, but this time he managed to keep his car on track.

He tried to pinpoint where it had all begun to go wrong, but couldn't exactly put his finger on it. It was all too recent for him to dissect it analytically, though he often tried.

There was one thing for certain – he had made a complete fuck-up of his personal life and career, and they were both presently in one tangled, horrible mess that even Ariadne herself couldn't have unravelled.

On that first night of the murder enquiry he'd gone to Natalie's and ended up staying over. When her alarm had gone off at seven, he'd dashed home for a quick wash and a change of clothes, and given an open-mouthed Kate some lame excuse which she obviously didn't believe.

He had lied to her. Maybe that was the real start of it all. With a lie to someone he'd never lied to before.

From that point his home-life began to crack.

Lie followed lie, deceit followed deception, until his head was spinning and his emotions were in such a turmoil he might as well have had his head in a spin-drier.

Yet lying became easy. The words tripped glibly off his tongue, and it all seemed so straightforward. In the space of several days he was convinced he'd fallen in love with a young woman he hardly knew, other than carnally. And he'd fallen out of love with his wife whom he'd known since school and always regarded as his friend, confidante and lover.

The children became a dead weight around his shoulders. He had no time for them at all and they began to suffer too. They avoided him if at all possible.

He eventually began to hate going home.

Everything that was so familiar to him became despised.

He was in love with Natalie. A new woman in his life. A new impetus. And she loved him, her hero, wanted him, needed him, wanted to be his wife.

The sex was brilliant, like no other he'd ever experienced. He was swimming in a sea of sensuality with Natalie, caught up in a tide, drowning. They couldn't get enough of each other. Every time they looked at each other they wanted to fuck. It overpowered him. Drove him.

He began to use the murder enquiry as an excuse for not going home. He was genuinely working long hours, but could have got home every night if he wished. He didn't wish. Often he would book into a motel in the east of the county and Natalie would come across and stay the night with him.

It all felt so right. At least he made himself believe it did.

He didn't give Kate and the kids a second thought. They simply became unimportant to him as he began to lose his sense of values and judgement.

His judgement went on the back-burner at work, too.

Even though he had been ordered not to hand out overtime, he did so. By the end of the first month each man had worked in excess of eighty hours, totalling over eight hundred hours which had to be paid from somewhere.

And yet the investigation seemed to get nowhere.

He was losing all control of it; couldn't keep his mind on it. He regularly had to confront a sea of blank faces as detectives under his direction floundered and turned to him for inspiration – inspiration which never came.

The pressure grew on him from all sides.

Family – work; wife – daughters; Detective Constables – Detective Chief Superintendent; wife – lover.

All breathing down his sweaty neck.

He did not know which way to wriggle for the best.

Yet he thought he had a bolt-hole of sanity to escape to, or so he believed.

He eventually left home after a particularly fraught period with Kate when, at the end of it, he confessed everything. She took it all with great dignity and poise. She cried, of course. She was devastated. Her life had suddenly crumbled around her, although if she were ruthlessly honest with herself, she had seen it coming but had avoided it.

She forgave him immediately. She knew that you didn't just fall out of love with someone, but he couldn't see that. She held him in her arms that night and rocked him gently as he cried too. But he found he could not stay. His betrayal had been too great and the cracks it had caused too wide to paper over. And he loved Natalie.

'We can't ever go back to what it was,' he remembered telling Kate.

'But we can go forwards,' she insisted.

He was having none of that. His foolish stubborn streak could not be shaken.

He moved in with Natalie.

Bliss. Initially.

Then the nightmares started again as the stress of his marriage bust-up and the disintegration of the murder investigation crept clammily onto and all over him.

He woke up with a start, sweat pouring down him.

He'd seen the faces again. Those children clawing at the windows. Begging him for help. Fish caught in a bowl. Yet he couldn't help them. He had been powerless and they had died.

There was something new, too.

The head of that drugs dealer exploding all over his chest. Brain and snot and blood. The way his head had been distorted before finally bursting open. Frame by frame, in slow motion.

Then Ralphie's execution by the wall. Then that breathless chase down Blackpool Front, his clothing splattered with blood.

The woman taking the bullet meant for him.

Pointing that shaking gun at Hinksman – then having to fire it.

In his dream he could see his forefinger curled around the trigger, pulling it. He could see the hammer going backwards, the cylinder slowly revolving and the hammer falling and *bang!* He had shot someone.

He woke with the sound of the gun going off reverberating around his cranium like thunder.

At first Natalie was wonderful and understanding. She couldn't do enough for him. Comforted him. Held him. They made ferocious love after that first nightmare and he slept well afterwards, drained of all his strength. It was a black sleep.

After a dozen nightmares the sheen began to wear off for Natalie. She wasn't so wonderful after all. She grew tired and irritable and told Henry to pull himself together. She began to wonder exactly what she'd taken on here, as though she'd been deceived. A man possessed by demons? He was supposed to be tough. He was a hero, wasn't he? Not a wimp.

The love-making after the nightmares fizzled out. Instead she turned over and yanked the sheet over her head. He would lie there awake, dreadfully tired, but terrified of sleep.

Then he would get up and tiptoe to the tiny lounge of her flat where he would slide into the warmth of a bottle of whisky – and remain there.

In the end Natalie asked him to leave. She didn't understand, as it turned out, didn't want to understand. She had her life to live and didn't want the burden of a man verging on middle-age, who actually hated going to nightclubs if the truth were known, and who was probably having a nervous breakdown.

He moved into the flat over the vet's surgery. It was small, cheap, adequate, warm, slightly smelly, furnished.

Here he could indulge himself without infringing on other people's needs or emotions. Here he began a life clouded by alcohol and cheap sex whilst considering the question – Am I having, or have I had, a nervous breakdown?

Never having had one before, he couldn't be sure.

When FB called him to his office at Force Headquarters and dismissed him from the murder enquiry, and also told him he was being transferred from RCS back to normal CID duties, Henry broke down.

He cried like a baby in front of FB.

The astounded Detective Chief Superintendent immediately called the Force Welfare Department who dispatched a counsellor to FB's office. Within minutes she confirmed Henry's worst suspicions.

'You mean I *have* had a shed collapse?' he blurted. 'That's a relief. I thought I was going barmy.'

Henry was allowed to park outside the Crown Court after his car had been searched for bombs.

After several further searches of his person, he entered the building and settled himself down in the Shire Hall to wait for the trial to begin.

He truly believed he had got over the worst of it. The nightmares were still there occasionally, but they were less of a problem now and much more vague, less real.

All he needed to do was get his drinking under control and then his sexual excess – not necessarily in that order – and maybe, just maybe, he could regain control of his life and get back with his wife and girls, whom he missed desperately.

He knew that the trial would be the first test of his mental state.

Here, he would find out if all those ghosts and devils he believed were being laid to rest would get resurrected to haunt him when he stood up to give evidence and relive those experiences once again.

Chapter Eighteen

Agent Eamon Ritter had made a conscious, considered decision.

He was going to kill Sue Mather.

His life had become intolerable since she had seen him down at Bayside. He kept bumping into her, or so it seemed to him, both in the FBI building and out of it. Every time he turned a corner or came out of a door, she was there. Fat and unmistakable.

Too many times for it to be a coincidence.

She was definitely following him, of that he was in no doubt. And she knew, or at least suspected, he was on the take.

Yet why hadn't she done anything about it? Over six months had passed since Bayside. Perhaps she was tormenting him, toying with him. Then when she was good and ready, she would either bubble him or go for a piece of the action.

He'd actually considered approaching her and offering money, but he soon put that out of his mind. Just supposing she was straight? He would have played right into her hands.

No, he decided to stick at the viewpoint that she was upright and honest and what she was doing was building up a file of evidence against him before moving in for the kill. Bitch.

He sat at his desk in his office, rocking back and forth, pursing his lips as he considered his position.

There was no way he was going to give up Corelli's money. He was tied to it.

Firstly he had his lifestyle to maintain. It was discreet and subtly expensive, causing no one to raise an eyebrow. His modest house was well-furnished and he and his wife had decent, but second-hand cars. It was the finishing touches which told the story – the expensive CD-players in the cars, the original paintings on the walls of his house, the conservatory which could not be seen from the road, the top-of-the-range golf clubs, his designer clothes, which looked not a great deal different from off the peg – but oh, feel that quality. And the small apartment and boat on Grand Cayman which nobody in the office knew about. All these things needed money, more money than he could ever earn.

And secondly, if he pulled the plug and said, 'No more,' Corelli would drop him without a moment's hesitation to the FBI.

He had to go on.

The pencil he was holding snapped as he imagined his hands breaking Sue's neck.

The bitch had to die.

Even when a case comes to court, the wheels of British justice turn painfully slowly. On the first day of Jimmy Hinksman's trial, for no apparent reason, proceedings did not begin until 2.15 p.m.

That did not seem to bother the assembled press or public in the Shire Hall, restricted in their numbers to thirty and twelve respectively. There was a buzz of excitement, an air of anticipation, and a few hours' wait would not put a damper on that.

However, it did serve to wind Henry Christie up. He knew he would not be called to give evidence until the later stages of the proceedings, but he wanted it to be underway. All this waiting around, killing time, was stress-inducing as far as he was concerned.

After lunch the High Court Judge, Mrs Ellison, took her place on the Bench. She looked quite regally stunning and imposing, despite her sixty-eight years and slight frame.

Her wig, red robes and stern expression told their own story. Here was a woman not to be trifled with. This was her court and she ruled it without compromise. Unless it suited her.

The row of QCs, prosecution and defence, bowed to acknowledge her, all dressed in a similar fashion.

It was tradition taken to extreme.

Mrs Ellison indicated that the prisoner should be brought up.

A hush fell across the court. A couple of artists prepared their sketch-pads and pencils.

Henry braced himself. This was the first time he'd seen Hinksman since the committal hearing at Blackpool Magistrates Court.

He held his breath.

Two prison officers led Hinksman up from the holding cell below the court.

He gazed stonily into space, allowed himself to be manhandled and sat down in the dock, flanked by the officers. His handcuffs had already been removed.

Then his eyes began to rove around the court. From Judge to QCs to their briefs, to the security precautions . . . and finally, to Henry.

Their eyes met, their gazes interlocked.

Henry felt his flesh creep.

Hinksman sat back and, unexpectedly, his face broke into the most pleasant smile imaginable . . . which quickly changed into a sneer of contempt. He kept Henry's gaze, raised his eyebrows and mouthed the words, 'YOU ARE DEAD.'

There followed four days of legal submissions by the defence which were countered by the prosecution and vice versa, rather like the opening of a fencing match where the competitors were sussing out each other's strengths and weaknesses. It was all very eloquent and polite and at the same time dull. This legal parrying bored the spectators.

They weren't interested in nitpicking points of law and procedure. A good multiple murder case was what they all wanted to hear.

It was Friday before the jury was sworn in.

Even that did not prove to be simple. Hinksman's QC objected to eight of the original twelve for obscure but legally valid reasons, and they all had to be replaced by substitutes from the pool of jurors.

In the end there were seven men and five women. Two of the men were black. One of the women was Chinese.

At 4 p.m. everything was set to proceed.

So the Judge adjourned for the weekend.

Hinksman was led out of court after the Judge had left. He indicated to his QC that he wanted to speak to him.

A few minutes later the QC, whose name was Graham, came down to the holding cage for a hushed consultation with his client.

'I want you to arrange several things,' Hinksman told him.

'Such as?'

'I want you to find out the name and address of each of the jurors. I want the address of the Judge and the addresses of all the independent witnesses, including the cops.'

The QC pushed his pince-nez to the top of his nose, a feeling of discomfort flooding through him.

'That is not something I can do. These are details which are not disclosed by the prosecution.'

'Well, you'd better do it.'

'Why?' asked Graham, dreading the answer.

'So they can be intimidated,' said Hinksman simply, with a smile.

'I . . . I don't think I can do that.'

'Yes, you can. You've done it before, I know you have. If you do, you'll get a bonus. Two hundred grand – in five-pound notes – paid anywhere in the world. And if you get me off these charges, you'll receive a million dollars, tax free again, anywhere in the world.'

Graham shrugged. 'Well, in that case, I'll get them to you as soon as I've obtained them.'

Henry walked out of court a drained man. Even though the trial had not yet started, he'd been obliged to spend the entire week outside the Shire Hall and would not be allowed to enter again until called in to give his evidence, which could be weeks away.

The wait was always a nerve-racking time. Then, when the trial actually began, you wondered what the witnesses before had said and if you were going to make a fool of them or yourself by contradicting them or not 'sticking to the script'.

His week, therefore, was spent pacing the corridors of the ancient building or putting his feet up in the police room and chatting to the other police witnesses, overdosing on tea or coffee; or simply wandering around Lancaster. He took some heart from seeing that some witnesses were in a worse state than himself – particularly the civilian ones.

He was glad to get out of it for the weekend, and looking forward to spending it with his daughters who were over the moon about him living above a vet's.

An exhausted Karen Wilde arrived home that evening to the sound of her phone ringing. She could clearly hear it as she walked up the garden path, but she did not hurry. It couldn't be work calling, otherwise they would have 'bleeped' her. So it must either be family or a friend, neither of whom she felt like talking to at that moment. It had been a long week – a minimum of ten hours per day – and she was whacked.

Her plan was bath, supper, bed, sleep.

In fact she even slowed her pace to the door and put her key into the lock in slow motion, hoping desperately that whoever it was would give up.

The ringing continued.

'Damn,' she said, entering the house. She picked up the phone and gave a curt, 'Yes?' She recognised the voice on the other end immediately and her stomach did a yo-yo.

'Hi Karen, how are you doing?'

'Karl,' she stuttered.

'So, how are you?'

'Fine, fine,' she said, hurriedly pulling herself together. 'Where are you phoning from? You sound a million miles away.'

'Manchester Airport. I've just touched down from Miami, hell of a flight, and I'm about to get a cab to a hotel nearby. I'm over here for Hinksman's trial – thought I'd see how you were feeling.'

'Fine, yes. I expected to see you sooner.'

'Your prosecution department told me not to come until the second week.'

'It's not even started properly yet,' said Karen. Her mind was racing. She made an instant decision, one she knew she might regret. 'Look, Karl,' she commenced hesitantly, 'I know you're tired, but can you stay awake long enough for me to come and pick you up? We could have a meal together perhaps, maybe talk, you know?'

'Yeah, well, sure,' he said, taken aback.

'I'll be about an hour and a half, OK? I've only arrived home this minute myself.'

'Yeah but—'

'Don't ask, Karl. Just wait for me. I'll be at the International Arrivals meeting point in ninety minutes – OK?'

'Why surely, ma'am.'

'And do you know something, Karl? I've been dying to hear you call me ma'am for ages.'

She hung up and raced to her bedroom to get changed.

At the other end of the phone Karl hung up slowly, the bewilderment on his face fading slowly to a broad grin. It was all he could do to stop himself leaping into the air and shouting, 'Yee-hah!'

* * *

'So how's the crusade against Mr Corelli going?' Karen asked in the stilted manner which had been a feature of their conversation so far.

They were sitting at a table in the dining room of Donaldson's hotel and had reached the coffee stage without either of them having eaten or drunk very much at all.

Donaldson sighed. 'Not well. He's a very devious son of a bitch. He knows all the tricks in the book – the best one being to kill off any potential witnesses against him. Works like a dream. We're fairly sure he's dealing with Lenny Dakin over here and that it's a good profitable business. But the where, when and how of it constantly eludes us.' He shrugged.

'How's your partner's partner? I heard about the letter bomb.'

Donaldson looked into his coffee. 'To be honest, Chrissy's face is all messed up – one half of it, anyway. And the upper part of her body . . . It's heartbreaking, especially for Joe. He loves her.'

'No nearer catching the offender?'

Donaldson shook his head. 'Naw, but we're sure it's down to Corelli – a warning to us, you know? Joe's been working his tail off ever since, but he's getting nowhere. It's very sad. Every waking moment is spent either dedicated to bringing Corelli down or getting Chrissy back together. He's a very driven man at the moment. His whole personality has changed. It's like working with a demon. He'll crack if he doesn't ease up, have a breakdown.'

'Oh, talking of which, Henry Christie's been at court all week. I've seen him a couple of times, but we don't talk. I treated him quite badly.'

'He's not one to bear grudges. I'm looking forward to meeting up with him again.' Donaldson paused, then asked, 'Why did you say, "Talking about which"?'

She explained Henry's difficult last six months, most of which she'd heard second- or third-hand.

'Yeah?' said Donaldson, head tilting back as he considered the story. 'I can see that. He was under strain. He was on the edge.'

'Weren't we all?' commented Karen.

'Yes, we were.'

They eyed each other for a second, then Karen dropped her gaze and stared at her fingers.

'I tried to see you before I went back to America,' he said.

She nodded numbly and swallowed.

'I also telephoned you dozens of times from the States, left messages on your machine. You never returned them. Nor did you reply to my letters.' He was accusing her, but gently, without pressure.

She sat there blinking rapidly.

'Did you hear what I said when you ran into the elevator that night? I shouted it loud enough.'

'I heard,' she admitted, 'and whether you want to believe it or not, that's what kept me going. That thought. Those words.'

'So why did you run away from me?'

'The girl in the room.' Karen took a deep breath, found it difficult to go on.

'Look, I just needed someone and she was available. I know it sounds cruel, but she fulfilled a need there and then. A one-night stand, if you like. I was beginning to react badly to Ken's death. I needed some sort of release, someone to cling to, I suppose. She meant nothing to me. I meant nothing to her.'

'I'm sorry,' said Karen softly. 'That night's gone now. I can't change it, nor can you. I was very upset and confused and finding you with her made it worse. You see, I needed someone to cling to as well.'

'And I wasn't there for you,' said Donaldson, regret in his voice.

'But what you said gave me strength. I knew I'd be seeing you again, maybe to straighten things out between us. Anyway, maybe I'm being presumptuous. Maybe there's someone else in your life by now. If that's the case, I could handle it.'

'There's no one else. There's been nothing for six months . . . except the thought of you.'

'So do those words still apply?' Karen looked at him. Her eyes were shimmering and lovely. His breath was taken away by her beauty which seemed to overpower him.

'Y-yes, they do,' he said, stumbling over his words.

'Then say them again. I need to hear them – but this time say them loud enough for only me to hear, not a whole hotel.'

'I love you.'

'Now say it louder.'

'*I love you.*'

'Louder!'

'I LOVE YOU, MA'AM!'

Everyone in the dining room stopped what they were doing and stared at this crazy couple who'd burst out into a fit of giggles.

When their laughter was under control and everyone had returned to their own business, Karen said simply, 'I love you too, Karl.'

Dave August, dressed in civvies rather than uniform, strolled down from his office at Force Headquarters into the large garage at the rear of the building. His official car was waiting for him – a Jaguar. He dismissed the driver and slid in behind the wheel. This was not unusual for August who had made it one of his quirks that he liked to do his own driving whenever possible. And anyway, as his intended use of the car that day was completely unofficial he didn't want any witnesses; a previous Chief had lost his job for misusing police transport, amongst other things.

He clicked it into Drive and purred elegantly out of the garage doors, a broad smile on his face.

His last six months in the office of Chief Constable had been very smooth indeed, far smoother than he could have anticipated, particularly after that drunken night with Karen.

But nothing untoward had come of it.

Initially he had panicked, thinking that if she'd decided to make an allegation of any sort, he would be finished. If nothing else it would have exposed their affair and he would have had to resign. He braced himself for a few days but nothing happened. He quickly swept her discipline problems under the table and transferred her to the north of the county, out of the way. That combination of factors had obviously been enough to pacify her. After all, he'd mused, she might have thought she'd been raped. You never could tell with women. They were so touchy. So unpredictable. He'd been sleeping with her for months, after all. It was just a drunken fuck, one that got out of hand. So he'd slapped her a bit too. Well-entitled, he'd reassured himself.

If she'd chosen to squeal about it, he could have been in trouble though. But there was nothing. Not a word. Just a longish period off sick for her. Now he was sure the whole thing was dead and buried. She was back at work in Lancaster and doing pretty well, by all accounts. Good luck to her. He held no malice against her. And the time had long gone for her to make any complaints.

So he was safe. He was flying high again.

The Jaguar rolled into Preston town centre and pulled outside the Crest Hotel. Dave August leapt out of the car and trotted into the foyer.

She was there, waiting for him. As soon as she saw him, she stood up. 'David,' she said, crossing over to him. She kissed him lightly on the cheek and smiled prettily.

'Janine, you look lovely,' he enthused.

'Thank you,' she said shyly, colouring up.

'Shall we go?' He had bought expensive ringside seats for a boxing match in Manchester as his new girlfriend was a fan of the sport. She said it made her feel excited . . .

He beamed and crooked his left arm. She slid hers through it and they walked out of the hotel, side by side.

'A Jag! This is exciting.'

August gallantly opened the passenger door for her.

'You are a real gentleman,' she said. 'I need to kiss you.'

She flung her arms around his neck and kissed him squarely on the lips, holding him slightly longer than necessary. Then she slinked into the car, her skirt riding up, leaving the Chief Constable in no doubt that she was wearing no underwear.

Karen and Donaldson rode in silence up to his floor, holding hands nervously, hardly daring to catch each other's eye. He fumbled for his room key in his pocket as they walked slowly down the corridor.

He put the key in the lock.

Before turning it, he stopped and said, 'You don't have to do this, Karen. I don't want to rush you. I can wait for as long as it takes.'

For an answer, her arms slid around his neck. Their mouths touched. Hesitantly at first. Then her hips moved against his groin seductively. He felt himself grow to bursting. She felt hot and pulsating inside.

Then she pulled away, gasping slightly.

He unlocked the door.

After the boxing, August and Janine were invited to what was described as a 'little get-together' at a private house in Wilmslow. It was a big house, one of those neo-Georgian affairs with a well-laid driveway with an entrance and an exit. Out in front of the house was a row of classy cars; the Jaguar slotted in perfectly with them.

August and Janine then walked arm in arm up to the front door, which was open. The sound of disco music wafted to their ears from the back of the house.

'Is this where I meet all those police-loving businessmen you promised?'

'I'll do my best,' she said. 'It's a pretty big charity do. Anyone who's anyone'll be here and they'll have paid

234

handsomely. There'll be councillors, sportsmen, business-men . . . all in a good cause.'

'And why haven't I paid to attend?'

'Because I know the organiser,' she said mysteriously.

As they entered the house a photographer snapped away.

Inside it was a mass of people, shoulder to shoulder. The music was loud, but it was a good beat. There were clouds of cigarette smoke and the unmistakable tang of cannabis.

August's eyes went from face to face. Many of them had been at the boxing. He half recognised a couple of footballers and an MP whose name he couldn't recall.

Janine led him out through the throng to a large patio at the rear, which doubled as a dance floor. Beyond the patio was a large swimming pool; beyond that was a marquee which seemed to be the focus of food and drink.

A waiter bearing a tray thrust a glass in August's hand; another held a tray full of sandwiches, pies and sausage rolls under his nose until he made a selection.

He drank the wine in one. It was immediately replaced.

'Now, darling,' Janine said, 'I promised to introduce you to some people. I won't be long.'

She left him open-mouthed by the pool and hurried back into the house, where Lenny Dakin was waiting for her.

The businessmen spent an hour with August. One said he had the largest Volkswagen dealership this side of Birmingham and was interested in sponsoring vehicles for the special constabulary. The other said he owned a firm specialising in industrial, commercial and domestic sec-urity. He wanted to sponsor neighbourhood watch schemes by providing cut price security items, even free ones to pensioners.

August was hooked. The ease of it amazed him. Getting money out of the private sector was usually like getting blood out of a stone. But this! Pure gold.

Both men promised they would contact him the following week.

Business concluded, the two out of work actors left him beaming with pleasure into his beer. They collected their fee – £100 each – were told to forget this night ever happened, and left the party. Neither one had any idea why the charade had been carried out. Some sort of practical joke, they assumed.

Janine rejoined August who was sitting at a table by the pool.

He shook his head in admiration. 'I've got to hand it to you. You are brilliant. And sexy. And intelligent. It was a freak of Fate, us meeting like that and hitting it off so well, wasn't it?' He was referring to their first encounter two weeks before during a flutter he and a couple of friends were having at a casino in Blackpool.

'Mm,' she agreed. 'It was a freak.'

'Why did you agree to have dinner with me so readily?' he enquired. 'You didn't even know who I was.'

'Yes, I did, actually. I've seen you on TV many times. I wasn't going to miss the chance to get to know you. You're an interesting guy, to say the least.'

Janine hoped she sounded convincing. The effects of the cocaine Dakin had allowed her were wearing off now and she needed another snort.

Bastard, she thought. I'll be glad when all this is over.

'Anyway,' she said, raising her eyes to his again, 'now that I've kept my promise, I want you to make one to me.'

'Anything.'

'That you'll let me fuck your brains out.'

August nearly came there and then. 'Here?' he croaked.

'My place. I have a house nearby.'

'I didn't know that.'

'There's a lot you don't know about me, Davey darling.'

'In that case, I promise.'

'That was lovely,' Karen said softly.

'Yes, it was.' Donaldson was tired and dreamy.

They were lying facing each other, holding hands, a single sheet draped over their bodies.

'I was frightened that it would never happen,' she confessed. 'I was terrified that I wouldn't want a man to touch me again after what I went through.'

Donaldson rested a leg across hers. He kissed her neck.

'I'll help you every step of the way, if you want me to,' he promised tenderly.

'Yes, I do. I want you in my life all the time, for everything, not just that.'

'Sounds fine by me.'

'But I want to ask you something . . . do you think I should prosecute Dave for what he did to me, or just let it lie?'

'Er, how could you do it now?' asked Donaldson. He propped himself up on one elbow. 'It would be your word against his, wouldn't it? Pretty damned difficult to get a conviction, especially after six months.'

Karen took a deep breath. 'Just after it happened I was in deep shock and I didn't really know what to do about it. I went away for a month to Greece – Skiathos, but before I did I went to a rape crisis centre in Manchester. They were very kind to me. It's a fantastic place, in its own way. I had a few days' counselling there and made a statement while it was all fresh in my mind. And I saw a doctor too.'

'So?' Donaldson was puzzled.

'A specially trained doctor who specialises in sexual assault cases. She took photos of my injuries, made her own notes and took samples, swabs for evidence – and kept them all. It's the sort of place where they understand that the victim isn't always completely together mentally and may not be in a position to press charges. So they take the samples and store them at the correct temperatures, just in case the victim wants to pursue it at a later date.'

'You mean all the forensic evidence is still there, intact?'

She nodded.

'Well I'll be damned!' he exclaimed. 'That's handy.'

'I feel I may want to press charges, but I'm still not sure. I'm still in two minds about it.' Tears stood in her eyes.

'Hey, calm down, don't upset yourself.' He stroked her hair.

'Sorry. I need to discuss it with you, but not now, not here – I've a lot of love-making to catch up on – but soon. Do you mind? I'll understand if you don't want to get involved.'

'I want to get involved all right,' he said, 'physically *and* mentally, OK?'

She slipped a hand around the back of his neck and eased him towards her. 'I love you,' she said. They began to kiss.

Dave August stirred and rubbed his eyes. He looked at his watch. Six-thirty in the morning. He pushed the sheet back and swung his legs out of bed. Then he realised where he was. Janine's house, somewhere south of Manchester. A smile spread across his face as he glanced round at the sleeping female next to him in the large bed.

Carefully he pulled the sheet off her and looked at her bare flesh with a tinge of pleasure.

He felt himself move again.

But no. He had to leave.

Janine stirred and moved over the bed to rub her bare breasts against his naked back.

'I need to be going,' he said reluctantly. 'You said you'd give me directions to the motorway. I don't know this area at all!'

'Later,' she murmured, and gently slid her hand around to grip his twitching penis, taking it firmly in her palm. She squeezed it, began to manipulate it. It expanded rapidly.

August placed a hand on one of her breasts.

As soon as August and Janine left the house some twenty minutes later, a removal van pulled up outside. Six men descended on the property. In less than an hour every piece of furniture and every fitting had been removed and placed in the back of the van. A 'For Sale' sign was erected in the front garden and the van, men on board, drove away.

The house was back on the market, being sold by a small chain of estate agents, ultimately owned by one man.

Lenny Dakin.

Chapter Nineteen

'Daddy, I know I like it 'n' everything, but why are you living over a vet's?'

'Don't ask stupid questions, Leanne,' her older sister Jenny admonished her. 'Mummy and Daddy have split up because Daddy's become a drunk and an adulterer, and you need to live somewhere, don't you, Daddy?'

'Yes, dear, I suppose that sums it up,' said Henry, restraining himself from a smile despite the accusations.

'Well, I know all that,' Leanne said dismissively. She was sitting in the back seat of the Metro with a couple of dolls in her lap, and they were all en route to the Lake District. 'But why over a vet's?'

'Because it's cheap and interesting,' he said.

'When you get divorced,' began Leanne, about to pose one of those dreaded questions, 'will you marry the vet? She seems like a nice lady. I'd like her to be my second mum. I could have all sorts of pets to mend, couldn't I?'

'Whoa, hold your horses,' said Henry. 'Your mum and me aren't divorced yet. We might be getting back together.'

'Mum said that hell would have to freeze over first.' Jenny grinned at her father. 'But she was in a real bad mood when she said that.'

'Oh really?' said Henry. He felt his guts twist.

'And not only that,' interrupted Leanne again, 'why are you driving this crappy car?'

Henry burst out laughing.

★ ★ ★

Henry had rented a log cabin owned by one of his work-mates, situated high and lonely in the hills above Hawks-head in an idyllic position. He'd been there on many previous occasions with his complete family and the girls particularly enjoyed it.

The single-track path leading to it was long and arduous. The Metro struggled valiantly over the bumps and up the incline and made it more or less intact. They unpacked quickly – they were only staying the night and had a minimal amount of gear – and Henry assembled his fishing tackle.

'Right – you two be OK for a couple of hours while I go up to the tarn to fish?'

'Yeah,' they said in unison.

'Good. I'll be back by four at the latest. Then we'll go over to Windermere on the ferry for tea. Tomorrow we'll have a look at Beatrix Potter's place. OK?'

'Yeah,' they said. 'Excellent.'

'Good.'

'Tight flies, Daddy,' chirped Leanne. 'Don't be long.'

With a grin on his face at her child-like mistake, he hunched his equipment onto his back and over his shoulders and headed towards the trees, breathing deeply of the cool, pine-laden air. He felt as if this was the first day of the rest of his life. He'd felt the same way on many other occasions over the last few months though – and most had turned to rat-shit, so he wasn't foolish enough to totally believe it; yet somehow today *did* feel different.

He'd made a start by deciding to cut out two things that seemed to cloud his life at the moment – alcohol and women.

He was determined to woo Kate again and get back to a normal happy existence. The bachelor life didn't do much for him, he had to admit. He longed for the warmth of family life; being with the kids made him miss it even more.

But how to get back into Kate's good books?

That would take some doing.

Betrayal couldn't easily be forgotten.

And he knew things could never be as they had been in the past; it was the future that interested him.

Once into the trees, coolness and darkness reigned. The pine tang in the air became almost overwhelming, like a drug. The ground was firmly soft to walk on and he dawdled along, halting occasionally as he spotted some bird or beast. He broke back into open sunlight soon after and pushed on upwards.

He felt glad to be alive.

He'd made a few important decisions and things could be rosy again if he played it right. Once the trial was out of the way, the road ahead would be clear, he hoped.

After twenty minutes' fairly hard walking, getting up a good sweat, the tarn appeared below him. He trod cautiously down a scree and approached the water, breathing heavily.

A few minutes later he was on the banks.

Looking across the surface of the water he thought, I bet no one's fished here in an age, and his heart bumped when he saw the 'blimp' of a trout feeding on the surface only ten metres out, then another further away. Out loud he said, 'You little beauties won't be expecting me, will ya?'

He laughed and the echo of it danced across the water.

An hour and two undersized fish later, he'd drawn his fly line in and was making a couple of false casts when, as he brought the rod up to 90 degrees with the line running out behind him, ready for that final forward cast, the rod snapped in two and collapsed around his ears. There followed an echoing *crrack-ack-ack* in the air from over the tarn.

Just as Henry realised what was going on, the water at his feet exploded violently.

He threw down his tackle and ran, scrambling wildly towards the trees.

Somebody was shooting at him.

He dived full-length onto the ground just as a bullet slammed into a nearby tree. Splinters flew.

Henry's thoughts whizzed around his head like a silver ball skittering around a pinball machine. If it wasn't a lucky shot that had broken his rod, his assailant was a fantastic shooter and could easily have taken him there and then – he could have taken his whole fucking head off. Unless he was playing with him . . . wanting Henry to know he was going to die. My rod! Henry thought savagely. The bastard. My lovely rod. He's destroyed it!

Anger roared into him, replacing the fear. It was like the devil taking over a human soul.

This was the Mafia way with witnesses. Terrify them, or kill them. He remembered Hinksman's silent threat on the first day of the trial. Now it was coming true.

That bastard won't beat me, Henry thought. If it's the last thing I do, I'll see him rot in jail. Or preferably get fried in the States.

He made a decision: he was going to win this afternoon, no matter what the cost. And winning, at that moment, meant taking the man with the gun.

Carefully he turned round, crab-like, 180 degrees, keeping low. Having done this without mishap he drew his right leg up, placed his foot on a root, making sure he had good leverage for propulsion. He took a deep breath.

He was ready.

He shoved himself up and ran, zig-zagging, head down like a rugby player going for the line.

The shooter let loose. The air around Henry's body exploded with the *crack!* and *whizzbang!* of the bullets.

He sprinted on. He felt like it was lasting for ever, that he was in some weird sort of time-warp.

He was nearly there, keeping his eyes riveted on the place where he wanted to be, throwing himself the last couple of metres. The gunman kept firing remorselessly. It was while Henry was airborne that a searing hot pain shot up his back.

Oh fuck – he'd been hit.

He landed awkwardly, twisting his left wrist, then life

went blank . . . The bullets stopped. Their echoes ricocheted around the tarn and drifted away to nothingness, like spirits leaving the world. Silence descended. All birdsong had ceased.

It's hard enough for a person to get a hand up their own back at the best of times. For Henry, lying on his front, pinned down by a sniper, with a painful wrist and a sore head from his blundering fall, and a bullet wound in the back, it was near sodding impossible.

He probed bravely around to find the wound; it seemed to be a deep groove, about four inches long, in the muscle below his left shoulderblade. Though there was extreme pain he had no trouble shifting about.

He thought, it hasn't gone in! It's nicked me and stings like buggery, but it hasn't gone in. He laughed in relief. 'Thank fuck for that,' he breathed happily.

Sweat dripped into his eyes. He brushed it out with a blood-soaked hand, making it worse. Nearby was a large clump of fern leaves. He ripped them out of the ground and wiped his face and hands with them.

A burst of fire clattered dangerously over his head, only a matter of inches above.

He tried to think clearly, logically. He was still in danger, but he was here, in a better position strategically, and the odds had evened up slightly, even if the man with the gun still remained the clear favourite.

He snaked further into the trees. When he thought he was completely safe he raised himself to his haunches and started to make some progress around the tarn. Anger kept him going. Nobody takes pot-shots at me and gets away with it, he thought viciously.

A good twenty minutes later with half a mile's rough travelling through trees behind him, he was within metres of where he believed the gunman had been laid out. He peered through the foliage. Saw nothing.

Taking out his Swiss Army knife, he unfolded the longest blade with shaking hands. Now he was hunting for real, not for sport, and another man was the target. Mild-mannered Henry Christie had become a predator.

He tested the sharpness of the blade with a finger. Satisfied, he edged forwards on all fours, an inch at a time, dead slow.

It had all been in vain. The would-be assassin had gone.

Henry stood up and walked over to where the man had been lying down, the grass flattened by his weight. He'd even left his gun there.

Henry picked it up. 'Jesus,' he whistled, 'a fucking Kalashnikov.'

As he studied the gun, a twig cracked behind him.

He cursed, dropped the gun – it was no use without a magazine in it – and spun round wielding his pathetic knife.

Too slow.

The man charged into Henry from the undergrowth like a rhino from a thicket, bowling him backwards. The knife went flying from his grasp. Suddenly high foliage and sky swept past Henry's eyes and he found himself on his back, face up, with an immense guy on top of him, the man who'd tried to shoot him.

The man's head reared back and then rocketed towards the bridge of Henry's nose. In that instant Henry saw he had wild, demented eyes and a twisted smile on his face.

Henry flicked his head to one side and held the man back as best he could with one hand.

The head-butt deflected into the edge of Henry's right eye-socket. At least he hadn't got a broken nose.

Once more the man reared back.

Henry smacked him hard in the mouth with his right fist, but he was only stunned for an instant. He got a grip of Henry's arms, straddled all seventeen or eighteen stones of himself across Henry's chest, and almost tenderly placed one arm at a time under each of his knees.

Henry was like a butterfly pinned to a board.

'I'm going to kill you,' the man informed Henry.

Henry believed him.

One of his hands went to Henry's throat, and his fingers closed unhurriedly on the windpipe. Slowly, but surely, Henry was being throttled by a man who was enjoying his work.

He gasped, gurgled, struggled for air. His vision misted over. Blackout, followed by death, wasn't far away.

It was amazing what such a realisation could do to a person.

Everything that Henry had left went into what he did next.

He smashed his right knee up into the man's backside.

He'd wanted to connect with his privates, but that would have been physically impossible. However, the effect was just as good. The impact sent him shooting over Henry in a messy forward roll.

As the hands came off his windpipe, air whooshed down. Henry scrambled to his feet as quickly as possible. He staggered weakly and turned to his attacker, who was up on his knees already. Henry lurched towards him and executed a double-fisted swipe across his face that sent him sprawling again.

Blood flowed from the man's mouth, coupled with spittle and a tooth. He shook his head and looked meanly at Henry who stood over him. Then, suddenly, he dived for Henry's ankles – and nearly had them. Henry managed to step smartly backwards and all the man managed to do was grab thin air.

So Henry kicked him in the side of the head as hard as he possibly could.

Twice.

Henry was going to end it now. He had to.

While the man crouched on the ground, recovering, Henry picked up a large, oval-shaped rock. Lifting it high in both hands, he brought it down with all of his fading strength on the crown of his assailant's head. There was a horrible splintering noise and the big man was felled like an ox. He was probably as good as dead, but Henry wanted to make sure.

He hit him again with the rock. Then he found he couldn't stop himself. He continued to hit him. There was no point to it, but he couldn't hold himself back. He kept hitting and hitting until he collapsed next to him, exhausted.

It began to rain lightly.

A lifetime later, soaked to the skin, Henry staggered through the trees, and up the path. The cabin was ahead of him, nestling innocently in the trees, the Metro parked in front.

He stopped in his tracks, fearing the worst. *Suppose the killer had visited the cabin on the way?*

He ran to the door and burst in.

The girls were sat in front of the electric fire, contentedly playing draughts. They looked up, their beautiful faces suddenly transformed with looks of horror at what they saw.

A man. Dirty. Bloody. Wet. Bedraggled. Not their father.

Leanne screamed.

'Jenny,' said Henry. His voice came straight from the hell where he'd been.

Her mouth fell open.

Dizziness overcame him. He teetered. His limbs weren't working; they were suddenly jelly and couldn't hold him up.

He pitched headlong onto the floor of the cabin.

Henry surfaced several hours later. He had vague recollections of flashing blue lights, two-tone horns and a sensation of speed, but nothing more. When his eyes focused they saw a nurse in uniform and a tube sticking out of his arm.

He tried to speak, but the words wouldn't leave his voice box. His throat was very badly swollen and sore.

The nurse smiled. 'Carlisle Infirmary, Casualty Department,' she said brightly, reading his mind. 'Your children are in the waiting room with your wife and they're fine, so don't worry. I'll get a doctor now and once he's seen you he can decide whether or not you're fit for visitors, OK?'

Henry nodded. Well, that was everything taken care of, he thought. Nurses just seem to know everything.

When Kate and the children came in to see him, it was clear they'd all been crying. His wife was dabbing at her eyes and the end of her nose looked red-raw from snuffling. Henry wanted to grab her and hug her. He knew, however, that she would not allow it.

'You look a bit better now, Dad,' said Jenny, eyeing him critically. She managed a weak smile.

He laid his good hand on her head. 'Thanks to you, that is,' he said. He went on slightly falteringly, 'Well done for getting me to hospital, love. I owe you one.'

'No, you don't. I love you,' she said heartbreakingly.

He'd been told of Jenny's cool head and quick reactions. She had covered him with a blanket, given Leanne strict instructions to stay with him and she'd run over two miles to the nearest public phone box and called an ambulance. She had then run back to the cabin where a petrified Leanne held her father's head on her lap whilst pressing a towel onto the wound in his back. She had been sobbing and was covered in blood.

Henry looked at Leanne. 'And you, pet – thanks for looking after me.'

'It was nothing,' she said bravely, her lips quivering with remembered fear.

'That'll do,' said their mother stiffly. 'Now you two give your Dad a hug and a kiss and go and wait for me in the Matron's office.'

They reluctantly obeyed.

Kate perched herself on the edge of the bed, near Henry's feet and they regarded each other for a while in silence.

'You'll have to come nearer if you want a conversation,' said Henry. 'I can't talk very loud.'

She sighed and moved closer, not allowing him to touch her when he reached out to do so. He accepted the rebuff without comment.

'Two pretty amazing kids,' he said.

'Yes, they are . . . Look, Henry, what's going on? What have you got yourself into? The doctor told me he's called the local police in to see you, at your request, because you'd been shot. You must tell me what's happening!' She was afraid and confused.

'It's tied in with the Hinksman trial, I think,' he said painfully. 'Silencing witnesses – intimidation. But I doubt I'll ever be able to prove there's a link.'

'Oh Christ! So what happened today?'

Slowly, Henry told her everything.

'You think you killed him, then?' she asked when he'd finished. She put her hands to her face. 'You killed a man! I don't believe this.'

'It was in self-defence,' he croaked. 'I didn't have a choice in the matter. It was him, or me. I made sure it was him.'

'And are we in danger, I mean me and the girls?'

'I don't know,' he said truthfully. 'Probably it's only me they want. I'm the man who can do the damage.'

'So what shall we do?'

'Carry on as before, but keep a close watch on them. Tighten up security at home . . . I don't really know, Kate. I just don't know. I wish I did.'

'What's going to happen to you now?'

'I'll speak to the local cops and tell them what's happened. Hopefully they'll believe me, won't be daft enough to charge me with murder. The evidence should support my story. I'll have to see how it goes.'

'How will you get home? You can't drive with your wrist all plastered up.'

'Dunno. I'll find a way. Taxi. Bus. Train. Plane. Walk?'

'I'll come up for you.'

'You don't have to.'

She heaved a weary, full-bodied sigh and looked away.

After a pause, he said, 'What about us, Kate? Is it really over?'

'I don't know,' she said heavily. 'You betrayed me. You were unfaithful.'

'I'm sorry. I've said it a million times and I'll say it a million more times, if that's what it takes. I love you and I want to get our lives back on track. I let you down badly. I hurt you. I hurt the kids. I know all that. Don't you think I've suffered, too? I'm mixed up to hell about it all . . . but I know where I truly belong. I miss you like hell . . . I want to touch you, kiss you, hold you, reassure you, make love to you, court you, live my life with you, die for you . . . hmph! Talk about dying. You know what the worst part is, eh? Thinking you won't be there when I die . . .'

'Henry, don't—' She was sobbing again.

'Mr Christie?'

Henry looked up beyond Kate's shoulder. Two men had appeared at the foot of the bed. Well-dressed. Nice suits. Clean shaven. Short hair. Henry pinned them as detectives immediately. He smiled.

'Yes. Hello, fellas.'

They did not smile. 'DI Fletcher, this is DC Tumin. Carlisle CID.' They flashed their warrant cards.

Henry nodded, wary now.

'I'm arresting you on suspicion of murder. I'm not gonna bore you by reciting that new caution, mainly because I can't remember it. You know you don't have to say owt, but if you do it may be given in evidence – and if you don't say owt, then it'll do any defence you might have no good. Understand?'

Chapter Twenty

The trial at Lancaster Castle, due to begin properly the following Monday morning, came to a standstill quite quickly, much to the smiling pleasure of Hinksman who was led back down to the holding cell.

Several members of the jury had complained to an usher – who'd passed the complaints on to the court clerk – that strange things had been happening to them over the weekend. Two had windows broken at their homes by unidentified persons, two received unusual phone calls and three had tyres slashed on their cars. Taken separately, each incident amounted to nothing more than a minor annoyance; taken together, they were more than a coincidence. It was very sinister and unsettling. The jury was being got at.

In the chambers, the Judge saw FB. He promised to look into the matter and told her that he would arrange for each juror – if they so wished – to be escorted home by police each evening and back to court next morning for the duration of the trial. He also said he would provide each of their homes with an alarm linked to the police radio system. Such an alarm, once activated, would immediately alert every police officer on that frequency who could respond without delay. The cost would be excessive, but would have to be borne. Better safe than sorry.

FB also told her what had happened to Henry Christie that weekend.

She listened, appalled.

The trial did not begin until 2.30 p.m.

And Henry Christie was sat in court.

He looked a mess. The eye-socket which had been head-butted stuck out as big and red as a cricket ball and his throat was a swollen mess of dirty purple bruises. His left wrist was in plaster, and held across his chest in a sling.

He waited for Hinksman to be brought up from the holding cell.

Only then did he leave the court as he was required to do.

Only when he had made eye-contact with Hinksman.

Only when he had made it quite clear that he would not be beaten.

Everybody's eyes were on him as he hobbled out of court.

The Judge covered a grin and called for proceedings to begin.

Outside the court, Henry made his way to the police room where Donaldson was waiting, together with Karen.

He sat down and gratefully accepted the proffered cup of tea.

'Now then, Henry, you old son of a gun, bring me up to date,' requested Donaldson.

Henry took a sip of the tea, leaned back and told them his story.

Two uniformed Constables had guarded Henry on Saturday night through to Sunday morning – just in case he decided to run away. Henry, pumped full of blissful drugs, slept like a baby in a dark, dreamless void. He awoke refreshed the following morning, when he was discharged from hospital and taken into police custody.

He didn't blame them for arresting him. He would have done the same. Someone had died a violent death; explanations were needed.

It didn't stop it being an unpleasant experience. He was treated well and courteously, but there was no quarter given just because he was a fellow cop. He was grilled by experienced detectives whose techniques were very, very good. Henry could have played games with them, but he didn't.

He was open and honest and admitted what he'd done. He argued self-defence and everything pointed to his story being right.

The presence of FB in the background helped, too. He came to assist as soon as he heard.

At the end of the day after nine hours in custody, several of those hours being spent brooding in a cell, Henry was released without charge but warned that a report would be submitted to the Crown Prosecution Service for advice. Informally he was told by a Detective Chief Inspector that the 'job was going nowhere' – police terminology meaning that he would not be prosecuted. In his heart of hearts Henry knew that this would be the case, but it was a relief to hear it anyway.

True to her word, Kate came for him and drove him back to his flat above the vet's, despite his insinuations that he would be better cared for in the marital home. She was having none of it.

Alone in his flat, with the barking of a dog recovering from a hernia operation downstairs for company, he toyed with a bottle of Scotch. In the end he binned it in favour of some analgesic tablets, a hot drink of milk and bed.

He slept better than he would have thought possible.

There was nothing particularly eventful about Dave August's return to work that Monday morning. He'd spent a dull weekend with his family, and was glad to get into the office, which he did at 7.30 a.m.

At 10 a.m. he had his usual briefing from the ACC who'd been on duty over the weekend. There was little to bring to August's attention, other than to update him regarding Henry Christie and request protection for the jury in the Hinksman trial. It was clear that they were being nobbled.

'That's all we need!' exclaimed August. 'What about protecting the witnesses, too?'

'That's in hand, I understand.'

'I'd be tempted to give Christie authority to carry a gun

home with him under the circumstances. He may need it . . . it's something I'll have to consider.'

'Could be a good idea.'

'Hm. Anything else? No? OK, thanks for that.'

The ACC collected his reports and left the office. August checked his appointments for the day ahead. He was quite busy. He sighed and his mind turned to Janine. They'd made no firm plans for the week ahead, but she'd said to call her whenever he felt like it. She was working in Cumbria all of this week, and when she'd dropped him off at headquarters on Saturday morning, she'd given him her mobile phone number.

He wanted her there and then. He could imagine it – her bent forwards, holding onto the edge of the desk, him thrusting into her, both of them crying out with the pleasure of it all . . .

What a night they'd had. Pure carnal pleasure which had been increased by his introduction to cocaine. At first he'd resisted, but when he'd seen the effects on her, and been reassured that it wasn't addictive, he'd given it a try.

It had been fabulous.

He dialled her number, but it came back unobtainable. Strange, he thought, but decided to try again later.

The sight of all that paperwork in his in-tray depressed him. He scooped it up and laid it in front of him on the desk.

A couple of reports merely required his signature. The next piece of correspondence was a large, A4-sized Jiffy envelope, addressed to him personally. It had arrived via the external mail, post-marked *South Lakes*. He lifted it up, interested. It was fairly heavy.

He peeled the envelope open and shook the contents out. There was a video-tape, VHS, TDK make, with a label on it that said boldly COPY, plus a series of photographs which had been taken over the weekend, of him and Janine kissing and embracing in public.

August suddenly felt very queasy. Typewritten on the

sheet of paper which accompanied the video were the words, *This is a very edited version of events. Hope you find them interesting. Will contact you in due course. NB – this tape is a copy. It is for your eyes only.*

August stood up and crossed to the TV and video-player in the corner of his office. He inserted the cassette and waited apprehensively for the picture to appear.

Initially the screen was a lined grey haze.

Then an image came on. Very sharp. Very clear. Very professional.

A man and a woman. Naked. Kneeling, face to face. The woman was working his erect penis with deft fingers. The man moaned: the video had a soundtrack. His face was screwed up tight in the agony of sexual ecstasy. He came, ejaculating across the woman's lower belly. The sperm dribbled down to her pubic hair. The man sagged exhaustedly and the couple embraced. He laid his head on her shoulder and turned his face towards the camera. The screen faded to blackness. The whole thing was less than ninety seconds long.

The face of the woman had been erased from the video.

But the face of the man was very clear and identifiable.

The screen flickered back to life after a pause. This time it showed the same couple kneeling side by side over the bedside cabinet, apparently snorting cocaine.

This was a thirty-second clip. Then it all went black again.

August pressed the rewind button and played the tape once again. He held the last frame of the masturbation sequence for a few seconds and found himself staring helplessly into his own eyes.

He ejected the cassette and strode back to his desk, dazed and confused. He picked up the phone and dialled Janine's number. Unobtainable.

August stood holding the phone to his ear, his eyes gazing out unseeingly across his beloved rugby pitch.

All he could see was his sperm splashing across Janine's stomach – and the end of his career.

* * *

Henry Christie drew his story to a close. Karen and Donaldson had been good listeners.

'So who was the guy?' Donaldson enquired.

'Don't know yet, maybe never will. Fingerprints haven't thrown anyone up, so it's possible he may have no previous convictions.'

'Henry – you did good,' said Donaldson with a smile. He punched Henry on the shoulder.

Henry looked at them. They were grinning from ear to ear, continually exchanging sidelong glances. They were obviously very happy together. Karen's eyes were shining. She was a completely different person from the strung-out individual Henry had encountered all those months ago. The ruthless career woman who gave no quarter had been replaced by a relaxed person with no edge whatsoever.

Henry liked the change. He had never felt comfortable with her until now.

'So what's your news, Karl? What's happening on your side of the water?'

'Aww,' he said dismissively, 'Corelli's still givin' us the runaround and we don't seem any closer to catching him. I'll fill you in later. There's something much more important to tell you.'

'We're engaged to be married,' blurted out Karen. She reached for Donaldson's hand.

'Yep,' said Donaldson. 'You're the first to know.'

Henry was pleased for them. They were two nice people. In fact, he felt a twinge of jealousy. 'That's good news,' he said warmly. 'You're good for each other, but isn't there a slight logistical problem with all this?'

'Well, yeah,' admitted Donaldson. 'We haven't quite worked that one out yet, but we will. As the saying goes, love will find a way.'

After lunch with a visiting ACC from North Wales, Dave August returned to his office trying to believe that the tape was all a practical joke, that Janine would phone and explain it all away.

But once behind closed doors again, dark despair began to creep over him like a shroud of mist. Carefully, he removed the envelope he'd received that morning. Now it was in a clear plastic bag. He unfastened it, shook out the video and the photographs and gazed at them on his desk. They offended his eyes, made him feel sick.

He again slotted the video into the player and watched the action, mesmerised. He worked out where the camera had been situated. Now he saw why it had all been so easy and what a fool he'd made of himself.

'Shit,' he said. 'Sex, drugs and a Chief Constable.'

Presumably there was going to be a blackmail threat somewhere along the line. He would be ruined if the compromising material reached the people who were now considering his application for promotion to the Inspectorate. And what if members of the Lancashire police committee got hold of it? Or the press? August's heart sank. And what about his wife? Or the kids?

Career, marriage, lifestyle – down the tubes.

He had everything to lose.

He began to sweat.

But what do I have to offer a blackmailer? he asked himself.

I'm not rich, so it can't be money.

The only thing I possess is *information* . . .

He thought about it further, but nothing specifically interesting came to mind.

He locked his top drawer when he heard his office door open. In stepped his new staff officer – Chief Inspector Wendy Cornwall, just about the ugliest female in the force – and announced that the discipline hearing was ready to kick off.

'Wheel 'em in,' he said. Some poor bastard of a PC was going to get hell this afternoon.

*　*　*

Henry found himself confronted by one of the most stunning-looking women he had ever met in his life when he left court that afternoon. It was the combination of gorgeous long legs, short skirt, silky blonde hair, upturned cheeky nose, bright eyes and a haughty, confident, no-nonsense look which did it, plus a subtle perfume which assaulted Henry's nostrils like an aphrodisiac.

She had the particularly American way of speaking in short, punchy sentences.

'Hi, I'm Lisa Want. I'm from the Crime Bureau of the *Miami Herald* and I'm covering this here trial for that particular newspaper. I'd just love to do a piece about you, Sergeant Christie. Y'know the sort of thing – hero cop, dig a little into your background, et cetera. The American public just love reading about English cops, especially when they're as good-lookin' as you are . . .'

'Say no,' said Donaldson, who had walked up behind him. 'Don't trust her – Joe Kovaks did and it nearly cost him his job.'

'Now don't you go listening to that bitter an' twisted ole FBI man,' she purred to Henry with a pout. She flashed her eyelashes and he could have sworn he felt the draught. Her eyes moved momentarily to Donaldson and the look in them, just for a nanosecond, was pure hatred. Henry noticed it.

'It's up to you,' said Donaldson, 'but I'd avoid her like the plague, scheming bitch.'

'I'm sorry,' said Henry, and he truly was because the prospect of spending time with her was very appealing, 'but I tend not to have a very good relationship with the media anyway.' He shrugged sadly, and he and Donaldson walked out of the court.

Lisa clenched her teeth and stamped a foot on the floor, muttering, 'Karl Donaldson, you are a first-class cunt.'

Over in Dave August's office, the discipline hearing was drawing to a close. The officer concerned had lost. August fined him heavily for discreditable conduct, severely reprimanded him and transferred him to another station. That would teach him to fuck the cleaner on the snooker table, even if he was now living with her. There was a time and a place for everything.

Forty mintues later August was driving through the streets of south Manchester, desperately trying to locate the house Janine had taken him to that night. But he couldn't even begin to find it, even though he had driven there and back himself.

He pulled into the side of the road and parked, attempting to relive the journey in his mind. It was all a sexual haze – as no doubt it had been intended to be. He'd been driving the Jag, blindly following her directions while she masturbated him; at the same time his left hand was fumbling rather inexpertly with her clitoris. Both had been in moaning ecstasy. It was a miracle they hadn't crashed.

When he'd left the house the morning after it'd been much the same scenario, except he couldn't get a full erection. The journey from the house to central Manchester – where she had asked to be dropped off – had once again been at her direction. And now, only a few days later, he couldn't recall any of it.

His forehead dropped onto the steering wheel.

'You complete and utter idiot,' he snarled at himself.

Janine settled back in the fishing boat and pulled off her long baggy T-shirt. Underneath she was wearing a skimpy bikini top and a pair of faded cut-offs. She reached down for a can of Diet Coke from the coolbox next to her and rolled the ice-cold can across her sweaty forehead. Key West was fast receding as the boat picked up speed on its way out for a morning's fishing.

She was aware of the sidelong looks from the two crew members, both men of Hispanic origin, as they prepared the bait and rods. She was very pale and desirable to them.

The cabin door opened and the attention of the crew

moved solely to their tasks in hand as the boss appeared from below, accompanied – as ever – by his bodyguard.

Corelli was carrying a bottle of champagne and two fluted glasses.

Janine tossed the Coke can overboard and took the glasses from him.

'This is good stuff,' he said. 'The best. Don't want to spill a drop.'

He opened the bottle carefully.

The cork popped off and Janine held out the glasses, which he filled.

He took one and said, 'This is by way of thanks for the part you've played in securing the eventual release of my friend, the plans for which, as you know, are well advanced.'

'It was a pleasure,' she said. They touched glasses and drank. Janine thought it tasted wonderful.

'So I believe,' he murmured, and winked. 'I've seen the video . . .'

They burst out laughing.

Joe Kovaks stood on the quayside watching Corelli's boat which was now nothing more than a speck on the horizon, even through powerful binoculars.

His face was grim as he lowered the glasses from bloodshot eyes.

He felt like he had never laughed in his life.

This was not the Joe Kovaks of old. In the last six months he had aged considerably. He had lost weight and his grey skin hung loosely on his cadaver-like face.

Knowing it would be many hours before Corelli came back, he made his way to Le Te Da where he managed to secure a seat on the front balcony. It was here, in the 1890s, that the Cuban rebel Jose Marti had made speeches to raise money for the Cuban revolution.

Kovaks ordered a light meal, coffee and orange juice.

While waiting, he leaned back in his chair and closed his eyes. He wanted to sleep for ever.

The worry over Chrissy, the sleepless nights, the constant vigils and the ongoing campaign to get Corelli had all taken their toll out of his energy reserves. He'd kept himself going in the circle of home-hospital-work-hospital on a concoction of sweet black coffee and adrenalin.

And what good had it done?'

Chrissy's recuperation had been a painfully slow process in more than one sense.

Although out of hospital now, she frequently returned for further treatment. She was still a mess, despite all the doctors had done. Her burned face and chest were a horrific sight, even to Kovaks, who had grown used to them. She herself wouldn't even look in a mirror. The pain she endured was dreadful and she could only sleep under the influence of drugs.

However, the medical side of it wasn't the only problem.

The mental side was worse.

This once bubbly, confident and delightfully naughty lady was now a shell of fear. She was terrified of going out, of picking up the post, of doing almost anything. She spent most of her waking hours slumped in front of the TV, flitting aimlessly from channel to channel, avoiding the mainstream of life.

Kovaks had been warned it would take a long time. Surely, though, he pondered, there should be some improvement by now?

It was wearing him down; he couldn't deny it. He knew he had to be strong for her, but the strain was telling on him and it was bubbling over into anger.

Because through it all Corelli sailed on. Untouched. Untouchable.

Kovaks knew he was dealing drugs in the UK now with the guy called Dakin. Could he prove it? Could he fuck. Just like he couldn't prove that Corelli was behind the bomb that maimed Chrissy.

Kovaks was tired and frustrated. Corelli was simply telling him to go to hell. And slowly but surely, this is where Kovaks was headed.

Even the Bureau had whittled down the operation on Corelli. The team now consisted solely of him and Donaldson, Sue having been transferred to other duties.

The waiter brought his meal.

He opened his eyes.

Something would have to be done; it was a desperate situation all round, requiring a desperate solution.

It was about time to administer some justice.

Agent Ritter was also planning his own desperate solution.

Having made the decision to kill Sue, he had now decided where the demise would take place. So many unfortunate accidents happen in the home, he thought.

There were only two more questions to be asked.

When would it happen?

How would she die?

Soon, he thought, in answer to the first one.

In great pain, was his answer to the next.

Chapter Twenty-One

At the end of the third week, the trial seemed to have gone fairly smoothly for the Crown. The witnesses had all been good and believable and had kept to their stories, even under severe provocation and pressure from Mr Graham, QC for the defence, who was performing at his peak.

Donaldson had been up to give his evidence. It had been a harrowing experience for him to relive the death of Ken McClure, particularly when Graham questioned everything down to the last detail. Donaldson's eyes had visibly moistened when he described the scene and last words of his friend. The jury had been right behind him and he sensed he could do no wrong. If nothing else, Hinksman would be convicted of killing McClure.

When Donaldson was asked if the man responsible for his friend's death was present in court, he'd lifted his hand and pointed his finger straight at Hinksman. 'That is the man who murdered my friend, Ken McClure.' It was a satisfying moment.

Hinksman merely stretched and yawned.

Graham immediately objected to the statement, saying that murder had yet to be proved. The Judge ordered him to sit back down, then she warned Hinksman that he wasn't far from being in contempt of court. He raised his eyebrows and smiled at her.

She made a note.

Donaldson's evidence was the last to be given on that Friday afternoon.

As the trial was adjourned for the weekend, Hinksman

indicated that he wanted a private consultation with Graham.

In the interview room, Hinksman asked, 'Well, how's it going?'

'In truth, not very well,' admitted Graham. 'The prosecution have got sentiment on their side. It does help. Too many innocent people have died.'

'How strong do you think their evidence is against me regarding Gaskell, the arms dealer?'

'So so,' said Graham, sitting securely on the fence. 'Although there's no direct witness testimony, there are the videos the police recovered from the guest-house which show you turning up at Gaskell's house. Then the ballistic evidence – the fact that the gun you had with you when Christie arrested you is the one which killed Gaskell. It all looks pretty bleak, to be honest.'

'Mmm . . . When is Christie due to give evidence?'

'Middle of next week, I estimate.'

'Well, you make damned sure he has a hard time,' ordered Hinksman. 'I want his evidence and his character dragged through the mud. Hear me?'

'I hear you,' said Graham dismally. He was unused to being given instructions on how to defend a case by his client. He knew he had to be patient with Hinksman, otherwise he'd probably get a bullet in the brain.

'And I want you to tell Dakin to move up a gear on the jury. I want them all shitting themselves this weekend.'

'I'll tell him,' sighed Graham. He was more concerned with the prospect of Henry Christie's evidence next week. He knew very little about the detective or his background.

'I'm not sure I'll have much mud to sling at Christie,' he told Hinksman doubtfully. 'I may be able to get into his evidence, but as to his character . . . I don't know.' He shrugged.

Hinksman smiled an evil smile. 'Don't worry. By Monday morning you'll have everything you need. Promise.'

★ ★ ★

By its very nature this murder trial was spectacular and newsworthy. It had all the ingredients of a juicy international story. The massive bomb which killed many innocent people; the violent deaths of police officers; the links with underworld crime in England and America; the death of an American gangster and his 'moll'; the death of a British arms dealer; the involvement of the FBI and the insinuation – nothing more – that Hinksman was a Mafia hitman, although the words 'Mafia' and 'hitman' were never to be used throughout the trial.

When it started, the trial made front-page news across the globe; as it proceeded it was always featured somewhere on page two or three. But it lacked a 'certain something', a spark.

It got that 'certain something' over the weekend, which blasted it right back to the headlines.

Firstly, all the jury members had their houses fire-bombed. No one was injured, but much damage was done and worry caused. Speculation was rife: would the next step be the taking of a juror's life? Would there have to be a re-trial?

Secondly it got that something that made the whole trial really come to life.

It got a personality.

It got Henry Christie.

He was exposed.

Carried initially by the *News of the World,* it was a tale that caught the public's imagination.

Henry's life and times were laid bare for all to see.

His drinking was dredged up. His womanising. His adultery. His violent temper. His marriage collapse. His nervous breakdown. All slit open for the world to see and drool over.

Hero Cop's Sex and Drink Binge! screamed the headline.

Henry, who had always thought himself to be Mr Very Average, had become newsworthy.

All thanks to the relentless digging of a female American

journalist called Lisa Want, on special assignment to the *News of the World*.

Henry's Sunday was spent alone with the more highbrow newspapers. He took the *Sunday Times* and the *Sunday Telegraph*, which were delivered. He rose at nine, prepared a pot of coffee and warmed up two Sainsbury's croissants before settling down to three blissful hours of uninterrupted reading.

It was his Sunday ritual.

At 12.30 p.m. he switched on the TV to watch the Grand Prix.

The phone rang.

It was FB. His opening words were, 'What the fuck have you done, Henry? Talking to the fucking gutter press! Have you gone stark staring bonkers?'

'Hold on,' Henry cautioned him. 'What the hell are you on about?'

FB reduced himself from a boil to a simmer and explained.

Henry put the phone down as FB finished. It rang again immediately. A journalist from a rival newspaper introduced himself. Henry told him where he should get off and slammed the phone down – but not before he heard the man offer him five figures for an exclusive.

The phone rang again.

'I have just told you to fuck off,' bawled Henry.

'Henry. It's me, Kate.'

'Oh, Jeez. Sorry.'

'Have you seen the newspapers today – in particular the *News of the World*?' she asked coldly. 'Our marriage is splashed all over for everyone to see. Our private life, Henry.' She was obviously very upset and close to tears. 'I honestly thought we were near to . . . to getting back together. But this! This! It changes everything as far as I'm concerned. How could you? Oh Christ, how could you?'

'Hang on, Kate. I haven't done anything. I haven't spoken to any journalist – not one. And I haven't seen the paper yet, either . . . so, look, give me half an hour, will you? Please. I'll go and get a copy, read it, then phone you back, OK?'

'Very well,' she said quietly in a way that gave Henry a shiver.

Henry closed his eyes as he replaced the receiver. He'd had no idea that Kate was thinking about getting back with him. To hear that and to have the prospect dashed in the same sentence was gut-wrenching.

The phone rang again.

He picked it up, shouted, 'Go fuck yourself,' slammed it back down, then left it off the hook and dashed out to the newsagents.

He purposely did not open the newspaper until he got back to the flat. He poured himself a coffee, sat down at the small kitchen table and then opened it.

The story was plastered over pages three and four.

Henry gasped.

The headlines were bad enough in themselves. The story below made him cringe with embarrassment.

There was a still photo which showed him assaulting the TV reporter on the banks of the River Ribble. That illustrated his violent streak.

The remainder of the story was made up from an interview with Natalie which detailed their affair, their sexual exploits – 'He was insatiable,' she said – and their final acrimonious split. 'I couldn't live with a broken man,' she claimed, 'and anyway, he dumped me. He used me then tossed me aside.' She talked quite extensively about his nervous breakdown and his terrible dreams. Henry hoped she had been well paid for this, because she'd need the money when she got sacked . . . he hoped. There were a couple of photographs from his time with Natalie. They'd been snapped by her friend when he'd been drunk and was drooling pathetically over Natalie. Henry winced when he saw them. They made him look just like he was – a man making an utter fool of himself over a younger girl.

It didn't stop there.

There was also a piece about Henry and Karl Donaldson taking Natalie and her friend out. Entitled *My Night of Sex With FBI Man*, it detailed Donaldson's exploits that night too, including the mystery lady banging on his hotel door in the early hours, demanding to see Donaldson and interrupting their lovemaking. The woman wasn't identified, but was described as a 'high-ranking officer in the Lancashire Constabulary who was, at the time, running a major investigation'. It went on to describe Donaldson, naked, chasing her down the hotel corridor. Henry knew it was a night Donaldson would rather forget, especially now that he'd made his peace with Karen.

Then there was the photo of Henry's two distraught-looking daughters taken a few weeks before, following the shooting incident in the Lake District.

'Bitch,' uttered Henry, shaking his head, reading on.

It got worse.

The scorned cleaner Maureen had her say, too. Her story made an ideally tacky footnote to the whole thing. Another 'used and abused after a night of sexual ecstasy, a night when I did things for him I'd done for no other man'. For no other man *that night*, snorted Henry. There was a picture of her in her overalls with a mop and bucket, looking as ugly as sin. God knows how I ever fucked her, he thought bitterly.

The worst of it was that he hadn't told Kate.

Miss Lisa 'Shit-Face' Want had been very busy indeed. Some of her facts weren't exactly spot on and there was a great deal of literary exaggeration, but all in all it turned out to be a much better profile than she'd promised.

Henry rushed to the toilet and vomited.

He hung over the pan, spitting and slobbering, almost crying. This, once more, was where his life had gone.

* * *

Dave August spent a very subdued weekend, returning to work at eight on Monday morning. Everyone's eyes seemed to be on him, as though they knew. He tried to shrug the feeling off: he was the Chief Constable, after all. It was only natural that he should be the centre of attention.

Jean was at her desk, sorting correspondence. He bade her a jovial good morning and she was glad to see that her boss had rediscovered some of his lost friendliness. His mood over the last week had started to put a crisp edge on her nerves.

'Shall I make tea?' she suggested before he reached his office door.

'Most certainly, Jean. Best drink of the day,' he replied.

She got up, smiling, and left. He paused with one hand on the door handle. Taking stock of himself, he turned it and confidently shoved the door open.

Everything was as it should have been. There was nothing untoward in the post or on his desk.

August sighed with relief.

He got the phone call at 9.05 a.m.

Henry Christie and Karl Donaldson arrived at Lancaster Castle together. Donaldson was driving, even though Henry had had his plaster removed first thing that morning and his wrist felt OK, if a little weak.

They were greeted by a crowd of eager journalists and photographers who'd been herded behind barriers by the police. Questions and flashes assaulted the ears and eyes of the two detectives. They held up their hands to shield their faces and said 'No comment' to all the enquiries.

Once inside the building, Donaldson turned to Henry and said, 'Fame at last, pal,' with a grin.

Henry couldn't help but laugh.

They both submitted themselves to the search procedures and entered the court.

Then they went to hunt for Lisa Want – but she was noticeable by her absence.

* * *

Henry entered the witness-box at 10.30 a.m. on Wednesday. He took the Bible in his right hand and said, 'I swear by Almighty God that the evidence I shall give shall be the truth, the whole truth, and nothing but the truth.

'My name is Henry James Christie. I am a Detective Sergeant with the Lancashire Constabulary, currently on the CID at Blackpool. Previously I was seconded to the Regional Crime Squad, also based in Blackpool.'

The QC for the prosecution stood slowly up. He shuffled his papers.

The court was hushed and expectant.

Henry had a quick look round.

He saw that Lisa Want had suddenly appeared in the press-box. He looked at the jury. They seemed to be good, decent people.

Then his eyes locked with Hinksman's.

Hinksman was fondling his chin thoughtfully with the fingers of his right hand, gazing at Henry. As Henry looked at him, Hinksman almost imperceptibly drew his first finger across his throat in an unmistakable gesture.

Henry allowed himself a slight sneer.

The Judge had seen the exchange. She made no comment on it, but noted it down.

The QC coughed and began to take Henry through his evidence.

Henry felt he had done well. The jury were obviously on his side, sitting there open-mouthed with anticipation and sympathy.

As he drew to a close the prosecuting counsel thanked Henry and said, 'Would you please wait there, Sergeant. I'm sure my learned friend will wish to ask you some questions.'

He sat down and handed over to Graham.

Graham, with his half-glasses perched precariously on the tip of his nose, stood up slowly, adjusting his robes as he did so.

Henry knew of his reputation – well paid, defender of rich villains and celebrities, ruthless – and was on guard immediately.

Graham pushed his spectacles up his nose to the bridge, then allowed them to slide back down again to the tip. He pursed his lips into a pucker. He nodded at Henry and said, 'Sergeant,' by way of a greeting.

Henry nodded back apprehensively. This is not going to be easy, he thought. Why don't you just get on with it instead of fannying around, you bastard.

Graham's lips then went tight across his teeth, like a dead man's smile.

'I'm very pleased to see, as is the court, that you have recovered from your injuries.'

'Thank you,' said Henry. He realised that this would probably be about as humane as Graham got.

'You certainly have been in the wars,' he commented. 'It's a wonder you made it here.' A titter went round the court. 'You have been through a very traumatic time, physically and mentally.' Though this was a statement it was phrased as a question – but Henry chose not to answer it. If you want to ask me questions, he thought, then ask and I'll answer.

When nothing was forthcoming, Graham added, 'Isn't that so?'

'Yes,' said Henry simply.

'Right, Sergeant, if I may, I'd like to take you back to the night in question – the night, in fact, when you shot my client.'

Suddenly it was as though Henry was on trial.

Henry stood stockstill. He avoided eye-contact with Graham; he knew that would be disastrous. Eye-contact led to verbal battles; once these battles were joined, the officer giving evidence had usually lost the war, unless he was very experienced and clever. Henry had given evidence many times, but was aware he was no match for a devious, slimy barrister when it came to word-games.

He desperately wanted to say, 'And the night when your client killed a whole bunch of people,' but he didn't.

He decided to stick to his usual courtroom strategy: keep it simple, don't stray from the written statement, don't lose your cool, don't answer back. Tell the truth – but if a lie *has* to be told, remember what you said.

'You were on a surveillance operation that night, you say, tailing a man who was eventually shot in front of you.'

Henry said nothing.

Graham then knew he would have to ask direct questions.

'Is that correct, officer?' he asked stonily.

'It is,' nodded Henry.

'And you followed this man into a public house in Blackpool, the –' and here Graham read out the name of the establishment from his brief. 'Did you drink any alcohol when you were in this bar?'

'Er . . . I can't remember,' said Henry.

'Wouldn't you have stood out like a sore thumb if you'd been in there without a drink in your hand? You were, after all, undercover.'

'I may have had a soft drink,' Henry admitted. 'I was on duty and I don't drink on duty.'

'So, no alcohol?'

'No,' said Henry. He actually remembered buying a bottle of Bud but wasn't going to reveal that.

Graham nodded, not impressed.

'When you followed this man and his associates out of the public house, you stated that you lost sight of them and then were dragged down an alley. Is that correct?'

'Yes.'

'Can you describe the alley?'

Henry thought a moment. 'It was about twenty feet wide and a hundred and fifty feet long, coming to a dead end. The exact measurements are on a plan, which I believe you have a copy of.'

'It is your recollections the court is interested in, not a map,' said Graham haughtily. 'Where exactly was this alley?'

'Between the pub and the next building along, which is a guest-house, I think.'

Graham's mouth pursed as he composed his next set of questions.

'What time of night was it?'

'About nine forty-five.'

'Remind the court, officer – what month was it?'

'October.'

'October,' said Graham ruminatively, drawing out the word, as though chewing the cud. 'Quite late on in the year, wouldn't you say?'

'It is a fact,' said Henry, deadpan, 'that the twentieth of October *is* quite late in the year.'

A couple of the jury giggled. There was a slight release in tension. Graham shot them a hard, warning glance. He did not like it. But he took control of himself and smiled good-naturedly, accepting the joke at his expense. He turned back to Henry, his features assuming the look of a hunter poised to kill.

'So, getting on towards winter. Nights drawing in . . .'

Impulsively, Henry cut in: 'If you'd like me to say that it was dark – yes, it was dark.' He regretted his words immediately, not only because he'd spoken otherwise than in answer to a question, but because courts are very formal, traditional, patient places and by his impatience he had just managed to rub everyone up the wrong way, including Judge and jury. Not a good move.

Graham allowed himself the flicker of a smile, just the corners of his mouth twitching. Only Henry saw it.

Graham was back in charge of the interaction.

He said, 'I would be obliged if you could refrain from jumping the gun, Sergeant.' He raised his eyebrows and cocked his head at Henry, as if to say, 'Do you understand, pal?'

Henry nodded. 'My apologies,' he mumbled.

Graham paused and perused his papers, allowing time for everyone in the court to settle and for Henry to become agitated. A pause can be a good weapon, if used correctly.

'So, it was a dark night,' confirmed Graham. 'What was the weather like?'

'Clear and fine.'

'Could you see down the alley?'

'It was fairly poorly lit and there were a lot of shadows.'

'Was there any actual lighting in the alley at all?'

'No.' At that point Henry began to see where this was leading and his stomach lurched. He might just conceivably lose this.

'So, you were dragged into the alley and a vicious fight ensued between yourself and several men. You have graphically relayed details of this struggle whilst giving evidence earlier, and we are all very impressed by your bravery . . .'

Just fuck off, Henry thought.

' . . . so I don't intend to pursue that. But at the conclusion of this fight, could you remind us what position you were in?'

'Face up on the ground, surrounded by people who didn't like me very much.'

'You also mentioned that you'd received a blow on the head prior to this and that you thought you'd passed out momentarily. Is that correct?'

'Yes.'

'How did you feel?'

'Frightened.'

'No doubt,' said Graham. 'Were you pretty dazed too, from the blow on the head?'

'Actually my head was very clear,' he said. 'My body was in a mess physically – but I was thinking very clearly.'

Graham nodded. Then pounced.

'You'd been beaten up, bashed about the head and body, quite badly injured, knocked unconscious – and you say you were thinking very clearly?' Graham barely suppressed a laugh. 'Do you expect the court to believe that, officer?'

'I'm a very cool customer in stressful situations,' said

Henry glibly and rather rashly. A complete and utter lie, one which was seized upon ruthlessly by Graham.

'A cool customer in stressful situations,' the QC repeated dubiously. 'Now that is not altogether true, is it . . . Sergeant?'

'Yes, it is,' said Henry without conviction.

'Well then, perhaps I could remind you of another incident when you showed yourself to be completely uncool in a stressful situation. Such as at the scene of the M6 bombing, of which my client is accused. You actually assaulted and threw a TV reporter down the banks of the River Ribble. Isn't that so? Not the actions of a man who is, quote "A very cool customer in stressful situations", are they?'

'That was completely different,' protested Henry eventually.

'Are those the actions of a man who is a cool customer?' Graham was insistent.

'Completely and totally different . . .'

'Did you or did you not assault a TV reporter?'

'Yes, but—'

'Thank you, officer,' said Graham victoriously.

Henry found himself to be shaking and grinding his teeth. He gripped the edge of the witness-box to stop himself falling over. His breathing was shallow. His nostrils flared. Suddenly this big courtroom was beginning to swallow him up. He wanted to flee. Leap over the side of the box and run. Run for his life. He was, again, showing exactly how uncool he was in stressful situations. His eyes roved round the room madly. To the Judge. Across the faces of the jurors. To Hinksman, who smirked. Back to Graham, a man he hated more than anyone else at that moment in time.

Get a fucking grip on yourself, Henry, he told himself. Get a fucking grip. Pull yourself together. Don't let this little shit win.

'I need to tell you about that particular situation,' he pleaded. He looked at the Crown prosecutor for support.

The man, who had been squirming until that moment, got the message and stood up reluctantly. He addressed the Judge. 'Your Honour, I feel that Sergeant Christie should be allowed to tell the court about this if he so wishes . . . After all, he did not bring the subject up. It was my learned friend here.'

Graham said quickly, 'Your Honour, the situation itself is not actually relevant, merely the witness's reaction to it.' The last thing he wanted was Henry going for the sympathy bid.

'No,' said the Judge with finality, 'the Crown is quite correct, Mr Graham. The officer should be allowed to expand a little if he so wishes.'

She nodded towards Henry who said, 'Thank you, Your Honour.'

The prosecutor sat down, hoping Henry wasn't going to make a mess of this, like he had done so far.

Joe Kovaks rubbed his eyes. He had been up all night, patrolling the streets of Miami, searching, but not finding. It was almost 7 a.m., five hours behind British time.

He was parked in a plain FBI sedan in the Lemon City district, north of Miami, killing the last few minutes of his tour of duty.

His temporary partner, Tommo, dozed next to him in the passenger seat, snoring gently. Sue had been reassigned unwillingly to other duties – some massive white-collar fraud enquiry where she could use her accountancy skills to their best advantage – and Tommo had been teamed up with Kovaks pending the return of Donaldson from England.

The sun was climbing up through the sky. It was going to be another hot day. Soon Kovaks would be going home – how he had almost come to hate going home! – and he would take Chrissy to hospital where she would undergo treatment for most of the day, some medical, mostly psychiatric. He would go back to the apartment and sleep while she was there, collecting her later in the day.

Kovaks yawned and reviewed the night's work.

Another fucking total waste of time. He'd combed the city for what seemed the millionth time, but he couldn't find her, the woman who was going to bring Corelli to justice . . .

He and Tommo had hassled countless prostitutes, pimps and drug dealers, because he was sure that it was amongst these people she would be found: selling her body, what was left of it, and that once-gorgeous mouth so that she could get pumped-up with enough drugs to see her through the next day.

But he couldn't fucking find her.

Kovaks was teetering towards the edge now.

Tommo opened his eyes and squinted sideways at Kovaks. 'You gonna answer that fuckin' radio or not?' he croaked.

'Eh?' Kovaks had been so deep in his thoughts that he did not hear the radio operator shouting his call sign. He fumbled the handset. 'Yeah, receivin'. Go ahead.'

'Yeah, Joe,' began the weary operator. 'Can you be making your way to the Jackson Memorial Hospital, Emergency Room?'

Puzzled, Kovaks said, 'Sure, but I'm off-duty at seven.'

'Well,' she drawled, 'it's up to you, Joe, but that little lady you been seeking for the past few days has just turned up there in the back of an ambulance – drugs OD.'

'On my way,' shouted Kovaks, throwing the handset down, the wheels of the car spinning almost before he'd finished speaking.

They were back on Henry's side following his graphic and emotional account of the M6 bombing and its aftermath in the river and on its banks. It was the first time Henry had related the whole story in full to anyone. He found it to be a cathartic, cleansing experience. Suddenly he felt as though a great burden had been lifted from his soul. He'd tried his best, but the situation had been against him. And now he could accept that. Stood in that courtroom, the eyes of the world on him, he had bared his soul – and it felt great.

He looked at the jury. Two women were actually crying.

Then he looked at Hinksman.

Again their eyes locked. But this time Henry felt in no way intimidated by him. I am a brave man, he told Hinksman silently. You are a violent man, but at heart you must be a coward. I am better than you.

Graham coughed. He desperately wanted to get the whole thing back on course.

'Now if I may bring you back to the night in question,' he said, not wasting time, not allowing the jury to reflect. He went straight for the jugular. 'We've established that you were in a dark alley, being assaulted by a number of people. You were on your back, having passed out briefly. What happened next?'

Henry's ordeal was by no means over.

'One of them had a gun to my face – my own gun, actually – and he was weighing up whether or not he should "pop" me.'

'"Pop" you, officer?'

'Pull the trigger, kill me,' explained Henry. 'Before he could make a decision he himself was dead with his brains blown out, mostly all over me.'

'Who shot him?'

'A man who came down the alley.'

'Do you see that man in court today?'

'Yes,' said Henry. He pointed. 'Him. Your client.'

'Now, come come,' tutted Graham disapprovingly. 'How can you possibly make that assumption? A dark alley. No lighting. A beating. You cannot say for sure that it was my client in the alley, can you? You cannot say for sure that he killed those people, can you?'

Henry hesitated. Then he said, 'I am sure it was.' No way was he going to be swayed.

'Did you see his face?'

'To a degree,' said Henry. 'Enough to identify him.'

'What happened after "this man" shot those people in the alley?'

'He turned and walked away.'

'Did he speak to you?'

'No, but he spoke to one of the men before he shot him. He said a few words in an American accent.'

Graham chose to ignore that. 'Did he turn back at all?'

'Briefly, at the end of the alley. He glanced back and I saw his face again – this time under street lighting. It was definitely your client.'

'And how long did you see his face for? One second? Two? Three?'

'About a second,' admitted Henry.

'About a second . . . and that gave you enough time to make a positive identification of Mr Hinksman?'

'Yes.'

'How far away was he from you?'

'About fifty feet.'

'And you were still laid on your back, is that correct?'

'Yes,' said Henry.

Graham shook his head. 'What happened next?'

'Hinksman turned and walked away towards the Tower. I decided to go after him.'

'So you lost sight of him.'

'Yes.'

'For how long?'

'Until I caught up with him on the promenade.'

'Which was how long?'

'A minute, ninety seconds.'

'Is it not just possible that the man you caught up with was not the same man who killed all those people in the alley?'

'It was the same man – Hinksman,' said Henry firmly.

'But you lost sight of that man. How could you possibly say it was the same man?'

'I recognised him, and apart from anything else, he was wearing the same clothing.'

Graham did not pursue Henry's encounter on the promenade with Hinksman. Too many people could back him up. Instead he concentrated on discrediting the identification of Hinksman in the alley. He knew that much of the evidence against Hinksman was good and that he would probably get convicted of most of the murders of which he was accused. Graham saw it as his job to do two things; get some of them reduced to manslaughter and get him off some of the charges. He had a strong case against Henry's testimony, as the sergeant well knew. There was no one to back up Henry's story because Ralphie's girlfriend had disappeared without trace (probably dressed in concrete, Henry believed), and therefore everything rested on Henry's eyewitness account, backed up by forensic and ballistic evidence which proved that the gun in Hinksman's possession at the time of his arrest was the one which killed Ralphie and his pals. The difficulty for the prosecution was in proving that Hinksman had actually pulled the trigger. If Henry couldn't convince the jury, then Hinksman would be cleared of four murder charges. Henry did not want this to happen.

Henry spent a further thirty minutes in the witness-box under cross-examination by Graham.

In the end Graham said huffily, 'It is obvious, officer, that you have decided to stick to your story no matter what, so I have no further questions for you.' Angrily he sat down, unhappy that he could not get Henry to budge – and not terribly pleased that he had been unable to carry out Hinksman's instructions and drag Henry's character through the mud.

Three hours after stepping into the box, Henry stepped out, feeling weak and hungry. The court had adjourned for lunch.

'Well done, pal,' said Donaldson. He'd been watching from the rear of the court.

'I feel completely drained,' said Henry. 'Lunch?'

'Afraid not. Karen and I have an appointment in Manchester at three. We'll be leaving now.'

'What's that for?'

'Can't tell you,' said Donaldson, tapping his nose.

* * *

'A mega-concoction of pills, anything she could lay her hands on, I'd say,' the nurse told Joe Kovaks. 'You name it, they were in there. Pill cocktail, could've been lethal if she'd've had 'em in her any longer. Got here just in time. We pumped her stomach out real good. Doc says no harm done.'

'So she'll be OK?'

'Yep. She's tired now and she'll need a few days in here, but she'll be fine, or at least as fine as a junkie can get.'

They turned into the ward. 'Third bed on the left.'

'Thanks, nurse,' Kovaks said.

He walked quietly down the ward. Curtains were drawn around the third bed along. He found the gap and stepped into the enclosed world. Kovaks gasped when he saw her. She looked very ill, all skin and bone and she seemed to be barely breathing. In fact he thought she was dead at first, but a twitch in one of her fingers told him otherwise. A drip ran into one of her skinny arms, the tube of which was not much less in circumference than the arm itself.

Kovaks sat next to the bed. His chair scraped on the floor.

She looked ninety years old. Kovaks knew she was nineteen. He shook his head sadly, remembering the feisty girl who used to give him as good as she got whenever he visited her to try and arrest Whisper when he'd been wanted on warrant. She hadn't taken any shit from anyone back then. Now she didn't even look capable of taking a shit.

Yes, Corelli had a whole lot to answer for, he thought grimly.

'Laura,' Kovaks whispered.

Her eyelids flickered, but stayed closed.

'Laura,' he said more forcefully. He touched her arm. It felt cold and clammy.

This time her eyes opened. Kovaks noted they were dead eyes, without depth or hope. She squinted sideways at him, not instantly recognising him, but when she did she sneered.

Kovaks looked at her mouth. Once thick-lipped and sensuous, even he had imagined the pleasure of a blow job with her. Now her lips formed a thin, hard line.

'What do you want?' she whispered tiredly.

'I heard you were in. I wanted to see how you were.'

'Well, now you've seen,' she said, 'so fuck off and leave me.' Her eyes closed wearily. She breathed out and her whole being seemed to deflate as though she'd breathed out her soul.

'There's only one reason you're here,' Kovaks said, 'and that's because of Corelli. He hasn't only fucked up your life, you know? He's fucked up hundreds, thousands. We need to talk, Laura, maybe not just at this minute, but soon when you're feeling better. We have to stitch that bastard up . . . please, Laura.'

She opened her eyes again. 'I've lost my baby because of him. She's been taken away from me, did you know?'

'No, I didn't,' he lied.

'She was all I had left after they killed Whisper. Yeah, sure, I'll talk . . .' A tear rolled down her face and dripped onto the pillow. 'He can't do anything to me now. If he killed me he'd be doing me a favour . . . so what do I have to lose? But not now, not now. I feel so sleepy. I need to sleep . . .'

Chapter Twenty-Two

The town of Garstang lies midway between Lancaster and Preston on the A6. A couple of miles north of Garstang is a layby. At 7.30 p.m. that same Monday evening, Dave August drove sedately into the layby in his own car and parked up. He switched the engine off, unlocked all the doors and rested his hands on top of the steering wheel so they were visible – as instructed.

He stared dead ahead. Afraid.

The digital figures on his watch moved to 7.35.

Briefly he considered starting up, slamming the car into gear and speeding away. But suddenly the passenger door was wrenched open and a man seemed to fall from nowhere into the seat next to August. The Chief Constable jumped. He hadn't seen anyone coming. No one had pulled up in a car. The man must have sneaked up from the hedge.

August faced the intruder, and didn't know whether to laugh or scream: the man was wearing an Oliver Hardy mask. In the end he did neither because a heavy, dangerous-looking revolver was pointing straight at his belly. Behind the mask August could see the eyes and the deep red slit of a mouth which, when it moved, sickened him.

The voice was hollow, distorted. 'Drive north.' The man obviously had no time for small talk. 'Keep your speed to forty.'

'Look—' August began plaintively.

'NO! Don't talk – just drive,' he snapped. 'Or some cunt'll find a dead Chief Constable in a layby. Now fuckin' drive.'

A few seconds later August and his companion were travelling the A6 in the direction of Lancaster.

Just before they reached Galgate, south of Lancaster, the man ordered, 'Turn in here.'

August nodded. His hands gripping the steering wheel were weak and perspiring. He pulled into a car park by the side of the road, overlooking the Lancaster canal. A large number of pleasure cruisers were moored by a quay below them, but there was no one around. It was very quiet, tranquil.

The man dangled something in front of August's face. It was a small hessian bag with a drawstring fastener. 'Put this over your head.'

He obeyed meekly, slipping the rough-textured material over his head, down over his face, blocking out all light. It was harsh and unpleasant against his skin. The man pulled the drawstring tight and fastened it with a knot.

A hand touched August's shoulder. He was told to swing his legs out of the car and stand up. As he rose unsteadily he caught his head on the doorframe but managed to struggle to his feet.

Another vehicle drew up.

He was manhandled into the back of this vehicle – a Ford Transit van – and lying on his side in the foetal position, was frisked by heavy hands. The back doors of the van were closed and the van drove away. He had orders not to move, otherwise he would be thrown out.

August tried to keep track of his journey.

He could tell that they turned right out of the car park, so they were heading back towards Garstang. After a couple of minutes the van slowed and went left. This was the motorway junction. If there was another left turn they would be heading north up the M6. There wasn't. August could tell from the acceleration of the van and the way it leaned that they were looping around the junction to travel south, back towards Preston.

They were on the motorway for about fifteen minutes –

continuous, straight-line, high-speed travel. No one spoke on the journey, yet August sensed there were two men.

The van slowed and came off the motorway.

August was fairly certain this was the Preston north turn-off. Soon after, he lost his bearings as they hit Preston proper, and ten minutes later, they stopped.

He heard some doors slide back.

The van lurched and stopped again. The engine was switched off.

They had driven into a building of some sort.

In his blackness he heard hollow footsteps. The building doors sliding back again. Murmuring voices. A laugh. Then the back doors of the van were opened. He was heaved out and dragged for a few metres, then forced down onto his knees, then onto all fours and then completely onto his front. The ground was cold and hard. Concrete.

Soon, he thought, I will see them. This is their weak time.

He was wrong.

A voice said, 'I am going to remove the bag from your head, do you understand? Because I am a civilised man and we are going to have a conversation. However, when I do this you will look at the ground, your nose will be pressed to the floor and you will keep your eyes closed. Do you understand?

'Yes.'

'I will hold a double-barrelled shotgun to the back of your neck.' The voice was male with a Scottish accent and sounded as though it was being reasonable. 'If you open your eyes and try to look round, or do anything silly, or make a sudden move, I'll pull both triggers and blow your head off your shoulders. There will be nothing left of your head. Do you understand?'

'Yes.'

Then August felt the cold barrels of the gun pushed into his neck, just below his hairline. He wanted to be sick. He swallowed something that tasted of vomit.

The hessian sack was yanked off his head and he lay there face down, nose to the ground, shivering with fright. Before he could stop them, his eyes had flickered open for a nanosecond, and he nearly whined in terror. But no one seemed to have noticed. He squeezed them firmly shut, enclosing and sealing the memory of that face . . .

There was a cough, a clearing of the throat, the shuffle of feet.

'So, Mr August, what did you think of the video? Good, wasn't it? Very classy. Make a fortune on the porn market, that.'

'What do you want?' said August tightly. He wasn't sure how much more he could handle.

'Straight to the point,' said the voice. 'I like that. All right, we'll play it your way. There's something you possess that we want. *Knowledge.* You're a Chief Constable. You know many things – and what you don't know, you can find out.'

'I don't know anything,' August was almost in tears.

'But you do, you do,' the man assured him.

'What?'

'A man is presently at court facing murder charges. He will soon be convicted. A man called Hinksman.'

August groaned. 'So? I can't stop that.'

'I know – and he'll be convicted. Stupid bastard deserves to be . . . However, that doesn't concern us. He'll be taken by police escort from Lancaster to another prison, won't he? Probably Strangeways.'

August did not respond. He waited for the bombshell.

'What I want you to do is tell me when the escort will be setting off from Lancaster, how many of them are armed and with what sort of weapons . . . you know, that sort of thing. But I want you to do something else for me as well.'

'What?' said August, deep in a nightmare.

'Ensure that the convoy takes a particular route – one which I will supply to you. There – simple, isn't it?'

'But why?'

The man jabbed the shotgun roughly into the back of August's neck. 'Why d'you fuckin' think?'

Joe Kovaks had made his first visit to Laura at seven-thirty in the morning. He had got home just in time to run Chrissy to the hospital for ten. By the time he hit the sack an hour later he was exhausted, with only four hours to sleep before getting up and collecting Chrissy. He was due back on duty at six, when he planned to ditch Tommo, his partner, and go straight to see Laura and get his plan underway.

He felt excited. Corelli's time was ticking away.

Laura looked 100 per cent better that evening – in other words, marginally better than a corpse.

Kovaks sat on the stool next to the bed and placed a bag of mixed fresh fruit on the cabinet.

She gave him a weak smile, said 'Hi,' then closed her eyes. The brush with death had taken its toll.

'We need to get Corelli,' Kovaks said softly. 'How many more lives will he destroy?' He spoke in a low, hypnotic voice. He knew she was susceptible right now. This was the time to strike, to get into her mind and influence her way of thinking. He was being a ruthless bastard and he knew it. 'Look at what he's done to you and Whisper. He killed Whisper, not me, Laura. He had him knifed to death and his tongue cut out because he had the courage to talk to me. And then he made you suffer. He'd been making you suffer anyway. Using you as a source of income. Making you use your body and your mouth. How many men did you fuck, Laura? One hundred? Ten thousand? How man men did you suck off? Twenty thousand? He abused you, destroyed you, forced you onto drugs so that you'd be dependent on him for everything – money, junk, somewhere to live. I know you did it for the baby, I know it was the only way. I'm not judging you, honey. All I'm doing is stating facts, Laura . . . and then what happened? When he'd had enough of you, he kicked you out onto the streets, out of your home. The cunt! Not much of a home, I know – but it was your place nevertheless.'

She began to cry softly, eyes closed in shame. Kovaks was bang on target. He couldn't stop a triumphant grin from spreading across his face. This might be easier than he'd feared.

'And you lost everything. The baby. Whisper. Your self-respect.' He was relentless, driving it home. 'And you almost lost your life, like he's deprived thousands of others of theirs. While he lives like a king! He doesn't do drugs. He's a fucking billionaire! Owns houses, cars, boats, planes, businesses . . . all on the back of people's suffering. We need to do something about him, Laura. We need to stop him. You and me. You and me. If we pool what we know, I'm sure we can do it.'

'How?' she sobbed. 'We can't touch him.'

'I don't know,' said Kovaks. He shook his head. 'But we can think of something.'

'I want my baby back,' she cried. 'That's what I want.' Her mouth twisted grotesquely as she cried. She buried her head in a pillow. 'I miss her so much.'

Kovaks laid a hand on her bony shoulder.

'It's OK, Laura. You've got me now. You can depend on me. I'm an FBI agent, aren't I? I can pull strings. I can get her back for you, I'm sure I can. Don't worry, but you must promise to help me. We must get Corelli once and for all. You and me, Laura. You and me.' His voice was hypnotic.

'I need my junk too,' she said.

'That's OK, I can get you anything you need.'

'But how are we going to get him?'

'I don't know yet,' he said.

But he had a good idea.

A further two weeks of witnesses giving evidence drove the trial into its fifth week. Much of the testimony was presented by experts – scientists, doctors etc. – and the officers who conducted the interviews with Hinksman. It was basically unchallenged by the defence. Graham put up a spirited performance, but he was rowing up Shit Creek with only his hands for paddles.

The last witness stepped down from the box at 3 p.m. on the Friday of the fifth week and the trial was adjourned for the weekend.

On the Monday of the sixth week Graham began his final speech for the defence. It lasted two days – two days in which he tried valiantly to discredit the prosecution evidence. He was very convincing, eloquent and believable – but on the whole he was fighting a lost cause; however, as he was being paid so well and had such a dangerous client, he tried his best.

He did have a good case to rubbish Henry Christie's evidence, though. Despite the supporting forensic and ballistic evidence, Henry's testimony was unsafe, he insisted. He referred to a famous stated case – R v Turnbull – which dealt with the subject of identification and the guidelines which the police should follow. Most of Henry's evidence did not follow these guidelines; therefore, Graham submitted, Hinksman should be found not guilty of the murders in the alley.

On Wednesday the Judge began her careful summing up. This lasted until the Friday and was fascinating to listen to. It was as though she was telling a story around a campfire. She enthralled everyone with her turn of phrase and clear voice. She made detailed reference to Henry's evidence and supported Graham's submission. She told the jury that they must be very sure that Detective-Sergeant Christie's evidence was sound. Any doubt and they must not convict.

Henry could only agree with her conclusion from a professional point of view. Personally he was extremely pissed off about it. But then again, he mused, she hadn't told them *not* to convict . . .

However, she more or less directed the jury to convict on all the other counts.

The twelve good and true men and women then retired to

consider their verdicts. By five o'clock they had not got anywhere. They had begun a process which was to last five days. Over this period they were taken to a secret location – an hotel on the outskirts of Lancaster – where they were guarded by armed police and dog-handlers. The Judge instructed them to remain there until they reached their verdicts. Only then could they return to court.

Late that Friday night, the jury retired to their respective bedrooms at the hotel to get a good night's sleep before continuing with their task the following morning.

At 6 p.m. in Miami, five hours behind British time, Sue finished her work for the day at the FBI building, collected a couple of personal belongings from her desk and made ready to go home.

She was extremely bored with the task now allotted to her – a fraud enquiry which had been ongoing for two years and which the Bureau had been unable to crack. For the last two months she had been combing balance sheets, profit and loss accounts, bank transfers and private bank accounts until figures had been coming out of her ears, but at least she had made a breakthrough. She was fairly sure how the fraud was being perpetrated, but uncertain how it could be proved in court.

Although pleased by the progress, she was actually bored rigid with the case. The short time she'd spent teamed up with Joe Kovaks and the Corelli Unit had been very exciting and had given her a look over the fence, where the grass was definitely greener. She longed to get back onto organised crime where the baddies pulled guns out, not pens, and it was blood that was spilled, not ink.

And she missed Joe.

After an unsteady start, to say the least, she and he had become good friends. She had managed to maintain some contact with him when she'd been transferred, but it had dwindled and she hadn't seen him for almost four weeks now. It made her sad, but she knew he was completely immersed in Corelli, especially after the tragedy with Chrissy.

As Sue stepped into the elevator, one other person was already inside, finger on the Door Open button.

Oh God, she thought. I do not like this guy. He gives me the creeps. However, she steeled herself and said, 'Hello, Mr Ritter,' pleasantly.

'Hello, Sue,' he said. 'Ground or basement?'

'Basement, please. My car's down there.'

'Mine too.' He smiled ingratiatingly and pressed the button. The doors closed slowly with a sinister hiss and the elevator descended.

Sue stared at the doors.

Ritter lounged against the side of the elevator, looking at her. Bitch, he thought. You fucking know, don't you?

'Anything planned for the weekend?' he asked her.

'No, not really. Some shopping, maybe. Catch a movie, that sort of thing.'

'Not going to Bayside, by any chance?' He laughed nervously.

Now why ask that? She recalled seeing him there once and him denying it, but that was months ago. Obviously it meant something to him – probably out meeting some woman other than his wife – but so what? He wanted to deny it, let him deny it.

'Spending some time with your fiancé – Damian, isn't it, from Fingerprints?'

'No, he's away,' she said. 'Gone to see his mother for a few days. I'll have a nice weekend all alone.' She smiled at Ritter, wishing he'd shut up but not wishing to be impolite.

Fortunately the elevator stopped on the second floor and two secretaries got in. They were going to the basement, too. Sue was relieved. She exhaled a long breath.

At the basement Ritter stood by the elevator door, finger on the button, and allowed the three women to walk out ahead of him. The secretaries peeled off to the left. Sue walked straight on towards the car park.

If she turns round, Ritter thought, she knows.

Sue couldn't help herself. She glanced quickly round and saw Ritter still in the elevator, watching her. Weirdo. She increased her pace. Why the hell did I tell him I was alone this weekend, she asked herself. She had an uneasy feeling.

Ritter pressed the button which would take the elevator to the administration floor.

In the general office Ritter managed to collar one of the clerks before she left. Ritter knew she dealt with annual leave.

'Have you got a moment?' he asked.

'Yeah, sure, what is it?'

'I left a fingerprint indent with one of the experts downstairs, a guy called Damian Faber. I've been trying to chase him up today for a result. Turns out he's on leave. I need to speak to him pretty urgently about it. Is there any chance you can get into your computer records and see if he's left an address where he can be contacted? I'd really appreciate it.'

'Yeah, sure, no problem. Won't take but a minute.'

She sat down by a computer terminal, switched the machine on and tapped quickly into the computerised leave records.

'Here we are.' She leaned sideways to allow Ritter to see the screen.

'Mother's address in Clearwater,' said Ritter. 'No phone number. Damn!' He jotted down the details, which also included Damian's home address and phone number. 'I am very much obliged to you,' he said to the clerk. 'Looks like I'll have to send the local cops round to roust him.'

'Looks like,' she said, logging out and switching off. She pulled on her coat and hurried out of the office, late for her date.

Ritter phoned Damian's home number. The answering machine clicked in.

'Excellent,' said Ritter to himself with a dangerous smile. 'He ain't there, so he must still be at Mommy's.'

It was going to be a short, violent weekend for Agent Fat Bitch.

Damian had decided to surprise Sue.

He'd taken a few days' leave in order to visit his mother in Clearwater because she claimed to be seriously ill and close to death. Seriously mad, Damian thought as he drove east along Highway 41 towards Miami and home in his battered Chevvy.

Two days with her had driven him nuts. He had originally planned to stay until Sunday, but her crazy ways decided him to return early, surprise Sue and have a weekend of debauchery.

The thought of her body – a body he had come to love even though she was immense – spurred him to press down a touch more on the gas pedal. The car surged ahead and at the same time he experienced a pleasant sensation at his groin. He reached forwards and turned the volume of the radio up a touch as the Stones cut into *Honky Tonk Women*.

The chimes on the front door of the apartment tinkled. Sue pulled on her thin pink cotton dressing-gown, the one Damian liked – especially when she was damp and it clung to her – and trotted happily to answer it. She peered through the spyhole and stepped back, puzzled but unafraid.

She unlocked and opened the door. 'Mr Ritter,' she said. It was more of a question.

'Hello, Sue.'

'What can I do for you?'

'I think we need to talk.'

'About what?' She felt suddenly vulnerable and tugged the belt on her gown tighter.

'I actually think you know,' Ritter said, raising his eyebrows. 'May I come in? We can hardly conduct a civilised conversation out here, now can we?'

Reluctantly she allowed him in, but only because he was an FBI agent and wouldn't be foolish enough to try anything stupid. He sidled slowly past her into the living room, brushing his arm against her breasts.

'Nice place you have here,' he commented. He went to the kitchen, then the bedroom and looked into both. 'Nice bed. I'll bet you and Damian do some megafuck work on that.'

Sue's mouth dropped open. She couldn't quite believe what she'd just heard.

'What can I do for you, Mr Ritter?' she said coldly, deciding to ignore it, just in case she'd misheard.

He spun round from the bedroom door and pointed at her. 'What can you do for me? First of all you can sit down.'

Something about the way he said those words made Sue's legs go weak. There was some sort of trouble brewing here. 'I'd rather stand. This is my home – I'll do as I like. And I'm asking you to leave. Goodbye, Mr Ritter.'

He covered the space between them in a couple of strides, moving so fast that Sue was unable to defend herself from the powerful blow that sent her spiralling backwards onto the couch. It had been a well-timed, well-connected slap – with all his might behind it.

She sat up, shaking her head. 'Damian,' she called out. 'Get in here!'

Ritter laughed. 'Maybe when he comes back from Mommy's. You're all alone, Sue. I know these things. I check – I'm a pro.'

'You're a madman,' she hissed. She was sure her jaw was broken. She started to clamber to her feet, intent on hitting back, but she was too slow. *Where was Damian?*

Ritter grabbed her hair and rammed her face down onto his up-thrusting knee. Her nose burst with a distinct crack and he tossed her back onto the couch.

'You really are obscene,' he said, standing over her, looking dispassionately down at her exposed body: her gown, covered in blood, had sagged open and ridden up.

But Sue was past modesty. She had never felt such incredible pain before. She whimpered like a kitten: 'What do you want?'

He smiled benevolently. 'That day at Bayside – why were you there? Were you watching me, seeing who I was meeting? Is that why you were there?' His questions were relentless.

'I was having a picnic,' said Sue.

'Liar!' His foot lashed out and he kicked her shins hard. She screamed in pain. 'Now – *why were you there?*'

'Having a picnic . . . boyfriend . . .'

Oh God Damian, where are you? Come to my rescue.

'You've been following me, haven't you? Building up a dossier. Who I meet, who I speak to. The boat I own – do you know about that too? What about my condo? Have you checked my bank accounts? I bet you have, you accountancy cunt. You know all about me and Corelli, don't you?'

'No, no, no,' she cried desperately. 'You're wrong, wrong. Oh, please Damian, help me.'

'He won't help you,' sneered Ritter. 'He's miles away, with Mommy. So, who else knows all this?' he demanded.

'No one . . . you're insane.'

He grabbed her by the hair again and yanked her into a sitting position. Then leaned down and glared into her eyes. 'Who . . . else . . . knows?' he repeated slowly. Spittle ran from the corners of his mouth. 'Where is the file?'

'There is no file. I know nothing about you or Corelli,' she said.

He flung her back contemptuously, revealing her shaking folds of flesh.

'Oh, you really are gross,' he said disgustedly. 'It'll be like sticking a pig.' And he pulled a knife out of his pocket.

Sue tried to scream but no noise would come; she tried to get up and run away, but fear had driven all responses from her body.

Ritter plunged the knife into her chest, piercing her

heart. By the time he'd removed it and plunged it in a second time, she was as good as dead. This didn't stop him from stabbing her in a frenzy of utter blind madness another thirty-eight times. And that was just the beginning.

Joe Kovaks drove into Liberty City at nine that evening and cruised the streets slowly, making sure that he wasn't being followed. He couldn't afford to be caught out on this one, either by his own side or the other. This was his little operation and its success depended on no one else knowing about it.

Kovaks looked cynically at the streets where in 1980 the whole world had been made aware of Miami's race problems; four days of rioting had left eighteen people dead. A white face here was still unwelcome. Now, even though he was streetwise, unafraid and armed, he kept his windows closed, door locked and never stopped at a traffic light.

Once he was satisfied he was alone, he drove out west to a rundown motel just on the edge of Liberty City and made straight for Room 103. After knocking in a particular way, he let himself in with his own key.

The room was untidy, but at least the bedclothes were clean. Laura lay motionless in the bed with the duvet wrapped tightly around her head. She hadn't heard him either knock or enter.

In the corner of the room a TV set blared out. Fast-food cartons, their contents half-eaten, were strewn on the floor. Kovaks switched the TV off and went into the kitchenette where, after clearing and wiping the work surface, he emptied the bag of groceries he'd brought into the relevant cupboards.

As he was doing this, Laura surfaced. Wearing only a pair of panties, she sat up, head in hands, rubbing her face.

'Joe, you got it? I need it, Joe!' she said through her fingers.

'I got it. Be patient.'

'Come on, man. I need it. You promised.'

'I always keep my promises.' Kovaks returned to the bedroom. 'But first you gotta do something for me.'

'Yeah, yeah, anything, Joe.'

'Clear the fucking place up or you get nothing – understand?'

It took a few seconds for his order to reach her brain. Then, without a murmur of dissent, she got to it. In a matter of minutes the room had been tidied. The fast-food cartons were in the bin, the bed was straight, clothes and shoes were put away.

Kovaks sat on one of the two easy chairs and watched her scurrying about the room. He'd always known about the power that pimps and dealers had over drug addicts, but had never imagined how easy it was to get in such a position of dominance. You had what they wanted and they'd do anything for you to get it. A very simple equation. Power went to the people who had the drugs and were not users themselves. People like Corelli.

Kovaks had always found it difficult to understand addiction, but thanks to his short association with Laura he was learning fast. In her lucid moments, the black girl was bright, intelligent and articulate. What had been her downfall was circumstance, lack of money, lack of guidance.

But he didn't really care about that. He had decided to use her and use her he would. He exerted power over her now and that's what mattered. She would do anything for him, just to feed her habit.

'There,' she said, standing up, pushing her dry hair back, 'done.'

She moved in front of Kovaks and stood there. Her body was still painfully thin. Her ribs protruded through her skin and her knees stuck out gnarled and unsightly. 'Anything else? I need it, Joe. Come on, man.'

He took hold of her wrist and pulled her gently down towards him. Her thin body was easy to bend.

'How much do you want it?' he teased.

'You know how much.'

'Will you do anything for me?'

'Yes, I will.' Her bloodshot eyes looked pleadingly into his.

He had been leading up to this, never actually saying it, always insinuating it, prodding, pushing her in the right direction.

'Will you kill Corelli for me?' he whispered.

She didn't even have to think. 'Yes, I will,' she gasped.

Kovaks couldn't suppress a grin of triumph. Laura had lived in this motel room since her discharge from hospital and Kovaks, at his own risk and expense, had nurtured her, clothed her, fed her, provided drugs for her and now she was completely reliant on him. He was her world. She loved him. He was her provider. And he didn't beat up on her, abuse her or want to fuck her ass.

She didn't know that he really did want to fuck her. But fuck her good and proper.

Kovaks reached into his pocket. He handed her a brown bottle which contained a bright green liquid, rather like Crème de Menthe. It was methadone, heroin substitute. Twice her daily requirement, provided by a 'doctor' Kovaks knew who owed him a favour.

She unscrewed the cap and swigged the contents in one, wiped her mouth and smiled at him as warmth spread into her stomach and from there into her bloodstream.

'What about my baby?' she asked.

'I'm negotiating. It looks good.' It was a lie.

'Joe, I love you,' she said dreamily. She put her arms around his neck and sank her bony frame onto his knees, curling up like a child.

'I want you to kill Corelli,' he whispered in her ear.

'I will,' she said. 'Give me a gun. I'll do it.'

'You're a good girl.' Kovaks sighed. Suddenly a surge of guilt whipped through him, but then it was gone. It was the only way, he assured himself. The only way.

* * *

Damian lay under the bed for twenty minutes before he dared to move. He was not a brave man. He'd heard the outer door of the apartment open and close but hadn't had the courage to emerge just in case it was a ploy.

He tried to stand up but his legs were so weak and shaky that they wouldn't bear even his meagre weight. So, on all fours, stark naked, he crawled slowly towards the door.

He was terrified of what he would see. The reality was far worse than anything he could have imagined.

The living room was swathed in blood. Slashes of it swept across the ceiling and right down the walls, like some sort of modern art form. The couch was drenched in it.

Damian gagged. Using the doorknob for support he levered himself to his feet and stood there wobbling unsteadily.

Then he saw her.

Sue lay on the couch, legs and arms splayed wide. Her throat was cut and the rest of her had been literally ripped apart. Her intestines had been dragged out and some organ or other was hanging, shimmering on the edge of the couch like it was still alive, ready to slither off.

Damian sagged back to his knees, then scuttled on all fours back into the bedroom and into the en-suite bathroom, where he managed to get his head over the toilet before being horrendously sick.

He got dressed quickly.

At the bedroom door he composed himself for his re-entrance back into the living room. He placed his hands around his eyes, like he was a kid pretending to make a diving mask, to give himself tunnel vision. Then he ran across the bloodsoaked carpet, down the short hallway and out through the front door of the apartment.

Kovaks was back at his desk by 11 p.m., having left Laura in a state of drug-induced euphoria. At midnight he took a call. He grabbed his jacket immediately and within half an hour was at the front door of Sue's apartment block.

The senior detective at the scene was Lieutenant Ram Chander, from Homicide. He was one of the few Asian-Indians on the force, a very good detective, completely ruthless and hard to offenders yet with a genuine compassionate streak where victims and their families were concerned.

Kovaks had worked with him occasionally, but they didn't have any particular bond. He was surprised when Chander came down in person to greet him. They shook hands.

'She was once your partner, Mr Joe?' Chander said. He spoke with an American accent but with the odd inflection which betrayed his Kashmiri roots as well as the Indian habit of referring to people by their first names but with the preface of Mr or Mrs as appropriate.

'She was,' Kovaks confirmed.

'Was she a good friend?'

'Yes.'

'Then I must ask you to prepare yourself for an upsetting sight,' Chander warned Kovaks. 'Would you like me to describe it for you first, or do you just want to go and see?'

'I'll go and see,' said Kovaks impatiently. 'I've come across some bad things in my time.'

'Well, Mr Joe, this'll be one of the worst,' sighed Chander.

Ram Chander was right.

It took Kovaks a good while to recover. Yes, he had seen worse, but when it was someone you knew lying there, cut open like a carcass at a butcher's, it was different.

He was on the landing outside the apartment, talking to Chander. Inside was a bustle of activity. Cameras flashed, videos ran, the ME directed operations and the forensic people got to work.

Chander was telling Kovaks everything he knew.

'The call came in just after nine,' Chander said, referring to his notes. 'One of the neighbours walked past and saw that the front door was open. Thought it was suspicious, that maybe the place had been burglarised. The only time you leave your door open here is to let yourself in or out. Anyway, very brave of him, he went to have a look and found her. We arrived shortly after.'

'Any leads?'

'Most certainly,' said Chander. 'The boyfriend is the prime suspect.'

'Who – Damian?'

Chander shook his head, which actually meant yes. Just occasionally, when he got excited, he reverted to this Indian way of saying yes. Fortunately Kovaks understood the body language.

'He was seen by a neighbour leaving hurriedly.'

'I can't believe that,' said Kovaks. 'Damian wouldn't hurt a fly. He's not big enough to kill her.'

'I have a detective down at your place making enquiries. Seems he was on leave and should have been at his mother's over in Clearwater until Sunday. Mother was contacted and said he'd left early. Looks like he wanted to surprise the victim.'

'Come on – what would be his motive?'

'Until we get him, we can't establish that. Maybe she was seeing someone else. Maybe she'd dumped him. Jealousy? Anger?' Chander shook his head sadly. 'It would not surprise me, Mr Joe.'

'Well, it would astound *me*, Ram. Keep me informed, will ya?'

'Surely – so long as you keep me informed too. The parties involved may be Federal staff, but the murder is still our jurisdiction . . .'

'No need to remind me.'

They shook hands.

The Coroner's men were just emerging from the apartment with the very heavy body bag. Kovaks dashed past them. He didn't want to see her being carried away.

At six o'clock, British time, on Saturday morning, six men, all hard, tough and uncompromising assembled in a yard behind a scrap-metal dealer in North London. There were three cars for them, two Jaguars and a Mercedes. They were good cars, but a few years old and unremarkable, except for the fact that they were the most powerful models in the range and they were scrupulously clean – from a criminal point of view.

The men paired off and chose a car.

Each of the cars had had some internal bodywork carried out. A special compartment had been skilfully fitted underneath the rear seats, which ran the full width of the vehicle, which was about ten inches deep and ten inches across. These compartments could not easily be found should the car ever be searched.

The men placed certain items of what they termed 'merchandise' into each compartment, laid the lids back on and slotted the rear seats back into place.

Then they each put a holdall into the boots of the cars.

They were ready to travel.

Each pair tossed up to see who would drive for the first half of the journey. The lucky ones curled up in the back seats to get some shuteye. As ex-soldiers, they were aware of the value of sleep.

They set off in a convoy initially and headed north towards the M1. Soon they were travelling individually because they did not want to draw attention to themselves as a single entity.

This way, if one got into trouble for some reason, the others would get away.

Each man knew his destination.

They were to meet up in Blackburn, Lancashire at noon. There was no great hurry. They would be briefed today, recce the site, see what equipment was available and what they needed to acquire, make their plans and then bide their time.

They were good at waiting. But from all accounts they wouldn't have to wait too long.

Chapter Twenty-Three

The jury reached its verdicts at lunchtime on Tuesday. The Crown Court was reconvened and the elected foreperson was asked to read the verdicts out, whether the accused was guilty of murder, manslaughter or not guilty as the case might be.

Henry was sitting in court alongside Donaldson and Karen. FB sat in the row of seats in front of them, surrounded by all the detectives directly involved in the case.

The court was full to the brim; Henry noticed that Lisa Want was among the journalists. She'd been noticeable by her absence recently. Henry held back the urge to leap across the court and break every bone in her beautiful body.

The foreperson was a lady in her mid-thirties. She spoke in a shaky, faltering voice.

The court clerk led her through the charges.

Hinksman was found guilty of the M6 murders.

A murmur of approval chunnered around the room.

Then he was found guilty of the murder of Ken McClure.

Someone almost clapped. The Judge looked sternly at that person.

Henry had a quick glance at Donaldson. A tear was running down the American's cheek. Henry saw that his and Karen's hands were intertwined. He felt happy for them. He turned his attention back to the court proceedings.

Henry began to grow tense. He wasn't sure how he'd react if Hinksman was found not guilty of the charges he had brought against him.

Manslaughter verdicts were brought for the killings of the police officers who had raided Pepe Paglia's guest-house to arrest Hinksman.

A stony silence greeted these verdicts.

He was found not guilty of the murder of Pepe Paglia.

That drew a gasp of disbelief.

He was also found not guilty of the murder of the arms dealer in Rossendale.

A few shrugs went round the court. That had been half-expected, but was a disappointment nevertheless.

Then, much to Henry's relief, he was found guilty of all the murders in the alley.

A roar of approval went up from the court.

Donaldson, next to Henry, patted his knee.

It took the Judge a few minutes to bring order to the courtroom. She was clearly annoyed at the disruption.

The foreperson resumed and found Hinksman guilty of the manslaughter of the woman on the promenade who had unfortunately stepped into the line of fire between Henry and Hinksman.

Hinksman had also been charged with numerous firearms and explosives offences, most of which were proved.

He was going to go to prison for a very long time.

The foreperson sat down, relieved to have done her duty in the spotlight. She looked like she was having a hot flush.

Hinksman stared over at Henry and shook his head sadly.

Then the Judge said, in her most authoritative tone, 'The accused will stand.'

Hinksman didn't move. He looked at the vaulted ceiling and whistled. It was something the Judge had been counting on. 'Officers,' she said to his guards, 'bring the prisoner to his feet.'

Henry whispered to Donaldson, 'The administration of justice is a wonderful thing, don't you agree?'

'Sure do,' said Donaldson. They shook hands.

Karen, who had heard the remark, leaned across

Donaldson and said, 'There's more justice to be administered yet.'

'What do you mean?' asked Henry.

She tapped her nose. 'Wait and see.'

They looked to the front of the court as the Judge began to comment on the case and then to pass sentence.

'It's over,' Henry said down the phone to Kate.

'I'm glad,' she said.

'Life sentences. Judge recommended that he never be released. And on top of it, two months for contempt of court for some of the gestures he made during the trial. It was highly amusing. And the Judge commended me for bravery – and others. She said some good things.'

'So what happens now?'

'Well, he gets taken to Strangeways and we're all going for a knees-up.'

'I didn't quite mean that.'

'Oh.'

There was a sudden silence as if the line had gone dead, as if someone had pulled the plug.

'You still there?' Kate asked.

'Yeah,' he gulped nervously. 'How're the girls?'

'Fine. They'll see you at the weekend.'

'Excellent. Good. Look . . . er, did you mean what happens next to us?'

'That's exactly what I meant.'

'I do love you, y'know.'

'Do you?' she sighed.

'Yes. And I miss you like mad. And I need you.'

'I love you too, Henry.'

'Can I come home?'

'We need to talk about it. I'm still not sure. I need some reassurances, some promises. You hurt me very badly. All my faith was rocked when you betrayed me. Everything I valued counted for nothing. I want you to come home, but I am frightened by the prospect.'

'Me too,' he admitted. 'I'm sorry . . . Look, I'm having a day off tomorrow. Perhaps I could come round in the evening; we could talk then.'

'The girls would be in the way. I have a better idea.'

'Go on.'

'I'll take a day off too. Then we'll have all day to chat, see how we feel, what we can resolve.'

Henry's heart leapt.

'Yeah, yeah, good idea,' he said eagerly. 'What time should I come round?'

'Ten?'

'I'll be there.'

The pips started to go.

'I love you, Kate,' he managed to say before the line went dead.

He hung the receiver up slowly with a wide smile on his face, juxtaposed with a feeling of trepidation in his guts. *At last*, he said to himself. *At last*.

As he turned away from the payphone which was in the Crown Court building, he bumped into Lisa Want who was standing directly behind him. His smile dropped; his face became a mask of contempt. He tried to shoulder past her but she stood her ground.

'Look, I'd like to say I'm sorry,' she told him. 'I heard you giving evidence – I hadn't realised what you'd been through, OK?'

He snorted in disbelief. 'I have no doubt in my mind that you do not have a conscience, and if you ever get the opportunity to shaft someone, you'd do the same thing all over again. Goodbye, Miss Sleaze-bag.' And he edged carefully around her, as if to avoid contamination, and strode towards the exit.

'Ungrateful son of a bitch!' she uttered, and stamped her feet angrily like a child.

Outside the court building the victorious team of detectives, including FB, but not Donaldson and Karen, were waiting for Henry. They cheered as he appeared. He modestly acknowledged this with a bow, then they all moved off towards the city centre, where it was their intention to take over a pub and get riotously pissed out of their heads.

Just as they reached the prison gates, they encountered a crowd of journalists and sightseers. A buzz of expectation went through them as the prison gates were flung open and the convoy taking Hinksman to Strangeways roared out and sped down the hill.

Some of the detectives gesticulated rudely at the rear of the prison bus.

Henry merely stood there, hands thrust deep in his pockets, staring at the back window. He was sure that Hinksman would be looking at him through the one-way glass. He allowed himself another smile and thought, Goodbye, you bastard. I hope you rot in hell.

Henry had probably smiled more times that day than on any other in the last six months.

The bus and escort were out of sight within seconds, the sirens acompanying them becoming less distinct.

Henry then shivered with a sense of foreboding. Something was wrong. His smile dropped. What was it? He looked up into the sky. The force helicopter clattered overhead, moving with the convoy.

The gang of detectives surged down the road. Henry caught up with them and tapped FB on the shoulder.

'Boss?'

'Henry, what is it?'

'Er . . . nothing, I hope. It's just . . . I've suddenly had a very bad feeling.'

'You'll be all right,' said FB, slapping him on the shoulder. 'C'mon, you just need a drink inside you. There's a lot to celebrate.'

'Yeah, sure,' said Henry. But as much as he tried, he couldn't rid himself of that feeling of impending doom.

Lisa Want watched the detectives strut down the hill like a group of lager louts. She was utterly furious with Henry: it was the first time *ever* that she'd apologised to anyone for a piece she'd written, and the last.

But she did have to admit that the guy was right: she would do it again. It was in her blood.

A nondescript man approached her.

'Lisa Want?' he asked.

She nodded. 'This is for you.' He handed her a package; she noticed that he was wearing gloves. 'The man in it is the Chief Constable of Lancashire. The woman is a hooker. You don't need to know her name.'

Then he was gone, leaving Lisa holding the tape.

The police convoy – two cars to the front and rear of the caged prison bus containing Hinksman – sped down the hill away from Lancaster Prison and the crowd of onlookers. The traffic-lights at the bottom of the hill next to Waterstone's bookshop were set on green for them. The convoy should have turned left and gone into the one-way system which rings Lancaster; however, a few minutes before the convoy had left the prison, the last police operation for the trial had come into effect. Officers had stepped into all relevant junctions and stopped all traffic, enabling the convoy to turn right against the flow of traffic.

It worked smoothly.

Within a minute the convoy was travelling south towards Galgate along the A6. Once south of Galgate, the plan was to get onto the M6 and drive like the clappers to Manchester and Strangeways.

A grim-faced Hinksman sat sullenly in the back of the van, subdued and angry. His hands were secured in front of him by rigid handcuffs. The inane chatter of the two officers who sat in the cage with him only served to fuel his anger. Captured by a pathetic detective whom he had grown to hate and vowed to kill, then beaten by British justice, Hinksman was a killer with a grudge.

He rocked back and forth as he thought about his predicament.

Sent to prison for life – and no one had made any attempt to free him. What the hell was going on? What had happened to Corelli, and to Lenny Dakin – the two men who had most benefited from his skills and abilities at causing mayhem and death? Where were they now, he asked himself.

Lenny Dakin was actually parked up in a stolen Jaguar XJS with false number plates on the slip road leading up to Lancaster University.

He was contemplating how easy it had been to snare August. The manager of his casino in Blackpool always kept him abreast of 'interesting' people who used the facilities on a regular basis, and August had been a regular for about four months.

Not being one to miss out on any opportunity, Dakin had set him up twice with women. If he'd wished, he could have had pictures then, but he hadn't bothered. He'd simply put August on the back burner for when he really needed to exploit him.

Then it had been very easy indeed.

Dakin sniggered and peered out of the front windscreen of the Jag. He had a fairly good view from that position up the A6 towards the city. Suddenly the convoy came into view. He glanced up into the air: the chopper was there. A handset from a CB radio was resting in the palm of his hand. He pressed the transmit button and said coolly, 'We're on.'

The village of Galgate lies astride the A6, south of Lancaster. There is a set of traffic-lights at a crossroads in the centre of it, where a country road crosses the A6 at right-angles. A pub is situated on one corner, shops on the others.

It is a quiet place, not particularly picturesque and to be honest, not somewhere you'd normally stop for anything.

But it is a place where, with a little thought and planning, a gang of professional criminals who specialise in springing prisoners from custody could ambush a police convoy if they so wished.

* * *

Dakin watched the convoy speed by from his position near the University. His heart began to beat quickly and he became very excited. He'd heard about this team, read about their exploits in the newspapers and now – after a great deal of difficulty in actually tracking them down through intermediary after intermediary – had hired them himself. And they didn't come cheap. He hoped they were worth their fee. He was about to find out.

The traffic-light control box was easy to break into with a small jemmy. The man had done it many times before. It took him only a matter of seconds and no one saw him do it anyway. Not that anyone would have thought much about it, because he was wearing a Lancashire County Council boiler suit and looked official, like he knew what he was doing with that toolbag at his feet.

The control panel was no different nor more complicated than thousands of others. The man leaned nonchalantly on the control box, whistling, and cast his eyes up the road.

When the convoy was about 200 metres away, he pressed a button. All the lights at the junction went to red and stayed there. He pulled a ski-mask on, reached into his toolbag and pulled out a light sub-machine gun.

This was the signal for another man who had been sitting patiently behind the wheel of a large furniture removal van, parked a few metres into the crossroad opposite, with the engine idling. He too pulled a mask on, released the brakes and then let the clutch out in such a stuttering manner that the huge van kangarooed out across the junction at right-angles to the approaching convoy, stalled, and stopped dead.

The convoy screeched to a halt. They had actually slowed down as they'd approached the lights, but weren't intending to stop.

Behind the last police car in the convoy, two masked men leaped out of the back of a Ford Escort van which was parked up by the roadside. They were dressed in overalls and wore running shoes. One carried a machine gun ready for use; the other an infamous Sa-7, surface-to-air missile in a launcher, a type beloved by guerrilla and terrorist groups around the world. He aimed at the helicopter.

For an instant the police drivers couldn't be sure whether this was for real or not. Was it an ambush? Or was it just an unfortunate incident?

When the rear door of the furniture van dropped open like a drawbridge, slammed down with a clatter and two men emerged from within, again masked, dressed in over-alls and carrying weapons, they knew it was for real.

They reacted as they'd been trained. Screaming into their car-to-car radio, 'Ambush! Ambush!' the drivers crunched the gears into reverse. There was chaos. The passengers drew their guns in readiness.

None of the police cars got anywhere to speak of.

The man holding the SAM pulled the trigger. With a deadly *whoosh!* the rocket streaked towards its target in the sky.

The other man who'd leapt from the stationary van at the back of the convoy had already run the few metres towards the rear police cars. No one saw him coming. He sprinted past the cars, spraying them with bullets which smashed through the windows and bodywork with ease, killing all the occupants within seconds.

It was a similar story with the two leading cars; these were dealt with in the same manner by the two men who'd come running from the rear of the furniture van. The only difference was that one police officer, reacting faster than the rest, opened his door and rolled out and got up into a firing position. Before he could aim properly, however, the man who'd sorted the traffic-lights had virtually cut him in half with a sweep of his machine gun.

The pilot of the helicopter and the crew of police officers didn't stand a chance. The rocket slammed into the under-belly of the hovering machine and there was a massive explosion of blue and orange flame and black smoke.

Literally shot out of the sky, the helicopter twisted towards the ground, plummeting down onto the railway line which ran behind the village.

The driver of the prison bus was petrified – literally. He sat in his seat, numb, his hands tightly holding the steering wheel. The policeman next to him was babbling incoherently into the radio. Fortunately the radio operator at force headquarters was a cool customer who had already dispatched assistance and alerted his supervisors.

The driver of the furniture van raced past the two leading police cars holding a double-barrelled shotgun. He stopped at the front of the prison bus, took aim at the engine block and fired both barrels into the radiator. The engine cranked to a mangled stop.

Inside, Hinksman smiled at his two captors and held out his hands.

'Beaten, I think,' he said smugly. 'I think it's in your interests to let me go.'

'No fuckin' chance,' one of the cops said. He reached out and grabbed Hinksman's handcuffs and twisted them. Hinksman screamed and fell forwards off the bench seat and onto his knees. One of the advantages of the rigid handcuff is that there is total control – via pain – of the prisoner, no matter how big, tough or strong he is. 'If I'm gonna die,' the officer hissed into Hinksman's face, 'I'm gonna hurt you first.'

He twisted the cuffs again. They bit into the flesh and nerve-endings of Hinksman's wrists. A little more pressure and the bones would break.

The traffic-light man sprinted to the rear of the bus and efficiently clamped six tiny explosive charges to the doors – one at each hinge and two near the lock and handle. Then he retreated a few metres.

The two officers who were trapped in the space between the inner cage where Hinksman was held and the back doors cowered. They had their guns in their hands.

The charges all detonated together, blowing the doors

cleanly off their hinges. The noise ricocheted around the interior of the bus, like thunder in a confined space, deafening and disorientating everyone.

The officers were uninjured by the blast but were winded by the explosion and overcome with smoke. They tumbled out of the back of the bus into the open air, gasping, choking, coughing and confused. They were shown no mercy. As their feet touched the tarmac they were mown down.

All that remained was to get the inner cage door open.

The traffic-light man stepped up into the back of the bus, a small chainsaw in his hands. Within seconds he had removed the door. He flung it, complete, out of the back of the bus onto the road with the assistance of one of his colleagues.

Throughout all this, the officer who had decided to inflict as much pain as possible on Hinksman had more or less hung onto his man. When faced with overwhelming odds he sensibly let go of the cuffs.

Hinksman held out his damaged hands. The saw neatly parted the cuffs.

'Give me a gun,' he said to one of the masked men.

He was immediately handed a pistol.

He turned on his captor and held the gun to the officer's head.

'No one gets away with causing me pain and aggravation,' he said through gritted teeth. 'No one.' He pulled the trigger twice and most of the back of the man's head splattered through the cage onto the driver, passenger and windscreen.

Then he turned on the other officer who had also been his gaoler. 'Just remember what I've said – and pass it onto Henry Christie.' He shot the man twice in the lower stomach, figuring that he would stay alive long enough to tell the story.

'C'mon,' the traffic-light man said, tugging at Hinksman's sleeve.

312

Hinksman nodded and jumped out behind him. They ran towards the traffic-lights and turned right where their transport awaited – a huge, powerful motorcycle with no rear numberplate.

Hinksman was handed a crash helmet. Moments later, as the back-seat passenger, he and the traffic-light man were accelerating away from the scene down winding country roads.

The rest of the ambush team had gone too. No one who saw the incident – and there were many witnesses – could exactly say where to. The men had gone, disappeared like ghosts, their shock tactics having had the desired effect.

Only two police officers were uninjured – the ones in the front of the prison bus. They climbed slowly out when they thought it was safe, both covered in the contents of their fellow officer's skull. One of them looked around at the carnage, sank down to his knees at the kerbside and allowed his head to flop into his hands. He was too numbed to cry. The other wandered up and down the road, peering into the cars, knowing that he could do nothing. He sat down on a wall, and lit a cigarette. In the distance was the sound of approaching sirens.

One hundred metres further back, Lenny Dakin got into his XJS which he'd parked on a side street.

That had been fantastic, he thought proudly. Fucking fan-tas-tic. Money well spent. Worth every fucking penny. The most exhilarating two minutes three seconds he had ever experienced.

And Hinksman was free.

'He has to die.'

'I know, Joe, I know. I just don't know if I can do it.'

'It's not a case of *can*, it's a case of *must*. Don't worry, you'll be protected. I'll be there – I'll see you're OK. Trust me.'

'I don't know . . .'

'Don't you trust me?'

313

'Yes, I do, Joe.'

'Don't I give you everything you need? Don't I feed your habit?'

'Yes, yes, yes.'

'So what's the problem? I'll look after you, Laura. He needs to die and we need to do it. He's the enemy. The destroyer. The user. Every other way of dealing with him has been tried, but justice has failed. It's failed you badly, it's failed me badly. Now we're going to administer the justice . . . you and me . . . you and me . . . *you*.'

'Yes, but—'

'What's he done for you? Nothing, absolutely nothing. He used Whisper, then killed him. He used you and you almost died. There are thousands more like you, thousands who need justice . . . and just think what'll happen when it's over. You'll get your baby back! The Social Services have promised me. And you'll be free . . . and that's everything you want, isn't it?'

'Yes, Joe. Me and my baby.'

'And all the dope you need.'

'Yes, yes . . . have you got some?'

'Only if you kill him.'

'I will.'

'Promise?'

'Yes. When? How?'

'Soon. Very soon, I promise.'

'Here, take this.'

It was a small plastic sachet containing white crystals of crack, one of the most addictive drugs known. And she was addicted. It wasn't her baby she wanted, not really. It was crack. She would do anything to satisfy her need for it. Murder included.

Henry had just taken a sip of his second pint of lager. It tasted good, as had the previous one. He was looking forward to the next ones. He felt good and was going to enjoy the celebration first and worry about getting back to the flat thirty miles away in Blackpool second. He glanced around the pub. It was small and narrow with a bar in the centre of the room. The atmosphere reminded Henry of pubs he'd visited in London. Most congenial.

He saw the uniformed Constable appear at the front door, helmet on, a worried expression across his face. A roar of disapproval went up from the assembled detectives who'd all begun to front-load Boddington's Bitter as though it was going out of fashion. The officer ignored them. His eyes roved the room and found their target. He walked quickly across to FB.

Once more Henry had that bad feeling in his guts. He placed his beer down on the bar and watched as the Constable and FB drew to one side, out of the hubbub. The Constable began to talk earnestly to FB, whose face dropped in stages: happy and carefree, all the way, step by painful step, to serious, concerned, deeply unhappy, shocked.

He patted the Constable reassuringly on the shoulder for the man seemed deeply upset by the information he'd imparted. FB then gave him some instructions, after which he left hurriedly.

FB looked across the room, his face pale and drawn. His eyes met Henry's, and he beckoned him over.

'What is it, boss?'

'Bad, very fucking bad,' said FB gravely. 'Hinksman's out. Free.'

'What do you mean?'

'He's been sprung. The escort got hit at Galgate and the team that did it slaughtered nearly all the bobbies.' FB was finding it difficult to breathe. 'All but three are dead. That's what the PC told me.'

Henry made a quick calculation. 'Fucking hell,' he uttered.

'I'm going to the scene now – there's a car en route to pick me up. You come too, Henry.'

Henry nodded.

FB turned his attention to the detectives squashed around the bar. He cleared his throat, called for quiet, and with tears in his eyes, made an announcement.

Laura was asleep now. Kovaks was relieved. What had been planned as a two-minute visit had taken him half an hour. And he had a partner waiting out in the car.

Kovaks closed the motel-room door and locked it with his key. Laura would be out of the game for hours now. He would re-visit her at the end of his shift.

Tommo was sitting in the Bucar, chain-smoking, eating a hamburger and sipping a coffee, all at the same time, whilst listening to a cassette which blared country music out deafeningly.

Kovaks slid in beside him. 'You're a slob,' he observed.

Tommo screwed up his hamburger wrapper and tossed it out of the window. 'Thought you said you'd only be a coupla minutes?'

'Sorry,' said Kovaks, offering no explanation.

'So was she worth it?'

Kovaks stiffened. 'Tommo, just shut the fuck up and drive. As I told you, it's my sister. She's gotta few domestic problems and she's holed up there to get her head together.'

'My ass,' snorted Tommo with a belch. He reversed the car out of its parking space and hit the road. 'There was a radio call for ya, by the way.'

'What did it say?'

'Dunno. I said you'd radio in when you'd finished fucking your little sister. I said you'd be about two minutes.' He cracked up with laughter.

'Don't push it, Tommo,' warned Kovaks. He reached for the cassette player and switched off Dwight Yoakam. Then he called in.

The radio operator was a sexy-voiced Texan lady.

'Yeah, Joe, urgent call came in for ya, 'bout ten minutes ago. Caller said he'd call 'gain exactly on ten-thirty.'

'Who was it?'

'Don't rightly know. Refused all details – but he sounded scared. Thought I recognised the voice, but can't place it.'

'Received,' said Kovaks. 'I'm on my way in.'

'You dickin' that piece of ass too?' Tommo asked with a leer.

Kovaks gritted his teeth and decided to ask for another partner until Karl Donaldson came back from England.

'Why the hell did they go via Galgate anyway?' Henry asked.

FB, pale, shaken, said, 'It was the Chief's suggestion. We had a meeting about it yesterday and we worked out the best route with the driver of the lead car.'

'But surely it would have made more sense to get on the motorway north of Lancaster? It's more direct. No winding, narrow roads. No towns to negotiate . . .'

'The Chief's argument was that if there was going to be any sort of attempt, they'd expect us to go that way. Going via Galgate was the less likely option, therefore safer.'

'It was a fucking stupid decision,' said Henry.

They were both sitting in the back of a traffic car which was speeding them to the scene.

'Not only that,' persisted Henry, 'whoever sprung the bastard was *expecting* the escort to go through Galgate. They were all set up and ready. They weren't just hanging about on the off-chance. Something's not right here.'

'I know,' said FB with a heavy sigh.

'Who actually knew that the escort would be taking that route?'

'Me, ACC Warner – Jack Crosby's replacement, the driver of the lead car, and the Chief Constable. We were the only ones at the meeting yesterday. The idea was that everyone else involved – the rest of the officers on the escort and the ones manning points – would get about fifteen minutes' notice just before the escort set off from prison.'

'Quarter of an hour,' mused Henry. 'Not long enough to put that sort of ambush operation into effect. Which means someone blabbed, someone inside the police . . .'

He looked at FB who had aged about ten years in the last ten minutes.

'I'm going to think out loud now,' said Henry, 'and I'm going to say something pretty uncomfortable. It's unlikely that the driver of the lead car talked to anyone because he's dead now, so it's either you, the ACC or the Chief.'

The traffic car reached Galgate.

FB and Henry did not immediately get out. They sat in silence for a few moments.

Eventually FB said, 'Well, I know one thing for sure.' He reached for the door-handle.

'What's that?'

'It wasn't me.'

Kovaks was sitting at his desk poring over some surveillance reports on Corelli. There was nothing particularly interesting in them, nothing he didn't already know about the man, but he looked through them anyway, just in case there *was* something important he'd missed.

It annoyed him that Corelli wasn't a man of regular habits. He needed to know where and when Corelli was going to be in a specific place and for how long, otherwise how could he plan his execution?

Corelli had many favourite haunts, but he visited none of them at a regular time. He was a butterfly. Flitting here, landing there, then taking off again. This was one of the reasons why the FBI had never caught and prosecuted him successfully.

Obviously he spent a great deal of time at his homes and places of business, but these were times when his protection teams were at their strongest and no one could get through the ring uninvited. For Kovaks' purpose, he needed to be away from these places, out in public.

Kovaks drew up a list of the places in Miami where Corelli ate and the amount of time he spent at each one. Then he averaged the times out.

In most places he spent less than an hour. But in two

restaurants he had a tendency to linger for about three hours at lunchtimes. The problem was that he hardly ever visited them. He'd been to both four times in the last two years.

It did seem, though, that whenever he did, he took his time.

Kovaks raised his eyebrows. 'Interesting,' he whispered to himself. 'If I knew when he was visiting one of them, things could maybe start rolling.'

Suddenly, for no accountable reason, the image of Sue's badly mutilated body snapped vividly into his mind's eye. The cops had still failed to track down Damian. Why didn't he come forward? Could Damian really be a murderer?

Kovaks found that very difficult to believe . . .

The phone rang, interrupting his musing.

'Special Agent Kovaks, can I help you?'

'Joe?' came a quiet, frightened voice.

'Yes, who's that?'

'It's me, Damian.'

'Damian!' Kovaks spluttered. 'Where the hell are you?'

'Joe, I need to talk to someone I can trust. Can I trust you?'

'Yeah, sure you can. Where are you? I'll come and—'

The line went dead; Damian had hung up. Kovaks looked sourly at the phone in his hand. He slammed it down and swore.

'This is the saddest tragedy that the Lancashire Constabulary has ever faced and mark my words, we will spare no cost and no effort to bring the perpetrators to justice. We will be relentless in our pursuit and every one of those responsible will be caught – every single one. Now, if you gentlemen will forgive me . . .'

An emotional Dave August wiped a tear from his eye, and ignoring the barrage of questions from the assembled press and TV men, he strode towards the scene.

The whole of the centre of Galgate had been cordoned off in a 200-metre radius of the incident on the road. On the railway line, all trains had been cancelled for the foreseeable future. High screens had been erected around the crime scenes so that no prying eyes or lenses could see anything they shouldn't as the forensic teams, Scenes of Crime officers and search teams began their gruesome tasks. None of the bodies had been moved yet.

August was in full uniform, looking proud and erect. He walked behind one of the screens and saw what lay beyond.

Nothing he had heard prepared him for what he saw.

What have I done? he thought frantically. Oh Christ, what have I done?

Clearly devastated by what he'd seen, he sank down to his haunches, removed his cap and wiped his sweating forehead with his sleeve. He wanted to cry. He wanted to run away. He wanted to bury his head in sand.

'Boss?'

August looked up. 'FB . . . this is awful. My men, slain in the streets like it's the fucking Middle East, not the north of England . . . Christ!'

'Yes, I know,' said FB. 'But can I just have a quick word with you about something else?'

'By all means,' August said, rising to his feet, his knees clicking, glad of the change of subject.

'I'll come straight to the point. It's already been mooted that this is an inside job, that information about the escort route was leaked from either me, you or Mr Warner. I know it's all bullshit, that it must have got out some other way, but we should be prepared to be investigated, to allow whoever follows this up whatever access they need to our private lives, don't you think?'

'Absolutely,' said August, and thought: Is this where the shit hits the fan?

He gave FB an odd look which FB interpreted as follows: Hellfire! He thinks *I* did it!'

Henry stood by the front car of the escort with his hands thrust deep into his trouser pockets, half-watching the conversation between FB and August, but not able to hear.

He stared vacantly at the killing field in front of him. This was a scene from Chicago, from the Bronx, not from Galgate, a one-horse place with a community copper who was wandering around the periphery of the scene as distraught as anyone.

His thoughts were curtailed by the arrival of FB who strutted up to him. He was unsettled, Henry thought.

'Y'know – I think the Chief thinks *I* leaked this!'

Henry chuckled, despite the situation. 'So, what's the plan of action for this?'

'Twofold, as I see it. One to recapture that bastard Hinksman and one to track down the people who did this.' He made a sweeping gesture with his arm.

'They're obviously pros,' observed Henry. 'I've heard there's an international team operating who specialise in this sort of job. Pulled that one early this year down south when that IRA man got sprung. To the best of my knowledge the cops in Hampshire haven't got the sniff of a result on that. It was much the same MO – but fewer dead cops. I think they did something in France too, just before Christmas.'

'Great,' said FB despondently. 'Anyway, I want you to take on the task of getting Hinksman back – if he hasn't already left the country.'

Henry held back a smile. It was just what he wanted. 'Can I pick one or two members for my team?'

'Yeah, why not. Who've you got in mind?'

'Karen Wilde and Karl Donaldson.'

Henry didn't have to wait long for FB's reaction. He boiled over immediately.

'No fucking way, Henry. That bitch killed Jack Crosby and I won't forgive her for that. And as for that Yank, the supercilious bastard – he isn't even a cop.'

Henry waited for the outburst to subside. Calmly he said, 'Jack Crosby killed himself. He smoked too much, drank too much, he was overweight, didn't take any exercise, worked too hard and pushed himself too far. It wasn't her fault he died. It was his own.'

'Hm,' snuffled FB, unimpressed.

'And she nearly caught Hinksman last time. If she'd got the support she deserved, he would have been caught much sooner and maybe, just maybe, we wouldn't have this . . .' Henry let his words sink in.

FB put his head to one side and said, 'You've changed your tune about her, haven't you? Don't forget, she disciplined you and kicked you off the initial enquiry.'

'I don't mind learning things about people,' Henry admitted. 'She knows as much as anybody about Hinksman, and Karl Donaldson is encyclopaedic. Let me have them. Give them a chance.'

FB nodded impatiently. 'OK, OK, I haven't the time to argue – but you keep me informed of every move you make, every breath you take . . .'

'Don't tell me,' said Henry. 'You'll be watching me.'

'Too fucking right I will.'

'Are you DS Christie?' A uniformed Constable had sidled up next to Henry.

'Yes.

'There's a message for you from the hospital. The PC who was shot in the guts has asked to see you. I've been told to pass on the message urgently. Apparently he doesn't have much time left.'

August stood by one of the screens which protected the scene from onlookers. He was hot and sticky and worried.

I've really done it now, he thought. Blood on my hands. Innocent men mown down like rats because of me. Because I was desperate to protect a career and a reputation. Everything gone through one lousy night with a whore. And I walked right into it, eyes closed, cock erect. What a stupid fucking bastard I am.

August looked at the driver of one of the cars, still slumped across the steering wheel. Part of the side of his face was missing, but his eyes were intact, wide open and staring accusingly. Right at August. He tore his gaze away with a little whimper.

August's mind raced on. They still have a hold on me, whoever they are, he thought frantically. If they want me for anything else, they've got me by the balls. If they gave that damned tape to the press, I'd be finished for good. Whatever happens, I must stop them being able to get at me again . . .

'FB,' he said loudly, 'on my desk, nine tomorrow morning, I want everything about Hinksman from Day One. I'm going to take a very personal interest in this investigation and from now on I'll be looking over your shoulder. I shall expect daily updates on all lines of enquiry – understand? I want to know *absolutely everything.*'

The motorcycle was abandoned near Garstang where both Hinksman and the rider transferred to a car. Here there was time for the remainder of the handcuffs to be snipped from Hinksman's wrists. He rubbed them gratefully and the blood flowed back into his hands.

Thirty minutes after driving sedately through country roads to Blackburn, the car stopped outside a terraced house in the Revidge area of the town. The driver handed Hinksman a key and said, 'That's where you'll be lying low until the next stage, whatever that is. There's enough food and drink for you for at least a week. Goodbye and good luck.'

Hinksman said, 'Thanks. That's a good firm you work for. How do I contact you if I ever need you?'

The man laughed. 'You'll find a way,' he said mysteriously.

'Understood,' said Hinksman.

They shook hands and Hinksman got out. The car pulled away from the kerb and Hinksman made his way to the front door of the house without looking back.

Ten minutes later he was joined by Lenny Dakin who had dumped the Jag and was now driving a legitimate car.

They greeted each other with much effusiveness and self-congratulation. A brilliant job. Superbly professional. It was as though they were discussing a Stock Market coup, not a shooting which had left more than half a dozen cops dead.

'I thought you weren't going to come through,' Hinksman admitted, 'when my lawyer said nothing to me.'

'I decided it was best that way. If he got cold feet and blabbed it would've jeopardised the whole thing. Better safe than sorry.'

They looked at each other then embraced elatedly, slapping each other's backs. When they came back to earth, Hinksman asked, 'What's next?'

'To get you out of the country.'

'How do you intend to do that?'

'Well, Corelli wants you back in the US as quickly as possible, but it'll have to be done at my speed. We have a delivery due at the weekend, so what I plan to do is use the reverse route for you. That'll get you to Eire, and from there it's relatively easy to get to the States, maybe via Paris or Amsterdam, whatever.'

'Sounds good,' Hinksman said approvingly.

'So in the meantime, just crash out here. You should be safe enough if you're sensible.'

Hinksman's nod turned smoothly to a shake. 'I have business to attend to. A debt to repay.'

'Now look.' Dakin's eyes narrowed. 'I've put my neck on the line for you, so don't fuck anything up.'

'As if I would,' said Hinksman reprovingly with a grim smile. 'I'll be careful and I'll be back in time. Trust me.'

A hand clamped down on Kovaks' shoulder, making him jump. He had been sitting at his desk, staring blankly into space, with the Corelli surveillance reports in front of him, ever since Damian's phone call. He turned round and there was Eamon Ritter accompanied by Ram Chander.

'Hey, day-dreamer,' laughed Ritter. 'I bumped into Ram

in reception. He said he'd come to see you about Sue's murder, so I brought him straight up. Look, I really am sorry about her, Joe. She was a damned good agent and though I didn't know her too well, she always had a pleasant smile for me. She was your partner for a while, wasn't she?'

'Yeah, she was. And thanks for the sentiment. How's the investigation going, Ram?'

'To be honest,' the Indian admitted, 'we don't seem to be getting anywhere and until we apprehend this Damian character, I don't think we will. That is why I came to see you, Mr Joe, to see if you have heard anything more.'

Kovaks looked at Ritter and instantly decided, what the hell, he's an agent too.

'Yes, I have heard something. Gotta phone call from your chief suspect not long before you walked in here. Sounds like he wants to talk to someone.'

Chander's interest perked up. 'Did he say where he was?'

Kovaks shook his head. 'Said he wanted to talk to someone he could trust, then I think he panicked and hung up. I've been waiting for him to call back, but he may not. He knows that all calls are recorded. He sounded scared.'

Chander sighed. 'OK, Mr Joe, if he does, please let me know immediately. Just remember, this isn't a Federal matter, it's my case.'

'Yeah, no problem,' said Kovaks.

After Ram Chander had left, Ritter sat down next to Kovaks.

'I didn't know that Damian was number one suspect,' he said. 'I knew they wanted to talk to him, obviously, but do you think he killed her?'

'No fucking chance,' said Kovaks with feeling. 'He wouldn't even kill a computer virus. Maybe he knows who did it, though. Maybe he witnessed it.'

'He couldn't have,' argued Ritter. 'Wasn't he on leave, at his mother's in Clearwater?'

'Apparently he left there and could've easily been back at the time of the killing.'

Ritter drew in a breath. 'So he could have done it?'

'Or witnessed it.'

'The cunt,' rasped Ritter. 'Look, if you need any assistance whatsoever, just let me know, willya? My workload's pretty light at the moment. I'd be happy to help you in any way I can.'

'Thanks, Eamon.'

He died before Henry could get to him. The nurses in the Casualty Department at Lancaster Royal Infirmary were just dismantling the medical equipment from around the bed and pulling drips out of veins which no longer pumped blood. Two of the nurses had tears in their eyes. A couple of young doctors stood at the end of the bed, conversing in hushed tones. An older doctor was filling out a form on a clipboard.

Two uniformed Constables and a Sergeant stood quietly by the door, all three overawed by the circumstances.

Henry walked to the Staff Only area where a Sister was working at a desk. He introduced himself and showed his identity. Henry noticed that she, too, had red rings around her eyes. He couldn't decide if it was tiredness or emotion.

'The policeman who just died,' he said, 'asked to see me. I wonder if you know what it was about. No one around his bed seems to.'

'I don't, actually,' she said. 'However, he was very lucid up to the last and asked for a pen and piece of paper. He wrote a short note on it and gave it to me to give to you. I think he knew he would die before you got to see him.' It was then Henry saw that the redness was emotion. 'He was in incredible pain,' she said, 'but he was very brave and very philosophical. He's a credit to the force.'

'Thank you,' said Henry, trying not to be moved. The last thing he wanted was to be drawn into this. He needed to keep an emotion-free head. 'Do you have the note?'

'Oh yes, it's here.' She pulled a piece of paper out of a pocket and handed it to Henry. 'I haven't read it.'

'Thanks.'

He went to the waiting room where he found a spare chair and sat down. He unfolded the note.

It looked like it had been written by a frail eighty-year-old with arthritic fingers. But it was legible.

DS Christie, he read. *He's going to come for you.*

Henry read it over several times before slowly folding it up and placing it in his jacket pocket.

'No,' Henry said out loud. 'I'm going to go and get him.'

Special Agent Eamon Ritter realised that he might have made a mistake, or possibly two, or maybe even three.

The first one had been failing to ensure that Damian had actually been in Clearwater and the second was not searching Sue's apartment properly. Now there was a distinct possibility that the little worm had witnessed the whole thing.

And what happens when you assume? he grilled himself mentally.

You make an 'ass' of 'u' and 'me'.

Standard FBI ground rules: *don't make fucking assumptions.*

And now, to compound all that, he'd made a third mistake by letting it slip to Kovaks that he knew about Damian's leave to his mother's in Clearwater.

Kovaks was very sharp: the chances were that he was probably meditating on that same disclosure at this very minute. Drastic measures were required – and these could include the sudden deaths of another Special Agent and a fingerprint expert.

Something was bugging Joe Kovaks, but he couldn't put his finger on it. He filtered through everything that had happened during the day: the visit to Laura, Tommo's infantile remarks, Damian's phone call, Ram Chander's appearance.

What the hell was it?

Twenty minutes later he still didn't have the answer. This is no good, he thought. I'm getting nowhere fast. He decided to take the rest of the day off. Give Chrissy a surprise.

He replaced the Corelli surveillance logs into a file and tucked it under his arm. He would take them home and study them there with a beer in his hand. Removing any official documents from the building, unless approved, was strictly against Bureau rules. But like most of the rules, Kovaks thought they were bullshit and often flouted them.

On the way home he would call in and see Laura, pep her up and discuss his idea of where to waste Corelli.

As he stepped into the elevator, the phone on his desk started to ring. He did not hear it.

Chapter Twenty-Four

Kovaks rubbed his temples wearily and stood up. He walked across to the large picture window of the apartment. From it there was a fine view of one of the inlets of the intracoastal waterway which ran up behind Fort Lauderdale. Yachts, motor boats, power boats, craft of all sizes and descriptions were moored there.

But Kovaks' mind was not on the splendid vista. It was concentrated solely on the violent death – not before time – of Corelli.

Was this really the right way?

Using Laura, a no-hoper, who had never really done anyone any harm – could he live with that? Using her, knowing that she would almost certainly die.

The problem was that he'd known her before she became a drug user and a prostitute, and he could clearly remember her as a spirited, pretty and more or less honest girl. Given time, trouble and patience she could return to her former self.

But there was no time.

She had to do it soon. Corelli had to be wasted.

Delay meant more lives destroyed.

Kovaks had purchased the murder weapon – a two-inch-barrelled Smith & Wesson model 31, Regulation Police, ·32 calibre. It was just under seven inches long and weighed 22 oz when empty. Laura needed to get in close and that meant a pistol or revolver, of a size and calibre she could hide and handle easily. And it had to be powerful enough to do the job. It was a wonderful gun to handle, though Kovaks found it too light for himself.

Laura had taken to the gun well. She knew a lot about them anyway. She'd spent their last session together practising, walking up to a lampshade with the empty gun tucked into her waistband, then drawing and pumping six imaginary shells into Corelli's head.

She found it very exciting. She wanted to do it for real.

'You must say nothing,' Kovaks coached her. 'You stroll up to him like it's a normal Sunday afternoon. Look relaxed. Smile. Pull the gun out at the last possible moment and shoot the bastard. Throw it down, turn and run. I'll be outside in a car waiting for you.' This lie almost stuck in his throat. 'Don't worry about the layout of the place yet. We'll go there for a meal ourselves a couple of times beforehand and find out where he usually sits. Now . . . squeeze the trigger. Yes, like that. Don't pull it.'

Kovaks didn't hear Chrissy emerge from the bedroom. She padded barefoot and silent up to him, wearing a short nightshirt which only just managed to cover her. She touched his sleeve. He jumped.

'Hi,' she said. 'What're you shaking your head for?'

'Oh nothing, just pondering.'

She slid an arm around his waist. It was as though a shock of electric current had passed through him. Surprised, but happy, he draped an arm around her shoulders and pulled her into him.

She smiled.

He couldn't believe it: a smile. He was almost overwhelmed with joy.

'I've been pretty awful to live with these past few months,' she admitted.

'You've had good enough reason. It hasn't been a problem.' It was a brave attempt at a lie.

'Oh yes, it has,' she insisted. She put her other arm around him and squeezed. 'You've been so good to me. I'm a lucky lady. You've put up with me and my moods and my medical needs, stayed with me through everything, no complaining, nothing. I'm very grateful to you, Joe.'

'You don't have to be grateful. It's my job – I love you.'

'Do you? Even now, with a face like this and a chest that looks like a burned turkey dinner?'

'Honey,' he told her tenderly, looking straight into her eyes, 'I'll admit that initially I was attracted by your looks, but I fell in love with the person behind them. I fell in love with the way you talk, the way you drag your feet, the way you have an answer for everything and a million more things. I'm still in love with that person, even if she is a bit burned.'

She swallowed. Her eyes became moist. 'I thought you'd leave. I was terrified you'd go. I wouldn't have blamed you.'

'Don't be a dork. I love you.' He spelled it out.

'I love you too, Joe.'

'Well, that's all right then.'

One of her hands went to the back of his neck and pulled his head down towards hers. They kissed. A tingle of excitement made Kovaks curl up his toes. It was their first real kiss for many months. Slowly their lips parted and became wet and they began to explore each other's mouths, tongues intertwining, sliding around each other like snakes.

'Joe, Joe,' said Chrissy, breaking off, slightly breathless. 'We need to make love.'

'I'll second that.' He bent down and scooped her up into his arms. Moments later they were on the bed and she was tugging hungrily at the belt on his trousers.

The next time Henry Christie looked at a clock it was 11.30 p.m. He had been busy all day setting up the incident room in the gymnasium at Lancaster police station. Then together with Karen and Donaldson he had brainstormed the lines of enquiry their team of detectives were going to follow the next day.

Henry was alone now; the other two had gone home. This was the last chance they would have for some time to get a good night's sleep. He stood with his hands on his hips in front of the whiteboard upon which all their ideas had been scribbled down. There was a lot to go at. Tomorrow would be an even longer day.

Then he thought: Tomorrow – Christ! My day off!

He picked up a phone and dialled a sleepy-sounding Kate.

'Sorry,' he apologised. 'I know it's late. I would've phoned earlier but I didn't get a chance.'

'No, no, 'sokay,' she mumbled.

'About tomorrow,' he began haltingly.

'You're not coming, are you? I thought as much . . . er, I didn't mean it to sound like that. I've seen the news, it's a dreadful business.'

'Yeah,' he said, stifling a yawn of his own. 'I'm well involved in the investigation, so you're right, I won't be able to come round. You do understand, don't you?'

'Yes,' she said.

'I have to catch this bastard before he catches me,' he said bleakly. 'I think I may have to kill him.'

'Henry, that sounds rather dramatic.'

'He's made it personal, love. He said he's coming for me.'

'Christ,' she breathed.

'Kate, I love you,' he said. 'When this is all really over, let's get back together. No more talking, let's just do it.'

'Yeah, OK,' she said simply.

There was a short spell of stunned silence on the line.

'I love you too, Henry. Please be careful, I want you back.'

She hung up.

Henry slowly replaced the phone and closed his eyes gratefully.

Kate snuggled down under the duvet, next to Leanne who had sneaked in about twenty minutes before, claiming she couldn't sleep. She had dropped off immediately next to her mother but the phone had woken her.

'Was that Dad?' she asked dreamily.

'Yep.'

'Is he coming back?'

'Yes, soon.'

'Does that mean I won't be able to sleep in here again?'

'Correct.'

'Oh, I don't mind, so long as he's back . . . I got told off for saying "Fuck" at school today.'

A minor arrest was about to be made on the streets of Blackpool.

It was the end of what, professionally speaking, had been a poor night for the prostitute whose name was Jane. She'd moved from pub to pub, mingling and soliciting, but all to no avail. No one, it seemed, had the money or inclination to pay for her services.

Frustrated by her lack of success – which was pretty unusual, but not completely unknown – she drank a good deal of alcohol. At closing time, well inebriated, she spilled unsteadily onto the streets and bought herself a bag of fish and chips. She then proceeded to eat them as she walked home. Quite often she missed her mouth when feeding it with handfuls of food and she ended up with a very greasy, uninviting face.

This, however, did not deter her from trying her luck with every man she walked past, whether he was attached or not. Her approach was brash and obscene and it went well with her appearance: a tight-fitting mini skirt in cheap leather, laddered stockings and a blouse that was unbuttoned below the line of her freely swinging breasts, leaving nothing to the imagination.

She managed to strike it lucky just the once. She collared a sallow youth, a holidaymaker hardly past puberty, and all but dragged him down a back alley. She sank to her knees on the cobbles, placing her chips carefully down beside her, unzipped his jeans and slid her oily mouth over his flaccid cock. Despite the odds, she was successful in bringing about an erection followed by ejaculation. This done, she collected her chips, claimed five pounds and left the poor boy standing there speechless, wondering what the hell had hit him.

333

Back on the streets, with a mouthful of fish to take away the taste, she tried her luck with one or two other men who swore at her and pushed her away.

Then her luck really ran out.

Her last few attempts at solicitation were watched by two plain-clothed policemen, one of whom casually walked past her. He was treated to her one-line come-on. When he introduced himself and arrested her, she punched him in the mouth and smacked the remains of her supper onto his head. She was forcibly restrained, put in the back of a police van and taken, struggling and screaming all the way, to Blackpool Central police office.

Once inside a cell, she immediately calmed down, laid herself out on the bed and fell into a heavy, drunken slumber.

After their lovemaking, Joe and Chrissy lay interlocked for a long time, him still deep inside her, both savouring the last twinges of pleasure before he withdrew slowly.

Then he lay face up and she nestled into his chest.

'That was lovely,' said Chrissy. 'I've been wanting to have you inside me for weeks now, Joe. Do . . . do the burns matter to you?' she asked timidly.

'No – not when you can fuck like that.'

She punched him gently in the ribs and giggled.

'How are you going on with Corelli?' she asked. 'I see you've brought some files home to work on.'

Kovaks sighed. 'As ever, he evades our clutches. Like he has a sixth sense.'

'Do you honestly think he was the one who sent the letter?'

He nodded. 'Oh, yeah. Just a warning. Business, y'know, nothing personal. But I won't give up on him. I'll get him one way or another.'

'I hope you're not planning anything illegal,' she said. 'You see, what I finally realised, Joe, was that he hadn't destroyed my life. If he'd taken you away, that would have destroyed it, but I still have you, and I'm happy. I just thought, What the hell am I doing sat here like a moron week after week, thinking about revenge, being bitter and twisted, when I should be thinking about the future. You and me, Joe. *That's* my future. Corelli can rot in hell. I even feel sorry for him. He's a sad man without a life. I've got you. I know it's taken me a long time to work it all out and I'm sorry for what I've put you through, but now I see. Let's just forget Corelli and get on with living.'

She snuffled and blinked the tears away from her eyes. It was the most she had said to Kovaks for many months and she sounded positive, like the Chrissy of old.

Kovaks felt an overwhelming love for her, and his throat constricted as suddenly he knew she was right. Revenge wasn't the way forwards. It was the way to hell. He lifted her chin so he could look into her eyes. 'So your future's with me, eh, kid?'

'If that's what you want.'

'Only if it involves marriage and kids and all that crap.'

'Is that a proposal of marriage?'

'Yup, I suppose it is,' he said shyly.

'Mm,' she said, pursing her lips thoughtfully. 'So let me get this clear in my head. You're asking me to marry you, right?'

'Sure am,' he said more confidently.

'In that case, I accept. But . . . '

'But what?'

'Between now and whenever the wedding day is, we've got a hell of a lot of fucking to make up and I'm going to get a piece of it right now.'

Driving exhaustedly from Lancaster to Blackpool in his Metro, which was constantly buffeted by heavy goods vehicles as they thundered past on the motorway, Henry Christie started to do 'nodding dog' impersonations. He opened a window and let the cool night breeze waft him into wakefulness. He didn't particularly want to end up squashed under the back wheels of a lorry.

Unfortunately, the fresh air had the effect of revitalising his senses and by the time he reached the outskirts of Blackpool he was very much awake. It was almost two o'clock in the morning, but he knew that even if he went to bed now he would be unlikely to sleep.

So he went cruising up and down the promenade and around town until somehow, he found himself driving into the back yard of the central police station.

He was about to turn around and head out when he thought, sod it. While I'm here I might as well have a look in, see a few people. He parked and locked his car and walked to the rear entrance of the building.

Though it was the early hours the place was still buzzing. The holiday season was underway and the influx of tourists had had the usual effect of increasing every officer's work-load. Henry wandered through the corridors and into the CID office where a couple of night-duty detectives were sat at their desks, ties removed, scribbling away. They were glad to see him and get the inside story on Hinksman and the escape. Henry, in turn, was happy to impart his know-ledge.

Eventually he yawned. Tiredness welled over him. He stretched, said good night, and took his leave.

A couple of minutes later he stepped out of the elevator on the ground floor and walked down the short corridor to the rear exit. As he emerged, the cage door of the custody suite on his right opened and a female tottered out in front of him. She had a high-heeled shoe in one hand, the other being on her foot, and a charge sheet in the other.

'You're all fucking wankers,' she screamed back through the door. 'Every single one of you.'

'You keep that up, my dear, and you'll end up back in a cell,' came the calm voice of the Custody Sergeant. 'So piss off.'

Muttering obscenities, she turned and tried to put her shoe on in the same motion. She lost her balance and careered into Henry who caught her and placed her upright.

'Let go, you cunt,' she said absently, then: 'My God! It's Henry Christie, isn't it?'

'Well hello, Jane. Long time no see. Still plying the same old trade?'

'How else would I make me livin',' she said mockingly, 'other than on me back – or in any other position required of me?'

They had walked down the rear yard past all the parked police cars until they reached Henry's battered Metro.

'This heap yours?' laughed Jane. He nodded. 'Gone down in the world, ain't ya?'

'Certainly have. Don't you read the papers?'

'No, why? Here – you goin' my way, Cuntstable? I could do wi' a lift,' she stated cheekily.

'You still living in that same dump?'

'Yep, the same one where you busted me for that speed. God, how long ago were that?'

Henry calculated. It had been when he was a PC. 'Eight years?' he estimated.

'Fuck me,' she said, shaking her head. 'Don't time fly when you're having fun!'

Henry unlocked the car. 'I'll take you as far as I'm going – then you'll have to walk the rest of the way.'

'You're an absolute gent,' she said, creasing herself into the passenger seat.

Once within the confines of the small car, Henry began to regret his generosity. She smelled quite awful. The mixture of body odour, cheap perfume, fish, chips and spirits nearly knocked him out. He wound a window down.

'What were you locked up for this time?'

'Oh, the usual,' she said unconcerned. 'Y'know – leopard never changes its spots. But I don't do drugs any more, thanks to you. I learned me lesson. Evil things.' She shuddered.

'At least I've done some good in my life,' he observed quietly to himself. He actually didn't know whether to believe her or not.

'I'm tryin' to give up whorin',' she said dreamily. 'Too fuckin' dangerous this game now. D'you know how many times I've been hammered? Six. Gettin' like America, this place. In fact, the last one who gave me a twattin' *was* a Yank. An absolute cunt, he was. Wild eyes. Mad as a hatter. Liked hittin' better than sex. Mind you, he was better at hittin'. Anyway, I ripped the fucker off good an' proper . . .' She turned to Henry who was only half-listening, his thoughts, though he didn't know it, on the same American. 'I'm tellin' you this off the record, OK? Pinched a rake of cash off him and did a runner. But he beat me up bad and I think he would've done worse if I hadn't legged it. Serves him right, and that smelly Italian landlord of his. Anyway, what I got off him was the start of me nest egg. Buildin' up nicely now, stashed away safe 'n' sound, thank you very much.'

By the time she'd finished wittering, Henry had arrived at the street where his flat was located. He pulled into a parking space about 100 metres away.

'You're a luv,' Jane said, levering herself out of the seat and slamming the door shut. Her voice seemed to be at megadecibel level; it made Henry squirm. 'Remember – if you ever want a freebie blow job, just call round. Best gob in town.' She slithered her tongue in and out a few times, gave a quick wave and turned, clattering away down the pavement on her dangerously high heels.

He watched her walk away, a smile playing on his lips. It was definitely an offer he wouldn't be following up.

There was a bang, then the sound of voices.

Hinksman awoke with a start. For a moment he thought he was still in the sub-zero darkness of the Iraqi desert, part of the Delta Force Scud-busting squads, sleeping in the shell of a burned-out tank. Then it all came back to him. He cursed himself for being so careless as to doze off.

He was actually lying on the cold metal floor in the rear of a stolen Ford Escort van parked near Henry Christie's flat. He raised himself an inch at a time so that he could see out of the front windscreen. Fifty metres away from him stood Henry Christie and walking towards him was the prostitute, Jane.

Must be my birthday, he thought, gloating.

He quickly dropped back onto the floor of the van and waited for her to pass. The click-clack of her heels approached, grew louder, drew level with the van and then receded. As her footsteps faded, Hinksman pushed himself back up.

Henry had disappeared to the back entrance of the vet's surgery.

Hinksman's mind worked quickly. He was in a quandary. He had been parked there for most of the evening, awaiting Henry's arrival home. Hinksman had expected him to be alone and it had been his intention to kill him in the back yard of the surgery. He'd been relishing the prospect of getting up close to the bastard and killing him face to face because in the short time he'd been acquainted with Henry he'd come to loathe him. He wanted to be right there at the death, not standing 100 metres away, shooting him. No. He wanted the feel of the knife going in, jarring the ribs, piercing the heart, twisting. That was what he desired.

But now things had changed.

The prostitute. The one who'd stolen from him. The one who'd escaped with all his money. The one who'd escaped with her life.

A surge of excitement coursed through his loins. Killing Henry would be sweet revenge, there was no doubt about that, and it would give great satisfaction. But killing the prostitute would be sheer pleasure – the kind he hadn't experienced in a long while. It was an opportunity not to be missed.

Quietly, he opened the back doors of the van and slid out. In the distance he could still see Jane. He began to follow.

Chapter Twenty-Five

Jane's flat was a one-room bedsit on the top floor of a seedy block in the back streets of Blackpool's south shore.

In one corner of the room was the bed – a mattress flung on the floor, covered by grubby sheets that hadn't seen a washing machine for months. In another corner of the room was a large settee that looked like it had once been very comfortable. Now it sagged badly, and it too was marked with the stains of her profession.

The corner opposite the door was the kitchen area, consisting of a cupboard, grimy sink, a two-ringed electric cooker and a battered fridge. The grotty wardrobe was the only clean thing in the room, clean because it contained the clothes and shoes that were her obsession. It was crammed full of assorted dresses, skirts, blouses, suits and shoes, mostly loud and glitzy ones she used for work. Without exception they were stolen from the major stores in Blackpool.

She came up the steps to the flat with a weary but silent tread. She had taken her shoes off right at the bottom because she'd had numerous accidents before when negotiating the narrow, poorly lit stairs in high heels and with drink taken.

The building was unusually quiet. Her neighbours, mostly unemployed teenagers, single mothers, drug addicts and an old-age pensioner on the ground floor, tended to keep odd hours. But tonight was quiet and dark.

She pushed open her door which was not locked, never had been, never would be, and entered her home. She was glad to see her bed. Not that it was particularly comfortable, but it left that rock-hard cell bed standing. She stripped off and hung her clothes up carefully, discarding the torn blouse and laddered stockings in a wastebin. Then she stood before the full-length mirror on the wardrobe door and surveyed herself uncritically while scratching her bushy black pubic mound and yawning.

Still naked, she padded across the landing to the shared bathroom. Out of the corner of her eye she caught a movement down the stairs on the landing below, but thought nothing of it. Probably one of her oddball neighbours skulking about. Didn't bother her. However, she did lock the bathroom door behind her. There were some things she liked to keep private. She emptied her bladder then had a quick, lukewarm shower and dried herself off with someone else's towel. She slid back to her room shivering, but feeling half-human again.

As she stood in front of the mirror, combing through her damp hair, she saw the door open behind her. She guessed it was that crank from the first floor who visited her at odd times of the day. He was a screwball, but she had no conscience about charging him double for a wank. She sighed. 'Come on in, Roger, don't be shy. I've just got time before I hit the sack – but it'll cost you twelve quid.' She waggled her ample bottom provocatively. Money, after all, was money.

The man came in.

Fast and hard.

Before she knew what had happened, she was on her back on the mattress, held down with a hand clamped over her mouth. Hinksman's face, glaring mad-eyed down at her, was only inches away from her own.

'Hello Jane,' he said. 'I'm back.'

She squirmed ineffectually. The hand stayed over her mouth, cupping her chin in its palm so that it was impossible for her to bite. He held her easily.

'You stole something of mine,' he said. 'Didn't you?'

He placed the forearm of his free arm across her throat and took hold of her shoulder for extra leverage. Slowly he forced the forearm down onto her Adam's apple. Just before she passed out, he released the pressure and slightly opened the fingers of his hand over her mouth to let air pass through.

She sucked greedily. Her pallor, which had turned pale like cartridge paper, now turned bright red.

'You did steal something of mine, didn't you?' he repeated.

This time she managed a nod.

'Good. Right . . . I'm going to take this hand away now and I want you to talk to me in a whisper. You scream out or even talk normally and I'll put it back and kill you. OK?'

A nod.

He peeled his hand away, one finger at a time. His forearm still rested across her throat.

'Where's my money?'

'Spent it,' she whispered. This was a lie.

'On all those dresses?'

'Yes.'

'Oh you stupid, stupid woman.' He shook his head sadly and sighed. 'So, what've you been saying to Henry Christie?'

'Henry Christie? What you on about?' Jane's eyes focused on his face as a whole. 'Oh God,' she uttered, 'you're the one who killed all those people on the motorway, aren't you? And all those cops. I didn't realise until now. Oh God, oh God.'

His hand clamped over her mouth again; his forearm pressed down onto her neck. The airflow was cut off quickly this time. She began to lose consciousness. Her head swam in a surfy sea, a warm, pleasant sea and it felt good to be dying.

Hinksman suddenly changed tactics. He jumped up and took hold of a bottle of Jane's vodka, just over a quarter full.

'Sit up and drink this,' he said, straddling her and handing it down to her.

She crawled into a sitting position, reached out a shaking hand and took the bottle from him.

'Big mouthfuls,' he insisted.

Jane knew, somehow, that this time there would be no opportunity to escape. He was too quick, strong and determined – and experienced. He oozed death. It leaked from every pore. Yes, Death had returned and was going to complete what it had started.

The only thing that warmed her was that he wouldn't get his money back, not one penny, not one cent of it.

She smiled and put the vodka to her lips again. If she was going to be murdered she might as well be oblivious to it. With the alcohol content in her body still relatively high, it wasn't long before she was completely drunk again.

Jane amassed all her faculties with one deep breath. Now she did not care.

'YOU'RE A FUCKING BASTARD WHO CAN'T SHAG FOR TOFFEE,' she screamed.

Before she had finished he'd ducked down to her level, wrenched her by the hair and taken hold of her head in both his hands. His right hand held her chin, mouth and nose. His left held the back of her head. He lifted and twisted in one easy, screwing movement. Jane's neck broke with a loud crack and she was dead.

He tossed her across onto the mattress. She flopped there loosely.

Hinksman wiped the fingerprints carefully off all the bottles he'd touched with a kitchen cloth and stood the bottles side by side on the sink. He stepped out onto the landing and listened. It was all quiet. He heaved Jane out onto the landing and pulled her to her feet at the top of the stairs. Her head flopped onto her chest. Spit dribbled out of her mouth. With a gentle push he let go of her and she went spinning down the steps to the landing below, arms and legs flailing everywhere. She came to an untidy bundle at the foot of the stairs.

Hinksman followed her down, stepped lightly across her and sped down the rest of the stairs.

Within seconds he was out of the building. Gone.

The greyness of dawn was just arriving.

Even though he wanted to, Henry couldn't get to sleep. A parrot in the surgery below was squawking loudly, shouting

343

obscenities, and in turn had set off a yapping terrier dog. The combination was unbearable. After half an hour of the cacophony he rolled off the bed and made himself a mug of tea. He switched on the gas fire, sat down in front of it and sipped the brew while staring at the flames.

About five-thirty the animals must have got tired and they ceased their noise. Henry sank back into the armchair, closed his eyes and, at last, nodded off.

An hour later Henry and the animals were reawakened by a loud knocking on the door. Henry staggered down the back steps and opened it. A bright-eyed Donaldson stood there, immaculately turned out. His smile drooped when he saw the unshaven mess that was his British counterpart.

'You did say six-thirty,' Donaldson said defensively. 'Long day ahead.'

'Yeah, yeah, I know,' muttered Henry. 'Come on in, give me ten minutes.'

'You look like something a cat's dragged in,' Donaldson observed.

'And you look like a dog's dinner,' said Henry. 'Did Karen get you dressed?'

He had a quick shave and a shower, threw on some clothes and fifteen minutes later was sitting in the passenger seat of Donaldson's hired car which sped down the motorway towards Lancaster. After a brief, perfunctory conversation, Henry's eyes closed, his chin sagged onto his chest and he fell asleep, drooling.

Donaldson laughed and tuned into Jazz FM.

As demanded, everything about Hinksman was on Dave August's desk at 9 a.m. sharp. The Chief Constable glanced at the boxes of files that FB had deposited and was itching to get into them, just to see if there was anything at all, anything that would guide him to the people who had made him do this awful thing.

But it was a task that would have to wait. The day ahead held other priorities: press conferences, then a visit to the

344

incident room. After that he planned to meet all the bereaved relatives personally at their homes. Just to give them a few minutes. To show he cared.

That was not going to be easy, knowing that, ultimately, he was the one person responsible for their deaths.

It was going to be a tough day.

Joe Kovaks was at his desk by eight o'clock that morning. He ignored the mountain of paperwork that he'd allowed to accumulate there. He wanted to get two things done.

First he wanted to see his supervisor and ask to be taken off the Corelli case.

Then he wanted to visit Laura and tell her about his change of heart. Killing Corelli wasn't the way forward, he now knew, and he had to convince her of that – which wasn't going to be easy. He'd spent enough time brainwashing her; now he had to try and reverse the process. The prospect was daunting. But the little sachet of white powder in his jacket pocket should make things easier.

For the first time in years his supervisor arrived late for work. Kovaks had been pacing the man's office like a cat.

'Hello Joe,' he said, removing his coat. 'What can I do for you?'

'Hi, look, sorry to be so blunt, Arnie, but can I make an urgent request?'

'Sure,' said the puzzled supervisor.

'I want off the Corelli case, as of now. The case papers are all up to date. That OK?'

'Fine by me, but why now? You've put a lot into this over the years. You in trouble or something? Someone leanin' on ya?'

'Not in trouble, but someone is leaning on me, yeah, but in a nice way. Can I tell you later, boss? I don't want to appear rude but I have an urgent meet with an informant. After that I'll come back and have a chat. OK?'

'Yeah, yeah,' the supervisor said, completely flummoxed.

'So I'm off the case?' Kovaks confirmed.

'As of this moment.'

'I love ya,' said Kovaks. He took the man by the shoulders and kissed his cheek. Before anything more could be said, Kovaks had turned and left the office.

Quickly the supervisor wiped his face dry, disgusted at the thought of being kissed by another man.

Car theft is a growth area in crime in Britain. It is a big headache for the police. There are always some people who leave their cars unlocked with the key still in the ignition.

People like Henry Christie.

When he'd parked in the early hours he'd been so tired, had so much on his mind and had been so busy chatting to Jane that he'd simply got out of his car, left the key in the ignition and forgotten to lock it.

Even if he'd remembered he wouldn't have been distressed. After all, who would want to steal a car which even the owner described as a 'heap o' shit'.

The answer was a young man called John Abbot. Aged fifteen, he was once again playing truant from school, engaged in his favourite pastime of robbing cars.

The 'robbing' was either stealing from them – which he did mostly – or, if the opportunity arose, driving the cars away and abandoning them somewhere when he got bored. Usually on the beach in the face of an incoming tide.

Abbot was one of Blackpool's most prolific car-crime experts and was verging on becoming a professional. He made over three hundred pounds per week selling the goods he stole from cars, and wrecked about ten thousand pounds' worth of cars each month, just for pleasure. He was rarely caught.

He was strolling through the streets of the south-shore area, trying car doors as a matter of course, when he came across Henry's Metro.

He couldn't believe his luck when he saw the key in the ignition. He had a quick glance around the interior and sneered at the state of it: torn seats, worn carpets and a radio which was just that – a radio. Not even a cassette player! No one would want to buy that.

'This car deserves to be trashed,' he said.

He slid in and reached for the key.

The engine fired at the third attempt and ticked over lumpily. He dipped the accelerator a few times and revved it gleefully. He selected first and moved off. There was a big smile on the young criminal's face.

He was not to know that this was the last car he would ever steal.

It was a long time since Joe Kovaks had felt so happy, certainly not since the letter bomb. It was like a new beginning, and he was looking forward to the road ahead. If this is what love feels like, he thought, give me more.

He almost skipped through the office to his desk. One or two people looked up quizzically from their work as his tuneless humming reached their ears.

The phone rang as he sat down.

'Joe Kovaks, Special Agent. May I help you?' he answered brightly.

'Joe, it's me,' came a weak voice.

Reality flattened Kovaks back into his chair. 'Damian, where the hell are you?' he hissed urgently. He'd almost forgotten about Sue's murder.

'Look, I can't talk on this line, you know that.'

'Hang on, hang on.' Kovaks fumbled in his jacket for his electronic diary. 'I gotta number here you can use.' He pressed a few buttons. 'Damian, you still there?'

'Yeah,' he said tiredly.

'This is the number of one of the phone booths opposite the office – you know, the ones we use for delicate calls?'

'Yeah, I know 'em.'

'You gotta pen?'

'Yeah.'

Kovaks read the number out and got Damian to recite it back.

'Is this kosher?' Damian asked suspiciously.

'Yeah. Leave it five minutes for me to get down there, then call the number, OK?'

'Right.'

Kovaks hung up and put his diary back inside his jacket. He immediately called Ram Chander in Homicide but was unable to contact him. He decided not to leave a message.

He glanced quickly around the office. 'Bill, do me a favour, will ya? Call Ram Chander and tell him Damian's recontacted me, right? Tell him I'm gonna try and make a meet with him. He'll understand. It's pretty urgent. Can you do that for me, pal?'

'No probs,' the other agent said, scribbling.

Kovaks left the office quickly. Eamon Ritter stood up and followed. In his hand he had a mobile phone which he began to dial.

Henry Christie sat staring dead ahead as Donaldson drove him back down the motorway. It was 5 p.m., and it had been a frustrating day. No progress had been made; and Henry was the subject of an official complaint, yet again.

He'd spent most of the morning with Karen, briefing the small team of detectives which had been assigned to their line of enquiry. Their first task was to go and see a tame magistrate and swear out two warrants which were to be executed later that afternoon.

Around lunchtime Henry walked up to the public mortuary at the hospital where Dr Baines, the Home Office Pathologist, was carrying out post mortems on the police officers killed the day before.

Baines was deep inside a chest cavity. His gloves, sleeves and apron were covered in blood. The scene reminded Henry of *MASH*, except there was no one to be saved here. They nodded to each other. Baines' hands emerged with a heart that had been shredded by bullets. He placed it carefully down by the body.

'Henry! How are you, old man?' he asked rather incongruously in a mock-Etonian accent.

'As well as can be expected under the circumstances.'

Both men looked down the room. There was a body on each slab. In one corner was a bloodstained pile of police uniforms.

'Glad to see you're fighting fit though,' Baines said. 'Believe you've had some, er, problems.'

'Yeah, but I'm over the worst now – I hope.'

'That double murder at Whitworth never got solved, did it?'

'No, we got nowhere with it. *And* I got kicked off the case.'

'I'm damned sure I know something important about that,' Baines said. He thought hard for a moment or two, eyebrows knitting. 'Nope, won't come, tried before. Anyway, must get back to work, so if you'll excuse me . . . Perhaps we should have a meal out sometime?'

'Yeah, why not?'

Henry meandered back to the station. FB was just driving into the car park.

'How's it going, Henry?' he asked as they walked into the building and made their way to the canteen for lunch.

'So so,' Henry shrugged.

'Just to let you know, just to warn you – I've let the Chief have copies of everything on Hinksman. He wants to know every move we make, so keep me informed please, bang up to date on everything, OK?'

'By all means.'

'So, what's planned for this afternoon?'

'Gonna scare the shite out of Lenny Dakin.' For the first time that day Henry's scowl was replaced by a grin. But it was a wicked one.

The warrants authorised the police to enter, by force if need be, two properties belonging to Lenny Dakin, and to search for a person unlawfully at large who was reasonably believed to be therein, namely Hinksman.

One warrant was for Dakin's home in the Ribble Valley and the other was for his flat over his supermarket in Blackburn. Henry knew of several other addresses but didn't want to overplay his hand at such an early stage. His idea was to panic Dakin, put him under surveillance and hope that he did something stupid, like lead the cops to Hinksman.

However, the afternoon turned into an utter shambles. Both premises were searched, but Dakin wasn't at either of them.

Henry and a squad of armed officers, including an unarmed Donaldson, hit Dakin's farmhouse. Another team, led by Karen, did the rooms over the supermarket.

As both teams reassembled back at Lancaster, a man purporting to be Dakin's solicitor telephoned the incident room and asked to speak to Henry. He demanded to know on what evidence the application for the warrants had been based.

'I cannot discuss anything over the telephone,' Henry said officiously. 'I don't even know if you are who you say you are.'

'Oh, I am definitely Mr Dakin's solicitor,' the man said. 'And there is also the question of compensation and theft. The front door of Mr Dakin's house has been severely damaged by police as they entered the premises . . . '

Henry held his breath. The door had been battered down and a joiner had been called to repair and secure it before the police left. Fortunately Henry had taken a Polaroid camera along with him for 'before and after' pictures.

'The door is several hundred years old, an antique in fact and is valued at two thousand pounds. We will be claiming that amount in compensation.'

'Bollocks,' uttered Henry, declining to disclose the existence of the photographs.

'And of course there is the problem of Mr Dakin's Doberman pinschers. Both dogs have disappeared, presumably allowed to escape by the police.'

Henry made no comment. The Dobermans had been a problem all right; they'd bitten two detectives' arses before being shepherded out of the house where they immediately hurtled away down the garden, over the wall, never to be seen again.

'A large amount of gold jewellery has gone missing,' the solicitor went on smoothly.

'Oh, for God's sake! Are you accusing me of theft?'

'Not specifically you, Sergeant Christie, not yet anyway. But by a process of deduction either you or one of your team or your whole team has stolen it. There will be an official complaint made shortly to your Discipline and Complaints branch. I've no doubt that when the Police Complaints Authority is informed, you'll find yourself deeply investigated.'

'Not half as deeply as your client will be,' Henry rasped.

'Tsk, tsk, threats now, is it? I'll add that to my list.'

Henry slammed the phone down.

'Fuck Dakin to hell and back!' said Henry.

'Don't worry about it,' Donaldson soothed.

They had reached Blackpool and were driving along the promenade.

'Right now, Dakin will be scared shitless,' the American decided. 'After all, it's the first time he's been implicated with Hinksman and, by association, with Corelli. Trust me. He won't be a happy man.'

Progress through traffic was slow but steady. They approached the traffic lights outside the Manchester Hotel at the junction of the promenade and Lytham Road. The lights went to red.

Donaldson's hands tapped the steering wheel while he waited for the green light. Idly he watched a car come down the promenade, then turn left into Lytham Road. It looked very familiar.

'Just like your pile of garbage, that one,' he said to Henry.

Henry looked across and saw the car sail through the lights. It only took a second. Then, 'It *is* bloody mine! And that little git John Abbot is driving it. Go after him,' he yelled.

'You look pretty much like death warmed up,' Joe Kovaks commented to Damian. He sat down opposite the little man and pushed a Styrofoam cup of black coffee across the table. Damian took it with a trembling hand.

'Thanks,' he said, and put the cup to his lips, but he was shaking so badly he couldn't take a drink. His eyes were constantly roving the restaurant – a McDonald's on the beach in Fort Lauderdale. 'You sure you're alone, Joe?'

The other man nodded reassuringly. 'Don't worry, I'm alone. Now have a drink of that coffee. Go on.'

This time Damian managed to get a mouthful. He looked terrible – thin and gaunt. Several days of stubble on his face. Eyes deeply sunken, bloodshot. Skin grey. Clothing unkempt and beginning to smell.

'Where the hell have you been keeping yourself?' Kovaks asked him gently. 'You know that cops all over the state are looking for you, don't you?'

'I don't need reminding,' Damian said. He removed his glasses and rubbed his eyes. 'Been sleeping here and there, roaming the streets during the day. Hiding when I see a uniform or cop car. Hardly eatin', never sleepin'. Got no money left.'

Then it all came flooding back to him. He began to cry, quietly at first, then with big body-raking sobs, drawing the attention of everyone in the place.

'Jeez, Joe,' he said through the tears, 'I loved her so much. I was in love for the first time in my life. I loved her – I didn't want her to die. Hell! Hell! Cut up to hell! Oh God, she's dead. I can't believe it still.'

Kovaks reached out and patted Damian's shoulder. 'OK bud, you cry, no problems.'

'I haven't been able to cry yet,' he said when he'd pulled himself together. 'I've been too frightened, watching my back all the time.'

'Damian,' said Kovaks. 'I got to know.'

'Yeah, I know you do.' He shook his head. His red eyes moistened again and tears fell down his face. 'I still can't believe it myself. I didn't do it, Joe. Honest to God. You gotta believe me. I would never have hurt Sue. She was so precious, so delicate, like a flower.'

'Who killed her then?' Kovaks interrupted.

Damian swallowed. 'You won't believe me when I tell you.'

'Try me.'

Damian told him.

Chapter Twenty-Six

At the same time as this revelation was being made, a car chase was just about to commence 3000 miles to the east in Blackpool.

The lights had just started to change; Donaldson slammed his foot on the accelerator pedal and cut dangerously across the oncoming traffic to slot in behind Henry's Metro.

Henry was fumbling to reach his radio which he had thrown onto the back seat. He hoped the battery was still charged up.

Abbot was only dawdling along in the Metro. He was going to make towards the motorway and head out towards Preston. Once on the motorway, he decided, he would 'screw the arse' off the car and try to get the engine to explode.

'The cheeky little bastard,' Henry said as he faced forwards again, clicking the radio on. 'Doesn't he know he's stolen a cop's car?'

'It's not exactly the sort of car you associate with a cop,' laughed Donaldson. 'More with a scrap-metal dealer.'

'Don't you start,' Henry warned Donaldson.

Both men were thoroughly enjoying themselves with this diversion. Henry spoke into the radio. Within seconds every mobile patrol in Blackpool knew what was going on. Some were already responding and making towards the area.

At that point Abbot checked his rearview mirror for the first time. He saw the Ford Escort close on his tail, two occupants on board, both male. He looked again more closely. The man in the passenger seat was talking into a radio.

'Shit,' he hissed, and pulled away.

'He's seen us,' said Donaldson. The Escort was more than a match for the tired Metro, which hadn't been serviced for well over a year and had nearly 90,000 miles on the clock. Donaldson had no trouble keeping up with Abbot, but maintained a safe distance between them in case he decided to slam the brakes on and cause an accident.

Abbot led them a merry dance through the side streets of Blackpool, but couldn't shake Donaldson who stuck there like a terrier.

'He'll bloody kill someone,' remarked Henry as they rounded a tight corner on a narrow street with parked cars on both sides.

On the next corner Abbot briefly lost control. He skittered sideways into a parked car, giving it a glancing blow and taking the wing mirror off the Metro before recovering.

'Oh my beautiful car,' said Henry painfully. 'He's damaged it.'

'It was falling to bits anyway,' Donaldson noted.

'Oh, thanks very much. That's my pride and joy, I'll have you know,' Henry said, feigning hurt. But there was a huge smile on his face. He was excited and had that peculiar empty feeling in his stomach and dryness of the mouth that he always experienced in situations like this. He put it down to adrenalin.

The car lurched as they took another bad bend. Henry's seatbelt snapped tight as he shot forwards. He lifted the radio, pressed the transmit button and gave out the new location and direction of travel. 'Preston New Road, towards the motorway.'

'The cavalry's here,' said Donaldson after a glance in the mirror.

A large, fast, sleek Rover 825i, liveried in the orange stripes of the Lancashire Constabulary Traffic Department, blue lights flashing, horns blaring, overtook Donaldson's car, cruised easily past Abbot and pulled in front of him. The big 'STOP' sign came on. It had no effect. Abbot simply refused to pull in. He flashed his own 'V' signs at the traffic man.

'D'you know,' said Henry, 'I see that little car of mine in a whole new light. I didn't know it could go so fast.'

'Obviously rising to the occasion,' Donaldson guffawed.

By the time they reached the motorway there were three traffic cars involved in the pursuit. Once on the motorway proper they had Abbot literally boxed into the slow lane: one in front, one behind and one car at his side in the middle lane.

But he still would not stop.

Behind them all, Donaldson kept up. 'He's gotta stop now, surely,' said the agent. 'Don't he know when he's beat?'

'Crazy young bastard.'

The traffic cars edged him onto the hard shoulder. Now he was completely trapped and all they had to do was slow right down to a stop – then he was theirs. Or so they thought. He did have one avenue of escape open to him, which was to drive up the steep grass banking by the side of the motorway.

He reckoned he could probably make it to the top of the grass, where he could abandon the car then leg it on foot across the fields. From his wide experience of traffic cops he thought this would be the best move because he knew how much they hated getting out of their big, warm, fancy cars and chasing people on foot.

Abbot peeled away from the formation like an ace fighter pilot and gunned the car up the slope.

The manoeuvre took the traffic officers completely by surprise, which was fortunate for them. It meant that none of them lost their lives.

Halfway up, the steepness of the slope meant that the mercury tilt switch attached to the detonator in the half-pound block of Semtex strapped to the underside of Henry's car was activated.

Contact was made. ⋆ ⋆ ⋆

Kovaks listened hard to Damian's story. How he had been to his mother's in Clearwater, but had returned early to surprise Sue. They had made passionate love within moments of his arrival and afterwards he'd gone to the en-suite bathroom to answer a pressing call of nature. Whilst in there, he'd heard someone at the apartment door, then voices in the lounge. Discreetly, he'd crept out of the bathroom and listened to what was going on. He had recognised Ritter's voice and clearly followed the accusations he made to Sue about her knowing he was on Corelli's payroll, then some talk about his condo and his boat. Sue had denied it all, saying she wasn't keeping any sort of a file on him. Then things had got nasty. Sue had screamed for help. Damian had crept to the bedroom door and looked through the crack. To his horror, he'd seen a knife in Ritter's hand plunging repeatedly into his girlfriend's body, blood spurting everywhere. Frozen in fear and panic, unable to help her, he'd eventually scuttled under the bed where he'd hidden until it was all over, sucking his thumb, curled up in a foetal ball.

When the attack had stopped he'd heard Ritter moving around the apartment, felt his presence in the bedroom. Then Damian had pissed in his pants.

He'd lain there shaking, eyes closed, praying that Ritter wouldn't find him and kill him too.

Then he heard the front door open and close.

And, when he was sure Ritter had gone, he forced himself to go and see Sue.

'And then I was sick and then I ran.' There were a lot of 'thens' in Damian's story. 'Every time I close my eyes, she's there: dead,' he said hoarsely. 'What a mess – and all my fault.' Tears poured down his tortured face.

'Don't punish yourself, Damian,' Kovaks said. 'You're only human.'

Damian looked up with pleading eyes. 'Do you believe me?'

'Yes, I do. One or two things have sorta slotted into place

here.' Kovaks' nostrils dilated as he thought. 'Yeah, I believe you.'

'So what do we do now?'

'First we get you somewhere safe where you can get a decent meal and a shower – and a change of clothes. Then we'll have a good long talk over a beer, get a few things written down. Then I have to think. Probably go to the cops first, let 'em know what's what.'

'But what if they're in on it too?' Damian shook uncontrollably. 'What if Corelli has them in his pocket, like he does Ritter?'

'No one could get Ram Chander in their pocket,' said Kovaks confidently. 'C'mon, trust me, Damian. We'll go to my place first. Chrissy won't mind and it should be safe enough for a few hours.'

They started to get to their feet.

'I think not,' came a familiar voice from behind Kovaks' shoulder. 'Sit back down, gentlemen.'

Kovaks reached for his gun, but before he could draw it, he felt the cold muzzle of a revolver jammed into the back of his neck.

'Sit down, Joe, or I'll make your brain into tomato catsup for their hamburgers.'

Kovaks sat down slowly. A wide-eyed Damian followed suit. Ritter edged in next to Kovaks, and with his free hand removed Kovaks' revolver.

Kovaks looked at Ritter, then beyond. He was not alone.

Ram Chander stood by the door together with two of Corelli's goons.

Kovaks closed his eyes.

Henry Christie was disgusted with himself.

Two minutes earlier he had been clinging to a toilet bowl at Blackpool Central police office and had been violently sick. Now, after swilling his face with cold water, he was looking at himself in a mirror over the washbasin.

And he did not like what he saw.

He should have been sick for the boy, Abbot. He should have been sick because a stupid young teenager had been blown to pieces on a motorway verge, his remains scattered far and wide.

But he wasn't. Henry had been sick for himself alone. A single idea dominated his thoughts.

That bomb had been meant for *him*, dammit! He glared angrily at his reflection, but behind the grimace he saw pure terror in his eyes for the first time in his life.

Hinksman was going to kill him and there was probably nothing that Henry could do to stop him.

With that thought Henry turned away from the mirror and dashed back to the toilet cubicle.

To the best of their abilities, the remains of John Abbot had been collected from the scene of the explosion by the police, ambulance and fire brigade. They had been bagged and sent to the mortuary where they had been unpacked and distributed over the tops of two post mortem slabs.

Henry Christie, together with Karl Donaldson, Karen Wilde, FB, a couple of high-ranking local detectives and a Scenes of Crime officer who was recording the PM on video, watched a pathologist pacing around a third slab. She had been brought in from Merseyside as Dr Baines was still busy in Lancaster.

Now the pathologist picked up a piece of charred flesh that could have been part of a hand or foot. She thought for a moment, surveying the reconstruction work, said 'A-ha!' with glee, danced round the slab and placed it. It was a foot. She was enjoying herself.

'I don't think I want to watch this,' said Henry. The smell of burned flesh was overpowering. He ducked out of the room without apology.

Karen followed him out.

'I just want to thank you for putting my name forward for this investigation, Henry. I appreciate it. And FB's been really nice to me too. He's even talked to Karl.'

'Good. I'm glad,' said Henry.

'You OK?' She linked arms with him.

Surprised but touched, Henry gave her a lopsided grin and admitted, 'No, not really.'

They were standing in the room where a large refrigerator took up the whole length and height of one wall. Inside it, bodies were stored on sliding trays. At the far end of the room a PC and an undertaker had just placed a body on one of the trays. The PC was writing a name on the leg with a felt-tip pen.

'I suppose,' said Henry, 'that I didn't really expect him to try something. It's shocked me. And a bomb again, on the motorway. That's just reopened a wound I thought I'd sewn up pretty well. Obviously I haven't. I keep seeing the kids on the bus again.'

'We're dealing with a madman.'

'One who knows exactly what he's doing,' Henry suggested. 'He's dangerous rather than mad. Don't forget, he kills people for a living. Madmen don't.'

They had been walking slowly towards the PC who, as they drew level with him, pulled a white sheet back over the body on the tray. Henry did a double take.

'Let me see,' he said quickly.

The PC obliged. 'Jane Marsden, local prostitute, shoplifter, drunk, and all-round lowlife,' he summed up. 'No great loss to society.'

'What are the circumstances?' Henry asked.

'Found about an hour ago at the bottom of a flight of stairs in the fleapit dosshouse she lived in. Probably been lying there all day from the state of her. She took some major straightening out.' The PC chuckled at the memory. 'Looks like she fell down drunk and broke her neck. Post mortem'll tell.'

'Anything suspicious?' Henry probed. He was trying desperately to recall some of the things Jane had been saying to him, things he hadn't really been taking in because he'd been too engrossed in his own thoughts.

'Not on the face of it. Why?'

Henry ignored the question. He drew the sheet further back. There was some bruising across her Adam's apple. Then he pulled it all the way down to reveal her naked, now wax-like body. He looked carefully at it and saw further bruising on her arms. It could have happened during the fall down the steps – the post mortem should be able to establish that – but Henry wasn't happy.

He covered her up.

He gazed into space and pursed his lips. 'Did you get Scenes of Crime to photograph the body at the scene?'

'Yep.'

'Right, when that officer in there has finished videoing the PM, get him to take some shots of her, will you? Point out those bruises on her neck and arms.' The PC nodded. 'Did you search her flat?'

The PC shrugged. 'Not really. Had a glance round, nothing more.'

'Is it locked?'

'No, couldn't find a key.'

'Henry, what's going on?' Karen interrupted.

'This gives me the willies,' he said. 'I actually saw this woman last night and gave her a lift as far as my place. She walked to her own from there.'

'Henry!' Karen said, shocked.

'No, I didn't, I'm not *that* desperate . . . it's just that when I last saw her, she wasn't all that drunk. She'd actually just been kicked out of the cells at Central . . . Look, something's not quite right here. She told me some half-baked story about ripping off a Yank who'd beaten her up.' He spread his hands. 'Maybe I'm barking up the wrong tree, but Hinksman likes beating up and killing prostitutes. And if my memory serves me right, he specialises in breaking their necks. Probably practising a technique learned from his Delta Force days. Perhaps here,' he pointed at the covered body, 'he's finishing off something he started a few months ago. I hope I'm wrong, because if I'm not, he's committed two murders since escaping.' He raised his eyebrows at Karen. 'Fancy a drive round to her flat? Might answer one or two questions.'

'Sure, why not? They'll be hours in there.'

The aroma of bedsits hit them as soon as they entered the ground-floor hallway through the open front door. It was a mixture of cigarette smoke, sweaty socks and underwear, and the unmistakable smell of lubricant used on male contraceptives intermingled with cannabis smoke. Here, in addition, was the musty tang of dampness.

They turned into the narrow staircase and began the ascent. It was almost 9.30 p.m. and it was getting dark. The stairs were lit by low-wattage bulbs operated by switches that 'sprang off' after about twenty seconds in order to save electricity. They trod carefully, as some of the treads were carpeted; some not.

On the last flight up to Jane's flat Henry inspected each step carefully. This was actually the only part of the staircase on which the carpet was well-laid and fitted. There was nothing on which a person could have tripped. Even so, the stairs were still steep and narrow, and possibly treacherous to someone who'd had a drink.

As expected, the door to Jane's flat was unlocked. They went in.

'Very salubrious,' remarked Karen.

Henry stood still and allowed himself to look the room over, his eyes taking in everything: the mattress, the bottles of booze, the sink, the settee, cooker and cupboards. Eventually his attention returned to the bottles which stood side by side on the draining board. He stepped over to them, and picked one up carefully by inserting his forefinger into the neck. He held it up to the light and rotated it carefully, inspecting it at different angles. He did the same with each bottle.

Karen was standing behind him. 'Got something?' she asked.

'Well . . . if she was drunk when she fell down the steps, it's safe to assume she'd been drinking after she left me – presumably from these bottles. I don't see any glasses about, so she must have swigged straight from the bottles . . .'

He moved aside for Karen, who bent down and looked at the bottles in situ.

'They've been wiped,' she stated, puzzled.

'Exactly. Even if she didn't take a drink from these last night, there would have been some marks on the bottles.'

Henry surveyed the room again. Years before he'd searched it for drugs and found some, but he couldn't quite remember where the stash had been. His eyes lit on a ventilation cover on the wall above the cooker. He smiled. Now he remembered.

The cover was metal with a sliding opener. He looked at it carefully and saw that there were recent marks in the screws which held it to the wall.

'Don't suppose you've got a screwdriver?'

Her reply was a wilting look.

Tut-tutting, he opened the kitchen drawer and rummaged through the meagre collection of utensils for something suitable to remove screws. All he could find was a flimsy table knife which twisted and buckled when he put it to use.

After much patience he managed to remove three screws from the ventilation cover, which then swung free on the remaining screw, revealing a square hole in the wall about eight by six inches.

Karen dragged a wooden kitchen stool across for him. He stood precariously on it and put his arm all the way into the ventilation cavity. He immediately found something. He gave a cry of victory and carefully, so that he would not drop it, extracted what he'd found.

'How did you know where to look?' asked Karen, impressed.

'Cheated,' he confessed. 'Did the place a few years ago for dope and found this hidey-hole then. There's a sort of lip a couple of feet down where she stored her stuff. Very tricky and pretty secure. I couldn't quite remember how far down the lip was.'

What he'd pulled out was a brown A4-sized envelope. He opened it and shook out the contents on the cupboard top.

'Jane's nest-egg,' he said sadly. 'Her passport to the better life.'

There were three bundles of Bank of England notes totalling about £2,000. What was more interesting was the wad of dollar traveller's cheques, a driving licence and six credit cards.

Henry handled them carefully. '*Voilà*,' he said. 'Recognise the name on the driving licence?'

'Yeah,' said Karen sheepishly. 'It's that poor guy I locked up after raiding his house with the support unit.'

'The innocent man, you mean?' said Henry wickedly.

'Don't rub it in. It's the driving licence Hinksman used to hire cars with. Don't recognise the names on the credit cards.'

'No, I don't either. Hinksman probably has plenty of identities, but he's used his own name on the traveller's cheques.'

'So she stole all this from Hinksman?'

Henry nodded and sat down on the settee. 'What we've got here is this: a dangerous man on the loose who will not tolerate anyone getting the better of him. Jane got the better of him by stealing from him – so he murdered her; I got the better of him by arresting him, and shooting him, and he's tried to murder me. The question I ask is this: has he finished yet? Has he made his point?'

Karen slumped down heavily next to him. 'I'd like to say yes.'

'But we know what the real answer is, don't we?' Henry said grimly. The terror was creeping up on him again.

'I'll say this for you, Joe, you're one hell of a cool son of a bitch.'

It was Ritter talking. He was sat next to Kovaks in the

back seat of the Bucar. Ram Chander was in the front passenger seat; one of Corelli's men was driving. Behind them was another car in which Damian was being transported. They were heading south towards Miami.

'This must be a pretty big shock for you, after all.'

Kovaks gave Ritter a contemptuous sidelong glance, then gazed back out of the window. He'd decided that to lose his temper would lose his life. Inside though, he seethed with anger and sadness. After a pause he said, 'How long you been working for him?'

'Long enough,' admitted Ritter. 'Long enough to have a healthy bank balance and a bolt-hole in the Caribbean.'

'Lucky ole you . . . and you, Ram? How about you?'

Ram twisted round and dangled his right hand across the seat-top. He was holding a gun which jerked dangerously around as he talked. Kovaks thought bleakly about the scene in the movie *Pulp Fiction*. 'A long, long time, Mr Joe,' he said.

Kovaks shook his head. 'Sad . . . fucking sad. So, Eamon, why kill Sue?'

Ritter's mouth twisted down at the corners. 'Simple – she was on to me. I had to do it.' He shrugged. 'Besides, I really enjoyed sticking my knife up her cunt.'

'Sick bastard.'

Almost before the words were out of his mouth, Ritter crashed his gun into the side of Kovaks' head.

'Aaah!' It felt like his brain had come loose from its fittings.

'Never ever call me that,' said Ritter angrily.

'She wasn't on to you,' Kovaks mumbled. 'You were paranoid.'

'Crap,' said Ritter, dismissing the statement. Suddenly he became buoyant. 'Hey, that Lisa Want! What a fuck, man! She gives head ree-al good . . . But you already know that, don't you?'

'Right, so you've been feeding her stuff too,' Kovaks grumbled through the palms of his hands.

364

'Couldn't resist, man. Just could not resist. She needed an inside source, so she got me. A fuck for information. Fair trade, I'd say.' He laughed heartily.

'You have very high morals,' said Kovaks. His mind rattled: so that was how Ms Want was always up to the minute with Bureau news and information. Wow – she was really scraping the barrel with Eamon Ritter.

'I even fed her all that stuff about Karl Donaldson and his English buddy screwing those policewomen. Y'know, that sex-crazed FBI Agent shit?'

For a moment Kovaks wondered what he was talking about. Then he remembered. And recalled how Ritter had joined the two agents for a drink one night soon after Karl had returned from England a few months before. No doubt killing two birds with one stone: picking up information for Corelli as well as titbits for Lisa.

He looked at Ram, then Ritter. 'So what's next?'

'Sit back and enjoy the ride,' Ram suggested.

'It's the last one you'll be takin',' laughed Ritter.

Ram looked quickly at Ritter – his expression puzzled Kovaks, for it seemed to have a significant meaning – then turned to face the front.

Kovaks settled down and began to figure out how he was going to get out of this . . . if he was going to get out of this.

Chapter Twenty-Seven

At the same time as Henry and Karen had entered the bedsit, the national and international news had just finished on BBC1. A couple of minutes of local news followed; the lead story concerned the death of John Abbot in a police pursuit. The item showed a clip of FB being interviewed about the incident, recorded earlier on the steps of Blackpool Central police station. FB was fairly vague about everything, though he did state that Abbot had been driving a stolen Metro which actually belonged to a police officer. FB offered no explanations as to the cause of the explosion. 'We're keeping an open mind at the moment,' he said. 'We don't really know anything for sure until tomorrow.'

The reporter pressed him for details of why the Bomb Squad were looking at the car.

'Just routine,' he said patronisingly. 'Now, if you'll excuse me . . . ' He walked out of shot, revealing the officer who was standing directly behind him: Henry Christie, looking rather ill.

Hinksman, sprawled in a chair in the safe house in Blackburn, sat bolt upright. Up to the point where Henry appeared on screen he hadn't really been taking too much notice.

'Mother fucker. You're still alive then.'

He threw himself back into his chair in frustration, clenching and unclenching his fists angrily. Finally, however, he couldn't help but laugh.

'You're a lucky son of a bitch, Sergeant Christie,' he said to the ceiling. 'But I ain't finished with you yet.'

There was a knock at the front door. For a second,

Hinksman froze. He checked through the curtains before answering and letting Lenny Dakin in.

Dakin looked flustered and agitated.

'It's tomorrow. The ship'll be coming through tomorrow. We'll meet it in the Irish Sea, collect my consignment and hand you over. From there it'll sail to Eire and you'll be able to get a flight from Dublin to Paris, then to New York. It's all arranged – false passports, money, everything.'

'Good.'

'What a fuckin' day I've had,' breathed Dakin. He helped himself to a Scotch and soda. 'I've had cops crawling all over my property looking for you. It's a damn good job I didn't put you up at the farmhouse.'

'Have they got you all worked up?' Hinksman chided.

'You bet they fucking have!'

'I thought you were a no-nonsense big-time criminal who could handle the pressure,' he teased.

'I can handle the pressure when necessary, but this isn't. You are a right royal pain in the arsehole at the moment and I'll be glad to get shut of you. You be here at nine tomorrow and you'll be picked up, OK?'

'No.'

'No? What the fuck do you mean?'

'Things to do, people to see . . . lives to wreck,' smiled Hinksman sweetly. 'You just tell me where and when you'll be sailing and I'll be there, probably with a passenger.'

'*What?*' screamed Dakin. 'Who? Are you fucking mad?'

Hinksman's eyes narrowed. 'Don't call me mad.'

By the time Dave August got back to his office at police headquarters it was midnight. He'd had a long, tiring day visiting grieving relatives, being bombarded with tears, questions and disbelief. He was worn out by the effort of appearing sympathetic on the surface whilst having to deal with his own inner turmoil at the same time. Once or twice he'd had the urge to blurt out, 'Blame me – *I'm* the one responsible.'

He'd been informed of John Abbot's death during the evening but had left it to FB and the ACC (Operations) to deal with. He'd look at it tomorrow. He couldn't believe it – what the hell else could happen? He was presently the head of a police force under mounting pressure and it didn't help that he was going through his own agonising crisis.

August sat down at his desk. He pulled a small bottle of Bell's out of a drawer and took a sip. The heat of the spirit seemed to revive him. He looked at the large pile of papers in front of him which constituted Hinksman's file. He opened the first folder and began to read by the light of his table lamp.

Somewhere in here, he hoped, was the answer.

At five minutes past midnight, a delayed flight from Miami touched down at Manchester Airport. It was some eight hours behind schedule, held up by 'technical problems' – a vague term which did not endear the company to the passengers in any way.

Tired and disgruntled, they disembarked and filed woodenly through the terminal building towards Passport Control.

Near to the front of the queue was a middle-aged woman who was in heated, but subdued, conversation with her timid husband. They were having a disagreement of sorts. She wanted him to do something, and as usual he didn't want to get involved. All he wanted to do was get home and get to bed.

'You are useless!' she told him – and not for the first time.

When they reached the desk and handed their passports over, the woman said icily to her husband, 'Well, if you won't, then I shall have to.' She looked at the Customs officer and leaned towards her with a conspiratorial air. 'Is there someone I can talk to?' she hissed, so that other passengers would not overhear. 'In confidence?'

'Yes, of course, what about?'

'One of the other passengers, who I think is on drugs.'

* * *

Henry Christie and Karl Donaldson completed their witness statements relating to John Abbot's death at about one o'clock that morning. The process had taken a couple of hours over numerous cups of sweet white coffee. Both men were exhausted, Henry in particular. He hadn't slept properly for almost two days and his mind was beginning to play tricks with his eyes.

He finished rereading his statement, blinked repeatedly and said, 'I've got to get some kip. My head's a complete shed.'

'Me too,' agreed Donaldson, yawning and stretching. His clothing reeked of smoke.

They were sitting at desks in the deserted CID office at Blackpool Central. Karen had left them about an hour before, completely wrecked herself.

Henry stood up. His joints creaked and clicked like an old man's. He walked across to a window, rolling his shoulders. He watched his reflection as he approached; he hardly recognised himself, wasn't sure who he was seeing. A stranger. Someone who had changed drastically in the last eight months. A man who'd gone from being happily married with two beautiful daughters and a beautiful wife, a contented lifestyle and good job, to a rundown adulterer who hardly saw his kids and lived like a hermit in a shit-hole of a flat that smelled of cat piss.

The only constant was that he still had the same job.

He tried to pinpoint the exact moment at which his life had changed for the worse. He reckoned it was that bomb on the M6.

He gazed blankly out of the window; in his mind's eye was every detail of that explosion and the faces of those kids. He knew now they were images that would stay with him for ever. And now he'd come full circle. Another explosion. Another motorway. And the link was the same two men: *himself and Hinksman*.

You're out there somewhere, he thought, and I want to find you. I want to hunt you down, but I don't know where to start.

He sighed and turned back to Donaldson. 'Where do we go from here?'

Before the FBI man could reply, the phone on the desk where he was sitting started to ring. Henry walked across and answered it. Two minutes later he hung up.

'Delete that last question,' he quipped. 'I might just have the answer to it. C'mon, grab yer coat.'

'Just one of those lucky things, really, if it turns out to be of any use that is,' the detective said to Henry and Donaldson as, forty minutes later, he led them through Manchester Airport to the police holding area.

'Initially we just thought she was a run-of-the-mill punter – y'know, trying to get a bit of stuff through. We searched her luggage and found some coke, a bit of crack, some heroin. Then we searched her body orifices. Well, not me personally, but I'm told there wasn't anything there that shouldn't have been.'

'So why call us?' Donaldson asked. He was beyond exhaustion. Really irritable.

The detective wasn't to be fazed. He had a bit of a story to tell and he was going to tell it, no matter what. 'Anyway, it was while a couple of female officers and a doctor were trying to search the girl that she started dropping names. She was scratching, kicking, all that shit, see, and she had to be forcibly restrained. Now she's threatening them, saying they'll get wasted for this, that she knows a hit man. A lot of rubbish on the face of it, but not when the names start coming.'

'Names like?' asked Donaldson.

The detective smiled. 'Hinksman? Well, we didn't attach much importance to that one. Every bugger in Britain knows his name. But then she was bawling about Corelli, Dakin, Stanton, you, Sergeant Christie, someone called Kovaks and you, Mr Donaldson.'

'Oh,' Henry and Donaldson said together.

'Starting saying things like the Mafia are giving you the run around. It was a lucky chance, really – she could easily have slipped into the system. It's just that one of the female officers she was wrangling with remembered the names from the last time you two guys were down here.'

'And what's the prisoner's name?' Henry asked.

'Er, Janine something-or-other. Fit little piece. If she wasn't a druggie, I'd give her one.'

'Has she said anything else?' asked Henry.

'There was one thing. She said she'd fucked your Chief Constable's brains out. A lot of crap, like I said.'

'Let's talk to her,' said Henry.

The detective shook his head. 'She's still floating in the stratosphere.' He pointed up to the sky. 'Not fit to be interviewed.'

'But this is urgent,' Henry said.

'Then you'll need a Superintendent's authority.'

Henry turned to Donaldson. 'Karl, you are hereby promoted to the rank of Superintendent. Do you accept this?'

'I do.'

'May I interview the prisoner?'

'You may.'

Dave August was getting nowhere slowly. He had spent over an hour leafing through the Hinksman paperwork, and his eyes were getting gritty, his concentration drifting.

He closed the folder he was reading and picked up the next one, headed *Unused Material*. It contained all sorts of scraps of information, intelligence and musings even, which hadn't been used in the court prosecution. It was a real mish-mash of stuff.

August swore softly and flicked through the contents with a grimace on his face. Then he closed the file, clasped his fingers, knuckles down, palms up on the desk-top and laid his forehead on the soft cushion they formed.

Within moments he was asleep.

The interview room had three chairs and a sturdy table with a tape-recorder on it. Janine was sitting on one of the chairs with her elbows on the table, hands held loosely over the sides of her face and ears. Henry sat down opposite her. Donaldson remained standing, arms folded, like a sentry.

Henry placed an unopened pack of tapes on the table, together with a sealed plastic bag containing the drugs seized from her. 'Janine, we'd like to have a chat with you.' He spoke softly, seductively.

'Who the hell are you?' she demanded.

'We're here to help you.' Henry noticed, with pleasure, that her hands were shaking. She was coming down.

'I'm up shit creek,' she said. 'I'll go down for this – importing or whatever. You can't do fuck-all for me.'

'Oh yes, we can,' countered Henry. 'But you've got to help us first. You see, this isn't a recorded interview.' He held up the unopened tapes. 'It's totally off the record.'

She gazed defiantly at him. 'Oh yeah?' she said disbelievingly. 'So what can you do?'

'Two things actually,' Henry said, matter-of-fact. 'First we can give you a fix – I can see you need one – and the custody officer needn't know about it; secondly, we can get all the charges against you dropped.'

Her eyes seemed to come alive. 'Are you taking the piss?'

'Trust me, Janine, we have the power. All you need to do is answer some questions. When you've done that, we'll slip you a fix. When we've verified what you say is correct, we'll arrange for you to be released without charge.'

He paused, letting his words sink in, then resumed, his voice hard: 'Thing is, if you don't cooperate, Janine, you'll get no smack and we will push hard for a custodial sentence. Just think – five years in prison, a lovely girl like you. We'll tell the court what a bitch you were – obstructive, violent, all that sort of shit. Get the drift? So, you can come out of this a winner or a loser. Choice is yours, babe.'

'What do you want to know?'

It was 4.15 a.m. when Dave August awoke. He felt terrible. He needed to wash his face and gargle with a minty mouthwash, which he did at the washbasin in his little sleeping annexe next to the office.

As he dried his face he looked at the camp bed. It hadn't seen much activity since Karen had left him. Bitch. Served her right. Without a shred of conscience, nor even the merest idea that he might have committed rape – after all, how could it have been rape after she'd let him fuck her all those times before? – he strolled back into his office, feeling more or less 'with it'.

The files on his desk were in disarray. He straightened them up and turned back to the one he'd been reading just prior to falling asleep.

As he skimmed through it again, feeling much more alert, he came across an old 1974 descriptive form – a piece of police bumf that is completed when someone is arrested – which related to a man called Dakin. August wasn't too sure about Dakin's role in the scheme of things (Chief Constables only ever want to know the wider picture not the ins and outs of investigations), and he wasn't too bothered. He speed-read the form without undue interest. It was an old-style form from Strathclyde police in Scotland, containing much more detail than the newer forms, even down to the colour of Dakin's socks.

August was about to add it to the pile when he paused. Something was triggered in his mind.

Firstly, it was a Scottish form. Interesting.

There was something else too, but he wasn't sure what.

He read it again, slowly. The officer who had filled it in had been very thorough, even to the point of describing and drawing the tattoo which Dakin had on the back of his left hand. It was in the shape of a heart with a skull superimposed on it.

August stared at the little drawing. His mind swirled back. The factory floor. The shotgun rammed into his neck. His face pressed into the floor, eyes tightly closed except for one millisecond when he'd squinted upwards and seen . . .

Heart and skull.

And the man with the tattooed hand had a Scottish accent.

Time to find out more about Lenny Dakin.

'Do you actually have the power to do what you said?' Donaldson asked Henry. 'Getting the charges dropped?'

They were back on the M6 motorway, speeding north, Henry at the wheel.

'Probably not,' admitted Henry. 'But I did get some smack to her and I'll do my best. If I can't pull anything off, so what? She's just a junkie. I won't be too concerned.'

'You're all heart,' said Donaldson with a short laugh. 'By the way, do you always break the rules? That interview wasn't really legit, was it?'

They both cracked up laughing.

'We don't ever break the rules in the States,' Donaldson went on. 'We can't afford to.'

'Neither can we,' said Henry bleakly.

The consequences of what he'd just done were too horrendous to contemplate if it came out. He'd lose his job and probably get prosecuted for supplying controlled drugs to a person in custody. A very serious offence. A very serious understatement.

He hoped that both Janine and the airport detective would keep quiet about it. Realistically, though, he knew it was probably too much to hope for.

They passed the turn-off to Blackpool and stayed on the M6. In less than fifteen minutes they'd be back at Lancaster.

'What d'ya reckon to all that blabbering about screwing your Chief Constable?' Donaldson yawned.

'Puzzles me,' said Henry. 'Perhaps it's one of her fantasies.'

'I wouldn't put anything past him,' said Donaldson.

'Which reminds me,' said Henry. 'What's happening about that er . . . business between him and Karen?'

'It's in the pipeline. That's all I can say.'

* * *

374

By 6.15 a.m. everyone was assembled in the gymnasium at Lancaster police station in readiness for a briefing.

All the detectives involved in the 'escape' enquiry were there, wearing scruffy clothes as requested, together with a heavily armed firearms team, dog-handlers and uniformed Support Unit officers. Also present was the Superintendent in charge of the division and a couple of communications operators.

Henry, Donaldson, Karen and FB were at the front of the room. Donaldson and FB kept a healthy distance between each other, despite FB's apparent acceptance of Karen now, he and Donaldson still did not see eye to eye. The American tended to bear grudges for a long time, especially where women and their treatment were concerned.

Henry gazed with mounting excitement tinged with trepidation at the tired but expectant faces in front of him. *This was it.* Somehow he knew it in his guts. This was going to be the real thing. No way could it turn out to be a wild-goose chase.

Karen had been tasked to do the briefing. When she asked for quiet, the room hushed immediately.

'Good morning, everyone. Thanks for turning out at such short notice. We are very impressed by your eagerness and I think that it will be rewarded today.

'OK . . . we all know about the escape from custody of a man called James Clarkson Hinksman three days ago after he'd been found guilty of the M6 bombing and the murders of several police officers and others. The escape was perpetrated by a ruthless professional gang who specialise in such jobs. It involved incredible violence, leaving many of our colleagues dead for no good reason. Obviously since then we have been working at full tilt to recapture Hinksman and apprehend this violent team.

'It's no secret that netting the team will be a long and difficult process as we believe they've probably dispersed abroad by now. However, with regard to Hinksman we have had a major breakthrough. This is why you're all here this morning.'

375

A murmur went round the room. Karen allowed it to settle before continuing.

'As most of you know, DS Christie and I have headed the part of the investigation aimed specifically at Hinksman. This morning DS Christie and Special Agent Donaldson of the FBI – who has been working closely with us on this – have received some Class A information which leads us to believe two things. Firstly, Hinksman is still in Lancashire. Secondly, he's going to leave the country today. We know how and where, but we don't exactly know when, other than it's today sometime. So I'll warn you now, this could be a very long day, but I'm confident that at the end of it we'll have a result. Any questions so far?'

There were none. But there were plenty of smiles on plenty of faces.

On the wall behind Karen was a large-scale map of Lancaster and its environs. She stepped to one side and turned to it.

'The information we have received today is this . . .'

She pointed to the map and began to reveal the police operation that had been hastily put together.

Dave August had everything from the Lancashire police files on Lenny Dakin: intelligence reports, photographs, more up-to-date descriptions, known associates, suspected involvement in crime, estimated wealth etc. There were copies of several surveillance operations which had been run jointly between Lancashire and other forces, but all these had been unsuccessful. He was a very careful man, very surveillance-conscious. One detective referred to him as the 'canny Scot'.

So, pondered August, he was a big-time criminal, of that there was no doubt. He read through an intelligence report submitted by Henry Christie, reporting that Dakin had picked up the American gangster Corelli at Manchester Aiport. Christie surmised that the two were in cahoots, probably planning ways to bring drugs into the country. He also surmised that Dakin had probably set up Danny Carver and Jason Brown to meet their deaths at the hand of Hinksman – but he had no evidence to back that up.

He may be Mr Big, August thought, but more importantly, this morning I have identified him as the man behind everything that has gone wrong with my life recently. This is the bastard who preyed on my weakness and exploited it.

When August's secretary Jean came in, he realised, much to his surprise, that it was 8 a.m. He was still sat there in the uniform he'd been wearing for the last twenty-four hours. He needed a shave and a shower.

Jean had a worried look on her face.

She walked across to August's desk and placed a newspaper on top of what he was reading.

'I think you should see this, sir,' she said without a smile. 'And there's a journalist outside asking to see you, an American called Lisa Want.' She spun round and left.

August frowned. This was not a newspaper he had ever read or would ever consider reading. It was complete trash.

Then the headlines hit him.

Chief Constable In Sex-And-Drug Orgy With Hooker!

'Oh my God,' he groaned.

A grainy colour photograph on the front page showed him facing the camera, standing naked with a woman kneeling in front of him. Her face and breasts, his privates and buttocks had been blacked out with a thick line, but the ecstasy on his face was horribly clear. It was a still taken from the video.

The article accompanying it was written by Lisa Want – again on 'special assignment'. Readers were invited to turn to the centre pages for more sensational photographs and a transcript of the soundtrack.

With a heartbeat increased to epic proportions and a quivering hand to match, Dave August did just that. His world, which was crumbling away, began to avalanche down a precipitous mountainside.

And there would be more to come.

He looked out of his window towards the sports field.

The day was overcast, clouds grey. Big spats of rain slapped loudly onto the panes.

The phone started to ring.

Both Henry Christie and Karl Donaldson received phone calls after the briefing which unsettled them. They were summoned down to the communications room on the floor below the gym and took their calls at the same time, but from different extensions.

Karen, standing in a position between the two, watched their reactions to whatever the news was.

'Daddy?'

Henry immediately recognised his eldest daughter's voice and the strained tone which accompanied even that single word.

'Hi Jenny, what's the matter, sweetheart?'

'I don't know, Daddy.'

He could hear fear in her voice.

'What d'you mean, you don't know?' he asked, keeping his own voice purposely light. He sensed something catastrophic was wrong. It wasn't like Jenny to phone him at all; she usually tagged onto Leanne's calls.

'We got up this morning and . . . oh, Dad! Mum's not here! She's gone. We don't know what to do.'

Henry felt something heavy drop in his stomach . . .

Meanwhile, in the same room, not six feet away, Donaldson was taking a transatlantic phone call.

'Just letting' ya know outta courtesy, Karl,' the faint voice 3,000 miles away at the other end of the line was saying. It was one of Donaldson's former partners, still a good friend.

'Speak up a little, Jack. Can hardly hear ya.'

'Bad news, pal, bad news. It's about Joe Kovaks . . . '

Henry and Donaldson hung up simultaneously. Each ran a hand over his own face.

'I can't believe this,' said Donaldson. 'Joe's gone missing. Last seen leaving the office ten a.m. yesterday, not called in since. Bucar's gone too. Not like him, not like him at all.

Chrissy hasn't seen him. I know he's a maverick, but he ain't stupid. Don't like it.'

Karen laid a worried hand on the back of his head.

Henry, stunned, said simply, 'I think Hinksman's got my wife.' He closed his eyes, dropped his head and began to pray.

A light flashed on the switchboard. One of the comms operators answered the call.

'DS Christie? Call for you.'

FB burst brusquely into the communications room. 'I've just brought the Chief Constable up to date with what's happening and where this thing's going. He didn't half sound strange—' He stopped mid-sentence and looked at the serious faces of everyone in the room.

Karen put a finger to her lips.

All attention was focused on Henry who picked up the phone and slowly put it to his ear.

'Henry, you're one hell of a lucky son of a bitch. That bomb was meant for you, but no doubt you know that.'

'It's a conclusion I reached,' said Henry stonily, immediately recognising the voice of Hinksman.

'An' I'm real sorry about the kid because I don't like killing innocent people unless it's absolutely necessary. It's so unprofessional.'

'So how guilty was the prostitute in Blackpool?'

'Hey, some detective! I'm impressed you know about her.' Hinksman's voice went hard, making the hairs creep on Henry's scalp. 'She stole from me. She lost her status of innocence. Rather like you, Henry, when you turned my money down, then when you shot me.'

'And how guilty is my wife?' whispered Henry, feeling the nausea grip his lower abdomen like a clawed hand.

Hinksman gave a short laugh. 'She's actually very innocent. I've told her it's nothing personal, but I need to use her. What surprises me is that you didn't take more steps to protect your family. You ain't even got a burglar alarm on your house. I as good as let myself in – not even a dog, for Christ's sake. And all those goodies to protect – TV, hi-fi, microwave – and those two lovely daughters.'

Hinksman allowed the words to sink into Henry's consciousness.

'Had a look in at that older one,' he said airily. 'Developing a real nice pair of titties. Might come back one day and rape the fuck out of her – just to make you suffer again. Because that's what all this is about, making you suffer for what you did to me.' His voice grew thick. 'I wanted to kill you face to face. I was waiting for you the other night, but I chose the hooker instead . . .'

'Then let's meet,' Henry cut in desperately. 'Let Kate go and I give you my word, just you and me.'

'Love to say yes – but no can do. I'm out of here – once I've finished with Mrs C, that is.' He laughed uproariously. 'So, unfortunately I'm going to have to make you suffer by proxy. Oh, and forget about tracing the phone – I'm on a mobile. Goodbye Henry. Missing you already.'

'Don't hang up,' screamed Henry. 'Hinksman!'

The line was dead.

'I told you to hold all calls, you stupid bitch. I don't want interrupting,' Dave August snapped down the line to his secretary. He was trapped in his office and it was getting smaller and smaller. The walls seemed to be sliding towards him like some sort of medieval torture chamber. He half-expected sharpened spears of steel to appear.

'Mr August,' Jean remonstrated. 'I'm doing my best. I felt I should let you know that the HMI has been on, as well as the Head of the Police Committee, as well as numerous others . . . and there are two gentlemen here to see you.'

'Tell them to fuck off.' He was sweating profusely. 'Is that bitch of a reporter still there?'

'Yes, out in Reception together with several others and the TV.'

'Tell them all to fuck off, or I'll have them thrown out.'

'Mr August, I can't do that,' she said desperately. 'I'm struggling out here to be as polite to everyone as I can. I'm trying to protect you so you can pull yourself together, yet all I hear from you are senseless, obscene instructions which are impossible to carry out. Mr August, I am very close to tears.'

Not as close as I am, he thought. He capitulated. 'Look, I'm sorry. I'm really sorry. My mind's in a bit of a mess at the moment as you can probably appreciate.' He took a deep breath. 'Who are the gentlemen you refer to? Not reporters, I hope. I won't see anyone from the press.'

'No, they're officers from Greater Manchester Police. They say they have something very important to discuss with you.'

'Right, right . . . give me five minutes.'

'I'm Detective Chief Superintendent Runshaw and this is Detective Inspector Tandy.'

August leaned across his desk and shook their hands. He had changed out of his uniform into a suit and had quickly shaved, nicking himself several times in the process. He looked a mess, but didn't give a shit. He invited the two men to sit down with a wave of his hand.

'Pleased to meet you,' he said, even though he didn't like the look in their eyes. 'What can I do for you?'

'A somewhat delicate matter,' Runshaw admitted. 'We've received a complaint from a member of your force, one of your officers, and we are investigating it following a decision by our Chief Constable in consultation with the PCA and CPS.'

'Oh? Sounds unusual.'

'It's actually a very serious allegation that's been made and it's an allegation against you, sir. It's one of rape.'

August nearly wet himself. 'What? That's preposterous.'

'A female Chief Inspector has alleged that you raped her in her home some months ago,' Runshaw went on.

'That's not true,' said August shakily. *Please, ground*, he thought. *Open up, swallow me . . .*

'Well, sir, the allegation has been made and we're

satisfied that there's enough evidence to make an arrest—'

'An arrest? Are you saying that you're going to arrest me? I'm a Chief Constable, for God's sake. You can't do that, especially on some unsubstantiated allegation by a bitter woman.'

Runshaw held up his hands, palms towards August in a pacifying gesture.

'Firstly, sir, I know you're a Chief Constable. Secondly, I or any other police officer could arrest you, so don't make that mistake. You are not above the law. However, if you would be willing to accompany us voluntarily so that we can interview you about the matter, that would suit us. No unpleasantness. That said, I must caution you.' And he recited it, word perfect.

August replied with a sneer in his voice. 'Her word against mine. You'll never prove anything.'

'Please, sir, don't jump to that conclusion.'

'You mean you have evidence other than her say-so?' He looked astounded as he watched the two men nod simultaneously. 'Such as?'

'Suffice to say there is more than just her say-so, as you put it.'

'Bollocks! Anyway, I'm too busy to be bothered with this at the moment. On the way out, make an appointment with my secretary for some time next week and we'll discuss it then. Goodbye, gentlemen.'

Cool, unflustered, DCS Runshaw said, 'I'm arresting you on suspicion of raping Karen Wilde, and may I add that I don't give a rat's arse that you're a Chief Constable. You could be the fucking Prime Minister for all I care. You're coming with us – *now*. Understand?'

For the second time that morning, as the enormity of what was happening hit him, Dave August's career tumbled before his very eyes like a ton of bricks off the back of a lorry. Whatever happened now, he was a goner. The combination of the arrest and the newspaper headlines had well and truly sunk him, professionally and personally.

He sat back slowly in his big comfortable leather chair and nodded apparent acceptance of the situation. But his mind was racing.

'Could you just give me five minutes?' he asked. 'Obviously I have numerous things to sort out and I can't just leave them in mid-air. I'll need to tell my secretary and staff officer what's going on; then have a quick word with an ACC to hold the fort. Will you let me do that?'

Runshaw looked at his DI and gave him the eye. 'DI Tandy will come with you, sir. I'll wait here if you don't mind.'

'No problem.'

August walked out of his office with Tandy on his heels.

'Jean,' he said, 'I'll be back shortly to let you know what's going on.'

'Yes, sir,' she nodded worriedly, completely mystified by the events of the morning.

In the corridor outside the office, August said, 'I need a wee.'

'I'll come with you, sir.'

'Suit yourself, but I'm not going to do a runner.'

He led Tandy to the gents toilet on the same corridor. There was no one else inside. Tandy hung back by the door whilst August relieved himself. He washed his hands meticulously and dried them under the hot-air machine. Standing there, rubbing his hands as instructed, flexing his fingers, he made a rash decision which in his present light-headed, unreal frame of mind seemed totally rational.

Might as well go out in a blaze, he thought.

He smoothed his jacket down and with a resigned smile on his face, sauntered towards Tandy, giving the DI no warning of what was to come.

It was a wonderful punch. Low, hard and rising, right in the solar plexus. He couldn't have placed it better if 'X' had marked the spot.

The wind hurricaned out of Tandy. He doubled up with an agonised gasp. August then grabbed hold of the scruff of the detective's neck, and drove him headfirst into the wall.

The DI flopped to the floor, dazed, gurgling incoherently. For good measure August kicked the unfortunate man twice on the head. The first kick knocked him cold, the second meant that Tandy would lose the use of his left eye for ever.

August then dragged him across to one of the cubicles where he dumped him, folded him up on the floor around a toilet and closed the door.

In his haste to leave the gents, August almost slipped headlong on the trail of blood across the tiled floor.

Outside, the corridor was clear.

He turned and sprinted towards the stairs, propelling himself down them three at a time. Within seconds he emerged in a ground-floor corridor. Here he paused and composed himself.

'Fucking career's ruined, life's ruined, what's it fucking matter?' he chunnered to himself.

A couple of people walked past him and nodded at him. He smiled benignly at them. Pulling his jacket together he walked briskly in the direction of the garage where his car was parked, passing the armoury as he did so.

The door was slightly open; someone was working inside.

August did a quick sidestep, unable to believe his good fortune.

'Play it cool,' he told himself.

The man inside was a firearms instructor from the training school. He was working at a small table, checking over some handguns which were laid out in front of him. August's eyes lit on a revolver, next to which was a box of ammunition.

'Hello, sir,' said the instructor, surprised, starting to rise.

August gestured for him to remain seated. 'No, don't get up. Just a flying visit as I was passing. All well?'

'Yes, sir.'

August pointed towards the revolver – a 4-inch barrelled Smith & Wesson ·38. Standard police issue. 'Mind if I pick it up? It's not loaded, is it?'

To anyone else the instructor would have said no. But

how could he refuse the Chief Constable? After all, he was the one who signed everyone else's permits.

August picked up the gun, gripping the barrel and cylinder as though he was going to use it as a hammer to knock in nails. In one flowing motion he whacked the heel of the butt across the instructor's head with as much force as possible. Surprise, as much as anything else, decked him.

August loaded the revolver and pocketed the remainder of the bullets from the box.

The instructor had risen to his hands and knees, shaking his stunned and cut head, flicking spats of blood everywhere. When August left the armoury and locked the door behind him, the instructor was flat out again, this time for the count. Blood poured out of another nasty gash on the back of his head.

Turning away from the door without looking meant that August collided with a woman who was walking from the direction of the canteen, bearing a precariously balanced plate with a cream cake on top of a cup of coffee. The contents of both plate and cup went flying into the wall. The crockery smashed into little pieces.

'Godamnit!' the woman shouted. 'Why don't you watch where you're go—' She then saw who had bumped into her. 'You . . . you're Dave August.'

August frowned at her and made to walk away. She wrenched him back to face her by his sleeve, yanking him to a standstill.

He brushed her hand off him, glowered angrily at her and said, 'I'm in a hurry, if you don't mind.'

'And I'm waiting for an interview with you.'

'And who might you be?'

'Lisa Want.'

'Oooh, the bitch who wrote that sleaze about me.' August was in two minds whether or not to punch her very, very hard when he had another avenue of thought. His eyes narrowed. 'How'd you like another exclusive?'

No hesitation. 'Yes.'

'Come with me. Quick, quick. Haven't got time to hang around.'

'What about this mess?'

'Leave it.'

He set off towards the garage at a fast pace. Lisa tagged on.

'What's all this about?'

'Just stay with me and you'll see,' he said.

In the garage he made straight for his official Jaguar. The keys were in the ignition, as always. He dropped into the driver's seat and told Lisa to get in the other side.

The engine fired up beautifully. He accelerated out through the garage doors, round the one-way system, past the HQ social club and bowling green, and seconds later he was out on the dual carriageway which ran by Headquarters.

'So what's this about?' she asked again.

'You got a tape-recorder?'

'Yep.'

'Well, put it on. I've got a story to tell: the downfall of a Chief Constable.'

Chapter Twenty-Eight

It was a dreadful morning. Thick grey cloud had scurried in from the Irish Sea and settled low over the Lancashire coast. Rain swirled and danced like a menacing spirit in the twisting wind, heavy and very wet. Not a day to be caught out in.

Henry wrapped his hands around the mug of coffee on the table in front of him. Donaldson was sipping slowly but continuously from a mug of his own. Both men, deep in their own thoughts, were sitting in a café called Lantern o'er Lune, staring out at the small port of Glasson Dock in front of them.

Glasson Dock is situated on the mouth of the Lune estuary, a few miles downriver from Lancaster. In former days it acted as Lancaster's port, but now most of its trade centred on pleasure boats.

All vessels coming in from the sea have to pass through the outer dock gates from the river into the main, deepwater anchorage. This is a manoeuvre which can only be carried out at high tide. Once inside, with the gates closed, they either tie up in the main dock to unload their cargoes, or in the case of pleasure boats, pass through a lock which lifts them to the level of the yacht basin. This process involves closing the main road in Glasson which actually passes over the lock. Once in the yacht basin – a large, square-shaped area of water with a marina in one corner – the boats either moor on the wall of the basin or in the marina itself.

Lenny Dakin owned a large sea-going motor-cruiser berthed at the marina. And if – a big IF – the information Henry had received was correct, he would be coming out to catch the tide; this meant that when he passed into the lock, he would be trapped for at least fifteen minutes.

But if Hinksman wasn't aboard, there wasn't much point in having him trapped.

Henry and Donaldson were wearing earpieces so they could listen to the radio transmissions from the various police officers who were hidden around the dock. Some were armed, but the main firearms team had been put on standby at a caravan site next to the road leading into Glasson, about a minute away from the dock.

So far they had been unable to say which boat belonged to Dakin. There were several good class cruisers and it could be any one of them. They didn't want to get in too close for a nosey just in case Dakin was spooked and the operation was spoiled.

Henry shook himself out of his reverie and consulted his watch.

'Not long before the tide turns,' he commented. 'If he doesn't go out on this one, then we'll be here another twelve hours. Makes me wonder if this is really going to happen.'

'It's all we've got,' said Donaldson.

'I feel so fucking useless just sitting here,' Henry said bitterly. He wasn't too far from tears. 'If Kate's injured or hurt or worse, I'm not sure I'll be able to handle it. I feel like cracking now.'

'Look, if this information is good,' Donaldson tried to placate and motivate him, 'this is the best place to be. He'll turn up and we'll grab him. I'm sure of it.'

Their earpieces crackled into life.

'Charlie Delta Two to control.'

'Charlie Delta Two, go ahead,' came the voice of Karen in the communications room at Lancaster. She had taken over the helm with FB by her side.

Henry and Donaldson listened carefully. This was the voice of the officer hidden in a hedge near to the roadside entrance to the marina.

'Target One approaching site. Three on board. Repeat: Target One approaching site, three on board.'

'*Yes!*' said Henry triumphantly, clenching a fist.

This meant that Dakin had arrived at the marina in his Bentley with two other persons.

There was silence on the airwaves for another two minutes. Then: 'Charlie Delta Six to control.' This officer had an elevated view of the marina from binoculars on a hillside.

'Go ahead.'

'Confirm Target One on site in company with two others, both male . . . cannot ID them but fairly sure not Target Two, repeat NOT Target Two.'

'Damn,' said Henry. This meant that Hinksman wasn't either of the two others.

'Don't worry,' Donaldson said. 'He'll come.'

'Charlie Delta Six – all three men have left the vehicle parked up and have climbed on board a motor-cruiser. Can't see the name. Now all out of sight.'

Karen acknowledged him. The radio went silent again.

Dakin was on board.

Henry rubbed his temples with the base of his thumbs. 'This is doing my head in.'

'Mine too,' Donaldson confessed ruefully.

Five minutes of radio silence passed. The weather seemed to worsen. Rain started to drive down.

'Charlie Delta Six to control.' He sounded quite excited. 'A motor-cruiser has moved off from the marina and is headed towards the lock.'

Instinctively Henry reached underneath his anorak and touched the butt of his revolver with his fingertips.

'Patrols are reminded to keep well out of sight of the incident area,' Karen warned sternly over the air. 'I repeat . . . ' This was a warning that everyone involved should keep well away from, and out of sight of, the lock – with the exception of Henry and Donaldson who were running the show.

From their position in the café the two detectives had an uninterrupted view of the lock, some 100 metres away.

The lock-keeper came out of his cottage. He dropped the barriers across the road to stop all traffic, though there was none at that time. He then got to work on swinging the section of single-track road, which bridged the lock, to one side and securing it with chains. It wasn't as hard a task as it seemed as the bridge was geared and on well-oiled runners.

As he was busy doing this, a motor-cruiser appeared at the lock-gates.

'Here he is,' said Henry, sliding down low on his chair and pulling up his collar. 'Looks like Dakin's at the helm.' He wasn't particularly *au fait* with nautical terms. 'I don't recognise the two others.'

'Gofers,' Donaldson said dismissively.

The lock-keeper had secured the bridge and now began to push open the upper lock-gates. They opened slowly and the boat slid majestically into the lock.

Donaldson whistled appreciatively. 'Nice boat.'

Henry agreed. 'He's in a profitable business – and if I can prove he bought it from the proceeds of crime, I'll get it seized.'

The boat was a Trader 50 which Dakin had owned since new, and was laid out with four double cabins. The twin Caterpillar 210 engine gave it a good long range at 15 knots. Its specification was excellent and included a generator, air conditioning, 48-mile radar, autopilot, galley equipped with three fridges, a freezer, washing machine and microwave, plus a dinghy, life-raft and awnings.

Dakin's two gofers – dressed totally inappropriately in T-shirts and jeans – wrapped ropes around the bollards on the side of the lock opposite to where Henry and Donaldson were sitting. Dakin seemed to be shouting obscenities at them. Their faces, when Henry could see them, registered apathy, as though they didn't want to be there.

The lock-keeper closed the upper lock-gates.

In a few moments he would transfer his attention to the lower gates, when he would open the gate paddles to allow water to flow out into the dock, out of the lock chamber.

Dakin was trapped. It would be an easy task to board the boat now.

'Well, shall we?' Donaldson turned to Henry, eyebrows raised. 'You're in charge, pal. Everyone's waiting on you.'

Henry gave a noncommittal shrug. 'If I knew he was on board, I'd say yes. But I don't want to blow it, because if he isn't, we've lost a good job for when Dakin comes back in loaded to the nines with drugs.'

'Yeah. I understand the quandary—' Donaldson was stopped in mid sentence by Henry's hand clamping on his arm. A van had pulled up on the far side of the lock. The driver got out and walked, head bowed against the wind and rain, towards the boat. It was virtually impossible to make out his features.

Henry said, 'It's him,' hoarsely. 'It's Hinksman.' He was sure. He felt his heart rate increase. 'Where's Kate? What the hell's he done to her?'

'You sure it's him?' Donaldson questioned, peering through the window.

'Positive.'

Hinksman stepped across onto the boat.

'Let's give him a second or two,' Henry said. He spoke into his radio to appraise everyone of the situation, telling them to hold back for his word.

Hinksman went into the cabin and started talking to Dakin.

A second car stopped on the other side of the road, near to where Hinksman had parked his van. The horn blared angrily. A man climbed out and walked to the edge of the lock.

'Jesus Christ,' uttered Henry in disbelief. 'It's Dave August, I'm sure it is.'

'What in the name of damnation is he doing here?' Donaldson said.

'Dakin!' August shouted. 'Lenny Dakin!'

'Fuck off,' one of the henchmen replied.

Dakin stepped out of the cabin with Hinksman just one pace behind him. 'What do you want?'

'You Lenny Dakin?'

'Aye.'

'You know who I am?'

'Should I?' he replied, though he did know very well.

'I'm Dave August. Chief Constable of Lancashire Constabulary.'

'Congratulations.'

'You have ruined my life, Lenny Dakin.'

August's right hand pulled out the revolver which had been tucked in his waistband underneath his jacket. He pointed it at Dakin.

'Now I'm going to ruin yours.'

'Let's move – now!' shouted Henry down the radio. The intention had initially been to give the firearms team a couple of minutes to race into position from the caravan site. That idea had gone right down the tubes. Things had definitely changed.

'I don't know what's going on,' he said to Donaldson, standing up and running towards the café door, 'but I think we'd better intervene.'

He drew his gun as he went through the door.

August yelled something completely incomprehensible.

Hinksman threw himself to one side at the first sight of the gun, but Dakin froze momentarily. A moment too long.

August fired.

Dakin was propelled back against the cabin; he slithered down onto his knees, facing August, clutching his right shoulder which spurted blood. Once again the gun in August's hand cracked – *smack!* – the sound almost deadened by the heavy rain. A bullet burned its way through the air to Dakin's chest, burying itself deep in his heart, tearing it to shreds.

This all happened in a matter of seconds.

Henry and Donaldson ran across the grassed area between themselves and the lock, unable to see exactly what had transpired because of the boat obstructing their line of sight.

They bounded over the footbridge spanning the lower gate of the lock and onto the opposite side where they were confronted by the scene.

August was standing there with the revolver hanging loosely in his right hand by his thigh.

Dakin's body was sprawled out on the deck, blood and rainwater mixing. He was twitching.

Dakin's two men were crouched down behind the wheelhouse, both quivering wrecks.

Henry and Donaldson came to a halt.

A couple of steps behind August was Lisa Want, drenched, a camera in her hand but not being used.

Henry was confused, to say the least. He couldn't work any of this out at all.

August turned and looked at him, a distant faraway deadness in his eyes. His face was streaming wet, his hair plastered down on his forehead. He had no particular expression on his countenance as he levelled the revolver slowly at Henry.

Henry went low, bringing his own gun up, prepared to fire to defend himself. But it was not necessary. He watched in fascination as August, in what seemed like slow motion, drew the tip of the revolver into his own mouth cavity and pulled the trigger.

It was almost like his hat had been blown off in the wind – but it wasn't a hat – it was the top of his head.

For several seconds the newly dead man remained standing. Then his body realised it was no more and collapsed.

Lisa Want screamed hysterically and began frenziedly trying to wipe August's brains off her chest.

Henry frantically looked round. 'Hinksman! Where the hell is he?' he screamed.

As soon as the gun appeared in August's hand, Hinksman followed the survival instincts which had kept him alive for so long. He immediately threw himself down to the deck, scrambling wildly away as Dakin was hurled back against the cabin. By the time August fired the second shot, Hinksman had vaulted over the side rail of the boat and was running for his van.

Hinksman had started the engine before Henry and Donaldson had even got as far as the lock. He accelerated away from the lock, away from trouble. Desperate to clear the windscreen as his vision through the glass was a complete blur, he fumbled for the wipers switch, momentarily confusing it first with the headlights switch, then with the indication controls.

'Fuck!' he cursed angrily.

'Ram that van! Stop him! It's Target Two!' Henry shouted hysterically down his radio, hoping that the transmission was being picked up and understood by the firearms team personnel carrier which was hurtling down the road towards the dock.

What Henry was advocating was completely against force policy. However, in those split seconds, he reasoned that it didn't matter too much because there wasn't a Chief Constable to enforce it.

'Ram the bastard off the road,' he screamed again.

He was chasing after the vehicle on foot.

The Sergeant who was sitting in the front passenger seat of the personnel carrier exchanged a brief glance with the driver, who was a PC. He said, 'Do as you're told.'

The Constable didn't need telling twice.

He almost stood on the accelerator pedal and the 3.5 litre engine seemed to growl as it surged forwards.

At last Hinksman found the stalk for the windscreen wipers.

The blades cleared the screen with their first sweep . . . and Hinksman's eyes widened as the huge blue personnel carrier bearing down on him filled his total vision.

He wrenched the steering wheel down to the left, but there was no way he could avoid a collision. The bastard was aiming straight for him.

Henry knew not to underestimate Hinksman, but he thought that it would have been impossible for even the American to get out of the van alive. The front end of it had

394

clipped the front fender of the personnel carrier and the van had been flipped over onto its roof. Its momentum had then carried it on over the kerb where it had smashed into the ladies' entrance to a block of roadside toilets.

It was a complete mess. The roof had been crushed and the front end stove into the toilets and the windscreen shattered. Looked like a good fatal RTA.

Henry stopped running. He holstered his gun. He walked cautiously towards the van, past the firearms personnel carrier which had skidded to a halt by the side of the road, virtually undamaged.

'Anyone hurt?' Henry called out.

'Nope.'

'Good.'

Then he couldn't believe his eyes when Hinksman, apparently uninjured, crawled out through the space where the windscreen had once been, and sprinted away.

Henry was only feet behind. He was almost near enough to lay a hand on Hinksman's shoulder.

They ran behind a pub. Hinksman leapt over a low fence, closely followed by Henry.

'I've got you, I've got you,' Henry said to the beat of his running pace.

Suddenly they found themselves on the edge of the outer dock wall. On their right was a fifteen-foot drop into the fast-ebbing, brown-coloured, swirling water of the River Lune.

Henry was gaining on Hinksman all the time. He was feeling confident. Hinksman, in turn, seemed to be slowing down; perhaps he was injured, after all.

Then without warning, Hinksman stopped, spun round on the spot with the agility of a soccer centre forward. The move caught Henry completely by surprise and before he could stop himself he ran right into Hinksman's arms.

Hinksman brought a knee up into Henry's testicles and rammed them home. Pain seared through his groin and he doubled up, letting go of the American. Hinksman then punched Henry in the back of his head and Henry dropped to the ground.

Hinksman turned and was about to run, but Henry was not having that. Despite the pain he reached out and grabbed an ankle with both hands, catching Hinksman off-balance, bringing him crashing face-down to the ground. Henry fell on top of him, trying to pin him there for as long as possible. Surely assistance could only be moments away?

But Hinksman was strong, agile and dangerous.

He elbowed Henry in the ribs, causing him to release his grip, and both men rolled towards the edge of the dock, clutching at each other.

In a flash of speed Hinksman was on top and Henry's head was dangling over the edge.

'Hold it,' came a voice. Assistance, Henry thought with relief.

Hinksman glanced up. Then he looked down at Henry, smiled and said, 'Let's go together.' With one final surge he took both of them off the edge of the dock into the river below.

They separated as soon as they hit the water, pulled apart with such incredible icy force that they were powerless to resist.

Henry struck out ferociously with his arms and legs in a desperate panic to remain on the surface. It was a futile attempt. He was drawn under with terrifying ease and he knew he was going to die. He clamped his mouth shut in an attempt to keep his lungs clear of water. He found it impossible. The dirty river water cascaded down his nostrils instead, making his mouth open in a gasp, then swallowing what seemed like the equivalent of a bucketful of gritty water into his stomach and lungs. It felt as if it was filling his head too. His body was twisted and turned, stretched, slewed and squashed, thrown around like a piece of clothing in a spindrier.

All in blackness. Everything freezing cold.

He knew he would be dead very soon. If not from

straightforward drowning, then from the numbing cold of the river. It was pointless to make any effort. He might as well give up. To struggle would achieve nothing.

Suddenly he was spat up to the surface.

Air shot down his gullet – sweet, sweet air. His eyes opened. He saw that he was in mid-channel, surging with the tide towards Morecambe Bay and the open sea beyond. He could see the open dock-gates of Glasson about 150 metres away. Several figures were looking out at him.

He tried to shout but his voice was lost in the heavy wind and rain.

A vortex twisted him round 180 degrees. Now he was looking at the opposite bank of the river, about 120 metres off.

A second later the invisible hands of a current dragged him under again.

This pull was long and strong and he couldn't fight it. He never expected to come up from it. He seemed to be under for ever, yet only seconds later he was on the surface again, looking towards the riverbank which appeared much nearer, about fifty metres away.

The water covered him again, this time with less force.

Even so, he was cold, weak and helpless.

Yet he began to fight it. Because he had something to fight for – to find Kate. He couldn't leave the world not knowing. This time he rose to the surface from his own inner strength and there was no panic in his struggle. A rush of power coursed through him like an elemental driving force. He fixed a point on the bank and began to use long, strong, methodical strokes, and utilising the general direction of the flow, struck out towards the bank which was now even closer.

The mud of the riverbank was deep, brown, sticky and smelly. But to an almost completely exhausted Henry Christie it was as glorious, beautiful and welcome as a tropical beach. One last push and he was out of the water.

He was alive.

Coughing and retching, he crawled out of the river on all

fours. He rose slowly to his feet and stumbled a few steps before weakness felled him face-down into the mud again. He was completely covered in it now, brown from head to toe like a wallowing hippo. But he didn't care. He was out of the water, alive, and more or less kicking.

With a great effort he rolled onto his back, too weak to move any further, lying there, gasping for breath, feeling the rain splatting onto his face. He began to shiver, but he'd already decided that, despite the risk of hypothermia, he was going to lie there until he was rescued. He closed his eyes and began to cough.

There was a clicking noise near his face.

Henry looked up into the muzzle of a revolver pointed between his eyes.

Donaldson was holding the binoculars so tightly to his eyes that they were beginning to hurt the sockets. There was a leak in them too, which didn't make it any easier, and the lenses were steaming up.

'Fuck this rain,' he blasted. 'Can't see a damn thing properly.'

He could make out the two figures on the opposite bank about a mile away, one standing above the other. But that was all. They were just stick men on a drawing. He knew one was Henry, knew one was Hinksman, but couldn't tell which was which.

He swore again and looked round as a rifle marksman trotted up beside him.

Henry let his head drop back into the mud with a 'plop'.

'Christ,' he gasped, 'I hoped you'd drowned.'

'Take more than a trickle of water to get rid of me,' said Hinksman. He was also covered in mud, was panting heavily, and coughing up mud and water.

Though very tired too, the one big advantage he had was that he was holding a gun and pointing it at Henry. The gun was coated in thick mud too, but Henry had no illusions about this. He knew it would probably still fire and wasn't about to take any stupid risks on the off-chance.

Hinksman wiped the gritty mud from his eyes and mouth. 'Well, last time we were together like this, the roles were reversed. So, Henry, how does it feel to have a gun pointed at you?'

'I love it.'

'Yeah, I'll bet you do, asshole,' sneered Hinksman.

'So what are you going to do? Kill me, like you killed all the other innocents?'

Hinksman shrugged. 'Innocent bystanders get killed occasionally. That's just the way it is, Henry. But I haven't got time to get into that debate now. So, Henry, here we are – just you and me. That's what you wanted, isn't it? Just us two, alone. I'd better watch myself . . . you're a pretty dangerous guy. We got lots in common, you an' me.'

'Oh, I doubt it,' said Henry. He started to sit up.

Hinksman took a step backwards. His foot sank in the mud and he nearly overbalanced. 'Don't you fucking try anything, or I'll just kill you now!' he warned.

'All I'm doing is sitting up, OK?' Henry said. 'Y'know, I really do think you're afraid of me.'

'In your dreams, chum. You couldn't scare a kid shitless.'

Henry looked across the river to Glasson Dock. He could see the tiny figures on the dock wall. Help seemed a long way away.

'They can't do nothing for you, Henry. It's just you and me – and our common interests.'

'We've nothing in common,' Henry stated. He drew his knees up and folded his arms around them. He was really shaking now, both with cold and fear. His voice had begun chattering as he spoke.

Henry felt his gun hanging in the holster under his left armpit. For the first time he realised it was still there and Hinksman obviously didn't know about it.

'Oh, but we do. For example, we've both fucked the same woman. Kate. Lovely lady. Lovely, lovely lady.'

Henry's chill disappeared, to be replaced by a burning

heat throughout his lower abdomen. The look in his eyes changed from fear to anger, then to danger.

'She's putting on a bit of weight around the thighs and midriff. But she's a nice, really nice woman. At least she was until she met me, then she became debauched, a real animal. Do you know, I couldn't believe you'd never had anal sex before. That really surprised me in this day and age.'

'You bastard,' Henry hissed. Very deliberately he laid the palm of his left hand over his right bicep and jacked up his right fist.

'I know, I admit it. I've done a lot of very bad things to her, Henry. Very bad indeed . . . but your colleagues in that big blue van have done something even worse, by ramming me off the road.'

'How do you fathom that?'

'They killed her,' he said with a fake note of surprise in his tone. 'You see, she was in the back of the van. You mean you didn't know? Trussed up like a chicken, naked as a jaybird an' all that, but definitely alive – until they forced me off the road, that is. I gotta quick glance at her before I climbed out. Real mess. Head all smashed in. She looked pretty dead to me, pretty fuckin' dead. And your pals did it. Not me, not me, Henry.'

'You liar.'

'Now why in hell would I lie at a time like this?'

Henry thought numbly, *and I told them to ram him off the road.*

'Shoot the one who's standing up,' Donaldson said to the marksman. 'That's Hinksman, I'm sure of it. One hundred per cent.'

'How do you know?'

'I know. Trust me. Shoot him.'

'No, I can't,' stuttered the marksman, cracking under the pressure of a real-life situation. 'It wouldn't be reasonable force. I'd have to justify it in court.'

'So? Fuck me! He's pointing a gun at your colleague.

Last time he did that he pulled the trigger and killed the poor son of a bitch. Now shoot him before he does it again.'

'No, I won't.'

'What is it with you English cops, for Christ's sake?' Donaldson screamed through the torrential rain. 'A pal of yours is being threatened by a maniac with a gun who's killed before and you're discussing what you might have to say in court. I don't believe this! Just pull the fucking trigger.'

'No, I can't. I couldn't guarantee a hit at this range and in these conditions anyway.'

Donaldson looked down pityingly at the marksman and made a decision. 'Sorry about this, pal,' he sighed and looked at the point just behind the man's right ear.

'In fact, I've changed my mind, Henry. I'm going to let you live. Killing's too good for you. If I kill you, you'll only suffer for a few more seconds and I'd rather you suffered for the rest of your life, knowing that the police killed the one you loved – *after* I'd raped her, that is. So stay where you are, Henry, and don't come after me – otherwise I will shoot you.'

He turned and began to walk across the mud towards the road.

Henry felt for his gun under his anorak. As he drew it he rose to his feet. He pointed it at the back of Hinksman's head, steadying it on the palm of his hand.

'Stop there. You're under arrest again. Drop your weapon – NOW!'

Hinksman froze. Then turned slowly around, gun in hand. When he was half-facing Henry, a smile broke out under the facial mudpack.

'I should never have underestimated you,' he admitted, shaking his head.

'No, you shouldn't. You should've killed me when you had the opportunity, because I wouldn't have ever given up on you. I'd have chased you to the end of the earth, and we'd have ended up in this position again.'

'I believe you, Henry.'

'Now drop the gun and put your hands up. As you can see,

my gun isn't shaking this time, and if you give me any cause whatsoever, I'll shoot you dead and feel good about it.'

'Well, you've certainly got the drop on me this time.' Hinksman's gun came up quickly.

Henry was hoping it would. He was ready, didn't hesitate. He fired a double tap. *Bam-bam!*

At the same time as his two bullets drilled into Hinksman's neck and chest, the large-calibre bullet from the rifle entered his face just below his right eye, removing the whole of the back of his head.

It seemed a long time before the *crack* of the shot caught up with the bullet from across the river.

The Bucar was discovered at 9 a.m. two days later, parked on a grassy knoll alongside a lake near to the main entrance to Florida International University, about ten miles from downtown Miami.

A campus cop had driven slowly past it a couple of times on his rounds and eventually decided to ticket it for being illegally parked.

He strolled up to it, unfolding his ticket pad whilst whistling and chewing. He had almost completed writing the ticket before he actually glanced inside the vehicle. Something unusual caught his eye: a hand on the passenger seat. On closer inspection he saw that the hand was attached to the arm of a body which was doubled up into the front passenger footwell, as though neatly folded into place.

The cop stopped whistling, dropped his pad and his gum fell out of his mouth. Then he saw the other two bodies laid on top of each other behind the front seats.

He did what a good cop should have done: sealed the scene and called for backup – after he'd finished vomiting.

The first detective on the scene was Ram Chander.

He strolled up to the Bucar and looked inside at the three bodies.

'I got a gut feeling about this one already,' he admitted to the campus cop. 'I bet we get nowhere with it.'

Epilogue

Amongst his many failings, Henry Christie acknowledged that his greatest was that he was not a romantic at heart. In all his married life he had never regularly bought flowers, gifts nor cards for Kate, other than at her birthday or Christmas. Valentine's Day merely passed him by; their wedding anniversary was just another date on the calendar. He had expected her to take his love for granted and that, he now saw, was probably one of the many reasons why their marriage had run into difficulties.

Now he was making up for lost time.

Whilst Kate had been in hospital he had showered her with flowers, cards and gifts, and continually let her know what he felt about her.

She had spent four weeks in hospital, the first six days in intensive care with major, possibly life-threatening injuries.

On her discharge she'd spent further weeks convalescing at home in Henry's care. He had taken special leave and with the assistance of Jenny and Leanne – whom he allowed to stay off school for the purpose – and a district nurse, Henry gentled her back to health.

When she was fit enough, he did what he thought was the most romantic thing he'd ever done – booked a second honeymoon and arranged for the kids to stay with their grandparents.

They watched the blazing sun disappear quickly into the Mediterranean. There was no moon, just blackness and a warm breeze. Both were dressed in shorts and T-shirts, nothing on their feet but the fine golden sand which filtered through their toes. They held hands.

The beach was deserted.

Henry felt euphorically happy.

They hadn't said anything for a while, but it was a contented silence.

'That was a beautiful sunset,' Kate said.

'I cannot disagree.'

She squeezed his hand. He bent over and kissed her briefly on the lips, but the brief kiss became a lingering, wet, exploring one, sending a charge of excitement through both of them. It was like their first real kiss.

When they broke apart, Henry said, 'I love you.'

'Mmm,' she murmured happily, a wide grin on her face.

They began to walk slowly down the beach towards the hotel.

'I don't want this to end,' she said. 'It's been lovely, but I do miss the girls.'

'Me too – on both counts.'

They walked a little further in silence.

'So, is it all over, Henry, this Corelli business?'

'For us, I hope so. Corelli's still operating and I've no doubt he'll team up with some other big-time British criminal to import drugs . . . but it'll take some time, I expect. I think we put a pretty big dent in his operation when the Navy pulled that freighter in the Irish Sea . . . but, from our point of view, I think we've probably seen the last of him.'

'Good, I'm glad. It was his evil that cast a shadow on us all, wasn't it?'

'Yeah . . . everything started with him.'

Kate interlocked her fingers into Henry's.

'Kate, I thought I'd killed you. If you had died, it would've been my fault. You see, I told that personnel carrier to ram him.'

They had stopped and were facing each other, still holding hands.

'You weren't to know where I was,' she said softly. 'Don't feel guilty. I'm alive, you're alive, we're back together and we've got a future . . . and that's all that matters. Us and the girls.'

Henry looked sullenly at his feet as he poked around in the sand with his toes.

'What's the problem?' she asked.

'He told me everything he did to you. Everything.'

'Henry, he hasn't done anything to me. He might have hurt me physically, but I detached myself from what he was doing. He might as well have done it to a piece of meat. He didn't touch me here.' She laid his hand over her heart. 'Only you can touch me there.'

'You're very strong and I feel so weak and pathetic.'

'Don't. What happened between him and me means nothing. It's taken a while for it to work out, but I'll tell you one thing, darling . . .'

'What's that?'

'It's about time you did touch me.'

'I didn't want to rush anything.'

She slid her T-shirt off and allowed her shorts to fall to the sand.

'Here?' he asked incredulously.

'Here and now,' she ordered him. She reached out, unfastened his shorts, pulled them over his thighs, down to his ankles. He pulled off his shirt and threw it to one side.

'Are you sure you're ready?' he asked. 'I don't want to—'

His words were cut short by the forefinger she placed on his lips. She moved up close to him, skin to skin. It felt like the most sensational thing in the world. Her hard nipples pressing into his chest, her moist bush pressed around his thigh and his hard penis pressed against her soft belly.

'I wonder if it's true what they say,' he said, as he gently lowered her down.

'What?' she mumbled.

'That sand gets everywhere.'

Corelli enjoyed Cuban food. One of his favourite restaurants was the Versailles which was in SW 8th street, just to the west of Little Havana on Calle Ocho. It had one of the largest Cuban menus in Miami and he could fill himself for around ten dollars on steak with plantains and rice. Even though he was extremely wealthy he still liked a bargain – and the Versailles was a bargain.

It was just on noon, and the restaurant was already very crowded. Nevertheless he had been shown directly to a table in one corner where he could sit, Mafia-style, his back to the wall, with an advantageous view of everyone coming and going. He had no particular reason to be worried, but old habits die hard, and you could never be too sure.

At the table were four others beside Corelli. Stanton, the bodyguard; Lucas, the man most likely to replace Hinksman; and two British businessmen who seemed rather cowed and overawed by the illustrious Italian. They had been thoroughly searched by Stanton and Lucas prior to being allowed to sit down. They were clean.

Specific business was discussed over the main course. This was one of the few public places where Corelli occasionally conducted his affairs. Over dessert and coffee they chatted about things in general.

After a pause in conversation, one of the Brits cleared his throat and began rather hesitantly, 'They say you had three FBI operatives silenced recently.'

Stanton stiffened. He looked quickly at his boss. Was this a subject that could be discussed – or was it taboo? Corelli raised a calming hand, indicating he did not mind. Stanton relaxed.

'People say many things,' Corelli said mysteriously.

'If it is true, we are very impressed,' said Brit number two. 'Occasionally the authorities need to know where they stand.'

'They were three troublesome people,' Corelli said. 'As it happens,' he went on, 'I did not have them silenced, I had them executed.'

The two Brits laughed nervously.

'I was judge and jury,' Corelli said, 'and Mr Lucas here was executioner.'

Lucas raised a glass. The two Brits felt their anal passages tighten and contract, but managed a smile each.

'I propose a toast,' said Corelli, picking up his own glass. 'To the FBI and law-enforcement officers the world over: may they continue to be so bad at the administration of justice.'

Everyone laughed and raised their glasses.

No one at the table paid any particular heed to the woman who entered the restaurant at that moment and walked towards them, snaking her way between tables. She was tall, elegant and walked like a model; swaying hips, confidence. Sass.

She was very well dressed in a blouse and tight mini-skirt which showed off her long tanned, shapely legs. She had a green silk scarf tied around her head and wore a pair of dark glasses.

Neither did they pay any attention to the skinny black girl who had been eating at a table with her back to them. Similarly attired to the first woman, she rose slowly from her seat.

The woman who had walked into the restaurant held a small purse delicately in front of her. She went straight up to Corelli's party and smiled. Her blouse was tight-fitting and made of sheer silk which showed her generous breasts at their best. Her nipples were erect and she was breathing shortly, almost panting, as though she was excited.

'Mr Corelli?' she asked.

Lucas became alert. Corelli laid a finger on his sleeve to check him. He smiled up at the woman, somewhat distracted by the figure.

'Yes, what can I do for you?'

Slowly she removed her scarf and allowed it to waft gently to the floor. She took her sunglasses off, folded them deliberately and slid them into her bag, keeping her hand inside.

'You sent me a letter a while ago,' she said.

Corelli saw the ravages of the first stages of plastic surgery all the way up one side of her face. He was repelled and his face showed it.

'And then you killed my man, Joe Kovaks.'

The hand in her purse came out holding the ·32 calibre Smith & Wesson revolver.

Lucas began to make for his gun.

Stanton went for his too.

The Brits sat rigid, somewhere in the middle of all this.

The gun in the woman's hand swung quickly in Corelli's direction. His eyes widened. He dropped his fork, tried to cower.

Lucas' gun was partly out. He was very fast.

Stanton cursed. His gun was stuck.

Corelli's eyes grew wider. His mouth opened to shout something. He had nowhere to go.

Neither Stanton nor Lucas saw the black girl wheel round from her table. Held low in her hands was a double-barrelled sawn-off shot-gun which she'd smuggled in underneath her top coat. She held it like a professional.

The Smith & Wesson discharged all six shots into Corelli's head in rapid succession, the trigger being yanked back in a frenzied, jerking movement. A bigger gun would have caused too much recoil in her hand for full control, but the relatively small calibre meant that, despite the anger, it was easy for her to ensure complete accuracy.

Corelli's head twisted grotesquely as the bullets whacked into him. One right in the centre of the forehead, two into the temple, one directly through his left eye and the final two in his face on either side of his nose.

The first barrel from the shot-gun took most of Lucas' head off. The blast toppled him backwards over his chair into the wall behind – already splattered with his brains; the second barrel removed most of Stanton's right shoulder which exploded as if an ounce of Semtex had been inserted in the joint.

The restaurant erupted in a whirlwind of panic.

Corelli was dead, slumped horribly back in his chair, with the last gasp of air gurgling out of his lungs in dribbling bubbles of blood.

The two women dropped their weapons and walked slowly through the chaos, unchallenged, free, not looking anywhere but dead ahead.

At Corelli's table, the two Brits, petrified with fear, still hadn't moved.